Diamond Mafia:

How a Good Girl Set It Off

Diamond Mafia:

How a Good Girl Set It Off

Genesis Woods

www.urbanbooks.net

Urban Books, LLC
300 Farmingdale Road, NY-Route 109
Farmingdale, NY 11735

Diamond Mafia: How a Good Girl Set It Off
Copyright © 2020 Genesis Woods

ISBN 13: 978-1-64556-233-7
ISBN 10: 1-64556-233-6

First Mass Market Printing July 2021
First Trade Paperback Printing August 2020
Printed in the United States of America

10 9 8 7 6 5 4 3

*This is a work of fiction. Any references or similarities
to actual events, real people, living or dead, or to real
locales are intended to give the novel a sense of reality.
Any similarity in other names, characters, places, and
incidents is entirely coincidental.*

Distributed by Kensington Publishing Corp.
Submit Orders to:
Customer Service
400 Hahn Road
Westminster, MD 21157-4627
Phone: 1-800-733-3000
Fax: 1-800-659-2436

Prologue

"Yo, you really think all four of them broads gon' be down with your plan?"

I sat back in my seat and eyed the small group of people who stood around a huge birthday cake, singing the age-old song to a little boy decked out in Gucci from head to toe. His wide eyes wandered around in amazement at all the people who circled him with smiles on their faces as they sang off-key. A little girl I was assuming to be his sister stood next to him. Her hair was layered in French braids with colorful beads at the end, and she wore an outfit similar to his, but hers was pink. You could tell by the little pout on her cute face that she was feeling some type of way about not getting all the attention, but she quickly got over it when her brother stepped to the side and allowed her to blow out each of the burning candles on top of his cake. The four women I was interested in proposing this job to all cheered the little girl on as she started to dance shortly after, tongues and phones all out while they snapped pictures and moved to the beat as well.

Wiping my hand over my face, I silently counted to five and sighed. This was why I liked to research potential workers on my own. Niggas like Ant could work your last nerve, always wanting to know the if, ands, buts, or whys behind certain shit happening. The only reason

I kept him around was because he was family, and the nigga was actually good at what he did.

"I think anybody would be down with making some money. Especially when there's *eighty million* reasons why they should," I expressed, putting emphasis on the amount of money we stood to make if everything went according to plan.

Ant looked back over toward the crowd of people, who were now all dancing and eating cake as the sounds of Ice Cube's classic song "Today Was a Good Day" rattled loudly from the trunk of a '64 Impala.

"You think I can crack one of these hoes before you get them to come on board?" He chucked his chin up. "The one with the short haircut is who I'm feeling. She got a thick little frame and is bad as fuck."

My eyes wandered over to the girl he was talking about. She was a sexy little piece, around five-seven, with smooth milk chocolate skin; eyes almond-shaped and bright like the sun; lips full, ass fat, waist small, and titties just right. I felt a sudden pull in my groin as my gaze continued to scan her thick frame from head to toe. As if she could feel my intense glare on her, she paused putting the hunk of cake in her mouth and looked around the park at her surroundings. For a split second, her eyes cut to where I was parked, but then changed direction when she couldn't see behind the dark tint on my windows.

"That one"—I pointed in her path—"is off limits."

"Off limits? But—"

I cut him off. "But nothing. That girl right there is the key to my plan actually going through. I'm not about to let you fuck up anything for me or the rest of the crew."

Ant sucked his teeth. "Nigga, you ain't slick one bit. Talking about *she's the key to my plan going through*," he said, poorly mocking my deep voice. "I know you, my dude, and I can tell from the look in your eyes that you want her all for yourself. That's why she's really off limits. Tell the truth and shame the devil, my nigga. Since when have you ever had a problem with me mixing business with pleasure? You know how many hoes I done fucked that have worked for you and you ain't said not one single word? As long as they—"

"Get to the money." We finished the last of his sentence together and laughed.

"I'm saying, though." Ant raised his hands, still chuckling. "Shawty look like she can be the next Mrs. Lewis if I'm keeping it all the way real. I'd wife her ass up in a second."

I looked back over at the crowd of people who were still partying and having a good time. The woman who'd had my attention since the first time I laid eyes on her a couple days ago was talking to a redbone chick who had just walked up to the little get-together. I watched as she smiled that beautiful smile of hers and hugged the girl tightly around her neck. She took the gift bag from the girl's hand and placed it on the table before pulling her over to the tree where the other three women she rolled with were standing.

"Aye, pass me that folder out of the glove compartment," I advised Ant as I looked at a text on my phone, ignoring his last comment. Once he handed it over to me, I opened it up and passed him three of the four pictures that were paper-clipped to the top. "I need you to study each and every one of their faces. In the next few weeks, I want you to find out everything there is to know about each of them— where they work, what type of car they drive, the brand of maxi pads they wear when it's that time of the month.

I wanna know who they're related to, who they're associated with, and who they're fucking even if it's off and on. I need to know everything."

Ant nodded as he shuffled through the photos. "I got you, man. But, uh, what about that picture over there, though? The one you got that tight grip on." I looked down at the photo of the chocolate beauty I held in my hand and then over to the tree where she was still standing. Snoop Dogg's "3's Company" was blasting through the speakers as the little birthday boy did his rendition of a crip walk with the woman I was assuming to be his mother c-walking right along with him.

"Don't worry about her. I'm going to personally look into her background," I said, grabbing at the fine hairs on my chin. "Like I said, she's the most important piece to this puzzle, and I'm not about to let you fuck that up."

Ant cut his eyes at me before grabbing the folder out of my lap and looking over the paperwork inside.

"So, other than this bullshit your tech guy was able to get off the internet, have you heard anything from them niggas you keep on payroll in the hood about these broads?"

I thought about his question for a second. "I haven't heard anything of importance yet. However, this one right here—" I grabbed the picture of the Keri Hilson lookalike. "Her nigga is someone we both have crossed paths with before."

Ant squinted his eyes at the photo, trying to see if he could place her face somewhere. He shook his head. "She doesn't look familiar at all. Who's her nigga?"

My lips curled into a slick grin. "Remember that muthafucka Big Titty Tina brought to your welcome home party a few months back?"

He nodded his head slowly.

"Found out she"—I pointed at the picture—"is his old lady."

He covered his mouth with his fist. "Nooooooooo. I know he ain't fucking around on her fine ass with Tina big ass?"

I shook my head and laughed. "Aye, don't do my homie Tina like that. You know she be pulling these dummies left and right. Be getting paid, too."

"I'm saying, though," Ant said, still amazed. His eyes zeroed in on the picture of the girl with caramel skin, honey-colored eyes, and long blonde hair. "Tina pussy and head gotta be hella fiyah if this nigga is fucking around on his fine-ass girl with her. Maaaaaan . . . I'm at a loss for words." He shook his head. "I don't even wanna talk about this shit anymore. Did you roll up on Tina yet?"

I nodded my head. "You know I did. Dropped a few bands on her too."

Ant sat up in his seat and rubbed his hands together, excitement all over his face. "Okay. And what did her *do-anything-for-money* ass tell you?"

"She didn't tell me much because she said the nigga is real secretive about his shit. However,"—I licked my lips—"she did tell me a little something that I think will get you started in the right direction when looking into ole girl."

He nodded his head as he turned his eyes back toward the party, which was still going on. "Well, what are you waiting for, nigga? Lay it on me."

I looked down at the picture in my hand and smiled. My dick was getting harder and harder each time I thought about the money we were about to make and the pretty face I intended to have in my bed before this was all over with. After zoning out for a second, I turned my attention back to Ant and said, "All right then, so check it . . ."

Chapter 1

Lucinda "Lucci" Adams

I get high, high, high (Every day)
I get high, high, high (Every night)
I get high, high, high (All the time)
High.

Styles P's classic "Good Times" knocked through my speakers as I sped down the 105 freeway, finally making my way back to the city from a twelve-hour turn-around trip I just did to Arizona. I'd been up for the last twenty-four hours doing what I did best, making that money. Now, normally I wouldn't make a run like this because my man Stax and I had a whole army of workers under us who got paid to do it, but when the money started to come up short and product started to slowly disappear, that's when one of us had to show face and get shit back on track. Since Stax was taking care of a different situation, it was my turn to make this trip.

Hopping off of my exit on Wilmington Avenue, I maneuvered my way through the back streets of ghetto-ass Watts until I arrived at the tiny stash house we had tucked deep in the heart of this small city. Fiends were walking around, looking for their next hit, while niggas who thought they were making money stood on the corner, clocking hours that we allowed them to get. Young girls pranced around in this summer heat wearing short-ass Daisy Dukes and crop tops, looking for the next baller to take them up out the hood.

I smirked and shook my head as I passed by my girl Kay Kay's little sister, Shauna, and the pack of rats she always kept behind her. The girl was always on this side of town, trying to get picked, but never got with a nigga worth anything. She already had two kids at home that she cared nothing about, but she was still out here busting it open for whoever was willing to pay like they weighed.

I pulled into the driveway of the trap house we mainly used to cook and bag our dope, happy to see Stax was already there waiting on me.

"What's up, Lucci?" Zig, one of our enforcers, yelled out as soon as my feet hit the ground.

I grabbed the black duffle bags out of the back seat of my truck and closed the door.

"What's up, Zig? Where it's at?"

He held his hands up in the air and smiled, pausing the dice game he and some of the other workers were in the middle of.

"Shit, you know I stay with that good green. You matching one or what?"

I chucked my chin up toward the house. "Let me go take care of this first, and then we can roll a couple up."

His thick lips curled into a sexy-ass smile before he nodded his head. "All right, bet. I'ma be out here when you get done in there with boss man. I need to holla at you about something too." A more serious look took over his boyishly handsome features. "Something went down at Tuni's spot on Sixth Ave last night, and shit ain't adding up."

I stopped in my tracks at the news and walked over toward Zig, who stepped away from his dice game and met me halfway. The YSL cologne he had on met me before he did. My eyes roamed over his six-foot-two frame and decadent chocolate skin. His signature low taper cut was looking like he'd just stepped fresh out of the barber's chair; thick gold link chain hanging from his neck with the matching bracelet around his wrist. A simple black T-shirt with the words #*MoneyMoves* across his chest and black 501 jeans was his outfit of choice, topped off with some tight-ass red sneakers that I knew probably cost a grip and a red bandana hanging out of his back pocket on the right. Even in the neighborhood we were in, Zig stayed reppin' his colors, and I liked that about him. I liked that a lot.

Biting down on my lip, I tried to suppress the low moan that escaped my mouth when he walked up on me, hovering over my body. The look in his eyes was one I couldn't describe as he eyed me up and down as well. I cleared my throat and stepped back a little when I started to feel curious eyes looking in our direction. Everyone knew I was Stax's girl and would lie, die, steal, and kill for that nigga. However, it didn't stop me from being attracted to this fine man standing in front of me.

"So, what happened on Sixth Ave?" I asked in a voice I didn't even recognize.

Zig smirked after realizing the effect he had on me. Instead of speaking on the situation at hand, he chuckled and said, "When you gon' stop fucking with that nigga Stax and come get up with a real nigga?"

"A real nigga?" I questioned, mind already going back into the trance Zig's fine ass had me in.

"Yeah, a real nigga. If you were my girl, you wouldn't be out here making the type of moves that you be making. Nah." He rubbed his hands together and licked his lips. "You would be out shopping with your girls, getting your hair done, and all that girly shit females like to do."

I cocked my head to the side, eyes in a low squint, as his words replayed in my mind. "It's obvious you don't know me that well. I've always been a get-money bitch and always will be. My man would know and understand that I don't like to just sit in the house and spend up all his money. It's a must that I have my own, and the only way to do that is to get out here and get it how I live." I walked up closer to him and could see the pure look of lust in his eyes, "So see, my dear Zig, you and I could never be. You want a good girl or one of those bird bitches"—my head nodded in the direction of Shauna and her friends walking down the street—"like them hoes, and I'm far from that."

Zig opened his mouth to say something but stopped when the dice game he had just left started to get a little too heated. Before he could even turn back around to address me, I was already walking off and headed back toward the rear of the house. I shook my head and laughed.

Zig and I grew up in the same projects, the Nickerson Gardens. We were cool and hung out a time or two, but nothing ever really happened between us. By the time I started taking niggas serious and really fucking around with them, Stax had entered my life and shut down all of the situationships I had going on outside of him. I was a thug-ass bitch who needed a thug-ass nigga. Zig was still working his way up, and Stax was already out there making moves, so the choice was easy for me to make. I just hoped that my decision to sleep next to a nigga who was as money hungry and cutthroat as me would never blow up in my face.

"What's up, Lucci?"

"Hey, Lucci."

Females greeted me after I stepped into the one-story rundown house and into the kitchen. Bitches Stax had on the payroll were asshole naked, cutting and bagging up our dope.

"What's up, Cyn and Moni?" I returned. They were the only chicks who talked to me out of the six that were there, and for good reason. Cyn and Moni were the only two hoes I didn't have to pistol whip for stepping out of line and trying to get at Stax behind my back. Since the beatdown of the last girl I fired, I hadn't had any real problems out of anyone. These bitches knew I was crazy and wouldn't hesitate to kill the fuck out of one of them if they tried that shit again.

Walking down the hallway, I passed up the two rooms Stax usually used to test out the dope with a few fiends and the main bathroom everyone had to use. Once I made it to the double doors at the end of the hallway, I knocked on the door a few times before opening it and walking in. Stax was sitting behind his desk, reading something on his phone and smiling hard as fuck. He was so into whoever he was texting that he didn't notice I was there until I dropped the money-filled duffle bags on the ground, causing a loud thump to echo around us.

"What's up, baby?" he finally said when his eyes landed on me. The phone in his hand was placed on his desk face down. "When did you get here?"

"Who got your ass smiling like that?" I asked, ignoring his greeting and question.

"Man Lucci, don't start that shit. You just got back. A nigga can't get a hug or a kiss?"

"Not until you tell me who the fuck has you skinning and grinning the way you just were when I walked in," I said as I walked closer to his desk. I reached my hand out to grab his phone, but he snatched it before I could get it.

"Lucci, you know better than that. Since when do we start checking each other's phones and shit? You know what type of thangs go on around here, so you know anything that happens on this phone"—he held up the blue-cased iPhone—"is strictly business. Now, if I were on the personal line, I could see you questioning me about some shit, but this phone, you know its business only."

I stared at Stax for a few seconds, knowing his Henry Simmons–looking ass wasn't telling me the whole truth, but I decided to let it go for now. I hadn't seen my man in the last twenty-four hours, and all I wanted to do was count this money and get some dick.

Stax placed his phone back on the desk and stood up. With his arms opened wide, he walked up to me and pulled me into his embrace. His cologne didn't have me stuck like Zig's did a few minutes ago, but it was familiar and welcoming, something I needed right now.

"How did everything go?" Stax finally asked as we pulled apart. He kissed my forehead and then grabbed my hand, pulling me over to his seat, where he sat back down and placed my ass directly on his dick. "Them niggas didn't disrespect you or come at you wrong, did they?"

I waved him off. "Everything went cool. Dayo tried to run game on me, but I nipped that shit in the bud as soon as his lying ass started the bullshit up. I had to whip my piece out on his right hand, too, because the nigga thought that just because I was a woman, our meeting was gon' go a certain way."

"Niggas ain't knowing about my down-ass bitch Lucci. Did you get the money he owed us?"

"Nigga, do you know who you talking to? Them niggas knew what was up as soon as I kicked in the door and walked in that muthafucka. Had to slap the little bitch sucking Dayo's dick. She wouldn't stop screaming. But once I pointed that gun at her ass, she shut right the fuck up."

Stax chuckled and slapped me on my ass, garnering a surprised yelp out of me.

"Stop, babe. My shit already hurting from sitting in that car so long."

"You want me to rub it for you?" he asked, placing his big hands on my thighs and massaging them.

I moaned. "I want you to do more than rub my thighs, baby. Your pussy needs some loving too."

"Is that right?" A slow smirk formed on his face as I stood up from his lap and began to undress. His eyes stayed on me the whole time until I was completely naked. He licked his lips when he looked down at my hairless mound. "You know I missed my pussy, right? Nigga couldn't even think straight without her around."

"Showing is always better than telling."

Before I knew it, Stax picked me up and laid me on his big oak desk, knocking all of his papers and shit onto the floor. My legs, which were already in the air, were pushed open and spread far apart before I felt the tip of his tongue playing with my clit. My back arched the second he pulled my pearl into his mouth and sucked on it so hard that I exploded all over his face.

Although I was enjoying the way Stax dined on what truly belonged to him, I couldn't shake the visions of Zig being down there instead. I would never betray Stax for no other nigga, because he would never do me that way; however, imagining Zig's thick, juicy lips sucking on my shit had me busting harder than I ever had before.

Chapter 2

Diamond Morris

"Hey, Diamond, once you're done with that customer, can you come to my office for a second?"

I internally groaned and tried hard as fuck not to roll my eyes at my assistant manager, who liked to micromanage the fuck out of me. Ever since corporate gave pimply-face Timmy his promotion, his ass had really been on one.

After bagging the customer's food and giving her change, I closed out my register and walked to the back of the store to Timmy's closet-sized office. Not even bothering to knock on the door, I entered his shit and instantly turned my nose up. The pungent smell of ass and some sort of medicated cream hit my nostrils as soon as I stepped in.

"You wanted to see me, Tim?" I asked in a not-so-enthused voice.

He typed something on his computer, fingers hitting the keys hard as hell before pushing his glasses up the bridge of his nose and looking up at me.

"Have a seat, Diamond."

I shook my head. "Nah, I rather stand."

He shrugged his shoulders and pushed his glasses up again. "Okay, well, I'm looking over your time card for the last week, and I noticed that you've been clocking in late every day except for today. Care to explain the reasons behind your tardiness, Ms. Morris?"

I thought for a second before I opened my mouth. If I told him the real reason behind me being late, he would probably question my ability to perform my job and whether I could still work there with having so much on my plate. On the other hand, I didn't want to lie to him. I mean, I did have a legitimate reason behind me being late in the last few days. Well, I should say weeks, if I was being completely honest.

I removed the pinwheel hat from my head and walked farther into his office. After looking around at the pictures of his ugly-ass family on the wall and the mountain of paperwork scattered around, I took a deep breath and gave him my explanation.

"Well Tim, I've been late this last week because I've been at the hospital—"

"You were in the hospital?" he asked, cutting me off.

"No. I've been *at* the hospital. You see, my twin brother had a massive heart attack a month ago, and I'm the only family he has. So, I go to see him and talk to his doctors about his progress in the morning, and then I ride the train here. After I clock out from Hot Dog on a Stick, I go straight to my second job at the department store downstairs. I work there until closing, and then I go to my third job I have at this small bar on the other side of town. Sometimes I don't make it home until three in the morning if the buses are running slow. I get home, sleep for about four hours, and then start the day all over again."

Tim looked at something on his computer screen and then back up at me. "So, you are working three jobs right now? Is there a reason why you need to work all three? Maybe if you quit one, things will be a little easier on you. Probably get to see your brother more and get a little more sleep."

"I need to work three jobs. It's the only way I can afford to pay my bills and my brother's hospital bills. His insurance only pays so much, and the rest has to come out of my pocket. And then the doctors are saying he has some brain damage, so when he does get better, he will have to have a nurse caring for him around the clock once he's discharged."

My eyes began to water as thoughts of my brother lying in his hospital bed flashed through my mind. Who would have ever thought that at thirty-one, someone as healthy as he was could have a heart attack? I didn't believe it when I got the call that he had collapsed while playing a game of basketball at the gym with his friends. I wasn't prepared for the tubes sticking out of his mouth and nose when I walked into his hospital room. Nor was I prepared to see him lying stiff with no signs of life in his body, either. The machine he was hooked up to was breathing for him now. In a couple of days, the doctors were going to slowly take it off of him to see if he could breathe on his own. I was praying like crazy that he came out of this. I needed my brother back. I needed his smile, his laugh, his love. I needed my everything.

"Wow, Diamond, I'm sorry to hear about your brother and everything you're going through."

"Thanks, Tim," I replied, wiping a lone tear from my eye.

He nodded his head. "Do you think that maybe you should be moved to a later shift instead of opening? That way you have enough time to handle your business in the morning."

I opened my mouth on the verge of saying something smart, but closed it when I felt my attitude start to spike up. Instead of saying what I wanted to say to this dork-ass muthafucka, I took a deep breath and responded in a less aggressive way.

"That wouldn't work for me because of my other jobs. If I started later here, that would throw my whole schedule off and make me late for those."

His eyebrow arched. "So, you're on time at your other jobs?"

"Not all the time, but for the most part, yes. My other supervisors understand and know the hardship I'm going through right now, so they don't really trip off of me coming in a few minutes late."

He scoffed. "You call thirty, sometimes forty-five minutes *a few minutes late*?" He used air quotes to mock me.

"No, but I can only get here as fast as the bus allows me to."

Tim shook his head before looking over at me with sympathetic eyes. "Look, Diamond, I feel for you and what you're going through. However, your tardiness is a concern to me. And now that I'm looking over your time sheets for the last month, this isn't the first time you've been late a whole week." Tim took a breath. "I hate to do this to you, but I'm going to have to place you on temporary suspension until myself and the higher-ups can come to a decision as to whether or not you're fit to stay working for the company. Right now, you're more of a liability than an asset. With all that you have going on and not having any reliable transportation, I don't know if you should continue working for—"

"Are you fucking serious?" I yelled, interrupting him, not giving a fuck about how aggressive my tone was now. "At Hot Dog on a Stick? Muthafucka, you act like this is a Fortune 500 company or something where they make real money. Nigga, you probably pull in two *G*s at the most on a good day. I'm the best goddamn employee you have. And now you wanna fire me?"

He raised his hands, palms stretched out to me. "Whoa. Whoa. No one said anything about firing. I said temporary suspension."

"Until you and the higher-ups can decide if I'm fit to stay here or not, right?"

Tim opened and closed his mouth a few times before speaking again. "Diamond, I'm just doing what—"

I held my hand up to stop him from speaking. "You know what? Save that shit. Save it before I put my foot so far up your ass that I can scratch your tonsil with my toenails." The look on Tim's face after I said that would've been funny had I not been so mad. "And you can save your little funky temporary suspension speech, because I quit."

He sprang up from his desk. "Now, wait a minute, Diamond. You don't have to quit."

"I'm supposed to just wait until you fire me then, right?" I shook my head and turned to walk toward the door. "You know, the only reason why I took this job was to help pay some bills. I'm thirty-one years old. I shouldn't even be working at no damn corn dog spot."

Tim mumbled something.

"What did you say?"

He licked his lips nervously. "I said we don't serve corn dogs. We serve *hot dogs* on a stick."

My eyebrows furrowed, and I could feel a nasty curl form on my lip. "Muthafucka, those things are corn dogs, just like that cheap cheese you dip in batter is a fancy mozzarella stick. Fuck outta here. I'll be expecting my last paycheck sometime tomorrow. Don't bother trying to send it in the mail either. I'll be here first thing in the morning to pick it up," I said over my shoulder as I walked out of his office and back to the front.

Grabbing a bag, I dumped in the freshly made corn dogs and cheese sticks my coworker had made for the long line of customers waiting on their orders. I filled my thermos with some of the pink lemonade, said my *fuck-you-see-you-laters,* and then left.

The sound of Tim screaming my name and the waiting customers' complaints were the last things I heard as I stepped on the escalator and made my way down to Macy's. Hopefully my manager there would let me clock in a few hours early to make up for the hours I was going to miss at Hot Dog on a Stick. What started out as a good day for me was easily turning into one of the worst days of my life, especially after I got the call that my brother had another mini heart attack, causing me to leave Macy's early and call out of my nighttime gig.

As I sat on the train on my way to St. Mary's Medical Center, I said a small prayer. "God, please make a way for me to come up on enough money so that I'm able to quit these jobs and take care of my brother without stressing. You know how bad I need Shine to come back to me. He's all I got, and I need him here. Please just let something work in my favor this one time, and I promise I won't ask you for anything else again. Amen."

I didn't know what was in store for me as far as getting more money, but I would gladly do whatever it took to get it. I just hoped it wasn't something that would land me in jail for the rest of my life or get me killed. However, knowing my luck, I'd probably end up working four more part-time jobs at the mall before some fast money shit like that ever happened.

Chapter 3

Robette "Bobbi" Smith

I was wiping down the display cases in the front of the store when the door buzzed, alerting me that security was allowing someone to come in. Placing the towel behind the counter, I smoothed the front of my black blazer down and put a bright smile on my face.

"Welcome to Bernfeld Jewelry Exchange, where diamonds are everyone's best friend. My name is Robette, and I will be your jewelry consultant today. How may I help you?"

My breath caught the second my eyes connected with the same man who had been coming into the store at least twice a week for the last month. He went under security and the owner's radar because he always bought something whenever he came in, but my hood instincts recognized a jack boy when I saw one. His fine ass had been casing the place and I knew it, but his secret was safe with me.

"So, we meet again, Robette," his smooth voice sang once he finally made it over to me.

I took in the three-piece Italian suit tailored only for his body. His chiseled chin and strong jawline was covered with thick, silky hairs. His tall, medium-built frame was a sight to see and probably grabbed the attention of girls everywhere he went. My eyes scanned over the fancy Rolex on his wrist and the sapphire-and-diamond cufflinks he purchased last week on the ends of his shirt. The brother screamed money in every way that you could imagine, but I could tell from the jailhouse tats on his neck and fingers that he was far from it. Nigga was probably born and raised in South Central like me but getting his money the best way he knew how—stealing it.

"Yeah, we do meet again, Mr. . . ." I trailed off, forgetting his name.

"Ali, but please, call me Naveen or Nav. Whichever you prefer." He grabbed my hand to shake, and just like last time, an electric shot zapped through my body.

"Mr.—" I cleared my throat. "I mean Nav, it's nice to see you again. Were . . . were you looking for anything in particular this week? Perhaps some diamond earrings for your mother or girlfriend this time?"

Nav smiled and bit his lip, eyes roaming over the display of diamond earrings in front of me. From studs to hoops to the fancy shit some of the stars wore on the red carpet, we had it all.

"That's a clever way to see if I'm single or not."

I smiled, and he returned it.

"I am a happily married man."

He raised his hand, and I noticed the platinum band around his ring finger for the first time. I tried to hide the shocked look on my face by turning my head to the side and pretending to cough, but I knew he had seen it by the playful gleam in his eye.

"Don't be embarrassed. You couldn't have known. I just recently got married. The weekend before last. That's why I've been in here so much. Had to buy a few gifts and things before the big day."

I slowly nodded my head and began to remove the diamonds from the display case so that he could get a better look.

"Well, um, congratulations on your nuptials, and I wish you many years of wedded bliss."

"Thank you, Robette. Now, if you were my wife, which pair of earrings would you like?"

For the next hour and a half, I assisted Nav with finding a post-wedding gift for his new bride that would be sure to have her gushing for days. After dropping a whopping ten grand on some bomb-ass studded hoops, a two-carat stunning tennis bracelet, and this beautiful emerald teardrop necklace that I would literally kill for, Nav finally left the store and left me to tend to the rest of the customers who were coming in to purchase our jewels.

By the time seven o'clock rolled around, I was tired as shit from selling, showing, inspecting, and cleaning diamonds. I was ready to pack up and take my ass home. On the way to the back room to grab my things, I answered my ringing phone.

"What's up, Diamond? Everything good?"

The quietness on the other end of the line told me that it wasn't.

"I . . . I almost lost him today," Diamond said just above a whisper. "But the doctors were able to keep him alive for the time being."

I already knew she was talking about her brother. He'd been in the hospital for some time now after that heart attack. My girl was stretching herself thin as hell working all those jobs to keep up with bills and shit. I'd offered her money, and so had Lucci and Kay Kay, but Diamond's stubborn ass wouldn't take it. She declined our offers so much that Lucci went behind her back and paid some of the mounting bills adding up. I was pretty sure the hospital informed Diamond about the payments, but she hadn't said anything yet.

"What happened, baby? What's going on?"

As Diamond explained everything going on with Shine, I text both Lucci and Kay Kay, telling them that we needed to head over to the hospital and give our girl some support. Once they both responded with okays, I continued to listen to Diamond and gather all my personal belongings so that I could leave.

"I just don't know what I'm going to do, Bobbi. Not only did I quit one of my jobs that I really needed, but the doctors want my permission to move Shine to some other hospital that's better equipped to keep him alive. The thing is, the transport is going to be risky as hell. They're saying he could die while being airlifted to another hospital." The line went quiet for a few seconds. "I can't lose my brother, Bobbi. I can't lose Shine."

"Shhhhhhh." I tried calming her down. "Everything will be okay, girl. Look, Lucci, Kay Kay, and I are on our way up there. Don't make any decisions until we are all there with you. I'm in line about to get scanned by the security guards, and then I'll call you once I make it to the car, okay?"

"Okay," she sniffled. "I won't make any decisions. Can you . . . can you just try to hurry up? I know traffic is going to be a mess for you all the way out there in Beverly Hills, but please get here as soon as you can."

"I will," I promised her as I walked up to the security guard desk and placed my things on the conveyor belt. "Look, Diamond, I'm about to get checked. Let me call you back."

She giggled. "I can't believe they check you guys like they're the TSA or something. It's gotta be hard as hell to steal diamonds out of a jewelry store. All those cameras they have on you guys every second of the day and security precautions. It's like Fort Knox up in there."

"Shit, it might as well be with all of the diamonds that come through here. I remember one time, we had to shut down because one of the actresses going to the Oscars had a necklace made with over five million dollars of yellow di—Wait. Diamond, let me call you back."

I released the call before she could say anything. After getting my body scanned with the wand, I walked over to the security desk where my things were being held, thumb wavering over Diamond's name so that I could call her back.

"Um, I'm sorry. Why are you guys holding my bag and coat hostage like that?" I asked one of the security guards when I noticed my belongings weren't on the conveyor belt anymore.

He cleared his throat after whispering something to his partner. "Uh, Ms. Smith, Mr. Bernfeld would like to see you in his office."

I looked around the room, staring back at my other coworkers, who were nosily looking over at me. "In his office?" I asked as I turned back around to face him. "Why?"

The security guard cleared his throat again. "Seems like you had something in your personal belongings that didn't belong, and he would like to have a word with you."

"Something in my bag?" I was confused. I'd never stolen anything, or tried to steal anything for that matter, so what the hell were they talking about? I reached my hand out over the desk. "Please give me my things. Let me see what you're talking about."

"Unfortunately, I can't give you your stuff at this time, Ms. Smith." He pulled my bag further out of my reach.

"Why not?"

"Because of the evidence."

"Evidence!" I screamed loudly this time. "What the fuck are you talking about, evidence? I ain't steal shit."

"Ms. Smith," he hissed, trying to control the situation.

"Ms. Smith my ass. Give me my bag. Show me what the fuck you found as evidence. I'm not about to leave my shit up here so you can plant something in it. Y'all got me all the way fucked up if you think I'm going to let that go down. Muthafuckas, I'm from the hood, the product of a street rat and a scammer, so you gon' have to come with something pretty wild to get one over on me."

"Ms. Smith"

"Nah, fuck that," I started, but stopped when the stern voice of Mr. Josh Bernfeld, part owner of Bernfeld Jewelry Exchange, called my name. I turned around in his direction with wild eyes, wondering what the hell was going on.

"Ms. Smith, if you just come to my office, we can talk about everything privately."

"Privately? I feel like I'm being treated like a criminal for something I know I didn't do."

He walked closer to where I was standing, hands up in surrender, eyes focused on my face, voice low and calming. He reminded me of those negotiators on the TV shows that try to talk down a hostage situation.

"Robette, please. If you would just follow me to my office, I promise that we will get everything under control and figure this out."

After thinking about it for a few seconds, I said, "I'll come, but I'm not leaving my bag up here for them to plant some shit in it."

Mr. Bernfeld walked over to the desk and grabbed my things. "Can we go now?"

I nodded my head and turned toward the direction of his office. A million things were going through my mind as we walked down the long hallway, my heels click-clacking on the linoleum floor. The line of fluorescent lights above me got brighter the closer we got to our destination. I stopped just as we reached the cherrywood door with the gold plaque on it that read JOSHUA BERN-FELD in big black letters.

Stepping to the side, I watched as he slipped his key into the knob and pushed the heavy piece open. Walking in first, I looked around the poshly decorated office with its grey, red, and black color scheme. It had been a hot minute since I'd been in there. The sound of the door shutting closed brought me back from my thoughts.

Just as I opened my mouth to ask what this really was about, my back was slammed against the door, and my blazer and shirt were ripped open.

"God, I couldn't wait to get you back here," Josh breathed into my ear as his hands fondled my breasts. "I've been watching you on the security camera all day. I saw you flirting with that tattooed thug, too. Is he your type, Robette? Huh? You think he can fuck you better than I can?"

"No," I breathlessly lied as he took one of my nipples in his mouth and sucked hard on it. "He's . . . he's married any . . . anyway."

"What does that mean?" he managed to ask with a mouth full of titty.

"It means—*oh*. It means I don't . . . fuck with . . . with married men." I could hardly get a word out. Josh had his hand on my nub, thumping it with his fingers. I was on the verge of cumming and was getting tongue tied in the process.

"I'm sorry I made such a big spectacle to get you back here," he apologized in between breaths. "But I didn't know any other way I could get you into my office without people questioning me having you back here for no reason."

So that's what all this was about. Although I was mad as fuck from being embarrassed in front of all those people, I didn't have the desire to address that right now. All I wanted was some dick before I left to go to the hospital. This was going to be the last time Josh and I had sex, and I really meant it this time.

What had started out as a little harmless flirting when I needed a few extra hours some months ago had easily turned into this three-month affair Josh and I now had going on. He was not typically my type. I'd never ever seen myself actually fucking him, but when my curiosity got the best of me after staying late to help with inventory one evening, Josh surprised me with his stroke game, and we'd been fucking ever since.

"Damn, I can't wait to put your pussy in my face and taste it."

"Me either. You got protection, right? You know if there's no glove, there's—"

"No love," he finished for me. "Yes, I have condoms. Bought a whole new pack on my lunch break."

I smirked at his audacity. "Okay, but we are going to have to make this quick. I gotta meet my friends at the hospital, and I don't wanna be the last one holding them up."

He let my nipple drop from his mouth and started attacking my neck. "You know all I need is ten minutes. Once I get up in that sweetness you got down here between your legs,"—his fingers brushed against my swollen nub, and my body trembled—"I can only last but so long."

"I know!" I squealed when he bit my neck and smacked my ass.

"It's good that you know. Now, go lie on the couch over there and open up for me. I'm ready to eat."

I wiggled out of his hold and made my way to the leather couch in the corner of his office. Looking at the time, I knew I had about thirty minutes to spare if I wanted to at least make it to the hospital before traffic started to really pick up. Hopefully, by the time we were done, I'd be able to make it to Diamond no later than forty-five minutes. With Lucci coming from the other side of L.A and Kay Kay coming from Long Beach, I knew we'd probably end up at St. Mary's around the same time. Until then, I was going to enjoy this last fuck and then be on my way.

Chapter 4

Kahlani "Kay Kay" Jones

Bobbi: We need to head up to the hospital asap.

Lucci: What's up

Me: Everything good?

I puffed on my cigarette a few times before looking down at my phone for Bobbi's reply.

Bobbi: Naw. Diamond needs us. Something's up with Shine.

Lucci: Okay. Give me a few and then I'm on the way.

Me: I'll be there. Gotta check the house first and then I'm on my way.

I laid my head back against the headboard and closed my eyes, wishing that I could be anywhere in the world but where I currently was. However, I had responsibilities to take care of, even if the majority of said responsibilities weren't mine. I couldn't let my family down seeing as I was the oldest of my mama's four kids and the one all my siblings looked to for help.

Where I should've had a normal life, shit went completely different for me. At thirteen, I was already fucking. At sixteen, I turned my first trick. At eighteen, I went to jail for prostitution for the first time, and at twenty-one I gave birth to a baby whose father was a blank face to me.

I didn't have not one problem giving her up for adoption after I pushed her out of my coochie. She deserved better, and I hoped she got it.

At twenty-five, I got locked up for a few years after being involved in a robbery my then nigga said was sure to have us living lavishly, and at thirty, I was released from prison only to have to go back to being the sole provider for my family again. The only difference this time was that I was working for myself. I wasn't about to let another nigga talk me into helping him break the law and then when we get caught, the hoe-ass nigga blamed everything on me.

I took another puff of my cigarette, already irritated with the trick I was fucking with tonight. His fat ass couldn't fuck a damn donut if he had to. His dick was so small it felt like my pussy was the size of the Grand Canyon whenever he slipped in.

Most people blamed others for their terrible upbringing, but in this case, I had no one to blame but myself. I had the opportunity to go live with my father in Arkansas or go into foster care, but I begged the judge and them other people to let me stay with my mother. Her ass was a straight tweaker, getting high any chance she could get with whoever and wherever she could get it. The bitch was even high at the hearing for my child services case. Came in stumbling and shit. I cleaned her up enough to look presentable to the judge and the rest of them white folks, but anyone who knew her could tell that she was flying.

By God's grace and some type of miracle, my mother was granted custody of me as long as she agreed to doing monthly checkups, drug tests, and counseling. Of course, when it was time for the checkups, I made sure the house was in order and had a nice amount of food in the fridge. When it was time for her drug test, I'd pee in a plastic bag that she would keep hidden under her big-ass belly flap and pour into the cup whenever we went down to the building where she got tested. And as far as counseling goes, let's just say my mother hardly showed up for a session. Lucky for me, my counselor was a man who had a thing for young pussy. I would break him off after a session, and he'd write up a fake report that satisfied the court and the Los Angeles Department of Social Service.

As if my life wasn't fucked up enough, my mama seemed to get pregnant every few years after she had me. My brother Kane, who was three years younger than me, was serving a life sentence right now for killing one of his homeboys who beat our mama's ass for stealing from his stash. My other brother, Trip, who was four years younger than Kane, didn't even get a chance to experience the hood life me and my other siblings were subjected to living in. His daddy swooped him up as soon as my mama pushed him out. I'd spoken to him a few times over the years, but he didn't keep in contact with us that much.

Then there was the baby of the family, Shauna. That girl was twenty-one and on the road to death and destruction if she didn't sit her hot ass down somewhere. She was sixteen when she had my nephew and seventeen when she gave birth to my niece, both by niggas who had women in their lives that they had no plans of leaving. Like a dummy, she believed that shit, though. Had their babies and was now left to take care of them by herself. Well, if I was being all the way real, I was taking care of my niece and nephew. It was my hustling that kept a roof over their heads, food in their bellies, and clothes on their backs. Their dumb-ass mama was still out in these streets, playing Russian roulette with these married and/ or already involved men, not knowing that these wives would kill your ass before they let you fuck up their family.

The bed dipping in on the other side of me told me that the fat fuck had come back from the bathroom. We had just gotten done with our first round of humping, which meant now he wanted me to suck his dick until he came and fell asleep. Usually that would be the time when I would collect my fee and get ghost on his ass, but tonight, I had other plans. Doughboy's fat ass always had a fat knot of money on him, as well as a few credit cards. The plan was to suck his micro penis so good that the nigga literally slipped into a coma. Once he was out, I would take pictures of his cards and ID, grab a couple bands from his stash, and then use his car to get back to mine, which was parked up the street at the Food 4 Less grocery store. Just like I didn't like a trick to know where I lived, I didn't like them to know the type of car I drove either. Nigga wouldn't run me down on the street after weeks of ignoring his phone calls.

Puffing my cigarette two more times, I snuffed it out on the ashtray next to my leg and turned my attention over to fat-ass so that we could get this party started. He caressed my cheek with the back of his hand for a second before pinching my chin.

"You are fine as fuck, Kay Kay. And you got some fiyah head and pussy, too. When you gon' stop fucking with a nigga's head and be mine? You know I can change your whole life if you just fuck with me."

For a big nigga, Doughboy was nice looking. I mean, he dressed nice, always smelled good, and had some of the prettiest white teeth I'd ever seen. He was a get-money nigga from up North, and to my knowledge, he didn't have any baby mama drama or a harem of females at his feet. The thing that stopped me from taking it further with him, though, was his dick. I couldn't be faithful to a nigga who couldn't make me cum. Nigga's dick was legit the size of a Vienna sausage.

"You already know what it is with me, baby. I'm a free spirit. Don't like to be tied down. Besides, you know how I make my money, and I don't have plans on stopping anytime soon."

He lowered his hand from my face and slunk his body down farther on the bed. "Yeah, I know. You wanna be turning tricks for the rest of your life, though?"

I wasn't offended by his question, because most of the niggas I fucked asked me that. I just got tired of having to answer it.

"I guess I will get tired of it eventually, but right now, it's what I have to do to provide for my family."

"What about a regular job?" he asked with a scrunched-up nose.

"If you can show me a job where I can make at least two Gs in two hours, then I'm there." He opened his mouth to say something, but I cut him off. "And before you say stripping, just know that I've already been there and done that. When bitches start jumping me after shows and stealing my money, it's time for me to hang up the stilettos and move on." I pulled a new cigarette from my box and lit it.

"For some reason, you don't strike me as the type of girl who would let that type of shit slide."

I laughed before blowing out a cloud of smoke. "I'm not. Have you ever been to that strip club Starz in

Gardena?" I asked, flicking my lighter. He nodded his head, and I continued. "The next time you go, ask them why Buttafinga isn't allowed to step foot in that establishment anymore."

His eyes lit up with excitement. "Oh, shit. What you do?"

I licked my lips and shrugged my shoulders. "Just ask them the next time you go. I'm sure a few of them bitches I had to slice up are still working there. Hoes think they run that joint."

"So, you one of them knife-and-razor-carrying bitches," he said. "I gotta remember that if you and I ever get into it."

"Nah. Me and you gucci. You understand what it is, and I only expect what's coming my way after our transaction is done."

"Which is?"

I took one last pull from my cigarette and put it out. "Which is money."

He looked at me for a few seconds before speaking. "Okay, well, since you said it like that, why don't you come over here and show this dick what the mouf do so I can pay you your money."

Without saying another word, I slid over to his side of the bed, grabbed his baby pickle–sized dick, and gave him what he came here for. Within five minutes, the nigga's whole body was shaking like he was having a seizure. I let him cum all over my titties before hopping out of the bed and getting into the shower. By the time I came back out, his ass was dead to the world and snoring like a damn grizzly bear.

Tiptoeing across the room, I found all of my clothes and slipped them back on. After tying my sneakers, I walked back over to his side of the bed, grabbed the money he had already set out for me on the dresser, and picked up his pants. The loud clunking sound of his belt buckle being moved froze me in my tracks. I looked over at Doughboy, expecting him to stir a little or even open one of his eyes, but when he didn't, real smooth-like, I took his wallet from his pocket and started taking pictures of everything I needed.

Once I was done, I placed his jeans back on the ground and made my way over to the Gucci backpack he always carried with him. Slowly unzipping it, I stuck my hand inside the heavy bag and began to pull out bundle after bundle after bundle of hundred-dollar bills. If I was counting right, I had easily just pulled about ten bands outta his backpack. On top of the two stacks he set out on the dresser for me, I was already at $12,000. I wouldn't have to turn another trick for a week or two with this kind of money. My niece and nephew would get some new clothes and shoes. I'd drop a few bills on Kane's books. Rent and everything else would be paid up, and I could also tuck a few bands in my rainy day stash.

Once I zipped his backpack up and positioned it back on the chair the right way, I grabbed his keys and quietly crept out the door. I knew when Doughboy figured out I stole some money from him, he'd be on the hunt. Luckily for me, the nigga didn't know where I lived, what kind of car I drove, or any of the spots I hung out at. I made it a point to meet him at the motel on 104th and Broadway for a reason. No one knew me on this side of L.A., so he would just have to chalk that loss of money up just like I did whenever one of my tricks shorted me on my ends.

Chapter 5

Lucci

"Wait, wait, wait. Y'all remember that time Kay Kay's ass got into that fight with Big Brenda and her crew?"

Kay Kay waved Bobbi off. "Your ass always bringing that up whenever we puffing on one."

"Because that shit was funny." Bobbi laughed. "Your short ass stood in the middle of them tall-ass Amazon bitches and was ready to fight each and every one of them by yourself."

Kay Kay pulled on the blunt. "You already know how I get down. I don't fear no man or woman but God. Bitches always had me fucked up back then. That hoe Big Brenda thought that just because she was a whole two feet taller than me and weighed somewhere close to a ton that I wasn't going to give her that heads up." She shook her head. "I knocked the fuck outta her ass."

I laughed. "You did. And as soon as her little crew tried to pounce on you, me, Bobbi, and Diamond came around that corner, swinging first and asking questions later."

"We sure did," Bobbi added. "I ended up fucking up my damn knee that day. Shay's fat ass fell all on my shit. I was outta commission for like six weeks." She shook her head. "Why did Big Brenda wanna fight your ass anyway, Kay? I don't think we ever got the real story."

Diamond, who was zoned out and in her own little world as we stood on the roof of the hospital, finally spoke. "She probably fucked the poor girl's man."

We all laughed.

"Is that what happened?" Bobbi and I asked at the same time.

Kay rolled her eyes at Diamond, who smirked in return. "No, I didn't fuck her man, bitch. Brenda was going out with Charlie Mack at that time, and although his ass was fine as hell, the nigga wasn't making any money. So no, I wasn't fucking him." She paused for a second and took a few pulls of the blunt we were smoking before passing it back to me. "I was fucking her daddy, though."

"Bitch!" I exclaimed. "I knew it. A few times when Stax and I pulled up to the Snooty Fox, I thought that was you in Mr. Mell's truck, ducking down, trying not to be seen."

Kay Kay nodded her head and threw a rock over the ledge. "Yeah, I saw your ass too. That nigga Mr. Mell was one of my best tricks. I always kept money in my pocket before he died."

"Your ass is crazy, girl," I said to Kay Kay before walking over to Diamond and handing her the blunt. The somber look on her face caused my heart to ache. "Hey, girl. How you doing? Any thoughts on whether or not you wanna transfer Shine to the other hospital?"

She shook her head, passing on the blunt. "I want to, but then again, I don't. I can't lose my brother, Lucci. He's all I have." Her voice cracked before she fell into my arms and cried her eyes out. "I promised my mama that I would look after him before she died. What kind of sister would I be if I make the wrong decision and he dies? God, I wish my mama was here. She would know what to do."

I rubbed Diamond's back as she continued to sob on my shoulders. I don't think that I could ever go through something like this in life. That's why I was kind of glad that I didn't have any siblings. What Diamond was going through right now would probably break the strongest person down bad.

I was so lost in my thoughts about my friend's situation that I hadn't noticed Kay Kay and Bobbi come to join in on our hug. The four of us had been friends since our first day of middle school. All of us had the same home-room class that year. I don't know what it was, but we all seemed to just click. After introducing ourselves to each other, we had talked about all kinds of bullshit that we had in common. It was in that moment that we decided to look out for one another during our time at Hamilton Middle School. We'd been inseparable ever since.

When one was down, we were all down. Just like that time we had to come together and handle Bobbi's child-molesting-ass uncle for raping her. Or when we would go from crack house to crack house looking for Kay Kay's mama whenever she would go missing in action. My girls even came together for me when I got shot a few years ago. They didn't go out to try and find who did it, but they did handle some of the day-to-day business I was missing out on while in the hospital, like picking up money and distributing new packages to my workers.

We had always been there for one another, and the shit wasn't going to stop now. After Diamond's body stopped shaking and her face was free of tears, we pulled from our embrace and just stood in our spots, watching the sun go down. There was a calm silence between us for a few minutes before someone decided to speak.

"Do you guys ever think about leaving California?" Bobbi asked, eyes marveling in the beautiful hues the setting sun was displaying in the sky. "Just getting out of here and seeing how the rest of the world looks?"

"I do," Kay Kay responded. "All the time. Just take my niece and nephew and get the fuck up out of here. Start life all over on some exotic island in another country. I'm starting to get tired of turning tricks just to make ends meet. I mean, I know I could get a regular job, but I don't want to have to save for a whole year just to make the type of money I can get from fucking different niggas in a week." She shrugged her shoulders. "Shit is getting old. Hell, I'm starting to get old. I can still pop, lock, and drop it, but these aging bones of mine be feeling brittle as fuck these days."

We all busted out laughing. Leave it up to Khalani to crack a nasty joke when we're all trying to be serious.

"You are so damn stupid, Kay Kay, but all bullshit aside," Diamond said, a smile finally gracing her face, "I get what you're saying. And as far as leaving California, Bobbi, I wouldn't mind doing that. Of course, Shine would have to get better first, but I'm ready to go. Wish I had enough money to buy me a nice little house on the beach somewhere in Hawaii. Hire a nurse to help take care of Shine and just enjoy our days in the water and sun."

"Shit, we can do it all if y'all jump on that Cocaine Mafia shit I was trying to get you on," I advised after lighting another blunt. "We could be rolling in dough right now. Stax got damn near all of Los Angeles County on lock. Parts of the OC, too. If we take over in Oakland, Sacramento, and maybe even San Diego, we can be making major bread."

Bobbi shook her head. "I already told you, Lucci. Those couple of weeks when we handled your pickup and drop-off schedule was enough for me. That shit had me paranoid like a muthafucka. I was just waiting for SWAT to raid my shit."

Kay Kay giggled. "Me too. I don't see how you do it. I almost shit in my pants when those big-ass Mexicans with the tattoos and shit all over their bodies and faces walked up to the car. I just knew they were going to take the drugs and not pay us."

I blew out a cloud of smoke. "Them niggas ain't crazy. They know Stax or myself would kill them and their whole family if that ever happened."

We stood quiet for a few seconds, each in our own thoughts again, before the conversations continued.

"I know that it's a no when it comes to the drug thing, but would you guys be down for *stealing* something instead?"

"Stealing? Stealing something like what, Bobbi? And does the shit being stolen come with a hefty jail sentence like distributing drugs does if we get caught?" Kay Kay asked.

Bobbi's eyebrow rose, and she smirked. "*If* we get caught, there'd probably be a long jail bid, but I'm not worried about that."

"Not wor—Bitch, you might not be worried, but I am. I'm not trying to go to jail anymore. That shit is for the birds."

"Calm down, Kay Kay. None of us are going to jail if we do this shit right."

"Do what shit right, Bobbi?" Diamond asked.

A small glint of mischief appeared in Bobbi's eyes. "I think we should rob Bernfeld Jewelry Exchange."

"Your job?" we all questioned at once.

Bobbi nodded her head. "Yep. Remember that nigga that's been coming in for the last few weeks named Nav that I told you guys about? I can feel it in my soul that his ass showing up damn near every week is because he's casing the place. And it's obvious he's still unsure about some things, or shit would've went down already.

I figure if I get in contact with him and we put our heads together, all of our asses can be swimming in millions."

"Millions?" Kay Kay echoed, excitement in her tone.

"Yes, you heard me right. Millions, my dear Khalani."

"And how do you know this nigga can be trusted or will trust us, for that matter?" I questioned. "I know if I was him, I would be looking at you sideways if you stepped to me about stealing some diamonds. I would probably act like I didn't know you or what you were talking about."

"Man, I'm telling you, he gon' be with it. Especially after I tell him that I can get access to the vault."

"And how will you be able to get that?"

She smirked. "I have my ways, Lucci."

Diamond took a few pulls of the blunt. "I don't know if I'll be down with this. I got too much going on with Shine and then all of his hospital bills that I'm taking care of." She shook her head. "If shit goes bad, who's going to handle all of that? I can't leave my brother hanging. I won't leave him hanging."

"C'mon, Diamond," Bobbi whined. "You guys are so busy thinking about all the shit that can go wrong that you're not seeing all the shit that could go right. All of those bills you're stressing over, working two or three jobs just to pay off, could literally go suck a dick once you have those millions sitting in your account. And Kay Kay, you wanna stop turning tricks but don't want to get a regular job because money is slow. If we get these diamonds, you won't have to pop that pussy on a handstand unless you wanted to for recreational purposes. And you, Lucci." She turned to me. "Your mind is always on making money, so I know there will be little to no effort convincing you once we get all of the details straight."

When none of us responded to her small speech, Bobbi walked back over to the chairs that were already up on the roof and sat down. "Look, I'm not trying to pressure you guys to do anything you don't want to do. All I'm asking is if you would just think about it. I'm going to see if I can get in contact with Nav and run this by him. If he agrees, would you guys at least come to a meeting to hear what he has to say?"

Kay Kay, Diamond, and I all looked at each other for a brief moment before turning toward Bobbi and slowly nodding our heads.

"That's what the fuck I'm talking about!" Bobbi screamed before jumping up from her seat and pulling us all into a hug. "These muthafuckas at Bernfeld ain't gon' know what hit 'em after we clean them out."

"I guess we should name ourselves Diamond Mafia, since y'all ruled out Cocaine Mafia," I suggested as I looked down at my phone. A text from Stax had just came through, telling me that he needed me home asap.

"Ooooh, I like that. Diamond Mafia. It has a nice ring to it."

"Diamond, you only like that shit because your name's in it. Maybe we should change it to Gemstone Mafia. I can already tell this bitch"—Bobbi pointed her thumb at Diamond—"is about to get on my nerves. Probably get some shirts made and everything."

"Come to think of it, that's not a bad idea," Diamond sassed as she tapped her finger on her chin and looked up to the sky. "Franchise on it and everything."

Kay Kay laughed. "This nigga."

"Aye, I'm down with whatever name y'all pick, so just let me know. And um, I'm about to raise up out of here. Just got a message from Stax. I need to go handle some business. Let me know if anything changes with Shine, Diamond, okay? And if you feel in your heart that he's not strong enough to be transported just yet, you tell them people no."

"But I don't have the mon—"

I cut her off. "Don't even worry about that right now. Whatever you can't cover, I'll cover." She opened her mouth to respond, but I held my hand up. "I don't wanna hear whatever it is you're about to say about not having the money. You're my sister, which means Shine is my brother, too. When you don't have it, you know me, Kay Kay, or Bobbi will have it for you. You're straight. He's straight too. A'ight?"

She nodded her head, and I gave her another hug.

"Besides, when we get away with stealing all of these diamonds, you can pay me back then."

Diamond smiled and pushed out of my embrace. "Thank you, Lucci. For coming up here with the good greens and for always looking out. You two as well," she said to Kay Kay and Bobbi.

"You already know." Bobbi stretched her hand out. "And with that being said, can I get a Diamond Mafia on three?" We all groaned, but she continued. "C'mon, y'all. Stop being a bunch of pussies. One, two, three."

"Diamond Mafia!" we all screamed even though the shit was real corny.

The smiles on our faces at that moment were full of the love we shared for one another and the promise of always having each other's backs. Had we known the path we were about to take was filled with lies, hate, and betrayal, none of us probably would've agreed to do this shit. You see, money had a way of severing even the tightest bonds, which meant lifelong friendships weren't too far behind.

Chapter 6

Bobbi

"Okay. I would like to see that link bracelet right there, the open square bar one right there, and the two-toned steel one that has *Dad* inscribed on it right there, please."

I opened the case in front of me to retrieve each of the bracelets the customer requested. Although I was assisting her, my attention was on the small crowd of men walking through the jewelry store. Josh's father, Matthew Bernfeld, the head honcho of Bernfeld Jewelry Exchange, was there today, giving a few Chinese investors a tour of the place.

Some of the most beautiful crystal raindrop chandeliers ascended above our heads looking like diamonds floating in the sky. BJE was most definitely a sight to see. Plush velvet flooring greeted you at the door. Modern-style furnishing was placed around the 10,000 square foot space for guests who wanted to take a quick break from browsing our vast array of jewels. The soft colors of pear, almond, and gold would never look good in my house, but for some reason, worked well there. I could tell that Mr. Bernfeld and whoever came up with the design concept for this place spent a lot of hours looking over swatches and spent a lot of money bringing the vision to life.

"Uh, excuse me," the customer I was half-ass assisting snapped. "Are you going to help me with what I asked, or are you going to keep looking over there at who I am assuming is your boss?"

I turned my eyes to her and had to catch myself from curling my lip and giving her back the same attitude she was giving me. I didn't have time to get fired for disrespecting a potential buyer, especially when there was still some shit I needed to know about the inner workings of BJE.

"I do apologize for my rudeness," I said with a fake smile and tone. "You are correct. That is my boss over there, and I wanted to make a good impression on him. You see, I just applied for—"

She held up her hand, cutting me off. "I didn't ask you any of that shit. I just wanna know if you are going to help me out or not."

Her voice was a little louder this time when she spoke, which caused Josh to look in our direction. His eyes went to her first as he tried to gauge what was going on. Once his gaze landed on me, he stared for a small second before looking back at the woman in front of me. I could tell from the way he scanned her body up and down that he was attracted to her in some way. I mean, who wouldn't be? She was a petite little thing with a slim-thick frame. Her purse and shoes alone told me that she had a little money, but it was her long-ass neon green stiletto nails and multiple earrings hanging from her ear that told me that she definitely had a little hood in her. Her hair was similar to mine in a low, slicked-back ponytail. Her skin was almost the same chocolate color as mine too, maybe one shade lighter. With her cute button nose, pouty lips, and big brown eyes, she kind of reminded me of Kyla Pratt, just with a lot more attitude.

"I apologize again, ma'am. Would you like to try any of these bracelets on?"

She scoffed. "Bitch, do I look like a man to you?"

"No, you—"

She cut me off. "If your answer is no, then why would you ask if I wanted to try the bracelets on?" She stuck out her arm. "You see how small my wrist is?"

"I do," I responded, slowly losing my patience. "I just asked because most customers—"

She cut me off again. "Well, I ain't most customers, so I don't need to try shit on. I'm pretty sure my husband can fit these."

"Oh, okay, so we're shopping for your husband. Will this be an anniversary gift? Early birthday gift? A just because gift?" I asked as Josh turned his attention back to his father, who was now moving farther toward the back.

A big smile formed on her face, and she held up her ring finger, which had a beautiful princess cut, three-carat ring on it. "It's actually a thank you gift. You see, my husband gave me the wedding of my dreams a few weeks ago." She gushed like a schoolgirl, attitude totally different from what it was a few seconds ago. "And as if that wasn't enough, he surprises me with this little piece last week." She raised her chin, giving me access to see the emerald teardrop necklace around her neck.

My eyes opened wide as I realized it was the same necklace I'd sold to Nav the last time he was there. The extra row of diamonds around the emerald pendant he had one of our craftsmen add before he left was a dead giveaway.

"I wanted to be a grateful little wife and surprise him with something just as nice, so here I am."

"You know, I actually helped your husband with this purchase," I revealed as I let the pendent fall from my fingertips. "Mr. Ali, right? I mean Nav," I corrected myself and smiled. "He's a real nice guy."

She cocked her head to the side, a look of confusion on her face. "How well do you know my husband?"

"I don't *know* your husband at all. He just came in here a few times and bought some very nice pieces. That's it."

We stood in an awkward silence for a few seconds. I could tell by the way she kept looking me up and down that she was trying to figure out if Nav and I had something going on further than I let on. The nigga was fine and all, don't get me wrong, but I'd never been the type of girl who enjoyed being the side chick.

I guess after she couldn't detect if I was lying or not, she decided to just let it go. I watched as she walked over to the next display case, which held the men's wedding bands, and began to look at those.

"Were you looking for anything in particular from this case?" I asked after grabbing the bracelets she wanted and walking over to her. Although I was a bit perplexed with her whole demeanor, I still wanted the commission money I would make off this sale. "We have a nice selection of bands for every occasion."

She didn't respond for a minute. However, when she did, I wasn't expecting to hear the question that came out of her mouth.

"Bobbi, do you like working here?"

Confused by the change of conversation, I hesitantly answered, "Uh, yeah, I guess. But um, how do you know my nickname? I never mentioned it to you."

"I know a lot more than you think I do. But that's neither here nor there. When my husband came in last week, did you two discuss anything in . . . particular?"

"Um, no disrespect, but where is this line of questioning going? And I'm still waiting on you to tell me how you know my name."

She reached into her purse, pulled out a card, and handed it to me. "I was instructed to give this to you. Don't ask me any questions, because I'm not at liberty to answer them here." She discreetly looked around the store one good time before looking back at me. "Call the number on the back. The person who answers will tell you what to do next."

"Wait a min—" I started to say, but she cut me off, changing the subject yet again.

"I'll take all three of those bracelets you're holding and this ring right here, the one with the black diamond setting and platinum band. If you can, could you please wrap my items in some paper after boxing them?"

I looked down at the black business card in my hand. "Ali Construction," I read out loud. "Wait a minute. What the hell is this all about?"

She ran her fingers over the display case and smirked. "You know, you ask too many damn questions. Just call the number like I said. Anything you wanna know will be answered once you do. Now," she said as she slid her shades back over her face, "can you get my shit ready? I still have a little more shopping to do."

Like I said, I wanted this commission, so I rang her up and wrapped her shit like she requested. Once Nav's wife left, I looked down at the card she'd given me. I wasn't too sure what this was all about, but whatever it was, I had a feeling that once I called the number on the back, my life would most definitely be changing.

***

I sat in the booth at the back of the small diner, waiting for Lucci and Kay Kay to show up. I had a very lucrative offer for them that I hoped and prayed they would be down to do. The only person I worried about was Diamond. The shit she was going through with Shine right now was really getting to her. The last time I called her and asked for an update, she said that Shine was still unresponsive and showed no signs of waking up. The doctors removed the breathing machine and were very hopeful that he would breathe on his own. Unfortunately, their opinions changed an hour later when he had to be hooked back up to the machine.

I hadn't been up to visit him since the last time we all showed up to the hospital. Between working my regular schedule and digging into some shit for Nav pertaining to BJE and their security, I hadn't had much time to do anything else. Hopefully, that would all change soon.

"Thank you," I said to the waitress who had placed some waters and coffees on the table. I took the liberty of ordering our beverages already. This conversation needed to start as soon as my girls arrived.

"Damn, bitch. This better be one hell of an emergency for you to have me out of bed this early in the morning. You know I don't get up before twelve and don't move unless the money is calling."

Lucci was the first to walk to the table, dressed in some skin-tight jeans, a pullover sweater, and these cute-ass Nike Air Max. Her blond hair was up on the top of her head in a messy bun, and her face was free of makeup. Based off looks alone, you would never know the type of life Lucci lived. Her ass was as gutter as they came, with the face of an angel.

"I'm surprised you showed up at all," I returned, taking a sip of my coffee. "Have you spoken to Kay Kay? I couldn't get a hold of her last night, so I just sent a text. I know she read it, but she didn't respond."

Lucci sat down on the burgundy vinyl seat and scooted over until she was sitting directly in the middle of the booth. Placing her bag on her side, she grabbed the sugar pack in the small bowl and began to make her coffee.

"She should've beat me here. When I talked to her twenty minutes ago, she told me that she was already headed this way," Lucci said right before she sipped her coffee and frowned. She then proceeded to add a few more packs of sugar to her cup. "Shauna's deadbeat ass didn't come home again, so she had to leave the kids with her mama real quick."

I nodded my head and continued to browse through the menu.

"I see you're still waiting for one last person. Did the two of you want to put in your order now, or did you want to wait?" the waitress asked after walking back over to our table.

Lucci lustfully eyed the poor girl up and down. I could tell the waitress was starting to feel a little uncomfortable by the way she kept fidgeting with her apron.

"You are sexy as fuck," Lucci complimented with a lick of her lips. "Me and my nigga would have some fun with you. Are you into girls?" she asked. The waitress nervously shook her head. "Too bad. The way your camel toe pushing through them slacks, I know your pussy is fat and juicy."

The waitress began to stutter a response at the same time as I spit my coffee out of my mouth. "Lucci!" I yelped, wiping the black liquid from my face. "Bitch, why would you say that?"

She shrugged her shoulders. "What? I'm only telling the truth. You know I'm far from shy."

"But still." I turned my attention to the waitress, whose cheeks were as red as a tomato. "Excuse my friend, uh . . . Jenny." I read her name tag. "She hasn't taken her medication yet. But to answer your question, we're going to wait until our other friend gets here to order."

Jenny nodded her head and turned around to leave our booth so fast that she bumped into the table that was behind her, knocking all the silverware and condiments to the ground.

"What the fuck is going on in here?" Kay Kay asked as she removed her jacket and sat down. "Lucci must've came on to the girl."

I laughed. "You already know how her and Stax get down. Always on the hunt for some new coochie."

"We're not always on the hunt." Lucci defended herself. She placed the menu she was looking over back down on the table. "I just like to have a good time."

"I bet Stax ass loves the fact that you like girls just as much as he does."

She shrugged her shoulders. "Yes and no. The nigga gets mad when I pay more attention to the bitch than him when we do have threesomes. He was all into it at first, but now . . ."

"But now what?" Kay Kay asked, drinking some of her water.

Lucci shook her head. "I don't know. Something's up with his ass. He been moving funny for a few months now. Disappearing at all times of the night. Getting sloppy with the pickups and drop-offs. The nigga's been very secretive, too. Always on his phone texting somebody, but as soon as I walk into the room, he either turns his phone off or darkens the screen and places it face down on the desk. Whatever his ass is doing, he better get that shit in order before I find out what it is. Stax ass knows I don't play about my freedom, my man, or my money, so he better figure something out."

Kay Kay and I nodded our heads in agreement and continued to listen to Lucci talk about what she thought Stax was up to. In the midst of the conversation, Jenny came back and took our orders.

Once the food was placed in front of us, we dug in. I waited until we all were almost done with our breakfast before calling Diamond on the speaker phone and informing them about why we were all there.

"Can you hear me, D?" I asked after the call connected.

"Yeah, I can hear you."

"Hey, Diamond."

"Hey, sis."

Both Lucci and Kay Kay greeted her.

"Hey, y'all. So, what's this all about?"

I wiped my hands and mouth with a napkin and finished chewing the food in my mouth before I spoke. "So, do y'all remember the conversation we had on the roof of the hospital a little while ago?"

"We talked about a lot of shit, Bobbi. Refresh our memories."

I rolled my eyes at Kay Kay. "Look, you all gotta just follow what I'm saying, okay? I don't want to say too much, because you never know who's listening." From the silence around the table and over the phone, I knew that I had their attention. "So, like I was saying, remember the conversation we had on the roof of the hospital? When we were talking about getting out of California and starting new lives or whatever?" After a chorus of *yeah*s,

I continued. "Well, remember when I told y'all about that fine-ass nigga Nav and what I thought he was up to?" Again, there was a chorus of *yeah*s. "Turns out that I was right. He was doing exactly what I said he was."

"How do you know?" Lucci asked, taking another bite of her medium rare steak.

"Because I talked to him over the phone the other day. He actually sent his wife in to give me his card. I wasn't going to call him at first, but something in my gut was telling me that I should."

Kay Kay frowned. "His wife? And he sent her in your job to talk to you on his behalf? Who does that?"

"Apparently he does. But that's neither here nor there. I brought you all here to see if you guys were for real about"—I lowered my voice to almost a whisper—"going after those diamonds."

Lucci sat back in her seat after drinking the last of her water and rubbed her bloated belly. "I already told you I'm with it. As long as the nigga has a dummy-proof plan and a stay-out-of-jail card handy, I'm with it."

I smiled at Lucci and gave her my hand to dap. "What about you, Kay Kay? You still want to get your niece and nephew up out of here?"

She looked between Lucci and me for a second before looking down at the phone. "Are you with it, Diamond? Because I'm only down if you're down."

We all waited for what felt like hours for Diamond to respond. And when she did, my blood started to boil.

"I know I was talking all that shit when we were on the roof high as fuck, but I really don't think I can do it, guys. Not with Shine like this. Had it been a year or so ago, you know I would be down for whatever, but if you can't guarantee me that we won't get caught up, then I'm not going to risk it. I'm all Shine has. I can't be here to look over him if I'm locked up in jail."

"But who said anything about going to jail?" I questioned heatedly. "You don't think we all will be taking a risk? You aren't the only one with responsibilities, Diamond. Kay Kay has her family to look after. I'm so far in debt right now with bills, student loans, and the IRS, I'm never going to experience having a full paycheck to myself. And Lucci just wants to be able to not have to work a regular nine-to-five to make ends meet. Not only that, but you're not the only one risking going to jail for the rest of your life. We are too."

Diamond was quiet for a few seconds. "I'm not saying you all don't have responsibilities, Bobbi. It's just that . . . my shit is different."

"How the fuck is your shit—" I started to say, but Lucci grabbed my arm, calming me and my attitude down. I took a deep breath before speaking again. "Aye, D. I apologize. I didn't mean to get all hostile a second ago."

"It's cool."

I took a deep breath. "Will you at least come to the meeting he's scheduled a few weeks from today? Hear what he has to say and maybe even ask some questions of your own."

"How do you even know we can trust this nigga? You don't know shit about him but that he has a wife and buys her expensive-ass jewelry."

I cleared my throat and silently counted to ten. Diamond and I usually didn't bump heads, but she was testing my patience with the way she was coming at me.

"You're right. I don't know much about him, but I do know enough to at least meet with the nigga and see what he has to say. I don't know about you, Diamond, but I could really use this extra money. Shit, we all can. But it's all up to you, sis. We're not committing to anything, just simply hearing the man's plan."

We all looked down at my phone, which was sitting in the middle of the table. From the look on Lucci's face, I could tell she was over the whole thing and ready to go. Kay Kay was just waiting on Diamond to give her answer so that she could give hers.

"So, what's it gonna be, Diamond?" Lucci asked while responding to a text on her phone.

"You're right, Bobbi. I could use the money. But as much as I need it, I'm still gonna have to pass. I'll just find another way to pay these bills."

"If Diamond isn't down, I'm not down either," Kay Kay added. Before she could say anything else, her phone rang. "What's up, Ma? Wait, what? Slow down. Where's Shauna? Where are the kids? Are they still there? Shit, shit, shit. Okay. I'm on my way. Mama, I said okay. Try to stall them or something. I'm on my way now. Fuck."

"What's going on, Kay Kay?"

Ignoring my question, she hopped up from her seat, throwing her napkin over her plate. "I gotta go. Child Protective Services just showed up at the house."

Both Lucci and I sat up in our seats.

"Do you need us to come with you?" I asked, picking my phone up and releasing the call from Diamond. She really pissed me off saying no. I had to figure out a way to get her to change her mind.

"Nah. I don't need y'all there getting all riled up with me. I'll call you after I find out what's going on." She bent down and pressed her cheek against mine and waved at Lucci. "Keep me posted on if Diamond changes her mind."

"We will," Both Lucci and I said at the same time.

Jenny walked back over to our table with the bill. "Did you all enjoy the meal? Your friend rushed out of here so fast, I was hoping it wasn't because of the food."

"No, she had to run. The food was great, thanks." Pulling my debit card out, I paid the bill and left Jenny a nice-sized tip.

"Where you going now?" I asked Lucci as we headed toward the parking lot.

She was so deep into her phone that she didn't hear me at first. I had to ask her again.

"Oh, I'm about to go handle some business. You know me, all about the money." We hugged. "And don't trip on Diamond right now. You know she's going through some things. I'll hit her up and put the bug in her ear again. Hopefully she changes her mind by the time the meeting comes around."

"Yeah, I hope so," I replied as I sent Nav a text message.

Me: We're all in. See you in a few

I knew he wasn't going to respond. Per his request, I was only to text him if my whole crew was down to get this money. I knew I may have been jumping the gun by saying that Kay Kay and Diamond had agreed, but I was praying like hell that they both showed up when it was time to meet up with Nav's sexy ass.

Chapter 7

Kay Kay

I saw the large crowd of people standing in the street as soon as I hit the corner. My mother was hanging halfway off the porch, holding on to my niece's leg, while my nephew was being carried to the open doors of a white social services van. The man holding my niece said something to my mother, which obviously fell on deaf ears. She still continued to pull at my niece's leg in spite of his obvious threats, and she was rewarded with a shove that made her tumble to the ground. That was enough for me to hop out of my car before I even put it in park and run right up to the asshole who had just hit my mama.

"Muthafucka, are you crazy?" I screamed in his face. My niece's cries became louder when she heard my elevated voice. "I'll slice your damn throat you put your hands on my mama like that again."

He opened his mouth to no doubt give me a smart-ass response, but a well-dressed, petite woman with beautiful bone structure, jet black hair, and skin the color of copper stepped from the passenger-side seat of the van and called my name.

"How in the hell do you know who I am?" I asked, already on high alert.

She looked down at the clipboard in her hand. "You're Khalani Jones. Female. Age thirty-one. Oldest of the four kids your mother birthed. Known troublemaker. Arrested for prostitution, burglary, and assault with a deadly weapon." Her eyebrow raised. "Spent a few years locked up behind those charges. High school dropout, and at one point, a teen mom who is currently unemployed yet takes care of herself and everyone in the family." I froze as she ran my life down and smirked. "Did I forget to mention anything?"

I cut my eyes at her. "Yeah, you forgot to mention who in the fuck you are and why you're taking my niece and nephew."

She handed her clipboard to the man standing behind her and stuck out her hand. "My name is Phyllis Hines, and I am your niece Dajah and nephew Devon's new case worker." When I ignored her outstretched hand, she took it back. While wiping her open palm against the length of her pleated slacks, she continued. "Ms. Kim, their previous case worker, unfortunately isn't employed with DPSS anymore, so all of her cases were handed over to me. I noticed in her reports that the last time she was out here for a visit was a little over four months ago, which isn't proper protocol for an open CPS case."

I rolled my eyes, just thinking about the reason CPS came knocking on our door the first time. Shauna's ass was out there fucking on somebody's husband, and his wife called the people on her. It was around the time I had just gotten out of prison and was staying in a halfway house. Shauna left the kids at home by themselves, and CPS just so happened to come to the house that day. It took us weeks and a gang of lawyer fees to get them back. By the time they came home, I was out of the halfway house and able to watch them from that point on.

"Okay, so what is proper protocol?" I asked, looking around at my nosey-ass neighbors. "Because I wouldn't think that ripping kids from their home and causing a big-ass scene is one."

She held her hands up in surrender. "A big scene was never my intent. I honestly thought that we were going to pull up and find nothing here." Phyllis took a small breath and stepped toward me. "I know everything that's happening right now may seem a bit much, Khalani, but I assure you that it all ties in with the wellness of the children."

"Wellness of the children? My niece and nephew are fine. Usually I watch them, but I had to step out for a few—"

"Where's their mother?" She interrupted me.

Her question caught me off guard for a second. People always assumed Dajah and Devon were mine because I had them so much.

"She's . . . uh. She's not here right now. I think she mentioned something about going to find a job."

"A job?" she repeated. I could tell she didn't believe me by the way her facial expression changed. "I was told that your sister is hardly ever home and that you take care of the children."

I opened my mouth and shut it. How the fuck did she know that, and who in the hell was out there telling my business?

"Nah, whoever said that lied," I voiced loudly, eyeing my nosey-ass neighbors. "My sister is a great mother and takes great care of her kids. I'm just one of those aunties who—"

She held her hand up, cutting me off. "No need for you to explain. I understand that, although the children's biological mother is alive and well enough to watch after them, the children are still cared for mainly by you. And although what you're doing is commendable, I still have dire concerns when it comes to their well-being."

"You're saying that as if I don't give a fuck about what my niece and nephew do or that I can't take care of them."

She cocked her head to the side with a smug look on her face. "Ms. Jones, do you have any idea of what the children were doing when I pulled up?"

I looked over at my mother, who was lying flat on the concrete. I could tell by the gloss in her eyes and the way her body kept twitching that she was high off of something. The only reason why I left the kids there with her was because she said that she didn't have any drugs or money to get lifted. I promised to throw her a couple dollars if she watched over her grandchildren for an hour or two. Had I known her ass was going to get ahold of some shit while I was gone, I would've taken the kids to the restaurant with me.

"Look, whatever it is that they were doing, I'm sure it's something that they won't ever do again. I can assure you of that," I tried to reason. I could hear whoever was in the back of the van trying to calm Dajah and Devon down as best as they could, but nothing was working. "Please, just give them back to me and I promise I won't let them out of my sight again."

"Ms. Jones." She walked closer to me. "As much as I want to leave the children with you, I'm afraid that I can't do that. You see, when we pulled up, Dajah was on the porch, using a dirty syringe to make her baby doll *feel good,* and Devon had a small-caliber pistol in his hands, pretending he was shooting at the *bad guys*." She used air quotes. "Thank God the gun wasn't loaded and Dajah used the needle on the doll instead of herself." She shook her head. "I'm sorry, but until we can determine whether this environment is safe for either of them, I'm afraid I'm going to have to take the children with me and place them in foster care."

"Foster care? No, please. Just . . . just give them back to me, please," I begged, eyes filling with tears. I remembered how scared I was when the state tried to take me away from my mother, so I could only imagine how my niece and nephew were feeling. I had to try something to get her to change her mind or at least look the other way this one time.

"Money!" belted from my lips. "I got a little bit of money. Maybe four or five thousand. It's all yours if you just let me have my babies back this one time."

Phyllis looked as if she were thinking about my offer for a second. "As good as five thousand dollars sounds right now, I'm afraid I'm going to have to pass." She pulled a card out of her pocket. "This is the number to my office, as well as the number to Child Protective Services. A hearing will be set for later on in the month, where a judge will determine whether the children will be released back into your custody. So, call either one of those numbers in a week for the date."

"What determines if the judge releases them back to me or not?' I asked, heart heavy as hell.

Phyllis looked around the front yard. The large crowd once gathered had already seen enough and started to disperse. My mother was still lying knocked out on the ground, high as hell, and Shauna's bitch ass was nowhere to be found.

"Your sister determines that, Khalani," she said over her shoulder as she started walking toward the van.

"Since you are not their legal guardian, it's up to your sister to prove that the children are in a safe environment and that she is able to provide for them mentally, physically, and financially. If she can do that, then the judge will grant her custody again."

"Okay, but what if—" I tried to ask Phyllis another question, but before I could, she closed the van door and instructed the driver to pull off.

I ran out into the street and looked at the van's tail lights until I couldn't see them anymore, the distancing cries of my niece and nephew still ringing loudly in my ears. I knew that it was going to take a lot of money and a good-ass family lawyer to get Dajah and Devon back. Fucked up part about this whole situation, though, was Shauna wasn't going to give two fucks that her kids were gone. Everything that needed to be handled would rest solely on me, which meant that I had to help Shauna get her shit together just like I did for my mama.

I was lying stretched out on the couch when my sister finally walked her ass into the house. A whole week had passed since the kids had been gone, and this bitch didn't have a clue. I flipped through the channels on the TV as she pranced around the living room, making all kinds of noise. I knew she wanted me to look at her and see the Fendi shirt and boots she was rocking. The bitch even had the Fendi headband around her Brazilian-bundle-weave head. She plopped down on the couch across from me and dramatically sighed when she realized her previous antics to get my attention were still getting ignored.

"It's quiet as hell around here. Where's Mama? Where are the kids?"

I shrugged my shoulders. "Mama's down at The Shack doing what she does best. And as far as the kids, CPS came and picked them up last week."

A shocked look covered her face for a second before she went back to smiling and admiring the iced-out bracelet on her wrist. "Maybe that's the best place for them to be. I hardly ever have time to look after them, and your life was slowing down because of them." She shrugged her shoulders. "This was probably a good thing."

I sat up on the couch and put the TV on mute. My head was starting to bang, and my blood pressure was spiking up to an alarmingly high rate.

"What the fuck did you just say?" I asked, telling myself my sister couldn't be that selfish. Hell, if she didn't want to be bothered with kids, she should've made them niggas strap up.

She looked down at her nails and then up at me. "You heard what the fuck I said, so don't act like you didn't."

I closed my eyes and wiped my hand over my face, trying to calm myself down. When my focus went back to Shauna, she was staring right back at me. Arguing wasn't going to help our situation, so I figured I'd try to approach this conversation a different way.

"Look, Shauna, I'm not even trying to go there with you today, or any other day, for that matter. It's obvious you've never gave a fuck about them kids since the day you pushed them out your pussy. You're so busy trying to snatch up a nigga to take care of you and finance your lifestyle that your children aren't even a priority." I took a deep breath and released it. "For the last couple of days, I've been talking to a lawyer. Since you don't want to be their mother and I basically am, he suggested that you sign over your parental rights to me. That way, I will be one hundred percent responsible for them and their well-being. If we do the paperwork now, I can take it to the court when it's time for the hearing."

Instead of responding to me, Shauna pulled her ringing phone out of her purse and smiled at the screen before answering it. "Hey, babe. Nah, I just got home. I was going to pack a bag and then come back to you. Okay. Oh, and thank you again for the mini shopping spree," she gushed while looking over her outfit. "I really love everything you bought me. Okay. Talk to you later, babe. Bye." She released the call and looked back at me. "Now, what were you saying about signing over my rights?"

"I was saying—" I stopped abruptly when gunshots rang out.

Shauna I and dove to the ground and covered our heads, eyes still connected, silently telling each other that we would be okay once everything was over.

I didn't know who was out there busting, but it sounded like they had a whole army of niggas going at it. The loud pings and bangs went on for what felt like hours. By the time the last bullet sounded off, I could already hear the police sirens on their way.

I was the first to get up from my spot under the dining room table. Shauna followed suit, her body still trembling a bit as we looked around at all the damage the house had incurred.

"Who the fuck did you piss off now?" we both asked each other at the same time.

"Bitch, you're the one sleeping with married men and thinking that their wives ain't gon' find out," I snapped. "I told you that you would fuck with the wrong one someday."

She sucked her teeth and opened the front door, stepping out onto the porch. I could hear the loud commotion of our neighbors starting to gather around.

"What the fuck does me sleeping with married men have to do with anything? How do you know the niggas you mess around with ain't married?"

"Because I make sure they're not. I don't need those kinds of problems in my life."

She grunted. "Looks to me like you got those type of problems anyway."

I looked at her with a confused expression on my face. "What the fuck are you talking about, Shauna? The niggas I fuck with don't know what kind of car I drive, let alone where I lay my head."

"Well, I guess somebody must've figured something out," she responded, pointing her finger. I followed the direction of her hand and almost shitted on myself when I saw my car.

"What the fuck?" I yelled, running toward my shit, not caring at all that my ass was hanging out of the boy shorts that I had on and my braless titties were probably bouncing all over the place in my thin wife beater. Out of all the cars parked on this side of the street, mine was the only one hit. "Not my baby."

Shauna walked up next to me, assessing the damage. She whistled low. "You must've pissed somebody off. Your shit looking like swiss cheese right now."

I pushed her out of the way as she laughed and walked around to the driver's side. The door was damn near hanging off the hinges. All the windows were busted out. The custom paint job I just had done, as well as the leather interior on the seats, were riddled with bullet holes. Swiss cheese was the perfect description of what my car looked like.

I turned around to the small crowd of neighbors behind me. "Did anybody see who did this?"

Ms. Emma, the old woman who lived across from me, pointed her finger toward the ground. "I didn't see who did it, but whoever it was dropped that piece o' paper on the ground that you're standing on."

I looked down at the lined notebook paper and bent over to pick it up. A million things were running through my mind. I was always very careful with hiding my life from my johns. The ones I was fucking on the regular didn't even have my phone number. I always called them from a burner phone when it was time for me to re-up on some ends, so I was really confused about who could've done this.

I opened the folded piece of paper and read what was written on it:

Bitch, you have one week to give me back the money you stole or I'ma pay a visit to your niece and nephew at their foster home and get it from them. Hit this number when you got my 20 stacks.

My body began to shake as I read the words on the paper for a second time. This drive-by was because of me. Over the years, I'd stolen money from a few people, so I wasn't sure who this was actually coming from. My mind went to Doughboy for a hot second, but I doubted his low-level drug-dealing ass had the resources to pull something like this off. Whoever it was, though, would no doubt come back looking for their money. And twenty bands at that? I couldn't let my niece and nephew suffer from some shit behind me. After paying $1500 to the lawyer and handling some other shit, I only had about

$3000 left out of the $5000 I had stashed away. More than ever, I needed to come up on some money now.

As the police began to pile on to the street, investigating the scene, I ran back into the house, picked up my phone, and sent a text.

Me: Is ole boy still trying to meet up
Bobbi: Yep
Me: Well, count me in
Bobbi: Already did

I smiled, reading Bobbi's response. The bitch already knew I would eventually come around. I just hoped that once we split this money from this diamond heist, I would be able to pay back whoever the fuck was after me for their money, get Dajah and Devon back, then get the fuck up out of California.

Chapter 8

Nav

"Nav. What the fuck, bruh? I know you hear me calling you."

I inwardly groaned as Tweety stomped her way up the winding staircase of the old firehouse building I used for business dealings. I heard her calling my name some time ago, but I didn't feel like being bothered with her or her shenanigans that day. For the last week or so, Tweety had been on my neck about Bobbi and her friends joining the team. When I first ran the idea by her, she was all on board for the additional help, but after learning that there would be four *females* added to the crew, shit started to become a problem.

I tucked the picture of Bobbi I'd been looking at under a stack of papers on my desk and waited for Tweety to storm her way into my office. Sitting back in my chair, I closed my eyes and began to rub at my temples, already preparing myself for the headache I knew was sure to come.

"Nav," she snapped as soon as she stepped over the small pile of duffle bags in front of the doorway. "What the fuck is up with you? Why do I have to call you more than once to get some type of response?" She walked straight up to my desk and crossed her arms over her small chest. Her hair was wrapped in one of those bonnet things she liked to wear, face heavily made up. I could tell by the way she was dressed that she was planning on going out somewhere. Her short black cocktail dress left very little to the imagination. I could damn near see the gap between her thighs because the hem was so short.

She sucked her teeth when I didn't answer. "Nigga, I know you hear me talking to you."

I rubbed my temples with a little more pressure and calmly said, "Yes, I heard you calling me. What can I do for you, Tweety?"

Her eyes scanned over my face for a few seconds before she looked down at the folders and blueprints scattered around my desk.

"I wanna know what's going on with the diamond job at BJE. Ever since I went to the store and gave that one bitch your card, you've been tight-lipped about the details."

"I haven't been tight-lipped about the details, or anything else, for that matter," I lied. "What would make you say that?"

She placed her open palms on the edge of my desk and leaned her body in so that we were almost face to face, knocking over a few of my picture frames and the cup that held my pens. I could smell the minty mouthwash she'd just used on her breath and the faint scent of the cocoa butter Dove she bathed with.

"Don't fucking sit there and lie to me, *Naveen*." My name rolled off her tongue with venom. "You don't think I know you and that Bobbi bitch got something going on?"

I chuckled at her accusation, which really pissed her off.

"You think that shit is funny? Nigga, you got me all the way fucked up if you think I'm about to sit back and let some new bitch come up in this organization and take my spot. I've been riding with you for years. Gave up the pussy to you and everything. You keep telling me that it's not the right time for us to be together, but now I'm starting to think that you've only been saying that to pacify me."

I finally opened my eyes and looked into those heated irises of hers. Tweety was indeed a beautiful woman. She was loyal through and through; probably would make a great wife to someone just as crazy as her. Unfortunately, that person wasn't me.

"Gave up the pussy? You make it seem like it was something I was begging you for. You and I both know that night was a mistake."

Like I said before, Tweety was a very beautiful woman—brown satin skin, a petite, tight little body with a gorgeous smile. Her personality was great, most times. Honestly, she reminded me of one of my boys with just a softer side. We moved as one, broke bread together, even vacationed and celebrated birthdays with one another. However, even with having all of that, Tweety and I never really vibed on a relationship level. At least not in my opinion. The one time we did have sex only happened because we were both drunk out of our minds after celebrating a job we had just pulled off. It was our first time hitting a lick and coming out with a smooth million each after getting the jewels off.

The morning after, when our highs had come down and the liquor was out of our system, I told Tweety that what happened between us that night should've never happened and wouldn't happen again. That day, she told me that she understood where I was coming from and respected the fact that I didn't see her as anything other than a partner in crime. But here we were, damn near five years later, with her insinuating that us having sex was more than what it was—just sex.

Her eyebrows furrowed and a look of sadness covered her face. "A mistake? It didn't feel like a mistake," she murmured, walking around the desk and turning my chair so that I was facing her. Tweety lifted her little dress above her hips and straddled my lap. Grabbing my face between her hands, she closed her eyes and tried to kiss me on the lips, but she got my cheek instead.

"So, that's how it's going to be? You really are going to sit here and act like you don't feel the connection between us?"

I grabbed both of her wrists and held them in my hands. "Tweety." I licked my lips and shook my head. "There is no connection between us. What you feel for me, I don't feel for you. At least not on that level. Do I love you?" I nodded my head. "Yeah, without a doubt. Would I kill for you? Absolutely, because I know you'd do the same for me. But will I ever want anything more than friendship from you?" I paused for a second, pulling my bottom lip into my mouth, eyes staring directly into hers so that she could see how serious I was. "No. You are my sister, and that's all you will ever be."

Tweety snactched her wrists from my grip, hopped off my lap, and pulled her dress down. I could see the gloss of unshed tears in her eyes and kind of felt bad for making her cry. I stood up from my chair, towering over her petite frame, and tried to wipe the lone tear that had managed to finally fall; but when I reached my hand out toward her face, she stepped back and shook her head.

"Don't. Don't try to act like you care now, Nav. I get it. You don't want me in that way." She wrapped her arms around her body, hugging herself, and stepped back some more. "I just thought that when you gave me that necklace and bought me those earrings, you were . . ." Her voice trailed off when she noticed the confused expression on my face.

"That I was what?"

She swallowed the lump in her throat. "That you were finally claiming me as yours. I don't know. I mean, you've never given me, let alone anyone else, a gift as exquisite as that diamond necklace. And then you bought the earrings to match. I don't know many friends that would spend over ten *G*s on a just-because gift."

The thing was, I didn't buy that set for her. I actually bought it for Bobbi. That day that I was in the store, I could tell that she loved the necklace the second she removed it from the display case and placed it on the velvet jewelry stand. The way her eyes lit up when she talked about the emerald teardrop jewel hanging in the center and the way her smile brightened when she tried the earrings on for me, I couldn't help but to purchase them for her.

The plan was to go into the store to count the security cameras and buy another expensive watch as a distraction, but my reason for being there quickly changed when I noticed the way her fingers lingered over the necklace display case and her eyes zeroed in on that lovely piece. The whole lie about me having a wife just stumbled out of my mouth. I didn't like the way her attraction toward me was instantly turned off when I mentioned that I had just gotten married, but it was too late to try to change my story.

I slipped the platinum band that was originally on my right finger to the left and held up my hand to show off the ring. When I sent Tweety in a few days later to give Bobbi my card, she took the lie to a whole different level. I'm not sure what-all she said to Bobbi on that day, but I could tell that it was enough to change Bobbi's whole attitude toward me.

I didn't want to hurt Tweety's feelings any more than they were by revealing who the jewelry was really for, so I opted not to tell her. Instead, I picked up a folder containing information on the security guards that worked for BJE and handed it over to her, changing the subject.

"So, I had my tech guy pull the security guards' records. Only one has priors. I got Ant watching him. I'm pretty sure once we offer him a few bands, he will be down with the plan."

Tweety looked at me for a second before nodding her head and looking down at the contents of the folder.

"What about the other security guard? You think he will be down if you offer him some money?"

I shook my head and picked up the cup of lukewarm coffee I had been drinking and took a sip. "I don't think he will. Nigga is squeaky clean and doesn't even litter." My focus turned to her. "This is where I need you to come in."

"What do you mean?"

"I want you to apply for the security position the company posted."

She opened her mouth to object, but I cut her off.

"Before you even shoot the shit down, just hear me out."

After I explained to Tweety why I wanted her in that position, she reluctantly agreed to do it and handed the folder back to me.

"So then, it's settled. I'm going to be doing security. What about the codes needed to open the safe? How will you get those?"

"I'll get them."

"How? I remember Ant saying that the owner switches the shit every week to something different. Never the same set of numbers."

"Would you use the same security code over and over again if you had seventy million dollars' worth of jewels locked behind a safe that may or may not keep thieving hands off?"

She shook her head.

"I didn't think so. But aye, don't worry about the codes. Like I said, I'll get them."

She looked at me skeptically for a second and then smiled. "I hate how secretive you are sometimes but I get why you are." Tweety walked toward the door to leave, but then stopped when she thought about something. "Oh, I almost forgot. What do you think about Greece?"

I shrugged my shoulders. "I don't. But what about it?"

"I think that's where we should go after we pull this lick." She winked her eye. "You know, to celebrate and shit."

"We will see," was my response before I sat back down behind my desk and pulled the picture of Bobbi from underneath the papers. I didn't want to get Tweety's hopes all high about us celebrating this next lick together, especially when I had plans on chilling with Bobbi. I just had to figure out a way to get her to believe that Tweety and I really weren't a thing.

Chapter 9

Bobbi

I stretched my arms high above my head and wiggled my toes to make sure they still had movement in them. My body was still a little sore from the workout Josh had just put down on me. Yeah, I know I said that the last time we fucked in his office would be the *last time*, but a bitch was horny, and Josh had invited me out to dinner after our shifts ended earlier. Had I declined, it would've been another night of leftover pizza for me, and I was so damn tired of freaking Dominos.

After we dined on steak and lobster at Mastro's, I could've easily taken an Uber back to my car, which I left parked in BJE's parking lot, and went straight home to rest; but when Josh suggested we head to his condo in Pacific Palisades for a nightcap, I was seriously considering taking him up on his offer. Sensing my hesitation, he proceeded to do that thing that I love with his tongue in my ear, and at that point, I was all game for the oceanside trip. What should've been a forty-five minute ride actually turned into a twenty with the way Josh was whipping his new S-Class up the 10 freeway. The speed gods were definitely on his side, because the police didn't jump behind us once.

As soon as we hit his door, Josh was ripping every shred of clothing away from my body. I was fully naked by the time we stepped into the condo. The cream-and-gold color scheme of the living room went by in a blur as he rushed me toward his bedroom door. I can't even remember how I got to the middle of the bed. All I know is that as soon as my knee dipped into the soft cushioning of the mattress, Josh's dick was pushing into my pussy. We fucked like wild animals for an hour straight before we stopped, rehydrated, and then went back to fucking again. It was that last ten minutes of me riding him that finally put him to sleep. And with an aching body and full belly, I dozed off not too long after he did.

Removing the large comforter from over my body, I let my legs dangle over the side of the bed before placing them on the cool hardwood floor. Some time during our nap, Josh had woken up and left me in his bed alone. I didn't know where he had ventured off to, but I needed to find him because I was ready to go. It was a little past eight o'clock, which meant I only had a few hours to get home, take a shower, get dressed, and then head over to Nav's spot. That was the night we were all meeting, and I didn't want to be late. It was already bad enough that we were going to be one woman down.

Diamond basically cut off all communication with us and the world after Shine passed away in his sleep earlier in the week. We didn't know where she was, how she was doing, or if she needed anything. I called her phone every day and left her a message, letting her know that I loved her. I still included her in the group text we had going about the meeting, just in case she decided to show up, but she never responded. I'd never experienced the loss of a loved one or family member before, so I was not about to sit there and say that I knew the pain she was going through; however, I did know that this was the time when she needed us the most, and pushing us away wasn't a good thing.

Looking around the plain yet masculine room, I searched for any single item of mine to throw on, but I didn't see shit. Slowly, I lifted my body up from the plush mattress and tiptoed over to Josh's dresser in search of something to wear. Once I found one of his oversized dress shirts, I slipped it over my body and went in search of him.

My eyes marveled at the expensive paintings that lined the hallway walls and the abstract art pieces that sat on top of some huge white columns at the end of it. The classical music playing in the background set the scene for the gorgeous ocean backdrop you could see through the floor-to-ceiling glass walls. Just like the hallway, the open floor plan that led from the kitchen to the living room, dining room, and balcony was a sight to see with its intricate details, starting from the gold accent pieces placed throughout the space to the modern high-priced furniture that looked fresh off of the designer's showroom floor.

I walked over to the sliding glass doors and stepped out onto the patio. A fire was glowing under the dark purple-and-blue-hued sky. The stars were twinkling bright, as the smell of the ocean breeze flowed effortlessly around me. I closed my eyes for a quick second, my mind clear and free of anything going on outside of me.

It wasn't until I heard the hushed tone of Josh's voice that I finally opened my eyes again. I expected to see him posted on one of the large rocks behind the bush beside me, but I had to walk a little way down the wooden-plank path to finally focus my gaze on him.

With his shirt off and only some swim trunks on, Josh sat on the beach with his feet buried in the sand. His knees were pulled up to his chest, while his arms hung loosely over them. His dark hair was wet and slicked back on his head, his body still covered with droplets of the ocean water, while his olive skin glowed under the light of the moon. I started to walk toward him and ask if he was ready to take me home, but I stopped when I noticed his father's stern face peering back at him through the phone.

"Son, when are you going to get over this sick fantasy?"

Josh sighed and dropped his shoulders. "Dad, I don't know what you're talking about. What fantasy am I supposed to be getting sick of?"

Mr. Bernfeld grunted. "You fucking on the help. First it was your nanny, and then the young girl who delivered the paper when you were in high school. After that was the little lady who tutored you in college, and now an employee. What is it about these black women that you can't get enough of?"

I couldn't see Josh's face, but I knew the expression on it was probably one of shock. He and I had been very careful about keeping our fuck-buddy relationship under wraps, so how did Senior know?

"Look, it's not a fantasy. I'm just really attracted to black wo—"

He was cut off. "What can a nigger do for you, son? A nigger that works for us, at that? How long do you think it would've been before I found out that you and that Roberta girl were messing around?"

"Robette, Dad," he corrected. "Her name is Robette."

"Rob . . . ette? What kind of ghetto name is that anyway?" He sighed when Josh didn't respond to his insult. "Look, son, all I'm trying to say is that you have to do better. I thought with this Robette girl being from where she's from and a little rough around the edges, that you'd pass over this one. The only reason I hired her was because I didn't think you'd give her a second look. She's as big as a cow, hair kinky and always in a weird style. Education barely scratches the surface of your Ivy League one, and she's from Compton. Compton? Of all places. I mean, Venus and Serena made a name for themselves with the tennis, so I guess the other ones can try to as well, huh?"

My hands smoothed down the curves of my size ten frame. Yeah, I had some ass, and my hips and thighs had a little thickness to them, but I didn't think that I was that overweight. My hands then went to the natural coiled curls that were wildly all over my head. Senior had complimented me on more than one occasion about my hairstyles and my beauty, so to hear him talk about black women the way that he was and call my hair kinky and weird had me feeling some type of way.

After a short span of silence, Josh finally spoke. "Dad, you caught me in the middle of my evening swim. Was there anything else we needed to discuss before I get back to it?"

"Actually, there is." His father cleared his throat. "Bernfeld Jewelry Exchange has been chosen by the Smithsonian Museum of Natural History to house their Hope Diamond collection while they are in town for the East Meets West jewelry exhibition. I wanted to let you know that the new security system for the Beverly Hills store is being installed as we speak per their request. Once Rebecca and I are out of the country in a few weeks, I won't have access to change the security codes for the vault or tap into the security feed. You will be responsible for all of that until I return. Do you understand?"

Josh groaned. "Yeah, I understand. But what codes are you going to be using? You switch them like every week, right?"

"I do, and for good reason," he claimed. "Now, in my office safe, I've left a list of codes I want you to enter for the weeks that I'm gone. Don't copy the list to your phone. Don't send a picture to yourself or anything like that. I need you to go into the safe, get the paper, memorize each of the codes, and then destroy it." He tapped his temple with his middle finger. "Your mind is the safest place for those codes to be."

"All right. I'm on it."

"Don't give me that passive '*I'm on it*' bullshit, Josh. Tell me you're going to do as I say."

"I'm going to do it, Dad."

After pondering Josh's words for a second, Senior said, "You better. Oh, and Joshua, before I let you go." His voice was deadpan and low. "That little fling you have going with Robette, make sure you end that shit before I get ready to leave town. If I have to, I'll terminate her ass and make sure she goes away quietly. I would hate to see you lose out on your inheritance because you can't get enough of her little black cunt."

Because of Josh's declaration to loving black women early on in the conversation and the way he kept whispering in my ear that he loved me, I just knew he was going to tell his father to suck a dick at his order, but when he stood up from his seat on the sand, dusted his shorts off, and raised his arms above his head for a stretch, I damn near fainted at the words that fell from his lips.

"You don't have to worry about that. Robette's already on her way out the door anyway. She was starting to become a little bit too clingy, so I took her out to a nice dinner at Mastro's tonight and brought her up to the condo for one last fuck." When he looked over his shoulder back toward the condo, I hid behind the bush. "Got her upstairs in the guest bedroom right now, knocked out. I'm about to go for another swim, and then I'm going to send her on her way. When she gets to work Monday, I'll have HR pull her in and give her her walking papers. Have Bert or Matt plant some earrings in her bag or something like that." He shrugged his shoulders. "She'll be gone before you make it to the airport. I promise."

"And just when I thought that you didn't know any better. My boy!" Senior cackled. "Those types of women aren't for keeping. They're not for breeding, either. At least not with a Bernfeld." Josh shared his laugh. "Well, I'll let you get back to it. I'll call you tomorrow so we can talk more about that new security system."

"Sure thing, Dad. Have a good night."

"You too, son."

After releasing the call, Josh scrolled through his phone for a few seconds before throwing it down on his towel and running to the ocean. As he dove in and disappeared beneath the dark tides, I hurriedly ran back up to the condo and grabbed my things. I couldn't believe what I'd just heard, couldn't believe that this asshole was really about to try and play me. I knew Josh and I didn't have a love connection, but I thought we at least liked each other.

The first thing I did after putting my clothes back on was to send a text to Lucci, asking if she could pick me up from the Pearl Dragon restaurant I remembered passing on our way here. The next thing I did was send a text to Nav, letting him know that I had some new info that he may need to hear. As I made my way through the front door, a reply text from both Nav and Lucci came in.

Lucci: Omw

Nav: Change of plans. Meet at this location in an hour.

I looked over the unfamiliar address and tried to place the area by the street name, but when nothing came to mind, I screenshotted the last part of my and Nav's text thread and sent it to the girls. I had a feeling that after this meetup, shit was about to get real. Josh and his dad may have thought that they were going to get the last laugh at my expense, but they had a whole 'nother thing coming fucking with me.

I took a pull from the blunt one more time before passing it to Lucci. We had just pulled up to the address Nav wanted us to meet him at and decided to smoke a bit of that premium before going in. My eyes scanned my surroundings. Besides Lucci's truck parked in the small lot across the street, there were three other cars, a motorcycle, and one of those big white work vans with tinted windows and double back doors. I looked in the direction of the two amber-colored streetlights flickering on and off, illuminating only a portion of the block. The buzz of the electric cords humming around us mixed in with the free-flowing traffic on the overpass above us.

My gaze turned back to the old rickety building across the way. You could tell from the faded brick pieces, the board-covered windows, and the weeds almost as tall as trees that the building had been abandoned for a while now. The two big garage doors looked as if they'd been replaced some time ago, but with the graffiti sprayed all over them and the busted, blacked-out windows, you couldn't really tell.

"You ready to go see what this nigga is talking about?" Lucci asked, stuffing the end of the blunt in her ashtray. She reached across my legs and opened her glove compartment, pulling out a small-caliber pistol. "Just in case," she whispered while stuffing the gun into the back of her pants.

"You're really bringing that in there with you?"

She shrugged her shoulders. "I never leave home without it. In my line of business, you always gotta have a piece with you."

"I understand that, but with this situation, I don't think you need to be packing. It's just a meeting," I emphasized while looking at my reflection in the visor mirror. I really couldn't do anything with my wild hair but use the scrunchie Lucci gave me and put it in a ball at the top of my head. The pencil skirt I had on was ripping at the split, and my blouse was wrinkled as hell. Good thing Lucci had a pair of flip flops in her trunk, or I would've been limping into this meeting with a broken heel and some holey thigh-highs.

"Meetings can get out of hand sometimes. You want one?" Lucci asked, pulling another gun from underneath her seat.

I pushed her hand away and shook my head. "Nah, Looch. I'm good."

She shrugged her shoulders. "Suit yourself. All I know is you can't trust anybody nowadays. Not even the nigga you sleeping with."

I wanted to ask her what she meant by that last line, because this wasn't the first time she said some subliminal shit that had me thinking that something was up with her and Stax, but some approaching headlights caught our attention. When we realized that it was Kay Kay pulling into the parking lot, Lucci and I both stepped out of her truck and met Kay at her door.

"Y'all ready to get this money?" Kay Kay beamed as she hit the lock button on the key fob. Her eyes danced wildly, her pupils dilated. Her hair was gathered underneath a red Phillies baseball cap, baggy jeans hung from her slim hips, and the T-shirt she had on was stained with whatever meal she'd consumed earlier.

Lucci's concerned eyes cut toward me before turning back to Kay Kay. "Uh, Khalani, you good, boo?"

Kay Kay paused for a second before popping her trunk and pulling out a black hoodie. She swiped at her nose. "Yeah, never better. Why do you ask?"

"Because you look high as fuck," I blurted out, not beating around the bush. "Your arms are all scratched up. Hair looks a mess, and then your clothes . . . Wait. Is that a bruise on your face?" I asked when I noticed the faint purple-and-blue spot under her eye. "What the fuck, Khalani? You getting your ass beat and you're out here basing now?"

She rolled her eyes. "Bobbi, man, look—"

"Don't 'Bobbi, look' me," I mocked, cutting her off. "As much shit as you talked about your mama out here doing her thing, I know you ain't out here getting down like that. Shit can't be that bad for you."

Kay Kay cocked her head to the side, eyes squinting a little. "First off, Robette, you don't know how bad shit is for me right now. Second, stay out my muthafucking business. I'm not out here digging all in yours." Her eyes scanned up and down my body, taking in my disheveled appearance. "And third, worry about how the fuck you're walking around these streets before you open your mouth to say anything about me."

I opened my mouth to respond but stopped when Lucci grabbed my arm and stepped in between us.

"All right, you two. Whatever y'all got going on, you need to squash it before we head in there." She nodded toward the old building. "We don't know what this nigga has in store for us, so we need to have our eyes and ears open, looking out for one another. Can you both agree to chill until after this meeting?"

I looked at Kay Kay, who was looking down at her nails, and rolled my eyes. "Yeah, I'm cool if she's cool."

"What about you, Kay Kay?" Lucci asked, stepping to the side so that we were facing each other again.

She shrugged her shoulders. "I'm good as long as she continues to mind her business."

"A'ight," Lucci snapped in my direction before I could say something smart in return. "Y'all both agreed to squash it, so let's go. We're already ten minutes late. Hopefully we didn't miss anything important."

Grabbing both of our hands, Lucci led the way across the street and to the front door of the abandoned building. After she banged on the rusty metal for a few seconds, a familiar face finally opened it.

"You're late," she grumbled with obvious attitude in her tone. "Nav doesn't like tardiness."

"Well, we got lost. Give us better directions next time," Lucci snapped, matching her tone. "Are you going to let us in or what?"

The chick who introduced herself as Nav's wife glared at all three of us before stepping back and allowing us to come in. After closing and locking the door behind us, she walked past a van identical to the one outside being worked on and said over her shoulder, "Follow me."

The sound of drilling, tools hitting the ground, and City Girls' "Act Up" could be heard throughout the large garage. The smell of burnt rubber mixed with oil lingered strongly in the air. I counted about four bodies in this room, and about three more in the small kitchenette we walked through next. All eyes followed us with lustful gazes as we continued to wherever this chick was taking us. When we got to a set of mahogany double doors, we stopped. She knocked on the one with the handle a few times before pushing it open and waving us in.

I looked around at all the TV monitors mounted on the wall, security footage from different jewelry stores flashing across the screen. There was all kinds of equipment spread out on the tables, along with duffle bags, ski masks, and black jumpsuits. Two figures stood in front of the largest screen, with another dude sitting in a leather chair doing something on the computer keyboard.

Lucci let go of my hand and pushed me forward when ole girl just sat her ass down on the plush couch in the middle of the room and opened a magazine.

I cleared my throat. "Um, Mr. Ali. I mean Nav—"

He held up his long, thick finger, cutting me off. Pointing at the screen, he asked the dude in the chair, "So, you think this will be the best way to go in?"

"Yep. I can cut the recording right here and loop it around to play some footage from earlier so that it looks like nothing is happening."

Nav nodded his head slowly before clasping the man's shoulder. "Cowboy man, you're a godsend."

"Aye, it's what I do."

Nav squeezed his shoulder. "That I know. A'ight, so go on and hook all that shit up." He looked down at his watch. "We're heading out in about half an hour. You think you can have everything set by then?"

"I'll have everything done in fifteen."

"That's what I like to hear," Nav told his friend before finally turning to us. His gaze swept over Lucci and Kay Kay for a second, and then landed on me. The way he licked his lips then pulled the bottom one into his mouth had me stumbling a bit.

"Welcome, ladies. Glad you could make it on such short notice. I see we're a body short. Will Diamond be attending?"

I was so stuck on how fucking fine Nav looked in the wife beater displaying his muscled arms and the black khaki work pants that hung low enough to show off his tapered waist that Lucci had to nudge me a little to finally answer his question.

"I . . . I'm . . . I don't think Diamond is coming. Her brother passed, and she—"

Nav cut me off and looked at the dude standing next to him. "Ant, I need you to do something for me." He whispered something into Ant's ear that had him nodding his head. After giving him a few more words, he turned his attention back to me. "Now, as you were saying."

"Uh, like I was saying, Diamond's brother passed away, and she basically shut us and the world out. We don't know where she's at or where—"

He cut me off again. "Cowboy, I need you to do something right quick before you finish that other shit." Nav wrote something down on a piece of paper and handed it to him. "Look into that for me." He turned his gaze to me again, arms now folded over his broad chest, showing off the sleeve of tattoos on both, muscles flexing every time he moved an inch. His legs were wide and in a bowlegged stance I'd never noticed before. "What were you saying now?"

I don't know why, but the cocky grin on his face immediately knocked me out of my daze. "Nigga, I'm not about to keep trying to answer your questions if you're going to keep interrupting me. That shit is rude as fuck."

His grin turned into a slick smile. "My apologies, baby. Just got a lot of things to handle before we go and handle this job tonight."

A look of confusion covered my face. "Why invite us here for a meeting if you're on your way to do a job?"

Nav walked over to the table with the duffle bags and equipment. "Because *we're*," he emphasized, "going to do a job tonight. A job that requires a six-man team. Hence, the reason why I requested that all four of you were down before accepting this meeting."

Lucci stepped forward. "First of all, who said anything about us doing a job outside of the BJE thing? And secondly, who the fuck are you to tell us what we're going to do?"

Ole girl who had been sitting silently on the couch stood up from her comfy seat, but not before sliding her hands between the cushions and pulling out a gun. At the sound of her cocking one into the chamber, Lucci whipped her gun from behind her back and aimed it right at her.

"Bitch, you ain't the only one carrying. Word of advice—you might wanna hit me first, because that's the only shot you're going to get off once I pull my trigger."

"Ladies," came smoothly from Nav's mouth as he stood between the pistols in the air. "There's no need for any of this. We're all on the same team."

"Same team? How, when she's pointing a gun at us?" I spoke up and said. "Tell your wife to put her shit down first."

Nav looked directly into my eyes, a glint of lust in them. "I would . . . if she were my wife."

"Well, then tell your bitch to put the gun down," I followed up and said. If this chick wasn't his wife, she had some kind of title. The way she fawned over and talked about him at the store that day told me that they had something going on between them.

His eyes were still trained on me as he walked up to Lucci's gun, pressing his chest into it. "She's not my girl, either. Tweety and I are just friends. Best friends, if I'm being truthful."

Had I not looked at Tweety the moment those words fell from Nav's mouth, I would've missed the crushed look that came across her face. When she realized that I was looking at her, she changed her expression real quick.

"I don't give a fuck who the bitch is to you. I'm not dropping my shit until she drops hers," Lucci said, cocking her gun. "You ready to take a bullet for her?"

Nav finally broke his gaze from me and turned to Lucci. "If I have to. However, you may want to hold off on that until I tell you why I wanted you guys here earlier than we originally discussed."

The room was as quiet as a mouse. The only thing you could hear was Cowboy's fingers working over the keyboard and the light sound of music flowing from the pods in his ears. When Nav realized that neither Lucci nor his best friend was willing to put her piece down first, he turned his head to the side and said over his shoulder, "Tweety, put the gun down."

"But, Nav—"

"Just put the gun down, Tweety. Damn." His voice was a little more stern.

She turned her lip up and smacked her teeth. "I told you this would be a bad idea, but your ass don't ever wanna listen. Always following your fucking dick," she mumbled that last part, but I heard her. "This bitch"—she pointed to Lucci—"is a hothead. That bitch"—she pointed to Kay Kay—"is high as fuck. And this bitch"—she pointed at me—"this bitch right here . . ."

"Call me bitch one more time," I threatened, stepping toward her.

"Bi—"

"Tweety!" boomed from Nav's mouth, causing a chill to run down my spine and Tweety's mouth to clamp shut. "What the fuck did I just tell you? Put the fucking gun down and shut the fuck up. You trippin', man."

"Nah, you trippin', Nav. Bringing these hoes on." She shook her head. "We were doing okay with just us."

He turned from Lucci, whose gun was now in his back. "That's because we were only doing two-man jobs. If we want more money, we gotta hit bigger stores, and that requires a bigger crew. Now, can you please put the gun down so we can get on with this?" He looked down at his watch. "We've wasted fifteen minutes on this dumb shit when I could've been explaining what's about to happen tonight and the role everyone will be playing."

Kay Kay, who had been quiet this whole time and just watching everything play out, stepped up and spoke. "You keep saying tonight. What's happening tonight? And whatever it is, will it get our hands on some money?" Her ass was sounding like a true dope fiend.

That slick smile of his graced his face again. "What's happening tonight is what I'm considering something like your initiation. Before I bring you in on the big job, I need to see how you operate with smaller ones." He chucked his chin up. "On the table over there is everything you need to get ready. Jumpsuits, ski masks, boots, and your tools. Everything should fit, so don't worry about that. I need you guys dressed in like ten minutes, and then we'll head out."

"Wait a minute." I held my hands up. "How do you know we're even ready to do a job? Shouldn't we at least practice first?"

Nav chuckled and walked over to me. The cologne he was wearing met me before he did. He grabbed a piece of my hair and twirled it around his finger. "You don't need to practice for a smash and grab."

"A what?" I asked breathlessly, getting lost in his eyes. Nav licked his lips and stepped closer to me, his mouth lowering to my ear so that only I could hear his next words.

"Now that you know that marriage stuff was all a lie, I can't wait to show you what being with me is really like. I've wanted you since the first time I laid eyes on you and can't wait until you let me have you."

My voice hitched in my throat, knees growing weaker by the second. Had Nav not wrapped his arm around my waist the moment he did, I would've indeed hit the floor.

Lucci cleared her throat, interrupting the sexual tension slowing building between us. "Yo, y'all can fuck and whisper sweet nothings into each other's ears some other time. We need to hear more about this job if you want us to be down."

Nav stared at my lips for a few seconds before looking back into my eyes. I could tell if we had a little more time and were there alone, he would have no doubt kissed me. Instead, he shook the thought off and released me. Walking back over to the center of the room, he turned to address us.

"Like I was saying, we're going to be doing what is called a smash and grab, hitting a number of stores at the same time and grabbing as much shit as we can get before the police start showing up. Each of us will have an earpiece in our ear, where Cowboy will be advising us of any issues at the store you're assigned to. You're going to have about ninety seconds to do ya thang."

"Cowboy will be watching the cameras,"—he pointed at the screen behind him—"as well as listening into the police scanner. Once he tells you that it's time to go, you need to leave. Doesn't matter what you see on your way out that may be of some value. You need to hightail it out of there. There will be two unmarked cars waiting in the alley going in separate directions. The car that you three are in will be heading south." He pointed to me, Kay Kay, and Lucci. "The car I will be in will head north. You need to figure out a place to stash the jewels other than your own home."

He looked around the room at all of us to see if we were following what he was saying. When no one questioned him, he continued. "Now, the plan was to hit the six stores in the jewelry district that get the most traffic. Lucky for us, they're all next to each other. However, now that we're down one man—"

"I can do it," Tweety voiced. I could tell from her tone that she was still a little salty with what happened earlier but wanted to show her loyalty. "I could fill in for their friend who didn't show up."

Nav shook his head. "We can't chance you getting caught up, Tweet. Especially with you having that security job interview with BJE on Monday."

At the mention of security and BJE, I remembered the shit Senior said to Josh.

"Nav, did you get that text I sent earlier about the information I needed to tell you about?" I asked.

He nodded his head. "I did, but right now, we're going to have to hold off on that." He walked over to the table and threw a black jumpsuit to each of us, including Tweety. "In a few days, I will hit you up, Bobbi, and have you bring the jewels to me. I will then meet up with my guy who wants the shit and get the money that we will all split."

"Split how?" I asked, looking over the tag in the suit. Sure enough, it was the right fit, a size ten. "And how much of a percentage do you get?"

He pulled a black T-shirt over his head and then a black hoodie. After putting a black skully on his head, he grabbed one of the duffle bags and crossed the strap over his body. "Because it's a small job, we will each get an equal split. With that in mind, you might want to target the pieces with bigger jewels in them and real gold. The more diamonds we have, the more money we'll get."

I looked at Lucci, who looked back at me. We both looked over at Kay Kay, who was already dressed in her jumpsuit and grabbing a duffle bag from the table.

"I don't know about y'all, but I need this money. I got too much shit going on right now that requires that shit, so I'm in," she said.

Ant, who I didn't even notice had slipped out of the room, walked back in with his all-black outfit on and handed a piece of paper to Nav. He opened a drawer behind a desk and grabbed two 9 mm guns. Handing one to Nav, he placed the other behind his back.

"We leave in five," was all he said before walking back out of the room.

"So, what's it gonna be? You in or out?" Nav obviously asked me and Lucci, since we were the only ones besides Cowboy who were still standing there in our regular clothes.

Lucci leaned over to me and whispered, "I'm in if you're in."

I looked at Kay Kay, who was silent but had a pleading look in her eye. Tweety still had a stank look on her face as she grabbed her duffle bag, making her exit out of the room, and Nav paused what he was doing, waiting on my answer.

"I guess I'm in. But will I get a gun since everyone else has one?"

Nav walked over to me, wrapped his hand around my waist, and pulled my hip into his side. "With jobs like these, you rarely ever need guns. We're only carrying them in the case that something pops off. You don't have to worry about anything, though, because if something goes down," he whispered lowly in my ear, "I got you." He tapped my ass. "Now, hurry your sexy self up and get dressed."

I don't know why, but butterflies began to flutter in my stomach. When I turned back to Lucci and Kay Kay, they were both looking at me with silly looks on their faces.

"That nigga gon' tear your pussy up whenever you decide to give him some. I can tell from the way that he walks his chocolate ass got a king-size Snicker between his thighs."

I laughed as I pulled my jumpsuit on. "Bitch, be quiet. Oh, and Kay Kay, how I came at you earlier—"

She waved me off. "Don't even trip, Bobbi. I know you were only looking out, so I'm not tripping." She paused for a second. "Truth be told, I'm not basing like you think. I have done a few lines here and there, trying to deal with the CPS situation and then this other shit I got myself into . . ." She trailed off.

"You ain't gotta explain," I told her. "As long as you trying to handle the shit and get out of it, then we're good. If you need anything from me, let me know. You know I got you."

She nodded her head. "I will. Now, can we go get this money and finally have Diamond Mafia's name ringing bells in these streets?"

Lucci laughed. "Yeah, let's hurry up and get this over with. Stax's ass keeps blowing me up," she said, responding to a text on her phone. "Nigga think I'm dumb."

Instead of asking her about her comment again, I finished getting dressed, grabbed my bag, and then headed in the direction that Nav had walked in. Lucci and Kay Kay were right on my heels. After saying a quick prayer for us and Diamond, I hopped in the back of the van the dudes were working on earlier. A seat was already saved next to Nav for me.

"You ready to do this?" he asked just as the van pulled off.

"As ready as I'll ever be," was my response as I pulled the black ski mask over my face and placed the hammer and crowbar I'd grabbed in my bag.

I could feel the adrenaline pumping through my body and had to take a deep breath to try to calm it down a bit. As if he could sense my nervousness, Nav grabbed my hand and gave it a light squeeze. When I looked up at him, he smiled and winked his eye before turning back to the driver and continuing their conversation.

I don't know why, but that little show of affection had me feeling a whole lot better. Maybe going into business with Nav wasn't such a bad decision after all. I could already feel a small connection forming between us. I just hoped he was able to keep Tweety's ass on a leash and far away from me. I let her disrespectful ass make it earlier, but I wouldn't hesitate to put the bitch to sleep if she barked again.

Chapter 10

Lucci

"So, what's about to happen now?" I whispered over to Nav as we stood at the back entrance of the stores we were about to rob.

"We have to wait for Cowboy to override the system and change the codes for the keypad. Once he does that, all six doors will open at the same time."

I looked up at the four security cameras on the walls above us, the tiny red dots blinking every other second. "And those?"

Nav pulled at the bottom of his ski mask. Even with the majority of his face covered, you could still tell that he was a very handsome man—thick lips, dark eyes, and that cunning smile. No wonder Bobbi's ass was slick infatuated with him.

"Already taken care of. You don't have shit to worry about, Lucci. You good."

I looked to my left at Bobbi and Kay Kay, who both chucked their chins up in return.

"Y'all good?" I asked once Bobbi diverted her gaze from Nav and looked back at me.

"Yep. I am. What about you, Kay Kay? You good?"

"I'm gravy. Just ready to make this money."

"Can y'all shut the fuck up? Y'all loud asses are gonna get us caught," Tweety hissed from her position on the end.

I rolled my eyes after she mumbled something I couldn't make out and looked back at my girls. "That bitch gon' get slapped the fuck up if she keeps talking shit," I joked as they snickered but then got serious. "Aye, Bobbi, what was that you said again about the high-end stuff?"

She fiddled with the duffle bag on her shoulder for a second before answering my question. "I said the high-end jewelry will be more towards the back of the store, so the first display cases you come to should be the first ones you smash open. You should also go for the watches and the necklaces with colored gems. Those will be the ones that get the most money once sold."

I nodded my head and then turned to Nav. "And how long do we have to grab as much as we can again?"

He looked down at the watch on his wrist, hands covered in the same black leather gloves as mine. His tall, athletic frame was covered in all black like me too.

"At the latest, ninety seconds. Once the system recognizes that the codes were changed by a different IP address, it will automatically set the silent alarm inside of the store until another code is entered. Since we don't have the other code, we won't be able to stop the alarm. So, the plan is to get in, grab as much as we can, and then get right back out. Cowboy will alert us of any police units approaching."

"Okay. And what about the drop-off spot? Where will that be, since you never mentioned one?"

"C'mon, Lucci. I know you and your man Stax got stash houses all over Watts and L.A. Pick one to leave the shit at for a few days and then wait for my call."

I reared my head back. "How the fuck do you know what I have?"

Nav chuckled before flashing that cunning smile of his. "You didn't think that I'd do a job like this without doing a little research on the people I asked to be involved, did you? I know everything I need to know about you,"—he looked at me—"you,"—he gestured toward Kay Kay—"and you." His lustful gaze stopped on Bobbi. When he licked his lips, I swear I could hear her pussy screaming.

I scoffed. "I see you're one of those niggas that trust a little too easily. Regardless of knowing what you may know about us, what makes you think we won't just take the jewelry and sell it to our own connect?" I asked, mad that this nigga probably knew more about me than I did about him.

Without taking his eyes off of Bobbi, he responded, "Because as ruthless as you think you may be, sweetheart, I'm far worse. You can try to play with me and my money if you want to, Lucinda, but please understand that I don't have a problem with killing you or whoever else I need to dispose of to get my shit. No one, and I mean no one, is off limits." His eyes finally cut from Bobbi back to me. When he glanced down at my belly and then back up to my face again, my hands immediately hovered over my stomach.

He couldn't. I shook my head as he smirked and went back to talking in hushed tones to Ant.

"Even though you rude as fuck, I appreciate the heads-up. Thanks for letting us know who we're dealing with," I said, rolling my eyes and wishing I'd brought my gun to shoot his smart-ass mouth.

I could feel Bobbi's curious gaze on me but didn't turn her way at all. I knew she would have questions in regards to the way Nav just low-key threatened me, but I wasn't ready to answer them, especially when I wasn't ready to share the news I'd found out the other day.

"Well, Ms. Adams, it looks like the reason you've been out of it lately and throwing up for the last couple weeks is because you're pregnant," the clinic doctor told me after reading my results off of the test I'd taken earlier.

"Pregnant?" I asked, confused. "Bu–but how can that be? I take my birth control pills religiously."

He looked down at the questionnaire the nurse had me fill out before looking back at me. "Says here you were taken Desogen as your form of contraceptive, yes?"

"Were? I still take them. It's the only pill I've been taking since my last doctor switched me out a couple years back."

"Did you know the FDA did a recall on that brand? Maybe about a month ago. Advised women taking them to return them to the pharmacy for a new pack or see your doctor about switching out."

"Wait, what?" I asked in disbelief. "I didn't hear shit about that." And it wasn't like I would, either. I was so busy in the streets that I didn't have time to watch the news or sit at home and browse the internet all day.

"It was a pretty big thing. Something about the wrong packaging and missing blisters."

As the doctor continued to tell me about the recall, my mind kept going over the fact that I was pregnant. I wasn't ready for a child, and neither was Stax. Both of our lives had no room for another mouth to take care of, so carrying this baby to full term was not an option.

After the doctor gave me a prescription for morning sickness pills and a list of other things I needed to get in order to have a healthy pregnancy, I left the clinic with a heavy mind and heart. Although I was feeling a bit nostalgic about the situation for a tiny second, a decision was already made. Before I left the parking lot, I called a different clinic and made the appointment for an abortion.

I thought about telling Stax but felt that it wasn't necessary. Me terminating this pregnancy would be something we both agreed on, so there was no need to tell him. Yet, I still wondered.

"All right, you guys." Cowboy voiced through the earpiece in my ear, bringing me from my thoughts. "Can you hear my voice clearly?"

A chorus of *yeah*s echoed around me.

"On the count of three, the doors will open, and you will have a little over a minute to raid the store, so make it count. I know it's a small window, but if you work fast, we can all come out with a few dollars in our pockets, okay?"

After we all agreed, Cowboy began his countdown. "All right. So, on my count. One . . ."

When my phone buzzed in my pocket, I already knew that it was Stax. For some reason, he had been blowing my shit up even more since we made it down to the jewelry district, and I didn't understand why.

"Two . . ."

He knew that I was out handling business and knew that I had a meeting with Nav that night. He also knew that I wouldn't divulge any information about what we talked about over the phone either, so calling me back to back wasn't even necessary.

"Three."

As soon as Cowboy said the last number, the locks on the doors clicked open, and I immediately walked inside, pushing any outside thoughts out of my head. I ignored the constant vibration in my pocket as I briskly walked down the short hallway and pushed through the second door that led to the showroom floor. My adrenaline was pumping, and my heart was racing fast as hell.

I scanned the dimly lit room for a second before zeroing in on the line of display cases closest to me. Without a second thought, I pulled the crowbar out of my bag and smashed open the watch display, followed by the case filled with ruby and emerald pieces. When I made it to the third case filled with an array of diamonds and pearls, I busted it open and began to stuff my bag with anything and everything I could grab. Earrings, necklaces, bracelets, rings, watches, and pendants were snatched up real fast. I even took a few diamond hair combs, hoping those would sell for a pretty penny too.

"All right, guys. The police are on their way. You have thirty seconds to grab whatever else you can get and then make it to the drop cars. Whatever doesn't fit, leave it."

I didn't even acknowledge Cowboy after his warning. I just continued to fill my bag with the loot.

"Ten seconds. If you're not heading to the door, you need to be."

I dropped my bag to the ground and struggled with the zipper for a second before it zipped up. The shit was heavy as hell when I swung it back across my body. The added pounds would for sure slow me down, so I started to make my way toward the exit. As soon as I stepped outside into the cool crisp air, I took a deep breath and smiled, welcoming in that crazy euphoric feeling that took over my senses whenever I broke the law and got away with it.

"What the fuck are you doing, Lucci? C'mon," Bobbi hissed just as the sound of police sirens started to get closer. "We need to get the fuck out of here."

I hopped over the rail that lined the ramp, landing on my feet. After straightening myself out, I took Bobbi's outstretched hand and ran in the direction of the car.

"Where's Kay Kay?" I asked as we splashed through puddles and jumped over debris. "Did you see Nav or anyone else leave out of their stores?"

Bobbi let go of my hand and switched her duffle bag from one side to the other. I could tell by the way she slowed down a bit that she was starting to become tired as fuck.

"Kay Kay is already at the car," she said between breaths. "She made it out of her store before me. Nav, Ant, and Tweety already made it to their car and left. I stayed behind to wait for you."

I held out my arm, and we bumped fists. "My girl."

"You already know," she returned with a smile.

We continued down the dark alleyway until we made it to the getaway car. Once we jumped in the back, the dude who had been working on the van at the firehouse pressed his foot on the gas and skirted out into the open street. Both Bobbi and I struggled in the back seat to get out of our jumpsuits but somehow managed to make it work. We fixed our clothes the right way and made sure our hair was intact after removing the ski masks. I pulled the latch behind Bobbi's head, causing the seat to move forward, and stuffed all three of our bags inside.

When the dude who was driving the car made it to the freeway without being spotted by the police or bringing any unwanted attention our way, I screamed loud as fuck, causing him to swerve a bit.

"Lucci, what the fuck?" Kay Kay fussed with her hands over her ears. "That shit hurt."

"Bitch, shut up and stop acting like a baby. We just robbed a jewelry store in sixty seconds and got away with it. Can you imagine how much money we can make if we keep hitting stores like this? Nigga, I think I may have found a new hustle," I screeched before slapping hands with Bobbi. "That shit was easy as fuck. How much do you think we made?"

Bobbi shrugged her shoulders. "I'm not sure. Depends on the connect and what pieces he wants and don't want. I know I grabbed at least twenty K. Hopefully we all did the same, since we're splitting it equally."

"Shit, I hope so, 'cause I got some things I need to take care of," Kay Kay replied as she messed with the radio.

"We all do," Bobbi agreed. "First things first, though. We need to get up with Diamond, finally locate her ass. I know she wasn't here tonight, but I think we should at least give her five Gs apiece. She could probably really use that money right now."

"I'm with it," I added.

"I'm not," Kay Kay protested. "Five Gs? Bobbi, you must really be out your rabbit-ass mind. Diamond ain't here, so Diamond don't deserve shit. Y'all can give her some of y'all cut if you want to, but she ain't getting shit from me!" Kay Kay barked. "Bitch ain't did no work. The fuck?"

I was shocked by Kay Kay's words, especially when she originally told us that she would only do the job if

Diamond was in on it. Her ass really must've needed this money to flip the script like that.

"Excuse me, ladies." The driver cleared his throat and said, "My apologies for interrupting your conversation, but Nav told me that you would give me the directions to where you wanna go once we made it to the freeway." His eyes connected to mine through the rearview mirror.

"Oh, yeah. Um, hop on the 105 when you can and get off on Wilmington. I'll direct you from there."

He nodded his head and turned his attention back to the road. Nav may have known about my stash houses, but I was pretty sure he didn't know where any of them actually were. So, instead of having dude drop us off in front of one, I was going to have him drop us off in the old McDonald's parking lot not too far from one of my houses and have Stax come pick us up from there.

Pulling out my phone, I wasn't surprised at the tons of missed calls and texts from his dumb ass. This nigga was really bugging. Instead of reading and responding to any of his messages, I decided to just call him instead. The phone rang about three times before it went to voicemail. When I tried calling again, the shit didn't ring at all, just sent me right back to voicemail.

"I know this muthafucka didn't just block my call," I said to myself. I tried one more time and became even more upset after getting the same results.

Because we were nearing our exit, I wanted to at least have a ride waiting for us already. So, after scrolling through my call log for a few seconds, I landed on the name of someone who I knew would look out for me.

"What's good?" Zig's deep voice sang through the phone. "Your nigga been hitting everybody up, looking for you."

"I know. And now he's not answering the phone. Are you with him?"

Zig said something to someone in his background before responding to me. "Nah. Nigga dipped out of here a few hours ago. Said he had to go handle some business."

I wanted to ask if he knew what business, but I decided to get to the reason for my call instead. "Look, Zig, I need somebody to come and pick me and my girls up from the old McDonald's on 108th. I'm going to be there in like eight minutes, so I need whoever there in four."

He was quiet for a second. I could hear the wind whistling in the background, the loud noise of whatever party he was at fading out the farther he walked.

"All these niggas been drinking and snorting powder. I'll come get you. I'm right around the corner and can be there in two minutes."

I smiled and couldn't help the little butterflies that started dancing around in my belly.

"Nah, Zig, I don't wanna pull you from whatever it is you were doing. You should tell one of them little niggas to come instead. You sound like you were having fun."

The loud sound of a car door being opened rang in my ear. The smooth sound of an engine coming to life could be heard shortly after.

"It's all good. Already on my way. Where do you need me to take you and your girls?"

"I'll let you know when we get there," I told him. Ole boy driving may have been looking like he was jamming to the music, but I knew he was listening to my conversation.

"All right, bet. See you in a few."

"See ya," I said before releasing the call and pushing the phone back into my pocket.

"Who was that?" Bobbi asked with a sheepish grin on her face. "And is the nigga single? He sound like he fine as fuck."

I don't know why her saying that low-key pissed me off, but it did. "You don't need to worry about who he is, especially when you have a fine-ass nigga like Nav trying to hump on your ass."

We both fell out laughing before getting into a whole conversation about Nav and his obvious thirst for her. By the time we made it to the McDonald's, Zig was already there, his big black-on-black Chevy Silverado blending perfectly in the dark area.

After grabbing our bags, we hopped out of the getaway car and into Zig's ride. The smell of weed invaded our senses as soon as the doors opened. A thick cloud of smoke released from his mouth as he eyed me and then looked away. His head slowly bobbed to Enchantment's "It's You That I Need" track bumping through the speakers. Zig's full and kissable lips mouthed the words as he looked out his driver-side window, waiting for us to get in.

No words were spoken other than the location of where I needed him to drop us off once everyone was settled. We all sat in a comfortable silence, lost in our own thoughts the whole way to our destination. My mind wandered over to Stax as the song continued to play. Zig turned up the volume, which I didn't mind. When I sneaked a glance over in his direction, he was already looking at me, an expression on his face I couldn't quite read. I turned my head and continued to look out the window, wondering if my decision to not fuck with Zig all those years ago was the wrong one. Stax's ass was moving real funny as of late. I hoped for his sake and mine that I wouldn't have to kill his ass for doing something stupid.

Chapter 11

Diamond

I lay across my bed, feeling like my world had been stolen right from underneath me. I had my face buried deep in my pillow, head pounding, naked body only covered by the dingy sheet I pulled from the bottom of my hamper since I hadn't washed in almost three weeks. My room reeked of alcohol, vomit, old food, and mildew from the damp pile of clothes I tried to hand wash in my bathtub but never hung up to dry.

I slowly turned over on my back and looked up at the ceiling fan spinning around. My mind was on nothing at all. I felt empty. I felt lost. I felt like I didn't deserve to still be living here on Earth, at least not without Shine. Losing him had by far been the toughest thing I'd ever had to deal with in my life. Seeing him take his last breath would haunt me until the day I died.

Picking up my phone on the nightstand, I checked the time. It was two in the afternoon, which meant I'd been asleep for damn near twenty-four hours. The sleeping pills I'd been taking weren't helping with just one dose, so I doubled up on them just to get some type of rest. I knew that doing that would probably fuck me up much sooner than later, but I didn't care. The pills, combined with the fifth of alcohol I drank every day, had been the only two things in my life to help with this pain.

My vibrating phone rattled across my nightstand and fell to the floor. Whoever it was would just have to try me some other time. I wasn't ready to speak with anyone or respond to any text messages either. I just wanted to be left alone, left to deal with losing my brother, my other half, my baby, on my own. Maybe pushing everybody away wasn't the best idea for me mentally or emotionally, but I didn't give a fuck, and I just wished people respected that.

Reaching for the half-empty bottle of Hennessy next to me, I popped the top and took a few swigs before lying back down and closing my eyes. As the smooth liquor rolled down my throat, tears began to fall down my face. My brother was actually gone and was never coming back. We'd been inseparable since our no-good mama pushed us out of her rotten-ass cat, awarded to the state right after they cleaned us off and whisked us away from the Central California Women's Facility in Chowchilla. We'd just turned two when our granny on our dad's side came and got us out of foster care. We stayed with her until the day she died on our fourteenth birthday. From there on out, it was Shine and me, sleeping in abandoned houses, stealing candy from the corner stores just to eat—basically, fending for ourselves. We didn't have any other blood relatives to take us in, and we for damn sure weren't going back to foster care, so we had to do what we had to do. Thank God Lucci, Bobbi, and Kay Kay looked out for us whenever they could.

I opened the Hennessy bottle and took another swig, this time a lot bigger than the last. Shit was crazy. I didn't even write my mama to let her know Shine had passed. The bitch didn't deserve to know, if I was being honest. She lost that right the day she chose prison over us.

Bang. Bang. Bang.

I groaned and rolled back over to my stomach as the loud knocks on my front door thundered throughout my small apartment. Only person bothering me this early in the morning had to be my landlord. I was three months behind on my rent, and I knew his ass was trying to serve me with an eviction notice. He caught me a few weeks ago when I was coming in from getting me another drink at the liquor store, but I'd been ducking and dodging his ass ever since.

Another round of loud knocks sounded on my door, and I continued to ignore them. I wanted to rest for at least another hour before I got up to go buy me another fifth of something and grab me a few snacks to eat. Hopefully my landlord's fat ass would be gone out running errands by then.

I'd just closed my eyes and was about to drift off into a nice little nap when the sound of my door being kicked in had me scrambling from under the sheet.

"Diamond!" I heard a familiar voice yell. "We know you're here, so you might as well bring your ass on out."

"Yeah, bring it on—What the fuck is that smell?"

"Really, Lucci?" Bobbi snapped. "We don't know if our girl is in here dead or alive, and your ass is tripping off of a smell?

"Yo, I can't stay here. I think I'm about to—uggggh!"

I heard Lucci vomiting her guts out.

"Fuck, man. You couldn't run your ass to the bathroom?"

"I . . . it's the sm—uggggggggh. I gotta . . . ugh . . . get outta here . . . uggggggggh."

"Lucci, take your ass back down to the car and tell Kay Kay's ass to come up here and help me clean some of this shit up."

I didn't hear Lucci respond, so I knew she must've been agreeing to what Bobbi said.

"And what the fuck is up with you? You've been throwing up since we did the job down in the district. Damn near left the majority of your insides on the ground when we did the thing in Chinatown. Now you throwing up all over Diamond's couch. Is there something you need to be telling us?"

A few seconds of silence passed before I heard Lucci do something I hadn't heard her do in a long time: cry.

"I was supposed to get an abortion two weeks ago, but I couldn't do it."

"So, you're pregnant?"

"Yeah." Lucci gagged.

Bobbi hesitated for a second before she asked her next question. "Is it Stax's?"

"What the fuck you mean, is it Stax's?" Lucci countered with a low growl.

I could tell by her tone that shit was about to pop off if someone didn't intervene in this conversation. So, instead of just lying in my bed and hearing everything play out, I got up, found one of Shine's old T-shirts to throw on, and stumbled my way to the living room.

When I got there, Bobbi had her hands up in mock surrender, and Lucci was leaning against the wall closest to the window, holding her belly, eyes burning a hole in Bobbi. They both had on some dark-washed denim jeans, showing off their shapely frames. While Lucci dressed hers up with a white off-the-shoulder sweater and some cute butterfly wing heels, Bobbi was more dressed down, wearing a fitted Rams T-shirt and some Air Max to match.

"Look, Lucci, I'm only asking because I see the way you look at that nigga Zig whenever you're in his presence. Y'all either fucking on the low or you wanna fuck him on the low." She shrugged her shoulders. "That's why I asked."

Lucci straightened her slumped posture on the wall and wiped the tears falling down her face. "I would never cheat on Stax. Ever. Even though I know he's out here doing me wrong." She sniffed and wiped at her face again. "I just look at Zig sometimes and wonder if my life would be better had I chosen him."

Bobbi opened her mouth to say something but stopped when she heard the noise I made, tripping over a lamp that was on the floor.

"Diamond? What the fuck? Where have you been?" Her wide eyes looked me over. "I've been calling, texting, stopping by." She reached her hand out and handed me the pile of notices that must've been taped to my door. "You had us so worried about you. Why did you shut us out like that? We could've helped you through this."

I stepped around some trash and a few old pizza boxes on the floor before going into the kitchen to get a glass of water. I pulled a mason jar from my cabinet and put it under the faucet. When I pushed the handle up, nothing came out.

"Your water's off, Diamond?" Lucci asked.

I shrugged my shoulders and walked over to my fridge to see if I had something in there to drink and was hit with a smell similar to rotting flesh. Bobbi stepped over toward me and flipped the light switch in my kitchen.

"Your electricity is off too?" Her concerned eyes stared into mine. "Diamond, how long have you been living like this? I mean, I know you haven't been paying your rent because of the notices I just gave you, but you haven't been paying your utilities either? How have you been bathing? Eating? Why didn't you call me? Or Lucci or Kay Kay?"

I went to go sit on my couch but turned around when Lucci's vomit caught my eye. The only other option for me to have a seat was on one of the end tables, so that's where I plopped down.

"One of y'all got a cigarette?" I asked, ignoring all of Bobbi's questions.

"Fuck a cigarette, Diamond. What's going on with you? I understand you're still mourning over Shine, but at the end of the day, baby, you still have to take care of yourself."

I dug around in the ashtray next to my feet until I found a cig butt long enough to take a pull from. After lighting it, I inhaled as much as I could before releasing a thick cloud of smoke.

"Neither one of y'all will ever experience a fourth of what I'm going through," I voiced, taking another pull from the butt and putting it out. "My connection with my brother was one I will never have again with anyone else, and the shit was taken away from me." My lips started to tremble, and I could feel the tears forming in my eyes. "My brother. My twin. The only person in this world who could feel what I felt. Imagined what I dreamed. Shared the same lifeline with. Did you know that whenever his heart would stop, that I could feel it?" I wiped at my face. "Not as bad as he did, but I felt it. Even . . . even when he took his last breath. I felt that too." I dropped my face into my open palms and cried for my brother.

Once I was able to pull myself together, I continued, "It wasn't my intention to push you guys away. However, you need to understand that when Shine . . . when Shine left this Earth, a piece of me did too, and I needed to cope with that in my own way."

The whole room was as quiet as a rat pissing on cotton. Bobbi stood over me, wiping tears from her face, while Lucci was now hunched down against the wall, trying to keep herself from vomiting again. We all sat in that comfortable silence for a few moments before there was another round of loud knocking on my somewhat broken door.

"Diamond Morris!" a loud voice boomed. "This is the Los Angeles County Sheriff's Department. As of today, you are no longer a resident of this unit and will have half an hour to grab as much as you can and vacate the premises before you are arrested for trespassing."

"What the fuck, Diamond? How far are you behind?" Bobbi asked while reaching for her purse. "Do you think your landlord will let me pay what you owe?"

Lucci grabbed her bag and took out a wad of cash, shoving it in my hand before answering her ringing phone.

"What's up, Kay? Yeah, we see the sheriffs. . . . Uh, actually they're at Diamond's door. . . . Nah, not for that. . . . Nope. Not that either. Girl, you should've brought your ass up here instead of waiting down in the car. . . . Yeah. Okay, bye."

Lucci threw her phone back into her bag. "Kay Kay's rude ass said what's up. She also said that she was on her way up here but decided to stay her paranoid ass in the car when she seen the popo."

"Her scary ass." I shook my head and chuckled. Standing up from my seat, I began to gather some of my things together.

"What are you doing?" Bobbi asked as she watched me open up a trash bag. "Why aren't you trying to go out there and talk to your landlord?"

"Because he ain't gon' listen. Plus, I'm already three months behind. The asshole been trying to put me out for a while now, so I might as well go. Ain't shit left here for me anyway. Why not move out and start over?"

"Start over? How are you going to do that? It's obvious you aren't working or have any money saved up. Where are you going to go?" Bobbi stressed.

I held up the wad of money Lucci gave me. "I know there's probably enough money here to get a room for a week or two at a hotel. After that, I'll just wing it from there. Y'all know I always find me a job."

"Nah, you ain't staying at no hotel." Bobbi grabbed the trash bag out of my hand and began throwing some of my things into it. "You can come stay with me. I got that extra room, and I—"

"No, Bobbi." I cut her off. "I don't want to be a burden to you again. You did enough for me when we were younger. All of y'all did," I said, turning to look at Lucci. "I don't know where Shine and I would've been had y'all not opened up your hearts and homes to us." My eyes started to become misty again.

"Diamond, you were and still are one of my best friends. Shine's fine ass was like my best friend, too, when I wasn't trying to get a piece of that dick."

I snorted a laugh, and both Lucci and Bobbi joined in. I think Shine kinda liked Bobbi crushing on him but would never say it out loud.

"You coming to live with me wouldn't be a burden at all. You know we will always have your back, which is why I'm still kind of upset that you basically shut us out. But we'll discuss that at a later time." She gave me a knowing look, and I smiled in return. "So, get everything you wanna take with you together and let's get the fuck up out of here. First thing first, though, your ass is gonna take a shower and wash that nappy-ass fro on the top of your head. After that, we'll get you settled in and then order some takeout and just chill for the night. Have a slumber party like we used to do back in the day."

"Can we talk about whoever Zig is and whoever has you glowing like you are?" I asked as I made my way to my room with Bobbi on my heels.

She laughed. "Yeah, we gon' talk about all that and then some. Now, let's get your shit together and get the hell outta here. You know I hate to be around roaches," she said, looking at the two baby bugs crawling on the wall. "Or any type of law enforcement. Bitch start getting hives and shit all over her body."

Chapter 12

Kay Kay

"Now that that's over, what is the next step for me?"

My lawyer looked down at his phone, scrolling over missed calls and emails as we walked out of the court building.

"Well, now that you have legal custody over your niece and nephew, we will petition an order to family court for a court date, where we will show the judge that you are fit and have the means to properly take care of them." He paused and looked down at me. "You did do everything I told you to do, right?" I nodded my head as we continued on our way down the stairs. "I'm not playing, Kay Kay. If you didn't obtain everything on that list, the judge might not grant that the children be released to you. How is the job thing coming along?"

"It's coming," I lied, knowing damn well I ain't been looking for a job. "It's just hard finding something that I'm actually good at."

"The last time I checked, working at a fast food restaurant or at one of those little retail stores in the mall didn't require much experience at all."

"Man, I'm too old for that shit."

His eyebrow arched. "Too old for what? Being a responsible adult? Providing for your children?"

"Nah, it's not that."

"It's not? Then what is it?"

I looked around at the passing foot traffic behind me, people in business suits and casual workwear rushing back from their lunch break and heading back to work. The bacon-wrapped hot dog vendor was bombarded with a new wave of antsy customers, while the homeless dude lying in the bushes groaned from not being able to take a nap. Horns blared from the middle of the busy street, the loud sound of drivers yelling for the next person to move. Just thinking about becoming one of these regular working-class citizens scared the fuck out of me. This was not something I could become accustomed to doing at all.

We stood at the edge of the street, waiting for his car to pull up.

"It's just that I'm not built for that type of work. Customer service isn't my thing." I shook my head. "You wouldn't understand. You chose a career where you have to work with people every day."

He stuffed his phone into the breast pocket of his blue blazer and smiled. "Then make me understand, Khalani. What is your thing?"

The way he looked at me and said my full name even after I told him to call me Kay Kay sent a small chill down my spine. Marvin Phillips was indeed a fine man with his smooth ebony skin, megawatt smile, and handsome playboy features. However, I could never take it there with him. Marvin deserved a good, wholesome girl to fall in love with, marry, and carry his babies, not some ran-through chick from the hood who would more than likely ruin his career and life.

"My thing." I thought about it for a second. "My thing is to get custody of my niece and nephew and then get us the fuck up out of California. That's all that I'm focused on right now."

"You wanna get out of California, huh? Where would you go?"

I shrugged my shoulders. "Somewhere far away from here. Maybe New York, Florida."

He nodded his head. "New York is cool. I went to law school there. Cold as fuck in the wintertime, but nonetheless, a nice place to live. Kinda pricey, though."

I didn't respond, just looked back out at the people walking around us. When his car finally pulled up, Marvin opened the door and waved his hand for me to get inside.

"I can have my driver drop you off where you need to go."

I stuffed my hands in the back pockets of my jeans and started to take a few steps backward. "It's okay. I parked around the corner at one of those lots that charge you ten bucks for the whole day."

"Well, let me give you a lift over there. We're heading in that direction anyway."

I shook my head. "Thanks, but I'm good. Might stop in one of these little retail spots along the way to see if they're hiring."

Marvin looked at me with an unreadable expression on his face before lustfully scanning my body up and down. "Well, you handle your business, Ms. Khalani, and hit me up if you need anything."

"I will," I acknowledged before turning around and merging into the sidewalk traffic.

I'd just gotten to the corner to cross the street and grab me a quick bite to eat when Marvin's car rolled up beside me and he stuck his head out of the window.

"I forgot to tell you. Once I get word on your new family court date, I'll give you a call and let you know the time and place we need to meet up at. Make sure you bring and do everything on the list that I gave you, okay?"

"Okay." I nodded my head and smiled.

He hesitated for a second, but then asked, "Can I take you out to dinner sometime? I know this is very unprofessional of me, but I would love to take you out on a date."

"As much as I would like that, Marvin, I'm going to have to decline the invitation for now. Maybe we can try some other time, like when I get my shit all the way together."

He bit his bottom lip. I could tell he wanted to press me more but decided against it. "Some other time, then. See you later, Kay Kay."

"See you later. And thanks again, Marvin."

Instead of responding, he gave me a sexy little smirk before rolling up his window and telling his driver to pull off. I don't know why, but for some reason, I started to get this funny feeling in the pit of my stomach like butterflies fluttering around. My heart skipped a few beats, and I could feel my cheeks start to flush. If it wasn't for the cab driver honking his horn for me to go, I probably would've missed my turn to walk across the street. I felt like I was floating on cloud nine and could probably get used to this feeling when the time was right.

I continued to gush and feel giddy about whatever this little affect was that Marvin was starting to have on me as I walked. I was so into the shit that I actually skipped stopping at the taco place and headed straight to my car. Maybe if I did get my shit together and start to live a normal life, Marvin and I could see where this little situation could go. I mean, reformed hoes deserve love too, right?

"Here you go," I sang as I handed Juan my parking ticket. He grabbed the small sheet from my fingertips, read the number, and then grabbed my keys.

"I go get car now," he spoke in somewhat broken English.

I scanned the lot for a quick second before spotting my new ride and stretching my hand out to him instead.

"I can go get it myself. It's just right there." I pointed, looking at the woman behind me with the crying baby hanging from her arm and the two whiny toddlers pulling at her leg. "Besides, she looks like she could use her car now."

The woman nodded her head in thanks before handing over her parking ticket. After retrieving my keys from Juan, I basically skipped over to my car and slid into the driver's seat. As soon as I shut the door, the visor above me fell open, dropping the little baggie of coke onto my lap, stopping all thoughts of Marvin.

I studied the white powdery substance for a second. Would one last binge really kill me? The only reason I'd brought it with me in the first place was for moral support, just in case the court decided to deny me custody of my niece and nephew. I knew that I had a solid case, and with Shauna signing the papers, it was a good thing, but you never know what could happen with this judicial system or my sister's grimy ass.

A light knock on the window scared the shit out of me. When I looked up, Juan was standing there, saying something I couldn't quite understand. However, I could tell by his hand gestures that he was asking when I was going to leave. Rolling down the window with one hand, I used the other to shield my bag of coke from his prying eyes.

"I'm sorry. I'm going to leave right now. I was trying to find the right radio station to listen to." I pointed to my radio. "I'm leaving now."

Without another word, Juan walked off, yelling something in Spanish to his co-workers. Not too sure what to do with my baggie, I threw it into the glove compartment, making a mental note to dispose of it as soon as I got home.

I had just shifted the car into gear and was about to back out of my spot when the loud sound of a gun cocking echoed around me. The feeling of cold steel being placed at the side of my head had me freezing in my seat.

"Didn't think I would find your ass, huh, bitch? Nah, you didn't," he taunted me. "Where the fuck is my money?"

"Doughboy, pl—"

He cut me off, shoving my head with the gun. "Don't Doughboy me, bitch. I thought shooting up your car would get your ass into gear, but I see you think I'm playing with your hoe ass."

"No. I don't think you're—"

"Shut the fuck up." He mushed me again. "And to think I was having thoughts of wifing your hoe ass. But then you turn around and steal ten stacks from me?"

I turned my head and was finally able to look up into the madman's eyes. That adoring gaze he always gave me was replaced with one of hate. For a quick second, he looked down at my lips, and his eyes softened, but when I stuck the tip of my tongue out to moisturize them, the heated fire in his gaze returned.

"Put this shit in park and scoot your ass over to the passenger side." I wanted to protest, but he shoved the gun harder into my temple. "And I don't wanna hear shit. Don't make me kill your ass out here in front of all these people. You already know how I get down."

Valuing my life, I changed gears and then crawled over to the passenger side and sat down. With his gun still trained on me, Doughboy opened my driver-side door and stuffed himself behind the wheel. He didn't even try to adjust the seat to his height or anything. His knees were hitting the dashboard, while the steering wheel dug into his belly.

"I think I'ma take this car and give it to my new little bitch. She needs something to roll around in."

"Doughboy, I will get you your money. I promise. Actually, I had it, but then this shit came up with my sister and CPS taking her kids. I really needed the money. My lawyer told me—"

The words were cut from my lips the second Doughboy backhanded the fuck out of me.

"Bitch, didn't I tell you I didn't want to hear any of your excuses? If it ain't about my money, then I don't want to hear it."

Tears instantly sprang in my eyes. I could feel my lip swelling up by the second. The coppery taste of blood slowly filled my mouth, letting me know that my shit was busted. Looking in my sideview mirror, I tried to see if I could see Juan or any of his employees, to try to signal for help, but it seemed as if everyone who was up there a second ago had just disappeared.

Doughboy pulled out of the spot, left the rooftop parking lot, and hopped right on the freeway. I didn't know where he was going and didn't want to get busted in the lip again for asking, so I just sat quietly in the passenger seat as we made our way through the midafternoon traffic.

Doughboy had been responding to someone through text on his phone when my phone actually rang. Because it was hooked up to the car's Bluetooth, his ass hit the answer button before I could decline the call.

"Uh, Kay Kay, say hello or something. Shit," Bobbi spoke into the phone with a laugh. "I told you her ass was probably somewhere getting dicked down," she said to whoever was talking in the background. "Kay Kay, if you can hear me, call me back, girl. We got some more money moves to make."

I tried to be slick and end the call before she could say anything else, but Doughboy grabbed my thigh so hard, digging his nails into it so deep that I knew he broke through my skin.

He mouthed to me, "Say something."

"Um, I'm here, Bobbi. I just got out of court," I mumbled, hoping Doughboy would relieve some of his grip. "What are you doing?"

She laughed at something before responding to my question. "Me and Diamond over here talking about the good ole days. Like, remember that time I tried to beat up Shine's girlfriend and ended up getting my ass handed to me instead? Nigga wasn't even fucking with me like that, and I was trying to defend my love. Had I known the bitch had a black belt in Tae kwon do, I would've never fucked with her."

"That's what your ass get!" I could hear Diamond yelling in the background. By the slur in her voice, I could tell she had been drinking. "I told you not to fuck with that girl in the first place, Bobbi. I told you."

"Yeah, well, I wasn't listening. All I saw was a bald-headed hoe with my man and had to rectify the situation."

"And got a rectified ass whipping!" Diamond hollered as she laughed loudly. "Aye, Kay Kay," she said between breaths. "Can you stop by Golden Bird on 120th and get me a slushie and some bites? I'll pay you back when you get here."

"Me too," Bobbi added. "And then we can talk about this meeting Nav got set up for this weekend. He said if everything goes right, we can all come out with about forty thousand each. I don't know about you, but I need that shit. Especially now that I'm unemployed. And I know you need some more money too. Shit, with all the lawyer fees, the new apartment, and that new car, I know your twenty *G*s is long gone by now."

I still had a couple of bands left, but not enough to take care of what I needed to take care of, if I were being honest. My mind drifted to Marvin and the list of things he told me to do that would make me look more responsible to the judge. *Get a job* was at the top of the list. I still intended on doing that, but for now, I needed to make this money.

Doughboy muted the call. "Bitch you had twenty *G*s and didn't pay me back my money?" I opened my mouth to respond but was rewarded with another backhand. "You must wanna die."

When I didn't say anything, he continued. "Yeah, you do. And what the fuck is you bitches doing to make that type of money in one night anyway? You know what? Never mind. It doesn't even matter, because your ass is gonna do the job, and I'm gonna take your whole cut. Call it interest. I was gonna make you suck my dick one last time before I gave you a few days to get my money, but now that I know you're about to come up on some major ends, your ass ain't going nowhere."

Bobbi and Diamond were so busy laughing and talking about old times that they must not have noticed when Doughboy released the call. When they tried to call back, he snatched my phone out of my hand, turned it off, and tucked it into his pocket.

Once we got to the small, one-story home that he took me to in Corona, I spent the next few days getting beat, raped, doped up, and basically tortured by Doughboy. Some days, he even let his friend in on the fun too. It wasn't a day that went by where I didn't pray for God to just take me away. My fuck-up had finally caught up to me, and I didn't have anyone else to blame but myself.

Chapter 13

Bobbi

I walked into the firehouse after the getaway driver I now knew as Ed let me in, and I headed right to Nav's office. Cowboy was behind the computers and TV screens again, tapping into security feeds, while Tweety sat her ass on the couch in her armed security guard outfit, flipping through a magazine.

"Hey, where's Nav?" I asked as I rounded the desk that had our tools on it and looked at the new bodysuits we were going to be wearing for the next job.

Cowboy turned his attention to me and smiled. "Stepped out about an hour ago. He said he'd be back by the time you got here."

I wondered why in the fuck Nav would tell me to meet him there at a specific time when he was nowhere to be found. What the hell was so important that it couldn't wait? I mean, it wasn't like he was my man or anything like that, so I really had no right to question him. We'd been talking here and there for a few weeks and even went out on a couple dates, but I wouldn't call what we had exclusive. We hadn't even shared a kiss yet. Seemed like every time we were close, Tweety's hating ass popped up, whether it was her calling his phone or barging into his office.

I sat on the couch across from the hating bitch and picked up a magazine, flipping through it. I crossed my leg and bounced it up and down, popping my gum and humming to the Faith Evans track playing.

'Um, do you mind?" Tweety asked after a few minutes had passed. "You hella rude with your ghetto ass."

"Pot calling the kettle black, huh?" I had learned that in dealing with Tweety, you had to give her the same type of energy she pushed out, or the bitch would think she had one up on you.

She closed the magazine in her hand and placed it on the table. Crossing her legs, she spread her arms wide across the top of the couch and smirked. "I eat bitches like you for breakfast and shit them out at lunch. You better do your research on who you talking slick to before I give you a firsthand taste of why Nav keeps me around." She looked down at her pussy and giggled.

I continued to bounce my leg and pop my gum, looking through a different magazine now. "Shit must not be hitting for nothing if he's kept you around this long and ain't made you his girl."

Her eyebrows furrowed, and I knew she was feeling the weight of my words.

"Instead of eating bitches like me for breakfast and shitting us out for lunch, you should be studying me. Learn how to keep the nigga coming back, not just fuck you once and act like it never happened." I knew I should've kept that little tidbit of information to myself, but I couldn't help it. Her smart ass deserved it.

I had asked Nav about his relationship with Tweety and if us getting to know each other would become an issue between their friendship. He assured me that it wouldn't, and he also told me that they had slept together once some years ago, but that was it. When I asked him if he had any kind of feelings for her other than platonic, he told me no, and for some reason, I believed him.

Tweety slid her hand between the couch cushions, no doubt reaching for her gun. I placed the magazine back on the table and waited for her to pull it on me, because I had something for her ass in return. Before she could, though, Nav came walking through the door, looking like a *GQ* model.

"Damn, sorry I'm late," he voiced, kissing the top of my head and walking over to Cowboy. "How long have you been here?"

I stood up from my seat and walked over to where he stood. "I've only been here for a minute."

He wrapped his arm around my neck and kissed the side of my face this time.

"Where were you at?" I asked.

Looking down at me, he smiled. "It's a surprise. You ready to go?" I nodded my head. "All right, let me holla at Cowboy for a second, and then I'm all yours."

A loud-ass, dramatic sigh caused both of us to turn our attention to the couch.

"What's up, Tweet? How's the new job treating you?"

She rolled her eyes at me. "It's going good. Your boy Josh already trying to get in my panties, though. Invited me out to his condo in Pacific Palisades and everything this weekend."

"Oh, yeah?" Nav responded absentmindedly as he looked at something on the screen that Cowboy was showing him. "You going?"

There was a shocked expression on her face. "You want me to go?"

He shrugged his shoulders. "Why not? We need more information on their new security system set up, and since Bobbi doesn't work there anymore, that leaves that task to you. We also need the codes to the vault. With the Smithsonian pushing the exhibition back to next week, I'm pretty sure that asshole hasn't memorized the numbers like his father asked him to."

"Knowing Josh, he hasn't," I said.

"Why do you say that?" Nav asked.

"Because," I shrugged my shoulders. "He hates what he does. Working for the family business has never been a dream of his, so he tends to lollygag when it comes to handling the responsibility of running the store. Shit, sometimes he left me the keys and had me closing up, just so he could go party with his friends."

Nav thought for a second. "We need to get his ass to trust you, Tweet. Maybe set up a fake robbery when y'all go on this date, or do a home invasion in the middle of y'all fucking. Whatever. Either way it go, you'll be the one to save his life, which will put you on a whole different level with him."

"In the middle of us fucking? So, now you're pimping me out?" Her heated gaze turned to Nav. "I thought I was only supposed to be doing intel."

Nav sighed and wiped his hands down his handsome face. It was at that moment that I took in what he was wearing—some black jeans, a black V-neck T-shirt that fit his body just right, and a pair of black motorcycle boots. The only pieces of jewelry he wore were the gold diamond ring on his pinky and the gold link chain around his neck. A small hint of whatever tattoo he had on his chest could be seen crawling up his neck.

"Look, Tweety, I don't know why you're tripping all of a sudden. You act like you ain't never slept with no one or did what you had to do to get certain information from a target. If you don't want to do it, that's fine. We'll just have to figure out another way to get into the vault."

Nav had an exasperated look on his face as he turned back to Cowboy. They talked in hushed tones for a few seconds before dapping each other up. When they were done, Nav turned back to me and stuck his hand out.

"You ready to go?"

I looked over at Tweety for a quick second and kind of felt sorry for her. You could clearly tell that she was in love with Nav, but he didn't feel the same at all.

"I'll do it!" she yelled at our retreating backs. "But after this, I'm fucking done, Naveen. No more. I want out."

Nav stopped in his tracks, his chin meeting his chest. "You're just upset right now, Tweety. I promise we'll talk in the morning."

She waved him off and sat back down on the couch. "Nah, I'm good. Got an employee meeting in the morning, so I won't be available. Gotta play my part, right?"

Nav scoffed. "I love you, Tweety."

She didn't say shit in return, just flipped the magazine open and started flipping the pages.

"She'll be all right," Nav assured me as we made our way outside to his motorcycle. When he handed me a helmet, I pulled it over my head and hopped on the back of his bike. "Hold on," was all he said before revving the engine and pulling off.

"Wow, Nav. This is beautiful," I said in awe as my eyes wandered around at the black and white photos hanging on the wall of his loft. "You took all of these?"

Nav stripped his leather jacket off his body and threw it across the small sectional in the middle of the room. "I did. Photography is sorta-kinda like a hobby of mine. I sometimes book gigs when I feel like it."

I stopped at a picture of a cute little curly-haired black girl feeding some baby ducks in the park. "Was this a paid gig?"

He rose up from his position at the fridge and looked over his shoulder. "No. I just happened to be in the park that day and couldn't help snapping a few shots of her. I got her parents' info after I took a dozen or so pics and sent them copies. I kept this one for my portfolio, though. Her infectious smile in that photo helps me out when I'm having a bad day."

Nav twisted the top off two beers and handed one to me.

"What about this one?" I asked, looking at a picture of a single sunflower in the middle of a field.

"That was for a paid gig. Some work I did for a web-site."

"Cool." I continued to browse his photos as we sipped our beers and talked about more of his photos. "Can I ask you a question?"

Nav had moved over to his couch, where he was watching muted sport highlights on ESPN. "What's up?"

"Obviously you're very talented behind the camera. Probably make a nice little living from the different gigs you do." I paused for a second, not sure of the best way to ask my next question, so I just asked, "Why do you rob jewelry stores? I mean, why risk getting caught doing that if you can make the same amount of money doing this?"

He smirked. "I could ask you the same question."

Before I could respond, his phone rang.

"Yo. . . . Okay, it's ready? All right. Thanks man." Nav stood up from his seat and stretched his hand out for mine. "C'mon."

I placed my empty bottle on his dinette table. "Where are we going?"

"Didn't I tell you I had a surprise for you?"

"You did, but I thought you bringing me here was the surprise."

Nav laughed. "Although you're the first woman who has ever been here, this isn't the surprise."

I sucked my teeth. "Boy, stop lying. I'm pretty sure Tweety or one of your other little booty calls have been here."

Nav abruptly stopped walking, which caused me to crash into his back. When he turned around and reclaimed his spot in my space, I stumbled back a bit. "Outside of the whole being married thing I told you in the store that day, I have never lied to you, Bobbi. Anything you ever want to know about me, just ask. I will never have a problem giving you an honest-to-God answer." He licked his lips, and I swallowed the lump in my throat. "So, like I was saying, you—not Tweety, not any other female—are the first and only woman I've ever brought to the place where I lay my head. The only woman who knows that outside of robbing jewelry stores, photography is a passion of mine." He placed his hands on my hips and pulled me closer into him. "I can trust you with my secrets, right?"

I nodded my head at the same time that I cleared my throat. "Y–yes," I stuttered. "You can trust me."

"Good girl," he said before bending down and capturing my lips in one of the most spellbinding kisses I'd ever had. When Nav slipped his tongue into my mouth and possessively wrapped his arms tighter around my waist, I knew then that I was a goner. If the nigga told me at that second that he wanted some pussy, he could definitely get it—medium, rare, or well done.

"Damn," we both breathed against each other's lips once the kiss was over.

Nav placed his forehead against mine and kissed the tip of my nose. "If we don't get across the hall right now, I don't think I'll be strong enough to hold out from fucking the shit out of you."

"Well, what's wrong with that?" I purred, heat emanating from between my legs.

He shook his head. "Because I wanna do something special for you. I promise after we're done, I'll do whatever you want me to do to your body for as long as you want me to do it. Cool?" His voice was husky and filled with lust. I nodded my head, giving him my answer. "All right then, let's go."

Intertwining his fingers with mine, Nav finally stepped away from me and led the way to the loft across the hall. After unlocking the door, he allowed me to step in first. My eyes went to the thousands of candles lit all over the room and the little photoshoot set up in the middle of it all.

"What is this?" I asked, walking into the place.

Nav closed the door. "This is my studio. Sometimes I do shoots here, but the majority of the time, I'm just developing pictures and shit. He placed his hands at the small of my back and guided me over to a six-panel Chinese dressing wall. "Everything you need to change into is behind there. When you're done, I'll be at the setup, waiting for you."

"Wait. We're about to do a photoshoot?"

He nodded his head.

"But—"

Nav's soft lips met mine, cutting me off.

"Mmmmm." I moaned when he broke our kiss.

"Just get dressed, baby. You're good."

His lips connected to mine one last time before I walked behind the dressing wall and changed into the nude bandeau bra that barely kept my titties secure and the matching thong. When I walked back from behind the wall, Nav was crouched down next to the porcelain slipper tub with his camera in hand. "Candlelight and You" by Chante Moore and Keith Washington was now playing in the background.

I took a deep breath, trying to control the way my hormones were raging at the moment. While I was changing into my outfit, Nav was on the other side of the wall, coming out of his. Dressed in only his jeans that hung loosely around his waist, Nav was a sight to see. From his inked-up, broad chest to the defined muscles in his arms, the deep V-cut at his waist to the tight and sculpted abs in his stomach, I was in awe. Even the fine, curly hairs of his happy trail was turning me on.

When he felt my presence, Nav turned around. His eyes looked me over from head to toe as he etched every curve of my body to memory.

"C'mere." His voice was raspy and filled with unadulterated lust. I walked over to him and took his hand. "You look sexy, baby. You ready to smile for the camera?" He held up the expensive-looking device.

"As ready as I'll ever be."

Nav smiled and led me to the bathtub, where I stepped in and sat down. The coolness of the porcelain slowly cooled my body heat.

Nav walked over to another corner in the room and picked up a big bucket that was filled with something. When he made it back to me, he began to pour what looked like thousands of sparkly diamonds over my body, filling the tub. After pinning my hair up in a ball and placing some beautiful sapphire studs in my ear and a gorgeous sapphire-and-diamond necklace around my neck, I posed my ass off for him and the camera.

By the time the mini photo shoot was over, I was completely naked in a tub of diamonds, getting my pussy licked from top to bottom by one of the finest men I'd ever met. I grabbed Nav's head and pushed his face deeper into my folds. His long, thick tongue thrashed wildly against my nub, eliciting a second orgasm out of me.

When he was done tasting my juices, Nav licked his way back up my body, stopping at my breasts for a few seconds before making his way back to my lips. As soon as my tongue slipped into his mouth, I could taste the remnants of my essence on his and moaned.

He'd just positioned the tip of his dick at my entrance when his phone started to ring loudly.

"Don't answer it," I whined into his mouth.

Nav kissed me for a few more seconds before pulling away. "I have to. Something might be wrong."

I groaned as he lifted himself off me and watched as he picked up his discarded pants, pulling his phone from his pocket.

"Yo," he said as soon as he answered. You could hear the annoyance in his tone. "Wait. Slow down, Tweety." I rolled my eyes at the mention of her name. "I can't understand what you're saying. Start from the top again? . . . Shit. Okay. Did anyone get hurt? . . . Shit. All right. I'm on my way." Nav released the call and began to put his clothes back on.

"You need to get dressed, baby. We have to go."

I stood up from the tub. The tiny diamonds stuck to my body, falling to the floor as soon as I stepped out. "What happened? Is everything okay?"

"No, everything's not okay. Somebody just shot up the firehouse."

"Wait, what?" I asked, trying to put my clothes back on while following behind Nav. "Shot up the firehouse? But why?"

He turned around to me so fast I almost got whiplash. "That's what I'm going to find out." He paused for a second as if a thought crossed his mind. "If you or your friends had something to do with this, I swear to God, Bobbi—"

I stepped into his face, lips tight and attitude now on ten. "What do you mean, me or my friends? Nigga, you're putting money in our pockets. Why would we want to shoot your shit up?"

He looked at me for a second before shaking his head and chuckling. "You know what? I am tripping. Forget I even said anything."

"Nah, we are not about to forget shit. Why would you automatically assume it was me and my friends?"

"Look, Bobbi, we've been conducting business at that place for years now and have never had some shit like this happen. You don't think it's suspect that after bringing you and your girls on that somebody shoots my shit up? Ed got hit three times. Do you know how bad this is going to affect the job I had lined up for tomorrow night?"

Nav opened the door to the loft back across the hall and grabbed his jacket and helmet, handing me the extra one.

"Wait one muthafucking minute." I countered, turning him to face me. "Me and my girls ain't got shit to do with anything. You need to be looking into your own crew."

Nav grabbed me by my neck so tight I didn't have a chance to respond. When he pushed my back against the closed door and crashed his lips into mine, I was speechless.

"I hope for your sake that they don't have anything to do with it. I'm big on loyalty and would hate to have to kill one of your friends for fucking with my money." He pecked my lips. "I would also hate to lose you. Now, come on. We gotta go." With that being said, Nav slapped my ass and walked out the door, leaving me to follow.

Pulling out my phone, I sent a quick text to Lucci, Kay Kay, and Diamond before heading down to his motorcycle.

Me: Meeting at my house in a couple hours. Be there!!!!

Chapter 14

Lucci

I looked at myself in the mirror and wiped at the corners of my mouth with the back of my hand. For the last ten minutes, I'd been in the bathroom, puking my guts outs while Stax questioned four of our top lieutenants about their trap houses coming up short. In the last couple of weeks, a little over fifteen *G*s had been stolen, and no one seemed to know where the money or product had vanished to. Stax swore up and down that it was me who dropped the ball on making sure the money and product was right ever since I'd started doing that shit with Nav, but he and I knew that that was some straight bullshit. In all of the years that I'd been doing the pickups, not once had the money ever been short. Now, all of a sudden, when he was the one responsible for running everything by himself, shit started to disappear.

I took a deep breath and sighed. Shit was starting to become too stressful for me with both of my hustles. And although I hadn't been back to the doctor since I found out that I was pregnant, I knew that all of this stress wasn't good for the baby. That's why I planned on stepping back from everything. I had to if I wanted to deliver a healthy child into this world. All of it would take a back seat—the drug dealing, robbing these jewelry stores, the street life period. I was about to be somebody's mother, and I couldn't do that from behind a jail cell or in a grave.

After splashing another handful of water over my face and patting it dry with a few paper towels, I made sure my clothes were on straight, fluffed out the curls in my hair, and secured my gun in the back of my jeans. Once I took one last look at my appearance and was satisfied, I walked out of the bathroom only to run into a hard chest. I stumbled back a bit but was able to catch my balance and not fall on my ass.

"I'm sorry. I wasn't look—" My words cut off as I looked up into the face of the person standing in front of me. "Zig, where did you come from?"

His soft eyes peered down at me. "I came to check on you. When I noticed ten minutes had passed and you still hadn't returned, I wanted to make sure you were okay."

I could feel my cheeks heating up, so I dropped my head to hide it from him. "I'm good. Thanks for looking out. But, uh, shouldn't you be in there?" I pointed to the conference room. "Helping Stax figure out who's been stealing from us."

A look came over his face like he wanted to tell me something but thought it better not to. "Honestly speaking, I don't think any of them niggas did it. They've never come up short when you were doing the pickups, so why now? What's changed?"

I could tell from the look in his eyes that he was expecting a response, but I wasn't going to give him one. His question coincided with some shit I had already been thinking but didn't want to believe.

"We should probably get back in there," I said instead, changing the subject. "You know how crazy Stax can get when he thinks someone is lying to him."

Zig looked at me for a second and then nodded his head. "Yeah, maybe we should get back in there. After you," he offered with a wave of his hand.

I gave Zig a little smile before tucking a strand of hair behind my ear and shimmying past his tall frame. However, before I could take another step toward the conference room, Zig gently grabbed my arm and turned me back around.

"How far along are you?" he questioned as he looked down at my belly and back up to my face. "And don't even try to lie, because this isn't the first time I heard you puking like you were a few minutes ago. You've also been rubbing your belly a lot. I don't think you even realize you're doing it, but you do."

I followed his line of sight down to my hand, and sure enough, I was circling my stomach with it. "I'm probably a little way into my second trimester right now."

"Why probably? You haven't been going to see your doctor?"

I shook my head as one of the young dudes from our crew walked by. He eyed me and Zig suspiciously but didn't say shit. Was probably about to go start a bogus-ass rumor with the other niggas he hung with.

"Don't worry about him," Zig acknowledged as if he read my mind. "He knows I would never cross that line with you and betray Stax."

"What if he doesn't?"

"He does," Zig assured just as the conference room doors came crashing open.

The force of the body being thrown out from the meeting space caused such a loud boom that both Zig and I grabbed for our guns. When we noticed that a lieutenant by the name of Ceddy was on the ground getting his face bashed in by Stax, our nerves came down a bit. Everyone was so into the beatdown that was happening in front of us that no one noticed the way Zig had a protective grip around my waist, shielding my belly with his hand. I stepped out of his embrace before anyone could notice and made sure there was a little bit of distance between us.

"That'll teach your ass to steal from me again. Nigga, get your ass up and take this punishment like a man," Stax yelled, wiping his bloody knuckles on his white shirt. "Get up, muthafucka, and talk that shit now."

Ceddy tried to say something, but with the way the bottom of his face was hanging, I could tell that the nigga's jaw was broken.

"You steal fifteen *G*s of my money and product and didn't think that I would find out?"

Ceddy said something, but with his jaw broken, you couldn't understand a word he said.

"What was that, nigga? We can't hear you," Stax taunted before letting out a loud, cackling laugh. He spun around in a circle, pointing at everyone who was laughing with him and egging him on.

When his eyes landed on me, the smile on his face brightened. "There you go, baby. Where you been? I was looking for you. You see this disloyal nigga right here?" Stax reached his hand out to me and I grabbed it. He brought me to stand over a bloody Ceddy. "You see this nigga right here? His ass doesn't deserve to live."

"Oh, yeah? Why is that?" I asked, playing along.

Stax laughed some more. "Because this nigga is the reason why our pockets are fifteen racks lighter. You see, while you were in the bathroom handling your business, the nigga confessed. Said he needed the money for his mama or something like that."

"For his mama, huh?"

Stax wrapped his arm around my neck, pulling me close to him. "Yep, and I was on his ass as soon as the words fell from his mouth. The nigga tried to get a little buck, but that's when I broke his jaw and threw him out the room. What do you think we should do with him?"

I looked back at Zig for some kind of answer but didn't get one.

"Uh, maybe . . . maybe we can let him work it off some way. I'm pretty sure we can come up with something we need handled."

Stax stopped laughing and looked at me, a confused expression on his face. "Did you just say work it off some way?"

I nodded my head, letting him know that that was indeed what I said. Stax studied my face for what felt like an hour before busting out in a gut-wrenching laugh.

"Let him work it off? Where is my Lucci, and what have you done to her?"

The whole crowd of people standing around us, except me and Zig, started laughing at that part.

"I know you're not starting to get soft on me, baby. Nah, not you. Take that pistol from behind your back and show all these muthafuckas what happens when they steal from us."

I looked around at all the people staring at me, waiting on my next move. "Stax." I shook my head. "I don't think that—"

"You don't think what?" He cut me off. When he followed my gaze to all the people standing around us, he scoffed, "What? These niggas ain't gon' say shit. You think one of them will snitch on you? These muthafuckas know better than that. Stop stalling and handle this business. It was your cut of the money he stole from anyway. Show them why these niggas from L.A. to the Bay don't fuck with us."

I stood frozen for a second. I wasn't about to commit a murder with over half a dozen witnesses in front of me. Stax was really bugging, trying to make me do some shit like that in front of a gang of niggas who could potentially rat me out one day.

"Stax—"

I was stunned a little when he snatched my piece from behind me and shoved it into my chest.

"Why you keep stalling, Lucci? Is there something you need to tell me?"

"Tell you something like what?" I snapped, mad as hell that he had just embarrassed me like that.

Stax looked down at the gun in my hand and smirked. "You was fucking that nigga or something? Why is it taking you so long to murk his thieving ass?"

I looked down at Ceddy, who now had tears coming down his face. I could tell by the frantic mumbling falling from his mouth and the way his hands waved wildly in the air that he was pleading for his life.

My heart started pounding, and my belly started to flutter. I wanted to soothe the little angel growing inside of me by rubbing my belly but didn't want to chance Stax noticing and questioning my actions in front of everyone. I was stuck and didn't know what to do. I couldn't look weak or show leniency for stealing in front of my crew. My heart knew that Ceddy didn't do it, but my reputation in the streets and my loyalty to this man would not let me make him look like a fool. So, against my better judgment, I cocked my gun and aimed it right at Ceddy's head. I closed my eyes and applied pressure to the trigger, but stopped when the sound of two bullets not shot from my gun whizzed by my head.

"That's what the fuck I'm talking about!" Stax cheered as he moved me out of the way and dapped up Zig. "My nigga, I was wondering when you were going to step in and take over. I mean, that's what we pay you for, right?"

I could feel Zig's eyes trained on me as he answered. "Right."

"That's what I'm talking about. But next time, nigga, watch where you shoot that muthafucka. Them bullets was too close to my wife's head. A few more inches over and your ass would've been on the floor next. You know I don't play 'bout my baby." Stax turned around and slapped me hard as hell on my ass.

"You little niggas clean this shit up and take what you just saw happen as a lesson. Stealing from me or my girl will get you murked, so if you don't want to die, keep those sticky fingers to yourselves."

Stax grabbed my hand, pulling me back toward the conference room doors. When I tried to get one last quick glance at Zig, he wasn't standing in his spot anymore. A million thoughts started running through my mind, and I needed answers, but first I had to check Stax's ass.

As soon as the double doors closed, leaving us in the room alone, I went in. "Nigga, what the fuck was that out there? Since when have I ever killed someone in front of witnesses?"

Stax waved me off and sat at the head of the large round table. He lit one of his cigars and leaned his chair back, blowing out a large cloud of smoke. "Lucci, you know them niggas ain't dumb. I would murder them and every single member of their family if I even thought they were going to snitch. You know I don't play when it comes to you."

His phone vibrated on the table, and he ignored it.

"You not gon' answer that?"

"Yo, why you always concerned with me answering my phone? You ain't never questioned me ignoring calls, so why question it now?"

I sat down in the chair closest to me because I was starting to feel a little lightheaded. "Because your ass has been moving funny, that's why."

He chuckled. "Moving funny? I haven't been moving any funnier than you have, especially after you started working with that nigga Nav. I see the money you're bringing in but can't know what y'all do."

I placed my hand on my belly and started rubbing it. "The less you know, the better. I'm about to stop fucking with that anyway. Doing my jobs with him and then trying to keep up with the shit we got going on is starting to become a little too stressful for me. I need a break . . . from everything."

"Yeah, you do, baby," he responded absentmindedly as he texted on his phone. "So, what are your plans for the night? Bobbi and them ain't trying to hang out with you?"

I watched as he smiled and damn near blushed at whatever and whoever he was texting on his phone. The nigga was so into the conversation that he was having that he never noticed me touching my stomach. My mind drifted to Zig and the conversation we'd had in the hallway. If Zig noticed my odd behavior, I was sure it would only be a matter of time before Stax did. So, after thinking it over for a second, I made the decision to finally tell him.

"Hey," I called out just as he put his phone down. "I need to tell you something."

He took a few puffs of the cigar and blew out some smoke. "Oh, yeah? What you gotta tell me, baby?"

Before I could get the words out, one of our young guns came into the room and asked Stax if he could speak with him for a second.

"Aye, Lucci, let me go holla at this nigga for a quick second, and then we can finish what you wanted to talk about, okay?"

Instead of waiting on me to respond, Stax got up from his seat, kissed my forehead, and then walked out of the room, closing the door behind him.

Because I hadn't eaten anything since breakfast, my stomach started to growl. I had a taste for some fried catfish but decided to eat a salad instead. So, after placing my order with a nearby restaurant and making sure the cleanup crew took care of Ceddy's remains, I scrolled through my social media pages until it was time to go pick up my lunch.

When I returned to the compound, Stax was still nowhere in sight. I picked over my food as thoughts of the day's events and everything else I had going on in my life rolled around in my head. At one point, Zig's handsome face popped up in my mind, and I could feel a small flutter in my belly. What he did for me that day was crazy and had me looking at him in a totally different way.

Just as those images of his sexy chocolate ass began to turn a bit naughtier than they should have, Stax came back into the office.

"Hey, babe. Sorry I took so long. That little nigga had a lot of questions."

I ate a piece of chicken. "A lot of questions about what?"

He waved me off. "Some bullshit. Nothing you need to be interested in. Did you order me something to eat?" he asked, changing the subject instead.

I shook my head. "I didn't know if you had eaten anything or not."

"I haven't, but it's cool. I'll just grab something to eat when I leave here and head over to the house on Tenth Ave." He grabbed a small duffle bag and his keys. "Oh, before I go, what was it that you wanted to say to me earlier? You know, before the little homie interrupted you."

I'd forgotten all about the conversation we were having earlier and almost thought about not having it once he brought it back up, but I couldn't keep putting off the inevitable. Taking a deep breath, I prepared myself to give Stax the news of our bundle of joy arriving soon, but got interrupted when the doors to the conference room came crashing in.

"Jamar 'Stax' Welks, you are under arrest for the murder of Donald 'Lugz' Jackson. You have the right to remain silent. Anything you do or say can be used against you in a court of law."

As the FBI officer read Stax his rights, I jumped out of my seat and tried to get the other officer searching the conference room to tell me what all of this shit was about.

"I'm sorry, ma'am, but your boyfriend is wanted for murder." The big, burly agent sneered as he handed me a search warrant. "You better sit your ass down before we haul you in too."

"Muthatfucka, who you think you talking to?"

The officer started to say something but was pulled away by another agent before he could.

"Baby," Stax called as they restrained him. "Call the lawyer and tell him to meet me wherever they're taking me. Make sure you lock up the laundromats and collect all of the coins out of the machine. You forgot to do it the other night." He spoke in code.

I nodded my head, letting him know that I understood everything he said.

As they took him away, I picked up his phone and called our lawyer, advising him of everything that happened and where he could meet them. Just as I released the call and stood up from the table, a message came in. Now I know that I shouldn't have opened the shit, but I couldn't help it, especially after seeing that the number wasn't programed in his phone.

213-555-3041: I can't wait to see you later. Make sure you have that lie ready for wifey too, because we fucking all night. LOL

I must've read that text over and over again one hundred times. I knew Stax was up to no good and doing me wrong, but to actually see it was a whole different type of hurt. I could feel the tears falling from my eyes. A light tap on my shoulder caused me to swipe them away and turn around.

"We're going to be here for a little while longer, ma'am. You're more than welcome to stay. If not, an officer will contact you once we're done," a different agent advised.

"Nah, I'm good. I'll wait until you guys are finished."

He nodded his head at my response and went back to searching through our things.

"Trifling-ass nigga," I said to myself, thinking about Stax.

Surely after all of this was done, I would no doubt need to vent, so I pulled my phone out of my pocket to call Bobbi but received a text from her instead.

Bobbi: Meeting at my house in a couple hours. Be there!!!!

The fact that Bobbi sent a message like that with no other explanation led me to believe that something had popped off with Nav and the shit we had going on with him. If the Feds were swarming in on Stax for a murder I personally know he didn't commit, they'd probably been looking at me too.

Chapter 15

Kay Kay

"I'm not playing, Kay Kay. You better come back out here with some valuable information for me," Doughboy urged as he removed a small bag from his pocket and tapped a line of white powder on the back of his hand. "We need to know the time, place, and location of the next store y'all are supposed to hit."

"Yeah, we need to know all that," Dough's homeboy, Yako, slurred from the back seat. His ass was gone off of the lean he was drinking but still in tune with our conversation.

"I hear what you're saying," I said from the passenger seat, eyes focused on the cars pulling up to the gated building next door. "But we—"

"But we nothing." I was cut off with a swift smack to the side of my face. The cocaine Doughboy had just put on his hand now covered my cheek, a light dust in my eye causing me to blink excessively. I licked my lips and got a taste of the residue left there. That small sample had my body fien'ing for more, and I hated myself for that.

"You sure do know how to keep a nigga's pockets empty, don't you? Look what the fuck you just made me do. That small bit of coke I just lost is coming out of your cut of whatever we take from your people. I hope you know that," he informed me while pouring another line.

I sat in my seat, dazed. Since Doughboy had basically kidnapped me and had me staying in what he called his dungeon, I was used to the quick smacks and slaps to the face by now. Anytime he got upset at something I said, did, or didn't do, the big, beast-looking-ass nigga would put his hands on me. Crazy thing is, he wasn't the only one, either. His homeboys had a problem keeping their hands to themselves as well. The real bold ones, like this bitch-ass nigga Yako, would rough me around a bit and make me suck their dicks, but none of them ever tried to fuck. I guess Doughboy wanted to keep some part of me to himself and told them that my pussy was off limits.

We were sitting in front of Bobbi's place, a cute little two-story duplex on one of the better sides of Inglewood. The neighborhood was quiet, traffic was low, the neighbors were friendly, and the kids playing outside weren't all loud and ghetto. This was a huge difference from the area my new spot was in. It was something I should've thought about when I was out looking for a new place to live. I mean, my new home wasn't a dump, but I probably could have found something better. I looked out of the window at the kids playing tag and thought, *Dajah and Devon would love it over here.* They deserved a piece of everything I didn't have as a kid, and I would do anything in my power to make that happen.

When Doughboy stuck his hand in my face, it only took a second for me to vacuum the new line of coke up my nose and welcome the high that I knew was about to come.

"Aye, I'm hungry as fuck, Dough. Let's hit up Fat & Juicy while we wait for her to come back out," Yako suggested, breaking me from my thoughts. His face was damn near next to mine as he leaned over the center console. "I need one of those chili and cheeseburgers asap."

Doughboy nodded his head as he snorted his line. "I can go for one of those, too." His eyes rolled over to me. "We'll be back in about an hour. That should be enough time for you to go up there and see what they're talking about. Have your phone on, and you better not tell them bitches anything about where you been these last few weeks either. You understand?" When I didn't respond, Doughboy mushed my head, causing it to hit the window. "Do you understand?"

"Yeah," I snapped back as Yako laughed loudly in my ears. My high was slowing coming down. "One hour. I got it."

"You better." He grabbed my thigh and squeezed it hard. "Now, get your fine ass up out of this car. If you do a good job, I'll let you snort a few lines off of my dick again before I beat that pussy up."

If circumstances were different, I probably would've gotten excited, but since I wasn't getting anything out of the deal but a quick nut and fix from his ass, it was just whatever. Pushing the car door open, I stepped out and felt the warm evening breeze blow over my face. The streetlights were just turning on, and the loud buzz of the electric cords could be heard all around. A few of the kids that were outside earlier were now gone, leaving a couple of the ones without streetlight curfews to get in a few more minutes of play. The back door of Doughboy's truck opened and shut. I could feel Yako's eyes on me as he transitioned to the front seat, but I didn't acknowledge his ugly Kodak Black–looking ass at all.

Walking up the stone pathway that led to Bobbi's home, I said a small prayer, asking God to forgive me for my sins and to place the same forgiveness in my best friends' hearts if they ever found out about the betrayal I was about to commit.

After walking through the gate and up to Bobbi's front door, I could hear the voices of Lucci and Diamond going back and forth. Although I couldn't make out what they were saying, whatever it was gave me pause for concern. Just as I raised my hand to knock on the decorative cherry wood door, it swung open.

"So, you decided to finally join us, huh?" Bobbi asked as she looked me up and down with her fist positioned on her thick hip. Short black cut off shorts showed off all of her thighs, while the red flannel shirt tied in the front gave you a glimpse of her waist. She stepped back, and my eyes immediately went down to the laced ankle booties on her feet.

"Those are cute," I complimented as I walked into her home, ignoring her question. "Where'd you get those from?"

"Uh-huh. Don't try to change the subject, bitch. Where in the hell have you been? We haven't seen or heard anything from you since the morning you went to court for the kids," she fussed.

"Yeah, Kay Kay. We were worried something bad happened," Lucci added. "Did you get to see the kids? What did the judge say?"

I grabbed a few of the grapes out of the bowl Diamond had in her hand before sitting on the couch next to her. I then ran down everything that happened in court the last time I'd seen them, including the part where Marvin asked me out.

"Damn. That's what's up. I hope the judge give you them kids, because Shauna's ass don't even want them. When I saw her the other day at one of the trap houses, she looked as if she didn't have a care in the world. I asked her about you, but she said that she hadn't seen or spoken to you in a while. And when I asked her about the kids, the bitch had the nerve to laugh. Ho acted like she didn't even know who I was talking about."

I shook my head, just thinking about my trifling sister. "Yeah. After she signed over her rights, she basically packed all of her shit up at my mom's house and moved out. Said she finally met a nigga with enough cash to finance her life the way she deserves it."

Bobbi, Diamond, and Lucci shook their heads at that news. We all sat in silence for a few seconds before I asked, "So, what was so urgent that we had to meet over here tonight?"

Bobbi picked up her phone to return a text as Lucci began to speak. "Well, before you walked in, I was just telling Bobbi and Diamond how the Feds raided one of my meeting spots today. Took Stax in for a murder I know he didn't commit."

Diamond raised her hand. "I'm still confused on the part where you say you know he didn't do it. No disrespect to my mans Stax, but he ain't no angel."

Lucci raised her hands above her head and grabbed a handful of her hair, putting it in a ponytail. She sat comfortably on the couch across from me, with one leg tucked under her behind and the other hanging over. The tank top she had on hugged her upper body the same way the fitted jeans hugged the bottom. She wiggled her cherry-red polished toes before she responded to Diamond's comment.

"I know he didn't do it because I was the one who murked that fool." She shook her head and waved off our questioning glares. "The nigga tried to set me up and thought that he would live to tell somebody about it."

A small chill ran through my body. "How do you know he was trying to set you up?" I inquired.

She shrugged her shoulders. "One of his boys came to me and told me."

"And you believed him?" Diamond asked.

"I didn't at first, because this nigga had been doing business with Stax and me for years and never seemed like the snake type, but after getting more information from his boy, I didn't have no other choice but to believe him. He knew too much about our meet-up and drop-off spots. Shit only Stax, myself, and the person we're selling to is supposed to know."

"So, what happened to his boy that told you all of this info?" I wanted to know.

"Killed that nigga, too. If you can turn on your friend, you for sure can turn on me."

I don't know why, but her words did something to me, and the way that Lucci stared at me with squinted eyes had me feeling real jumpy. I tried to busy myself with anything on my phone to keep down the anxiety I was starting to feel, and I was real thankful when Bobbi finally returned her attention to what we were discussing and changed the subject of the conversation.

"So, I wanna ask you guys something, and I need you all to keep it one hundred with me."

Diamond, Lucci, and I all shared a look between each other before nodding our heads, urging Bobbi to continue. "Okay, so a couple of hours ago, the firehouse got shot up."

Lucci opened her mouth to say something, but Bobbi held her hand up cutting her off.

"Before you guys ask any questions, I just want to know, did any of you have anything to do with it?"

Diamond spoke first. "I haven't even been there yet to be able to give the location to anyone, so it couldn't have been me."

"Me either," Lucci echoed. "Nav has been on the up and up with us so far when it comes to our cuts and everything else, so it wouldn't be a reason for me to do something like that."

"What about Stax?" Bobbi asked.

She rolled her eyes at Bobbi. "That nigga wouldn't make a move like that without talking about it with me first. We don't roll like that. Besides, he doesn't know anything about the firehouse. He only knows that we meet up somewhere before each robbery and then go our separate ways once the job is done."

All eyes turned to me.

"What about you, Kay Kay? You being MIA this whole time does seem a little suspect," Bobbi questioned. "Nav even asked me had I heard from you, and I lied and said yeah. Told him you were dealing with all your court shit and that's why you haven't been around." She paused for a second, then continued. "I wanna believe that shit to be true, but when you walk up in here with bruises on your face and looking like you've hardly had a night's worth of sleep, I'm having a hard time believing that."

"Yeah, Kay Kay. Unlike Bobbi, I wasn't gonna say anything in front of everyone, but you looking real rough, boo. Since when you start letting a muthafucka go upside your head?" Diamond asked before popping a grape in her mouth as her eyes intently scanned my face. "That shit looks fresh, too." She talked and chewed at the same time.

"That's because they are," Lucci pointed out. She shook her head. "The same nigga who's been giving her that dope is probably the same nigga putting his hands on her."

"Shut the fuck up, Lucci. I ain't on no dope, and instead of worrying about me, you need to be worrying about your man and whether or not he's in there spilling his guts to the Feds."

I knew that statement was a low blow, but I didn't care. I hated how the whole conversation seemed to turn to me.

Lucci smirked. "Stax ain't no snitch. That nigga probably is already on his way home anyway. We don't pay our lawyers those hefty retainer fees for nothing."

"You always walking around here like your shit don't stink. Like Stax ass hasn't put his hands on you before."

Lucci uncrossed her legs. "That nigga ain't crazy. Stax has never flat out hit me like the nigga who's whipping your ass does. He may have manhandled me a time or two whenever my mouth got too fly, but hit me? Never, bitch."

I smacked my lips. "Yeah, whatever."

"Yeah, whatever my ass. You mad because we are calling you out on your shit." Lucci laughed. "Funny thing is, everyone has denied shooting the place up but you. So, is there something you need to tell us, Kay Kay?"

I rolled my eyes at Lucci. "Bobbi hasn't denied it. I don't see your ass questioning her."

"That's because Nav already did," Bobbi answered. "He knows I didn't do it."

I sat in my seat, wishing like hell I had a line to snort. I needed something to take the edge off the way I was feeling and to help me disguise my paranoia. Swiping at my nose, I returned each of their curious glares.

"So?" Bobbi raised her hands in question.

"So what?"

"Did you have anything to do with the shooting? I mean, if you did, you need to say something now, Kay Kay. That way, we can be ready for whatever happens next, or at least try to convince Nav that the drugs you been doing somehow made you do it."

"Y'all need to stop with the drug shit, because it's not that." I hissed between my teeth while swiping at my nose again. "And what would it benefit me to have the firehouse shot up, Bobbi?" I asked instead of answering the question. "Y'all know I'm all about getting this money stacked up. I need that shit to get my babies back."

Bobbi eyed me for a few seconds. I could tell she wanted to ask me a few more questions but decided not to.

"All right, well, since neither one of us had anything to do with it, that means that there's someone else out there gunning for Nav and his crew. I don't know about y'all, but I'm not trying to get killed or go to jail doing this shit. I think we should start talking about an exit plan now. Do a couple more jobs, and then get the fuck out of California."

"What about the big BJE job?" Lucci asked. "Didn't Nav say something about us making a little over three million each if we pull it off?"

"Right about now, I'm cool on that shit. Things are starting to get too hot. The Feds swooping in on Stax. This shooting. Who knows what will happen next? I think after this next job, we should have more than enough money to start over."

"I agree with Bobbi," Diamond added. "I know I wasn't here during the first few jobs, but I'm here now. I'm ready to get this money and then get the fuck on. California is only a slew of bad memories for me right now anyway, and I wanna get away from all of that." Her eyes became misty, and her voice cracked. "Being here isn't good for my mentals, you know. Shine being gone . . ." Her voice trailed off as she began to cry.

"Awwww, D, it's okay," Bobbi whispered as she walked over to Diamond and wrapped her in a hug. "We all miss Shine."

Diamond's crying became harder. "I know, which is why I feel so bad for shutting you guys out the way that I did. I'm sorry for being so selfish when it came to grieving for my brother. You guys were his family just as much as I was."

"We were, but we also understand that everyone grieves differently. You shutting us out was your way of dealing with him being gone. Probably wasn't the best way, but yours nonetheless, and we forgive you. Don't we, you guys?" Bobbi looked at Lucci and then me.

"Yeah. We forgive you," we said at the same time.

Bobbi waved both of us over to join in on a hug, but I took that as my opportunity to excuse myself to go to the bathroom. As I sat on the toilet, thinking about everything that had happened and was going to happen, I started to become disgusted with myself. Maybe I should go in there and tell them everything Doughboy had planned to get the money that I owed him. I was sure they would understand my small lapse in judgement and help me figure out a way to be done with this Doughboy situation once and for all.

I handled my business and then washed my hands with a new outlook on this whole situation. If anybody would be forgiving of what I'd done, it would be my girls. I owed this to them, if not anyone else, to tell them the truth.

Just as I got ready to exit the bathroom and spill my guts about everything, a picture text came into my phone from Doughboy.

Doughboy: Just in case your ass is up in there thinking about whether you should stick to the plan or not.

I opened up the photo and damn near dropped my phone when a picture of my niece and nephew playing at some park came into view.

Doughboy: Just like I won't have no problem killing you about my money, I won't have a problem killing them either. Play with me if you want to, Kay Kay. Be outside in twenty minutes. I'm ready to go.

"Fuck," I cursed to myself as a soft knock sounded on the door.

"Kay Kay, it's Bobbi. I was just coming to check on you. I know things got a little heated out there, and I don't want you to feel like we're all ganging up on you, because it's not that."

After splashing a few handfuls of water on my face, I patted it dry with a paper towel and then opened the door. Bobbi stepped back and gave me enough room to walk out. When I turned to face her, she grabbed my arms and pulled me into a hug.

"You know I love you, right, and only want to help you, right?"

I nodded my head as I buried my face in the crook of her neck and circled my arms around her waist.

"Lucci and Diamond too, so when we bring up the drug use, there's no need to try and deny it. It's written all over your face that your coping snorts have turned into a full-blown habit. Just know that whenever you're ready to get the help that you need, we are all here for you, okay?"

I continued to hide my face in the crook of Bobbi's neck as silent tears began to fall from my eyes. Betraying them was going to be a lot harder than I ever imagined. However, Doughboy sending that picture of my niece and nephew to my phone made my decision that much easier to make. I raised my head from her shoulder, and both Bobbi and I wiped the tears from our eyes before sharing a laugh.

"Now that the mushy shit is over, can we talk about this job Nav has lined up for tomorrow night? I need all the pillow-talking details you were able to get."

Chapter 16

Nav

"So, did you get anything off of the surveillance footage?" I asked Cowboy as I studied the layout for the next job on my desk. Instead of robbing different stores at the same time like we'd previously done, we were focusing on robbing just this one tonight.

Cowboy was silent for a second. "Not really. Whoever it was either knew the cameras were right here,"—he pointed at the screen—"or was lucky as hell and managed to slip by undetected."

"What about the motion sensors? Did those go off?"

Apparently, the assholes who shot up the firehouse walked right up to the building and opened fire with some semiautomatic weapons. From the footage Cowboy showed me, they clearly knew what areas to target to hit somebody. Dressed in all black, they stayed in the shadows of the night. Once the guns started going off, all we were able to see were the small flashes at the end of the barrels.

"They didn't, which is weird as hell, especially for the type of system you have installed. But if you give me a couple more hours, I might have some more info for you."

I waved Cowboy off. "Hold off on that for right now. We need to get ready for this other job. Were you able to tap into the store's feed?"

As Cowboy explained everything he found out, I continued to study the layout of the jewelry store. If everything went according to plan, we were going to come off this lick with a little over 500K. I just needed everyone to be on their job while I worked on the safe in the owner's office. After getting updated on the information Cowboy was able to get, I walked out to the main room of the firehouse to address the crew.

Bobbi was the first one to notice me come into the room. It was like her body sensed it. The look in her eyes told me that she wanted me, but the way her nipples were pushing through the material of her bodysuit and the way her body shivered let me know that she needed me. Crazy thing is, I needed her ass too. The little sample I got yesterday wasn't enough to satisfy my appetite. I planned on picking up where we'd started as soon as this shit was over.

I cleared my throat, and it seemed as if everything going on around the room stopped. All eyes were now on me, anticipating what I was about to say. I looked around at everyone in attendance. Ant and Tweety were in the middle of a game of Spades. Lucci was sitting on top of the counter, typing away on her phone. Kay Kay was trying her hardest to look as if she wasn't high as a kite, and Bobbi's girl Diamond stood next to her, both dressed in their all-black bodysuits, ready to go.

"All right, so we leave in twenty. Kay Kay, Lucci, and Ant will hit the front of the store, while Bobbi and I will hit the back."

"Oh, so now y'all trying to be on some Bonnie and Clyde shit?" Tweety sassed, rolling her eyes. Ant lightly grabbed her arm, trying to get her to calm down, but she snatched it away. "Naw, man. Fuck that. I'm tired of keeping my mouth shut. This bitch ain't been on the team but for a second, and she get to partner up with you, Nav? That's supposed to be me by your side riding, not her."

I pinched the bridge of my nose. "Tweety, don't start that bullshit. Shouldn't you be getting ready for a date with Josh anyway? Why are you even down here?"

A look of hurt crossed her face. "So, it's like that now, Nav? Get some new pussy and just forget all about me?"

I scoffed and shook my head. "Ain't nobody forgetting about you, Tweety, but you need to cut this shit out, man. It's starting to become real old."

Tweety continued to burn a hole in the side of Bobbi's head as I addressed her. I thought her hate for Bobbi would blow over once she realized that I was actually serious about fucking with her, but it didn't. Something in my gut kept telling me that I needed to deal with Tweety before shit became worse, but the love I had for her as a friend wouldn't allow me to put her out like that.

"Yo, Tweet, come holla at me real quick." Ant finally intervened, grabbing her attention. "I need you to answer a few more questions about ole boy and where y'all going tonight."

She grunted before rolling her eyes and following behind Ant. "Yeah. Let's go. I need to get the fuck up out of here before I do something I won't regret."

Ant looked at me, and I slightly nodded my head, thanking him for the distraction. Once they left to the other room, I continued to address the rest of the crew.

"Now that that's over, did anyone else have any questions about what I said?" My eyes scanned the room until they stopped on the chocolate beauty whose pussy I could still taste on my tongue.

"I got one," Bobbi said, raising her hand. "What is Diamond going to do?" she questioned, pushing her friend forward a little.

"She's going to be the getaway driver. You do know how to drive, don't you?" My gaze turned toward her, and she nodded her head. "Since she ain't been here, I don't think that it's fair for her to jump in on one of our bigger jobs. With Ed out indefinitely, we need a new driver." I nodded my head toward the van. "You think you can handle whipping that shit through the streets without getting us caught up?"

She nodded her head. "Yeah, I can do it."

I smirked. "Pretty sure you can. Weren't you the getaway driver when you and your brother Shine led the police on a high-speed chase after stealing a car when you were younger?" Diamond's eyes bucked as I recalled a piece of info I had found out from her juvie file. "Said you got up to 120 miles per hour on the 10 freeway."

"How do you know—" she began, but I cut her off.

"I'm a thorough nigga when it comes to investigating the people I work with. Gotta know your full background if I choose to break bread with you. Is that going to be an issue?"

Diamond looked at Bobbi with questioning eyes before looking back at me. "Nah, it's not going to be an issue at all."

"So again, I ask, you think you can drive this van and get us to the drop-off spot without incident?" Diamond nodded her head. "All right, then it's set." I looked down at my watch. "In fifteen minutes, we're out of here. Does anyone have any questions?"

Kay Kay raised her hand. "Yeah, I got one. Did . . . did you find out who shot the place up?"

"Why? You got some information for me?"

She looked around the room nervously as all eyes went to her. "Nah. No." She shook her head vehemently. "I . . . I was just wondering why we were still meeting here after everything that happened. What if the niggas who came and shot the place up come back?"

"If they do, we'll be ready for them," I answered, thinking about the extra security I had placed around the building that they knew nothing about. "Which reminds me, that BJE job we've been planning for is out."

Everyone in the room started asking questions at the same time. I rose my hand in the air, silencing them.

"Until I can figure out who's coming after us, I don't wanna risk doing one of the biggest jobs of my life and some shit goes down. Once we get a handle on everything, we'll revisit the BJE job, but as for now, it's off the table." I didn't wait for anyone to ask questions. Turning around, I headed back toward my office to get ready for the rest of the night.

I had just pulled on my jumpsuit when a light tap sounded from my door. "Come in," I voiced with my back turned away from whoever was about to enter my office.

"Hey, I wasn't trying to bother you or anything like that. I just wanted to make sure that you were okay," Bobbi said as she made her way into the room, closing the door behind her. "You have everybody out there talking about you right now."

I zipped up my suit and made sure the burner phone I used for jobs was in my pocket. "Yeah, I knew that little announcement was going to have y'all talking." When I turned around to face Bobbi, I couldn't help the way my eyes roamed over her body. The new bodysuit fit her curvy frame to a T. Just thinking about the way her pussy was going to wrap around my dick had it twitch a few times. We needed to get out of this office before we ended up butt naked and not giving a fuck about the robbery. "What's going on? Did you need something?"

She walked closer to my desk, the fruity scent of whatever product she used in her hair meeting me before she did.

"I didn't need anything, Nav. Just wanted to make sure you were good. I mean, we're getting to know one another. Dating or whatever. It's okay for me to check on you, right?" she replied, tilting her head to the side.

"So, you call what we got going on dating?"

She shrugged her shoulders. "I mean, isn't that what we're doing? We go out, spend time together, talk and text on the phone all day. You know a lot of personal things about me, and I know a lot of personal things about you. In my mind, we are dating. Is that not how you feel?"

I finished getting myself together and then slipped the bag that held my guns and other tools over my head. Once I was sure that I hadn't forgotten anything, I walked over to Bobbi and wrapped my hands around her waist, pulling her body into mine. Lowering my head, I inhaled her natural scent and lightly caressed her neck with the tip of my nose.

"You and I are doing more than just dating, Bobbi. I told you that you are the only woman I've ever let come to my house. That should've told you right then and there that our relationship was on a different level."

She moaned and circled her arms around my neck, pulling my face deeper into the crook of her neck. When I brushed the tip of my tongue across her sensitive skin, her whole body shivered.

"Nav, you are going to be the death of me."

I smirked and placed light kisses across her jawbone. "Why do you say that?"

"Because you already got me so infatuated with you, and I ain't even had the D yet."

That comment caused a small chuckle to fall from my lips. Placing her hand on the print that I knew was now very visible, I guided her hand up and down in a slow motion, causing the semi-sleep beast to grow harder. I kissed her chin and then the side of her face.

"He already belongs to you. Just say when and I'll plant him so deep inside of you that my name will be permanently etched in your soul."

"Mmmmm," she moaned again, her grip on my dick becoming tighter. "How long do we have before it's time to go?"

Crashing my lips down on hers, I possessively covered her mouth with mine. Our tongues danced to a tune that could have me fucking up her whole life if we didn't stop this now. When she pulled on my ears, intensifying our connection, anything outside of what we were doing in that second was lost. I frantically unzipped her jumpsuit and palmed her melon-size breasts, the feel of the lace on her bra eliciting a low growl from my throat.

I was just about to place one of her Hershey-kisses nipples in my mouth when there was a loud banging on my door.

"Yo, Nav!" Ant yelled. "It's time to roll out, man."

I let my forehead drop to the space between her breasts and kissed it. Slowly backing up, I adjusted myself before helping her straighten out her clothes.

"You know I'm gon' fuck the shit out of you after we do this job, right?" I asked after grabbing the blueprints to the building.

Bobbi, whose face was still flushed, bit her bottom lip and nodded her head. "Looking forward to it." She hesitated for a second before asking, "Just so that we're both clear, if we're dating, that means that we . . ." She let her words trail off, waiting for me to finish her sentence.

Grabbing her hand and interlacing our fingers together, I looked deep into her eyes and said, "We belong to each other. Exclusively."

A smile tipped her lips. "So, I'm your Beyoncé and you're my Jay-Z"

I laughed. "Nah, baby. Pick another couple. Our backgrounds are a little dirtier than theirs."

She thought about her response for a second as I guided us out of my office. "What about Bonnie and Clyde? I mean, we are living a life of crime, right?"

I nodded my head. "I can get with that."

By the time we got to the main room of the firehouse, everyone was already in the van, waiting on us. Diamond sat in the driver's seat, ready to drive, while Ant sat next to her in the passenger seat. Kay Kay and Lucci sat on the left side of the van, leaving the right side for Bobbi and me. After getting settled in, we closed the doors, ready to roll out.

"You all remember your spots, right?" Ant asked over his shoulder.

Collectively, the girls all answered, "Yeah."

"All right." He looked at Diamond. "Drop us off at the end of the block, and then we'll meet you at the other end of the alley, okay?"

Diamond nodded her head in understanding.

"Now that we got that all out the way, let's hit it," he said.

With my hand still entwined with Bobbi's, I gave her a light squeeze and smiled. If we were going to be proclaiming ourselves as one of the baddest crime couples in the game, it was only right that we listened to some theme music to get us and the rest of the crew amped up.

"Alexa," I called out. "Play 'Bonnie and Clyde Theme' by Yo-Yo and Ice Cube."

I looked over at Bobbi, who was already looking up at me with the biggest smile on her face. When the all-too-familiar bass of Yo-Yo's hood classic began to flow through the speakers, everyone in the van started nodding their heads to the beat, mentally preparing themselves for what we were about to do. Bobbi and I may have only known each other for a short time, but I was more than sure that she was the girl for me. Her energy, personality, and mentals vibed with mine more than any woman I'd ever met. If she wanted me by her side, breaking the law and being her Clyde, then I was there for all of that shit until the wheels fell off.

Chapter 17

Bobbi

I had this real funny feeling in my gut that something was off. Call it women's intuition or whatever you want to call it, but I couldn't shake this feeling that something was about to go terribly wrong.

"Hand me the other stethoscope," Nav instructed me with his arms stretched out behind his back. "It's at the bottom of my bag."

I quickly walked around the large oak desk that I was going through and handed him what he requested. For the last five minutes, Nav had been trying to open the old-school safe by listening to the clicks of the dial. What he assumed was going to be a padlock actually ended up being the number-spinning dial joint. Good thing he came prepared for the shit.

"Do you think we should leave the safe alone and just grab what we can out of the front with Kay Kay and them?" I asked nervously. My eyes darted from the door and then back to him.

Nav stopped what he was doing and looked up at me. "You still feeling like something is about to go down, huh?" I nodded my head, and he smirked. "What I tell you before we hopped out of the van?"

I thought about it for a quick second. "You told me that if anything happens tonight, you got me?"

"Have I ever given you a reason to doubt my word?"

I shook my head again.

"Well, then stop tripping. I meant every word that I said, baby, so trust me when I say that I got you. Remember, Bonnie and Clyde equals homicide, right?"

"Right." I giggled at his play on Ice Cube's words from our theme song. Hearing him say that did make me feel a little better, but something was still off.

We'd only been in the store for about three minutes now and had about seven more to get what we could and get the fuck on. Because Cowboy was able to shut the alarm system off that reacted once we entered the store, we got in without a hitch; however, a call made to the police department by the security company to make a routine stop shortened the time we originally had to rob the place. That little hiccup was the first red flag that sent a wave of nervousness through my body.

The second was Kay Kay's ass. Since we all met up at the firehouse, she'd been acting weird as hell. When I tried to see what was up with her, she brushed me off and continued to text back and forth on her phone. I'm not even going to talk about the few times I saw her turn to the side when she thought no one was looking and snort that shit up her nose. She was high as fuck and a little too jumpy for me.

"I'm in," Nav said over his shoulder, breaking me from my thoughts. "There's only stacks of money in here. Did you find the keys to the file cabinets yet?"

Breaking from my thoughts, I continued to search through the top drawer of the desk until my fingers ran across a set of keys. It was obvious that the two short ones belonged to the file cabinets. I just had to figure out which one was which.

"I found them," I answered over my shoulder as Nav placed the last of the money in his bag. He stood up and walked over to where I was standing.

I stuck the first key into the lock and tried to turn it, but I couldn't. Once I inserted the other key in, the shit popped open, and Nav and I began to look through the drawers.

"I got this one," he said. "Open the other drawers and see if you can find anything in them."

Taking Nav's lead, I did exactly what he said and quickly opened the other file cabinet. The first drawer was filled with a whole bunch of paperwork, while the second one was filled with an array of empty jewelry boxes. When I got to the third drawer, my expectations for finding anything of value was low, until I removed the large cashmere blanket and grabbed the handle of the black security box it was covering. I carefully placed the box on the oak desk as my mind rolled over the possibility of three-digit number combos the owner probably set up. It would take us more than a few hours to try and crack that, but we didn't have the time. The thought of just taking the box with us rolled across my mind, but there was no doubt that whoever owned this thing had some kind of tracking device installed as well. So, after taking a deep breath, I said a little prayer and turned the three dials to the numbers above the ones that were displayed.

"Two, five, seven," I mouthed as I placed the pad of my thumb on the small silver button next to the dial and pressed it.

The second the latch released the pin and the lock shot up, my breath hitched, and my eyes opened wide.

Swallowing the lump that formed in my throat, I slowly opened the top of the box and reached inside. The smooth feel of velvet danced across my fingertips as I picked up the first small pouch, opening it and pouring the contents across the table. My heart was beating fast as hell.

"N—" I could barely get out. "Nav," I said again a little louder.

"What's up, babe? I didn't find shit in either one of these—" His words stopped as soon as he turned to face me, and his gaze shifted to my flashlight illuminating the desk. The tiny beams of light sparkling from each diamond that fell out of the bag rendered him speechless.

Nav walked up to the table and picked one of the dime-sized gems up. My flashlight followed his every move.

"Are these—"

"Yes." I cut him off, confirming his question of if the diamonds were real or not.

"How b—"

"About three or four carats, give or take."

"And how much—"

"Six to eighty *G*s per carat, depending on the weight and clarity," I excitedly said, cutting him off again. "I . . . I can't tell what it is now, but by the way that the light shines and reflects, these diamonds have been cut already and are ready to be placed in settings."

"Which means?" Nav asked as he continued to examine the gems.

"We just hit the fucking jackpot." I threw the three other velvet bags on the desk, their contents spilling out and blending in with the other diamonds. "Either the owner of this store was in the process of selling these to someone else, or he had a large custom order to do for someone." I shook my head. "Either way, that large bag he was about to get for these will now be ours."

"That's what the fuck I'm talking about," Nav hissed, grabbing me around my waist and pulling me into his body. "I told you you were worrying for nothing. See, if we would've bailed out on this job because of your nerves, we would've missed this big score."

I wrapped my arms around his neck and kissed his lips. "Yeah, you're right."

Nav grabbed a chunk of my ass and squeezed it before kissing my lips again. "Damn right, I'm right. Now, grab that shit and your stuff so we can get out of here. Cowboy just radioed in and said that the police will be here soon."

Turning out of his embrace, I stuffed the diamonds back into the velvet bags and secured them in my cross-body bag. Once we closed the drawers and made sure that nothing was left behind, we bolted from the office and made our way down the hall to the back exit.

"Wait," I yelped, turning toward the hall that led to the showroom floor. "What about Lucci, Kay Kay, and Ant? We need to go get them."

"They're already gone," Nav informed me, pulling the strap of my bag. "Cowboy said they cleared everything out and left out of the store a few minutes ago."

Nodding my head, I switched my direction back toward the exit and pushed my way through the metal doors. A sense of relief washed over me as soon as the cool air hit my face. Although this wasn't the first time we robbed a store, I never felt like we were actually home free until we were miles away from the crime scene. I could hear the loud wail of sirens way off in the distance and knew that we still had enough time to get to the van and leave the place unseen.

Feeling all giddy and happy about the biggest score we'd just come up on, I grabbed hold of Nav's hand when he reached back for mine and hurriedly ran down the alleyway by his side. With the van's headlights getting closer, my worries about something happening tonight were receding further into my mind. However, when Nav's pace toward the van abruptly stopped and he pushed my body behind his, that same worry began to creep back in.

A small shiver ran down my spine. That weird gut feeling I had earlier returned tenfold. Before I could even blink or try to see what was going on, Nav pulled his gun from his bag and aimed it at whoever was standing in front of him.

"Just give up your shit and no one else gets hurt," an unfamiliar voice said.

I tried to peek around Nav's body to see who was talking, but he jerked my arm back, urging me to keep still.

"Nigga, you got me fucked up. You gon' have to kill me first and take the shit from my cold body yourself if you want anything I have."

The mystery dude chuckled. "Nigga, you act like that would be a problem."

I couldn't see how many men were already standing at the end of the alley with dude, but I could tell by the sound of footsteps hitting the gravel that more than one person had joined him.

"Dough, just shoot this nigga and take his shit. My baby mama already been blowing me up, wondering when I would get home," another voice said.

"Nigga, shut your ass up and fuck your baby mama. We trying to get this money right now," the voice I now knew as Dough returned. "I'm trying to give this nigga the opportunity the rest of his crew didn't get."

At the mention of the rest of our crew, my mind immediately went to Lucci, Kay Kay and Diamond. If this nigga touched a hair on any one of them, his ass was as good as gone. Snatching Nav's other gun that he kept tucked in his back pocket, I rounded his body with the gun aimed, ready to go to war for him and my girls.

"Where the fuck are my friends?" I asked as all eyes went to me. I was now able to count five dudes in total. We were surely outnumbered but could easily take down two bodies if bullets started to fly.

"Damn," another one of the dudes said. "Who is that bitch? She bad as fuck."

Nav stepped forward and tried to shield my body with his again, but I sidestepped him. I could feel him staring a hole into the side of my face, but I wasn't going to take my eyes off these niggas. One had already disappeared behind the brick wall, and the other one eyeing my body up and down started to walk closer.

"Yo," he said, removing the toothpick from his mouth, gun in his hand but not aimed at anyone. "I could really use a bitch like you on my team. I like a ho who likes to get her hands dirty from time to time."

"Nigga, you got one more time to disrespect my lady and I'm gon' blow your brains out," Nav spat with so much venom laced in his voice.

When the dude who was being disrespectful smirked, I knew some shit was about to pop off.

"You gon' blow my brains out, man? Why? Because I called your girl a bitch? Or was it the ho part that really got to you?"

Before he could open his mouth to laugh at his lame joke or say anything else, the loud ringing sound of a gun going off echoed around us. A bullet had pierced his dumb ass right between the eyes. Nav turned his aim to Dough, ready to take him out, but he stopped when a bloody-faced Lucci was pushed into his grasp. I couldn't really assess the damage that had been done to her, but I could tell that she had been beat pretty bad, and with that dark, wet spot forming between her legs, I knew the baby she was carrying wasn't in good shape either.

"That was one of my best men you just killed. My intention was to only kill your driver, but now that you hit my man, it's only right that I take another one of yours." He raised his gun to Lucci's head, and I screamed.

"No! Please. Don't kill her."

His eyes went between Nav and me before rolling over to another one of his flunkies, who was shielding another body from us.

"If not her, then what about him?"

My eyes traveled over to a beat-up Ant. With his face in a deep scowl, he walked from behind the big trash can with his hands up and his eyes on Nav.

"Kill this nigga, man," he said between clenched teeth. "He already killed Diamond. Also shot Kay Kay and threw her body in the back of another car. This muthafucka didn't come here with the intentions on letting any of us live. Kill him and the rest of his homeboys and get the fuck out of here."

"Your boy here talks a lot of shit. Can take a good ass beating, too." Dough laughed, but Nav didn't.

I looked up at him and could tell by the pained look on his face that he was conflicted about what to do.

"Look, I don't wanna kill any more of your friends. Like I said, it wasn't my intention. The police will be here at any moment, and we all need to get the fuck on. So, just hand over your bags, and I'll let you go."

Nav lowered his head, then looked over at me, trying to see if I was down for whatever. In any other case, I probably would've went out with guns blazing, but seeing Lucci broken down and hurt, hearing that Kay Kay was shot and dumped in the back of someone's car, and learning that Diamond was dead had me reconsidering my actions. I didn't want to have to bury all three of my friends.

Slowly removing the crossbody bag from my frame, I threw it down to the ground. Nav, still conflicted, eventually did the same.

"Throw your guns down, too."

I was the first to drop mine. Nav was next. When Dough's flunky came and grabbed our shit from off the ground, he stood up and aimed Nav's gun at him. Moving with his front still turned to us, he walked backward until he made it back over to where Dough was standing.

"Now, see, was that so hard?" Dough asked with a fake smile. "It was nice doing business with you. Until next time." After pushing Ant and Lucci to the ground and shooting both of them in the back, Dough and his boys hopped into the car that pulled up and skirted away.

Without thinking, Nav and I ran toward our friends. While he and Ant talked about the niggas that just left, I rolled Lucci over. Tears rolled down her bruised cheeks as she tried to catch her breath at the same time.

"My . . . my baby," came out between cries. "I wanna . . . save my . . . baby."

"Shhhhh." I tried to soothe her. "Don't talk. Save your breath. We gon' get you out of here and to a hospital."

"Call . . . Stax," she managed to get out.

I nodded my head. "We're going to call him. We just have to get you to a hospital first, okay?"

Her lips started to tremble as more tears began to fall down her face. In all the years that I'd known Lucci, I had never seen her cry, and to see her this way was doing something to me.

"Nav!" I yelled over my shoulder. "We need to go."

When I looked back at him, he and Ant were slowly standing up from the ground. Ant had been shot in his shoulder but was still able to move quickly. After Nav helped me carefully pick Lucci up, we made it over to the van and opened the back doors. Diamond's lifeless body fell forward and hit the ground before any of us could react. Dropping Lucci's legs, I knelt down next to my friend and grabbed her in a tight embrace. Rocking back and forth, I prayed that her transition from this world was fast and easy, and I hoped that her soul was settled now that she was reunited with Shine.

"We have to go, Bobbi," Nav whispered into my ear as he squeezed my shoulders. "We can't take her with us. We have to leave her here if we wanna make it to the hospital in time to save Lucci."

"No, we can't leave her here," I cried. "Help me pick her up and put her in the back of the van!" I yelled to Nav as I began to lift Diamond's body with mine. "We can't leave her."

"Bobbi, we have to. The connection to Cowboy was cut, and we're basically blind out here. The police could be pulling up at any minute now. I know you don't want your girl to be found dead in the alley, but we have to leave her here. I promise once everything settles down, we can give her a proper burial. Anything you want. We just need to leave now."

I hugged Diamond's body one last time before finally standing to my feet and hopping in the back of the van. I didn't want to leave her there like that, but Nav was right. If we wanted to make it out of there without getting caught up and possibly save Lucci's life, we had to.

Closing the door behind me, Nav slipped into the driver's seat, taking off as soon as he brought the engine to life. Laying Lucci's head in my lap, I stroked her hair and slowly rocked her back and forth as my mind drifted off to Diamond.

"Ain't no way that wasn't a set up." Ant's loud voice broke me from my thoughts a few minutes later. "Somebody told them niggas about the robbery. They had to."

Nav continued to hightail it to the nearest hospital, running every red light we came upon. "I already know. We just gotta figure out who it was." His eyes connected to mine through the rearview mirror and stayed locked for a few seconds.

"Well, you know it wasn't me," Ant said first. "We been doing this shit for years, and ain't nothing like that ever popped off until we took in all of these new people."

Nav's gaze connected with mine again. "I know none of my people are on some snake shit, which leaves me to believe somebody in your circle is the one causing all this bullshit to happen. First the firehouse getting shot up, and now this. Bobbi, I already told you once, I don't play when it comes to my money. If I find out any of your girls or —" He bit his lip and shook his head. "Or you had anything to do with this . . ." He let his words trail off, not able to finish what he had to say.

"Me? Nigga, I was out there ready to give my life for you and them. How could you even fix your mouth to say some stupid shit like that? Let alone even think that I would try to set you up when you know how I feel about—" I stopped and thought for a second. This was the second time his ass had accused me of some foul shit without even looking into everything. "You know what? Fuck you, Nav. Fuck you and your whole entire operation. Fuck you, fuck this money, fuck all of it. I just lost one of my closest friends. Left her body in the alley for the rats to feast on until someone finds her. Kay Kay is possibly dead too, and Lucci is lying here in my arms, trying to hold on to life. Do you think any of us would set this up if there was any chance that we would get ourselves killed?"

Nav and Ant shared a look, but I didn't question them about it.

"Just get me to the hospital so I can make sure I don't lose another friend. After that, you can kiss my whole entire black ass."

The van was quiet for the rest of the ride. Everyone was lost in their own thoughts, trying to figure out what in the hell went wrong that night. Once we got to the hospital, Nav jumped out and waved down a nurse, who went right into action and brought out a gurney.

I jogged right along with the hospital staff as they whisked Lucci down the hall to the emergency room. Before I could leave them to do their job, Lucci lightly squeezed my hand, and I looked down at her.

"Nav is gon' be mad at you," she said with a smile that I returned.

"Why do you say that?"

"Be–because you told him . . . to kiss your ass."

I laughed and wiped the tears that were still falling from my eyes. "Don't you worry about Nav. I can handle him. You just worry about getting better and how big you want that Stax tattoo to be when you cover up that bullet hole."

Although it was weak, she smiled again. "Diamond? Is she?"

I shook my head. "Later, okay? We will talk later."

She nodded. "I love you."

"I love you too," was the last thing I said before the nurses pushed her through the double doors, leaving me out in the hall, looking through the small window.

I watched as the team of doctors and nurses cut Lucci's clothes off and began to work on her. When she started to flatline as they were trying to remove the bullet, I couldn't take it anymore and ran back through the hospital and out into the morning breeze. With my hands on my knees and my head hanging low, I tried to control the cries that fell from my lips, but I couldn't. It wasn't until a pair of strong arms lifted me up from my position and cradled me in his arms that I finally calmed down.

"Shhhhhh." Nav's deep voice vibrated through my ear. He pushed my hair out of his way and kissed the side of my face. "Everything's going to be okay, Bobbi. I'm sorry about everything I said earlier. Just let me be here."

I wanted to remove myself from his embrace so bad, but my mind and body needed his soothing comfort. I knew I should've just gone with my gut feeling earlier and tried to postpone the job until another night. Diamond, Kay Kay, and Lucci's blood was now on my hands, and I wasn't going to stop until I found that nigga Dough and everyone else who was behind this shit.

Chapter 18

Kay Kay

"Aye, Dough man, when is your connect gon' slide through with the money we're supposed to get for them diamonds? It's been three days already."

"Nigga, shut the fuck up and stop questioning me about my connect. They'll get here when they get here. Until then, find you something else to do, like clean up around here. It looks like a fucking pig sty."

I could hear what sounded like empty boxes being kicked around as Doughboy's heavy footsteps came closer to the room I was locked in. "And spray some air freshener in the air. That little bitch you be sneaking over when I leave got it smelling like stale coochie and rotten ass in there."

My appointed watchdog, Thumper, laughed. "It ain't my bitch with the stinky coochie. It's that snake-ass ho you got me looking after. I tell her to get up and take a shower every day, but the bitch refuses."

He was right. I had refused to take care of myself, but that was only to keep his grimy ass and the rest of them bitch-ass niggas up off of me. Even though Doughboy told them that I was off limits, that still didn't stop them from trying to fuck on me. It had been a week since the robbery, and I couldn't count on both hands the number of times that nigga Thumper tried to get at me. The asshole even tried to make me have a threesome, but once the girl got a whiff of my scent, she shut any contact between the three of us down.

I lay back on the bed with my eyes focused on the vent above me. My wrists and ankles were restrained to the bed by rope. The effects of the drugs they'd been pumping into my system every day was finally coming down. Keeping me doped up was the only way they could keep my ass from trying to escape and letting Bobbi and them know who was really involved with what went down.

I couldn't believe who Doughboy's connect was when I found out. The nigga didn't really need the information I gave him about the job that night at all. He already had it. I found out that I was only a pawn in this double-cross, and I had played right into the shit.

My mind drifted to Diamond and the look on her face when she realized that I had something to do with Doughboy and them showing up to rob us. Lucci and Ant were off to the side, getting their asses beat by the time I came around to the front of the van. Doughboy had his gun aimed at Diamond's head when he waved me over to where he was standing. At first, I was stuck. My body didn't want to move for shit, but when he cocked his gun and smashed it into Diamond's temple, my feet began to move.

"Thanks for hooking this up, baby," he said as he wrapped his arm around my waist and pulled me into his side. "We couldn't have done it without you."

The second he kissed my lips and Diamond's heated eyes glanced in my direction, I lowered my head in shame.

"So, you set this all up, Kay Kay? Your friends? You set us up for some bumpy whose dick you probably know more about than the nigga himself?"

I tried to open my mouth to say something, anything, to try to get her to understand, but nothing came out.

Doughboy *tsk*ed. "Don't do her like that, Diamond. Kay Kay knows a lot about me, don't you, baby?" His question was rhetorical, but I shook my head no. He smirked when I averted my eyes from his. "It's okay. She probably does know my dick more than she knows me. Which is why she probably thought she could get away with stealing from me. But it's all gucci now." He used the barrel of his gun to swipe away a few of the braids that had fallen into my face.

"Kay, baby, your debt will be more than paid after I hawk this shit and keep everything for myself. I might even fuck you a few more times before I throw you back out for the wolves. I can just imagine what that nigga Nav is going to do to you once he finds out you were behind everything."

I tried to remove myself from his embrace, but he pulled me in tighter. While he continued to taunt me about the slow and painful death I had coming, I could see Diamond trying to reach for something under the driver's seat. She was trying to do it as discreetly as she could while Doughboy had his eyes trained on me, but she wasn't as fast as she should have been. One quick, nervous glance from me in her direction was all it took for Doughboy to realize that something wasn't right. Before Diamond could pull the gun from underneath her seat, Doughboy returned his gun to her head and pulled the trigger.

At that second, it seemed as if everything started to move in slow motion. My heart dropped when Diamond's blood splattered across my face and her lifeless body slumped over in the seat. On instinct, I started swinging with all my might, landing blow after blow to Doughboy's head and face. I did enough damage to cause him to loosen his grip on me. When he did, I spun out of his embrace and tried to make a run for it, but I was shot in the leg before I could put any real distance between us.

Lucci's loud screams could be heard from underneath the bodies of niggas who were raining blows on her. She tried to get up but was slammed back down. I could hear her calling my name, trying to hear any sign of me being alive, but she never heard a peep, because as soon as my head hit the hard concrete ground, I blacked out.

That night had been playing over and over in my head since it happened: the look on Diamond's face before she was killed, Lucci's toe-curling scream when she witnessed me being shot, and the deep guilt I felt in the pit of my stomach for betraying the three people who had always had my back. I didn't deserve to live. Didn't deserve to be here while Diamond wasn't. I already knew my fate and had come to terms with it. I just hoped my niece and nephew ended up with the type of life I'd always wanted for them.

The sound of the door slowly opening broke me from my thoughts, and I wiped the single tear that had managed to fall down my face. Doughboy had entered the room and, like always, he went and sat in the chair next to the window. His eyes were trained on me as I looked anywhere around the room but at him.

"So, you still trying to act like you're disgusted with me, Kay Kay? Like you can't stand to look at a nigga?" I didn't answer after a few seconds, and he laughed. "Funny thing is, I hope you're that same way when you look in the mirror. Can't stand to look at yourself. You're the reason why everything has happened. You. Not your sister, not your mother, but you. Had you chosen not to steal from me and just been good with our little fucking arrangement, everything would've been cool. Hell, I probably would've turned the offer down to rob y'all had you been on the up and up with me. But nah, your ho ass was being too greedy."

Doughboy removed a small plastic bag from his pocket and poured the contents onto the silver spoon he kept on the dresser next to him.

"Did I ever tell you that my connect wanted me to kill you that night like I did your girl Diamond?" He shook his head. "But some part of me didn't want it to go down like that. Some part of me didn't want to let you go," Doughboy announced as he flicked his lighter on at the same time. The glow from the small flame illuminated the dark corner he was in. When the smell of burnt plastic started to surround me, I knew that it was time for my daily dosage of medicine.

"I had been kind of playing around with the thought of me and you getting this money and getting the fuck on. I mean, I can sell product wherever I'm at, and you—" He paused for a second. "You aren't the domesticated type, but I think you could've changed a little for me."

Doughboy stood up from his seat and walked over to the bed. The needle he was holding was already filled with my candy. I squirmed around a bit to try to get free, but like all of the other times I tried, it was to no avail. The restraints held me captive.

My throat was dry, but I managed to open it and say something. "Dough," I coughed. "Doughboy, please.

Please don't do this anymore. If . . . if you let me go, I . . . I promise I won't mention your name when . . . when Nav comes for me."

There was a twinkle in his eye and a smile on his chubby face as he thumped the syringe with his middle finger. "You promise not to tell, huh?" I was rewarded with a hard slap to my face for that lie. "Bitch, stop lying. The minute Nav comes for you, you gon' scream my name to the mountaintops." He leaned over and whispered in my ear, "Sorta like the way you used to scream it when I was balls deep in that pussy. I should fuck you one last time so that my dick is the last thing on your mind."

With his free hand, Doughboy used his middle finger to lightly caress my face then move down to my breasts and belly. When his touch got close to my pussy, he stopped and frowned. "Then again, I'm good. You ain't took a bath in almost a week, so I know that's your rancid shit stinking up the house."

I didn't even bother acknowledging his comment, because I knew that what he was saying was true. But that didn't stop me from trying to get him to fuck me one last time. I figured if he untied me and allowed me to go take a shower, I'd try one last time to escape this house and his ass for sure. I cocked my legs open, and the odor that followed wasn't the best, but I had to do something.

"Untie me, Dough. Untie me and let's fuck. One last time, like you said. I . . . I have to go take a shower first, but I at least want to experience something that feels good before whatever is going to happen to me happens. I know I'm going to die eventually—probably real soon—but just let me feel you one last time before it's all over."

For a second, it looked like Doughboy was considering my offer. His eyes roamed up and down my barely clothed body one last time before he shook his head.

"Nah, I'm good. I don't wanna have to wash you up to get rid of my DNA after I kill your ass. So, no."

"But I thought . . . I thought you said you weren't going to kill me. That's why you've kept me locked up here, right, and just doped me up every day. Doughboy, please. Let me prove to you that I can be who you want me to be. I promise I'll always have your back." My heart began to beat a little faster. I honestly thought he was going to let Nav do the dirty work of taking me out; that maybe, just maybe, he felt something for me and wouldn't be able to go through with taking my life. Guess I had it all wrong.

Doughboy looked around the bed until he spotted the rubber strip he used to tie my arm, ignoring all the lies spilling from my mouth. After securing the strip tightly around my arm and finding a vein, he inserted the needle. The warm liquid he had sucked into the syringe rushed through my body like a freight train.

"Doughboy, please," I cried out as tears began to fall from my eyes. "You said you weren't going to kill me." I could tell by the amount of time he kept the needle submerged in my vein that he was filling me up with more drugs than he normally did.

"I wasn't going to kill you at first, but now that I've had some time to think about it, there isn't any real reason for me to keep you alive. The boat on us being together has come and gone. I could never trust a bitch like you. And it's not because you stole from me. It's because of how easy you turned on your friends to get your ass out of trouble. I'm not about to live my life wondering if you're really down for me, or having to watch my back because you wanna rat me out to save yourself. So, for that, you gotta go. Don't trip, though. I respect you enough to put some clothes on your stankin' ass before I dump your body."

"Doughboy, please don't do this." I continued to beg. "If you don't want me in a sexual way anymore, maybe you can use me for something else. Like another setup." I tried to convince him. "You see the way I turned on my friends and got you all of that money? I'm sure we can do it again to someone else."

The second those words left my mouth, I could feel the bile rising from the pit of my stomach. I had to quickly turn my head to the side and throw up all over the bed to avoid choking on my own vomit. Just thinking about the way I had betrayed my friends made me sick to my stomach, and I hated using my disloyalty as a bargaining point, but I had to try something.

"You know, Kay Kay, that wouldn't be a bad idea. I know a few niggas that I could probably have you finesse and then rob blind." He thought about the offer for another second. "Then again, I think I'll have to pass on that. Like I said, you can't be trusted."

Doughboy continued to fill my body with the poison and waited around until the effects of so much heroin made me slip in and out of consciousness. It seemed like forever had passed before I finally started to feel my body shut down. I prayed to God that once my life was in His hands, He'd forgive me and make it so that Bobbi, Diamond, and Lucci would find a way to forgive me as well. I prayed that my niece and nephew found a family that was willing to take both of them in and love them better than I ever could. I also prayed that Doughboy and his connect got dealt with just like I did.

My eyes started to get real heavy when there was a light knock on the door.

"Come in!" Doughboy yelled over his shoulder as he placed the spoon back on the dresser and threw the needle away.

"Is it done?" an all-too-familiar voice asked, walking into the room. "I got a car out front, waiting to dump her stinking-ass body on the side of the 710. Make sure you get rid of anything that she touched so that this shit doesn't come back to us."

"Already done," Doughboy said as he picked up the trash can, ready to head out the room. "Did you bring my money? My niggas keep hounding me about that shit."

"Yeah, I got your cash. It's outside in the car. You'll get it after we take care of this bitch."

"All right, cool," Doughboy responded. "Aye, um, did you hear anything else about the other job them bitches were trying to pull off with that big jewelry store in Beverly Hills?"

"Nah," the connect said as they walked over to me and raised one of my droopy eyelids. "That nigga Nav is still saying it's a no go, but I have a feeling his decision will change, and when it does, you just make sure you and your boys are ready. I don't want any fuck-ups this time either. Y'all need to kill every single last one of them muthafuckas. We don't need no loose ends coming for us once this is all over. Do you understand?"

"Yeah I hear you. My boys and I will be ready."

The connect looked down at me and smirked. "Kay Kay, you make sure you send Diamond my love, and also let her know that those bitches Lucci and Bobbi will be joining you two pretty soon as well, a'ight?" My head rolled over, and the person laughed. "I'll just take that as an okay, since you're probably sucking the tip of death's dick right now. Thanks for all your help, boo. I couldn't have done any of this without your backstabbing ass."

The last thing I heard before my eyes finally rolled back was the fading laughter of both Doughboy and the connect. Them two muthafuckas may have been celebrating this win now, but I had no doubt that even in my death, it would be me getting the last laugh.

Chapter 19

Lucci

"Here you go, Ms. Adams." The nurse who wheeled me down to the lobby of the hospital handed me a cup of water over my shoulder. "I filled your bottle up, too, just in case we're out here a little while longer."

I wanted to snap at her for the smart remark, but I didn't. She was referring to Stax being over thirty minutes late in picking me up. I mean, the nigga was late, and I was getting a little upset myself that he still hadn't shown up after he text me almost an hour ago, saying that he was on his way. Stax was already about to hear my mouth about not visiting me in the week since I'd been there. If he knew what was best for him, he'd pull his ass up real quick and get me the hell home.

Business had been booming since we opened some of our trap houses back up. We even started serving this one area in Long Beach we'd been trying to get for a minute. However, Stax's ass wasn't that busy to where he couldn't be by my side while I was healing from the gunshot wound to my lower back or mourning the loss of our child.

My heart became a little heavy as my mind replayed the minutes that led up to the doctor telling me about the miscarriage. I had just opened my eyes for the first time in two days when the nurse stood over me, taking my vitals.

"Oh, Ms. Adams. You're finally awake," she said with a bright smile on her face, her pen still moving on the clipboard as she eyed my face with concern. "Are you feeling any pain right now?"

I looked around the cold, dark room, a small source of light coming from the muted TV at the foot of the bed and the night light above my head. "Where am I?" I managed to ask even, though the majority of my face was covered tightly with gauzes.

She smiled and placed the clipboard down on the stand next to my bed. Reaching across my body, she picked up a cup of water and pressed the straw against my lips. "Drink first, and then I'll answer anything you want me to."

I stared into her blue eyes for a few minutes before doing as I was told and taking a few sips of water.

"There you go, sweetheart. I wanted to at least wet your throat a little bit before you went into a coughing spell."

"Thank you," I whispered before taking a few more sips. "Now, can you answer my question?"

The nurse smiled as she fluffed the pillow behind my head. "Your friend said that you were a spicy little thing. I have to tell her that she was right. But to answer your question, you're currently a patient at Good Samaritan Hospital. A couple days ago, you were brought in with a gunshot wound to your back that exited out of your lower abdomen. Surprisingly, the bullet didn't hit a single organ. However, the . . ." Her words trailed off, and a weird look came over her face. "Let me go tell the doctor that you're awake. I know you probably would rather have him answer any other questions you may have."

I managed to grab hold of her arm before she could get some distance between us. "Why did you pause like that?

What are you not telling me? Did the bullet cause some major damage?" I asked as I wiggled my toes and the lower part of my body to make sure I still had movement.

She shook her head. "Ms. Adams, let me go get the doctor for you, please. He can answer all of your questions."

I looked into her eyes for a second. The gloomy look covering her face now caused my heart to beat a little faster. Something was definitely wrong. My hood instincts were telling me that. When the nurse's eyes slipped toward my stomach and then back up to my face, I figured out what she wasn't trying to tell me. I slowly lowered my hands down to my belly and sucked in the cry that spilled from my lips when I didn't feel the small pudge that had started to grow.

"My baby," I said a little above a whisper. "He . . . He didn't make it?" The question was rhetorical, but the nurse answered.

Placing her hands gently on mine, she said, "I'm so sorry, sweetie. I know how losing a child feels, and I wouldn't wish that on anyone." Her smile was warm but didn't radiate to my heart. "I'll go get the doctor now. I'll be right back."

Five minutes later, the doctor came into the room and basically ran down everything that had happened to me. The bullet that entered my body from the back went straight through me and my baby, killing him instantly. After giving me a few more details about my recovery time and the different types of medication that I would be on, both the doctor and nurse left, leaving me to grieve in the dark, cold room all by myself.

I called Stax that night and had to damn near beg him to come up to the hospital. Of course when he got there, two detectives were in my room, questioning me about what happened and if I remembered the faces of any of the men who shot me. Once I gave them some bogus story about what went down and lied about not seeing any of my attackers' faces, the pigs left my room. Stax's bitch ass didn't stay too much longer after that. When I told him about the baby, he didn't seem sad or upset at all. The nigga was so busy texting back and forth on his phone that he never said a single thing to me about any of it—me almost losing my life, us losing our baby, the niggas who robbed us. Nothing.

Sucks to say that Stax only came up there one other time, and that was to bring me some clothes to change into once I was discharged and to ask for my keys to the storage unit we used sometimes to store new shipment until we were able to get it cut and packaged. The nigga was more concerned about flooding the streets with dope than my well-being, and that had me feeling some type of way.

I had just pulled out my phone to call the nigga again to see where he was, but I released the call when a sleek black-on-black Challenger pulled up and stopped directly in front of where I was waiting. The music playing in the car was low, but I could still hear The Commodores' classic, "Zoom," flowing through the speakers.

"Is this your ride?" the nurse asked as she stood behind me, her hands on the handles of the wheelchair, ready to push me to the passenger side.

I shrugged my shoulders and shook my head. "I don't think so. My boyfriend and I don't own a car like this." The little bitch thought I didn't hear her smack her lips, but I did. "Do you have somewhere else you need to be or something? Because your attitude since we've been out here has been real stank. Now, I know I'm in this wheelchair bandaged up and shit, but don't let that fool you. I got enough pain meds in my system to raise up out this seat, slap fire from your ass, and then deal with the aftereffects later."

She opened her mouth to respond but stopped short when the driver-side door of the Challenger opened and a large cloud of smoke escaped into the air.

"Zig?" I questioned as he stepped out of the car. "What are you doing here?"

He rose his arms above his head and stretched them toward the sky, taking a long yawn before he answered my question. "I'm coming to pick you up." He walked around the car and up onto the sidewalk. The black joggers he wore were doing very little to hide the large print hanging down his thigh. The black wife beater showed off his muscled and tattooed arms. I looked down at the red weed socks he had on and his Nike slides.

"You just get out of bed or something? Where's Stax?"

Zig shrugged his shoulders and said with another yawn, "I don't know where that nigga is. All I know is that he text me about fifteen minutes ago and asked if I could pick you up from the hospital and bring you up to Sixth Ave. Said he'll come get you from there." Zig grabbed a hold of my wheelchair. "I got it from here, li'l mama," he told the nurse chick, who was just standing there, all dreamy-eyed and shit.

Stax telling Zig to bring me over to the spot on Sixth Ave. was understandable, because he had this thing about letting people know where we laid our heads, but I was still confused on why he couldn't make it to pick me up himself. Not trying to stress Zig out with my personal problems, I allowed him to help me into his car and

buckle my seat belt. The scent of his cologne filled my
senses as he leaned his body across me and made sure
I was strapped in tight. As he grabbed my bags off the
ground to put into his trunk, I could see Thirsty Nurse
trying to make some kind of conversation with him. They
chopped it up for a few seconds before he handed her
something and slid into his car.

For the first few minutes, Zig and I were both silent
and in our own thoughts as the slow grooves continued
to entertain us. It wasn't until Alexander O'Neal's song
"Sunshine" started playing that I decided to break the
silence and say something.

"Either you're really in love with a girl, or someone
really did a number on your heart."

Zig looked in my direction for a quick second, then
back at the road. "Why do you say that?"

I pointed to the radio. "Because you're always listening to these oldies but goodies whenever I'm in the car
with you. The few times you've come to pick us up after
we hit a jewelry store to the times you pulled up to one of
the traps with this shit blasting, you're always vibing out
to this type of music."

He wiped his hand over his face before looking over
his shoulder and switching lanes. "I've always listened to
these kind of tunes. The only shit my granny used to play
when I was growing up. Grown folks' music." He looked
at me and smirked. "Why do you care about what's
playing in my car, though?"

"I don't really," I returned as I looked out the window.
"It's just kind of weird for a stone-cold killer to always be
listening to love songs. That's all."

Zig chuckled and said, "Killers have hearts too, Lucci.
We just don't wear them on our sleeves like the rest of

these niggas." He didn't say anything else after that, just went back to being in his own thoughts as I continued to stay in mine.

Twenty minutes later, we pulled up to the stash house we had on Sixth Ave. The neighborhood was buzzing with people, walking around and doing their thing. Kids were riding bikes up and down the street. I heard the loud, buzzing noise of a lawnmower mowing and the loud screams of some hoodrats arguing. At first I thought it was Shauna and her crew about to get down, but I saw that it wasn't once we rolled passed them.

Zig pulled up into the driveway of the modern-style home and placed his car in park. He'd just grabbed the door handle to exit the car, but he stopped when I placed my hand on his thigh. His eyes zeroed in on the intimate gesture, then came back up to me.

"Oh, my bad." I blushed as I pulled my hand back. "I didn't mean—"

He cut me off. "Nah, you good. I don't mind your hand being there. What's up, though?"

I was speechless for a second. "Um, when you talked to Stax earlier, do you know if he was already here or not?" I looked toward the back of the house and then around the block for Stax's car but didn't see it. "I don't know why he would tell you to bring me to this spot if he wasn't going to be here on time to get me."

I'd been texting the fool since Zig picked me up from the hospital but hadn't gotten a call or a response text yet. Zig lowered the back of his seat and laid an arm over his face, covering his eyes. His legs opened slightly, as one foot was positioned on the brake, while the other was outside of the car, keeping the door from closing all the way.

"I didn't ask him all that. Did you try calling the nigga?"

I hit Stax's name on my phone, expecting to hear it ringing, but I was sent immediately to voicemail instead. I tried to dial his number a few more times but got the same results.

"Here, try mine," Zig said, handing me his phone. I tried calling Stax's number from his line but was hit with the voicemail as well. I handed Zig his phone back.

"Where the fuck is this nigga?" I questioned as I looked around at my surroundings and winced from the pain I felt in my lower back. "Damn, I need to pop a few of these pills and then lay down. I don't have time for this extra bullshit."

"You good?" Zig asked as he reached for something in his back seat. When he handed me a bottle of water, I thanked him and cracked it open.

"Yeah, I'm good, just in a little pain. Being shot ain't no joke," I told him after swallowing a few pills and guzzling down the water.

"It isn't. But you're handling it well," he offered with a small smile. His facial expression became serious shortly after. "Aye, I know you probably don't remember me saying this at the hospital, but I'm sorry about the baby. I know you were just getting used to the idea of being a mom."

My eyebrows scrunched. "You came to see me at the hospital?"

He nodded his head. "Yeah. I came a few times. Ran into your girl Bobbi twice. Those yellow rose arrangements in the trunk are all from me. Bought you a new bouquet whenever I stopped by. Read somewhere that yellow roses create warm feelings and provide happiness, so I brought you some."

There were five arrangements, which meant that he came to see me five times. All this time I assumed that Bobbi or Stax sent the bouquets, only to find out that it was Zig all along.

"Wow. Um, thank you, Zig. I really appreciate—" I stopped when there was a light tap on the driver-side window. On instinct, I reached my hand under the seat to grab my piece but laughed when I realized I wasn't in my car.

My eyes went directly to Zig, who was already staring at me, a sexy smirk on his face as he nodded his head. "Your ass stay on alert."

"I got to. When niggas is gunning for you left and right, it sorta comes second nature. I already got caught slipping once. I'm not about to let it happen again."

"I'm not either," he assured before opening his glove compartment and placing my gun in my lap. "Thought you might want this. You can put it away for now, though. I already know who this is."

Zig looked up at the hooded figure and cracked the window. "What's up, Styles?"

"Nothing, man. I got that info you wanted." He ducked his head and looked over at me. "What's up, Lucci. I see you out the hospital and shit. Bitch niggas couldn't keep a real one down."

"You already know, Styles."

"That's what's up."

Zig raised the window. "I'ma chop it up with him for a second. If you need me, just holla."

I nodded my head and sat back in my seat as Zig exited the car and walked toward the side of the house. I tried calling Stax again, but this time I blocked my number. When I heard the voicemail pick up after the first ring, I knew his shit had been completely shut off.

"What the fuck?" I asked myself as I scrolled through my phone. After hitting a few of my workers, asking if they'd seen Stax, and sending a text to Bobbi, asking if Nav had gotten any more information on the niggas that jacked us, I tucked my phone back into my purse and waited for Zig to come back to the car. In the time that I was waiting on Zig to return, I must've dozed off, because it wasn't until he slid back into his car that I stirred from my sleep and looked over at him.

"Everything good?" I asked with a light yawn. When Zig didn't respond, I wiped my eyes to get a better look at him. "Hey, is everything okay? What did Styles want?"

Zig sat silently, ignoring my question for a few moments. I could tell by the look on his face that he was in deep thought. He pulled out his phone and connected it to the Bluetooth in the car and placed a call to someone.

"What's brackin', blood?" A deep baritone voice flowed through the speaker. Loud laughs and music could be heard in the background. "You stopping by the party or what? It's a gang of bitches here, asking about you. I don't know how long I can hold my boys off. You know these niggas love crackin' new pussy."

Zig put his car in gear, backed out of the driveway, and drove to the next street over before pulling over.

"Zig, what are you doing? Why did we leave the house?" I asked, still hoping Stax was on his way to pick me up. "What's going on?"

Zig held his finger up, silencing me.

"Who's that you got with you, blood?" the nigga on the phone asked. "I know you not bringing a bitch with you to the function. All this pussy you got waiting here, and you bringing some? Nigga."

I opened my mouth, ready to spaz out on this nigga calling me out my name, but Zig raised his finger for a second time, silencing me again.

"Aye, Black, first things first, watch yo' mouth, nigga. You know I don't tolerate that disrespectful shit, and even though you my cousin, I'll beat your ass behind this one. Now, say you're sorry to Lucci."

He hesitated for a second, but then said, "Damn, man, I was only playing. But uh, I'm sorry Lucci."

I nodded my head, content with the way that Zig had just checked his cousin behind me, so he continued.

"Now that we got that all squared away, did my nigga come to your spot today?"

I could tell Black had moved to a different area at the party because the noise had kind of died down.

"Your boy? Oooh, you talking about Stax, that fuga-zi-ass nigga you sent my way for some business. Yeah, he came by. Probably about an hour ago. Bought a few of my new pieces that I didn't want to part with, but the nigga threw down a bag of cash, and I couldn't refuse. Paid double the price. He had this bad little bitch with him, too. I know you always talked about how fine his girl is, and nigga, you weren't lying. I'd smash her little ass all night if she gave me the chance. Nigga ain't my homie."

I could feel my cheeks heating up as Zig's wide eyes turned to my direction. His cousin was spilling some tea on their private conversations about me, and even though I was curious to know what little bitch Stax had riding around with him, I wanted to hear more about what Zig had to say about me.

"Focus, man. Stop thinking about pussy all the damn time. Now, did the nigga happen to mention where he was going after he left you?" Zig asked, quickly changing the subject.

Black thought about it for a minute. "He didn't directly tell me, but I did hear him mention something about grabbing some shit up in Covina before they left. After that, I had Bear escort him out. My Spidey sense was telling me that something was off with him, so he had to go."

"Yeah, something's off all right. Thanks, man. I'll hit you back." Before Black could say another word, Zig released the call.

"Do you know what place he might be heading to in Covina?" he asked me.

I wanted to lie but decided not to. "Yeah. He's heading to our home. Only place he could be going to out that way."

"Wait. I thought y'all stayed in the Heights?" Zig asked with a confused look on his face. "At least that's what the nigga told me when he had me take him there one time."

I shook my head. "Nah. Not unless he bought some property I don't know about. We only have the spot out in Covina."

"All right, well, while you tell me how to get there, I'm gonna fill you in on what Styles just told me. After that, I want you to fill me in on everything that happened with this last job y'all did. I know you know by now that the shit was a setup. And I just got word that—" He paused for a second, not really sure on whether he should continue with what he was about to say.

"Just got word that what?" I urged, my stomach already starting to do flips.

Zig grabbed my hand, and for some reason, all of the anxiety I was feeling began to transfer to him. I looked down at our entwined fingers and back up to him. There was a look in his eyes that I'd never seen before.

"Man, I don't know how to tell you this without sounding like a hating-ass nigga, but Stax, his bitch ass ain't the one for you. Never has been. Not with the type of caliber woman you are. His ass been on some grimy shit for the last few months, while you been busting your ass, trying to make sure you and him stay on top." The grip he had on my hand became tighter.

"Something in my gut kept telling me that this nigga was up to some foul shit, so I had Styles look into some things for me. All of that product and money that's been coming up missing in the last couple of months is because of Stax. He's been using, and his habit has gotten a lot worse in the last couple of weeks. The day he wanted you to kill Ceddy in front of all of those witnesses was confirmation enough for me that the nigga was on some bullshit. You never put your queen in a position to be taken down, especially when you have one as loyal as you."

Zig's words played in my head for a second. He wasn't telling me anything I hadn't already thought about, but just hearing it from someone else put a lot of shit into perspective.

"You don't sound like a hating-ass nigga, Zig. You're just looking out for me like you always have. I appreciate the heads up. And to keep it all the way funky with you, I've been noticing a change in Stax for some time now as well. It got worse after the Feds came and picked him up."

"You know he's cooperating with them, right? How the nigga was released so fast from their custody. At least that's what Styles just hit me with."

I lowered my head and kissed my teeth. I'd come to this conclusion a while ago. "My heart wants to believe that he isn't because of the way that we came up, but my street sense is telling me something else."

"Well, what do you want to do about it?" he asked, slowly merging into traffic as I pointed in the direction he should go. My other hand was still intertwined with his.

"The only thing you can do when there's a rat in your house—take him out before he gets you."

I loved Stax with all my heart and soul, but I would kill that nigga dead before he ever got the chance to have me locked up behind bars for the rest of my life. With all the shit that had happened to me in the last few weeks, you would think I'd be ready to hang my guns up and just start to live a normal life, but for a chick like me, normal could never happen. However, once I took care of this Stax situation and got back at the niggas who tried to kill me, I wouldn't be opposed to taking an extended vacation to get my head back in the game.

Chapter 20

Bobbi

Shit was starting to become a little too much. Had I known that everything that happened in the last few weeks was going to go down, I never would've suggested to Lucci, Kay Kay, and Diamond that we should try to rob BJE, or even contacted Nav, for that matter. I mean, don't get me wrong, I was really feeling the fuck out of him and could see what we were building being something great, but this whole Diamond Mafia shit and robbing these jewelry stores wasn't worth the headache, heartache or pain.

I paced the floor in my living room as I waited for Nav to arrive. He had called me about an hour ago and said that he needed to talk to me and Lucci and wanted to meet at my house. I didn't know what was going on with him and his little crew, but it must've been some bullshit too. Cowboy was MIA. Seemed like he just vanished after Diamond was killed and Kay Kay was taken. Tweety was still working for BJE and getting close to Josh, but I didn't see the need in that anymore since we missed the whole diamond exhibit a few days ago. I was so over this whole get-money-quick scheme and ready to move the fuck on.

I had just begun to straighten the decorative pillows on my couch for the third time when something on the

TV grabbed my attention. Taking a seat on my oversized chair, I grabbed the remote and turned up the volume on the TV.

"In other news, police are still seeking information on a string of jewelry store robberies that they believe this woman,"—A picture of Diamond flashed across the screen— *"Is connected to. The body of thirty-one year-old Diamond Morris was found shot to death in the back alleyway of Ongpin Jewelers, a high-end jewelry store police say was robbed just minutes before Ms. Morris' death. Residents around the area couldn't identify the deceased as a local, but police are speculating that her murder is indeed tied to the robbery."*

When the reporter went into more details about what the police were trying to find out about the robbery, I turned the TV off, laid my head back on my chair, and closed my eyes. Just seeing Diamond's face on that screen had me in my feelings again. It had been seven days since we buried her, and my heart was still heavy with grief. I never in my wildest dreams would have imagined that Diamond would be gone behind some shit I suggested that we do. A part of me felt like I was responsible for her death, while another part wished it was me that had gotten hit instead. That nigga Doughboy and whoever else helped in robbing us was going to get theirs if that was the last thing I ever did on this earth. A muthafucka wasn't going to take my friend away from me and still walk around this bitch like everything was okay.

I must've sat in my chair for thirty minutes, laughing and crying at the many memories that replayed in my mind about my friend, when there was a soft knock at my door. Already knowing who was on the other side, I opened the wooden frame and stepped right into Nav's open arms after he took one look at my face.

"What's wrong, beautiful? Why are you crying?" he asked as I inhaled his scent. Just being comforted by him seemed to make the sadness slip away.

"Just thinking about Diamond. I miss my friend, Naveen."

He pulled me into his arms tighter as the tears began to fall again. "I know, baby. And I'm sorry that you're going through this. But just know and understand that each and every one of them muthafuckas involved in her murder and stealing from us will be taken care of. You hear me?" When I didn't respond, Nav pulled away from me until he was able to see my face and palmed my cheeks. "Do you hear me, Bobbi? You know that I would never let anyone hurt you again, and if by some chance they were able to, I would kill whoever had a hand in upsetting you. You know that, right?"

When I nodded yes, he kissed my forehead and pulled me in for another hug.

"Let's go inside. I need to talk to you about something before Lucci gets here."

After standing in his embrace for a minute longer, I slowly turned around and made my way back into my home. Once Nav locked the door behind him, he grabbed my hand and led me over to the couch. We both sat in silence for a few minutes before Nav decided to speak.

"So, for the last couple of days, me and Ant have been doing some digging. The way those niggas had the scoop on us, someone on the inside had to be working with them."

"I was thinking the same thing," I said as I tucked one leg underneath the other and pulled a pillow onto my lap. "It was too easy for them to have us outnumbered and outgunned. "Plus, they knew too many specifics. It was like they knew the exact time to be there, which way the getaway car was going to be parked, and who to eliminate or go after first."

Nav nodded his head. "I said the same thing. I usually don't tell you guys the specifics of a job until the night of. No one's allowed to have their phones on them, so that made me question how those niggas were informed with that information."

I reached over to my coffee table and picked up the glass of wine I had been sipping on. "What did you find out?"

Nav wiped his hands over his face before releasing a breath. "Before we get into all of that, I just want to say to you for the one hundredth time that I'm sorry for how I came at you that night in the van before we drove Lucci to the hospital. I know I promised the first time I did it that I wouldn't do it again, but the events that happened that night had me all thrown off. In all of the years that I've been doing this, I've never had something like that happen to me. And then with Tweety saying all the shit she's been saying . . ." He shook his head and laid it back on the couch. "I let her get in my head when I should've been ignoring the fuck out of her."

I took a sip of my wine and placed the glass back on the coffee table. "What has she been saying?"

Anyone with eyes could see that Tweety and I didn't have any type of love for each other. Shit got real bad once Nav told her that we were an item. I thought the last conversation she and I had in Nav's office that day backed her ass up, but I saw I was gonna have to have another little talk with the bitch.

Nav took my hand into his and kissed it. I blushed before looking into his dark eyes and getting that tingly feeling all over my body. This man was sexy as hell and he didn't even have to try hard to be. Like right now, he was dressed simply in some sweats and a black-and-red Bulls shirt that matched the Jordans on his feet. His hair was cut low, and his beard was a little on the scruffy side, but it still looked good to me. Skin wasn't blemish free but adorned with war wounds I was sure he'd had since childhood.

He sighed. "You know Tweety still has issues with me choosing you over her, even though I've always made it clear that she and I would only ever be friends." Nav ran his free hand over his head. "She wants you to be a bum bitch so bad just so she can say *I told you so*," He imitated her annoying voice, and I laughed. "But she doesn't know you like I do. I mean, with what I know so far, you're far from bum bitch status."

"And snake bitch status too, right?" I wanted to make clear.

"Snake bitch status too." He smiled that gorgeous smile of his, and I returned one of my own. "I don't know where you and I will be years from now, Bobbi, but I hope it's somewhere on a fly-ass beach, in our fly-ass beach house, raising our fly-ass kids and just enjoying life and each other."

"So, you really do see a future with me?" I only asked the question because the nigga did try to accuse me of setting him up not once, but twice.

Nav sat in silence for a moment as he thought about my question. His fingers caressing the back of my hand sent all kinds of zinging sensations to my pussy. Although Nav and I had been kicking it for a few, we still had yet to have sex, and my body was craving him like crazy. We came super close that one day he did the photo shoot in the tub of diamonds, but since then, we hadn't had any real time to get a lovemaking session on.

"From the moment I laid eyes on you at the park that day, I knew you were going to be mine."

"At the park?" I asked, confused. "When did you see me at—"

Before I could get the question fully out of my mouth, Nav shut me up by pressing his lips to mine and tonguing me down something serious. I wanted to stop his assault on my mouth and come up for breath, but with the way he had my mind, body, and soul feeling right now, I'd die a happy death from lack of oxygen.

With the swift precision of a cheetah, Nav unfolded my legs, stretched my body on the couch, and nestled himself between my thighs. The thin knee-length tank dress I had on was pushed up over my hips and my panties pushed to the side. The second Nav's finger circled around my clit, my back arched and my toes curled.

"Nav," I purred in his ear. "Baby . . . ooooh. What . . . what . . . shit . . . what are you doing?"

He kissed me all over my face and then bit down and sucked hard as fuck on my neck. Although my skin was as chocolate as his, I was sure there was a purple hickey now on display for everyone to see.

"I need some pussy, baby. Give me some pussy, Bobbi." His breath was husky and low as he begged for my goodies in my ear. "I need to feel you. We need to feel each other."

I don't know if it was the begging he was doing or the way that his fingers continued to assault my clit, but I couldn't form a single word to say shit. Nav didn't have to beg me for anything, either. Even though this was going to be our first time getting down, my pussy had been reserved for him ever since he made it known that we were exclusive.

Raising his body up off of me a little, Nav was trying to pull his sweats down as easily as he could with one hand. Once he was able to get them down far enough, it wasn't long before I felt the heaviness of his hard dick resting against my pussy lips. On instinct, my legs opened wider, welcoming the added weight between my thighs.

Pulling my arms above my head, Nav laced our fingers together and looked me directly in my eyes. "If you don't want me to ruin your sex life for any nigga that ever comes after me, speak now or take all of this dick and claim it as yours."

I didn't say anything at all. I just pressed my lips against his and wrapped my legs around his waist, silently giving him my response. Nav's dick knocked at my entrance until my opening expanded enough to let him all the way in, the thick veins on his shaft making their permanent engraved marks like hieroglyphics on my walls. His bulbous head pressed against a barrier I didn't even know was there, causing a little bit of pain, but not enough to make me tell him to stop.

I was in pure ecstasy, an out-of-body experience that I never felt before. As Nav skillfully pushed in and out of me, claiming my whole being as his own, I couldn't help but to feel sorry for Tweety's ass. If Nav gave her at least a taste of half of what he was giving to me right now, I could surely understand why she was acting so crazy over him. Too bad the bitch would never get the chance to sample a piece of his dick again. Nav's sex now belonged to me, and I'd be damned if anybody else got to experience it for a first, second, or third time.

"Look at me," he huskily whispered above my lips, his hips moving to a rhythm I could dance to forever. "Let me see your pretty eyes when you cum, Bobbi."

I enjoyed a few more of his strokes before doing as he requested and looking into his face. The way Nav's eyes softened when he hit my sweet spot and my walls began to quake around his dick had me cumming harder than I knew I could.

"Nav." I moaned his name over and over again as he began to pound into me, his strokes shorter than before but still hypnotizing, to say the least.

"Yeah, baby. I'm almost there too."

"Naaaaav."

"I know, Bobbi. I know. I got you, baby."

"I . . . I . . . baby . . ."

"Cum with me, beautiful. Cum with me."

I didn't think I had another one in me because my body still felt so drained from that first one, but Nav switched his stroke up and started to piston into my super wet pussy, pulling another powerful orgasm out of me.

We lay basking in each other's energy for about five minutes as our bodies came down after we both climaxed. Nav stared into my eyes the whole time, making me feel a little self-conscious.

"Don't do that," he spoke when I tried to avert my eyes. "Our souls were talking. You didn't feel that?" I shook my head no and he kissed me on the forehead. "After sex, you're at your most vulnerable state, and if you have a connection to someone, your soul talks to the other person's soul that way. You ever wonder why you can convey how you feel to someone without saying a single word?" I nodded my head. "It's because people's souls communicate through their eyes."

Nav stood up from his position between my legs and pulled his pants up. With his hand stretched out to me, I grabbed a hold of it and let him pull me up from the couch. We stood in the middle of my living room, caught up in the rapture of our sex afterglow, when there was a loud banging on my door. Nav kissed my lips one last time before patting me on my ass.

"Go get yourself cleaned up, and I'll let Lucci in," he said over his shoulder.

"How do you know that's Lucci at the door and not one of my other niggas coming to see me?" I joked.

"Because you don't want them niggas' blood on your hands." His voice was low, but his tone was sharp. "Play with me if you want to, Bobbi, but I suggest you don't. Now, go get cleaned up."

I laughed at his jealous ass. "Wait. What about you? Shouldn't you get cleaned up too?" I asked, thinking about my juices I knew covered the bottom part of his shirt and some of his pants.

Nav stopped his stride to the door and looked down at his clothes. His nostrils flared as if he were smelling something in the air. "I like your scent on me," he admitted. "Plus, it'll help keep my dick tamed until our company leaves and I can get all up in my pussy again. Now, go handle your business for the last time. We got some shit we need to discuss."

"So, Nav finally gave you some dick, huh?" Lucci asked as soon as I returned from the kitchen with her glass of water and my second glass of wine.

"What makes you say that?" I wondered, eyes rolling over to my dining room, where Nav and Zig were having a hushed conversation. Every now and then, Nav would look over his shoulder and wink his eye at me.

"Well, for one, the nigga keeps looking over here like he's trying to make sure you don't run away. And two, I peeped how you kept tightening your fist every time I looked down at that big-ass bulge Nav got swinging between his legs when I first walked in here." Lucci's gaze drifted over toward Nav. "Nigga packing a canon over there. Your ass was kind of limping and shit when you walked to the kitchen, too."

I snorted and covered my face in embarrassment when both Zig and Nav looked over at me. "Bitch, I swear you get on my nerves. Ain't nobody limping over here."

"Shiiiiid," she chuckled before taking a sip of water. "It's cool, though. That glow you probably haven't noticed on your face is a good thing. Especially with everything we've been through in the last week or so."

I nodded my head and took a sip of my wine. "How you feeling, Lu? I mean, since you brought up the subject of last week. Are you still having a hard time accepting the fact that Di—" I got choked up for a second. "That Diamond is gone."

Lucci looked down at the small puppy in her lap and ran her fingers through the shiny brown-and-black fur. "I'm dealing with it as best as I can. Did Nav's people get any word on Kay Kay?"

I shook my head. "Nope. His people that work at the police station said that they haven't received a Jane Doe that fits Kay Kay's description. I called her mom a couple days ago, and she said she still hasn't heard anything. When I tried Shauna's number, the shit was disconnected."

"Damn. I pray every day that wherever she's at, she's okay. We already lost one friend. We can't lose another one."

I continued to drink my glass of wine and listen to Lucci tell me about her new dog until Nav and Zig finished their conversation. After dapping each other up, they both turned in our direction to join us on the couch, but when Nav's phone started to ring, he took a detour to another room and took the call.

"You good?" Zig asked Lucci as soon as he made it to her side. "You need some more pills or me to go get you something?"

She shook her head. "I'm good, Zig. Denairo could use a trip outside to use the bathroom, though. I don't think Bobbi would appreciate him pissing and shitting on her carpet."

"I sure in the hell wouldn't," I added, causing Zig to chuckle.

He removed the puppy from Lucci's lap. "I'll be back in five minutes. Call me if you need anything, okay?"

"All right." Lucci smiled as Zig bent over and kissed her on top of her head.

We watched as he retrieved one of the blue doggy poop bags from Lucci's keychain and made his way out my front door. Once he shut it behind him, I looked at Lucci and smiled.

"Looks like I'm not the only one who done got some dick up in here."

She reared her head back and smacked her lips. "Me and Zig? Girl, no. We're just friends. Haven't crossed that line yet."

"So, you *do* wanna cross that line?"

"What? No." She shook her head, trying to convince herself to believe the lie falling from her lips. "I didn't say anything like that."

"But you did say *yet*. And we both know *yet* means you want it to happen and will wait patiently until it does."

Lucci rolled her eyes. "Bitch, shut your ass up. You know I'm not worried about no nigga right now. Especially after the way Stax ho ass just did me." I could hear the disgust and hate in her tone. "I gave that nigga so many years of my life. Did so much shit that could've gotten me killed or put in jail for the rest of my life just to make sure we were good, and he basically says fuck me and leaves me out for the wolves. Can you believe that, Bobbi?"

I nodded my head because I could believe it. Stax was a cool dude. Never did anything to me, but I always thought that Lucci deserved better. While she was out there, risking penitentiary time and cheating death, Stax's ass was sitting back and reaping all the benefits of her hard work. Don't get me wrong, Stax was that nigga in these streets and was as ruthless as the next, but if it weren't for Lucci, he wouldn't have half the reputation that he did. For him to turn snitch for the Feds and then skip out of town, basically leaving Lucci with nothing to continue living her life with, Stax would always be a fuck boy in my books from now on.

"Girl, don't even worry about Stax and the fuck shit that he did. I got a little money saved up, and if it's only enough to jumpstart us getting the fuck out of California and starting our lives over somewhere else, then so be it." I reached my hand out and grabbed hers. "I already lost one friend and don't know if the other one is okay or not. I refuse to lose my last one or see her go down behind her bitch-ass ex-nigga, who couldn't take his time like a G, so he started singing like a canary to the police."

Lucci sat up in her seat and placed her glass of water on the coffee table. "The Feds been on my ass, too. Taking me down to their offices for questioning." She shook her head. "Asking all kinds of questions about this murder and that murder. This drug spot and that drug spot. When they started asking questions about Diamond and whether or not I knew anything about the jewelry store robberies, I told them to call my lawyer if they had any further questions and left. Do you know that nigga told them to ask me about Diamond Mafia? Said that if they applied some pressure to me, I would probably be able to point them in the right direction on who all is involved."

"Shut up. Stax told them that?"

"Yep. Good thing I never told him Nav's name or showed him where the firehouse was. Nigga probably would've had us all locked up."

Lucci and I continued to talk about Stax, Diamond, and Kay Kay until Zig came back into the house. After he made sure Lucci wasn't in need of anything again, he took a seat on the couch beside her. All of us started talking about the puppy and how cute he was. Nav came back into the living room with his phone still up to his ear.

"Who was that?" I asked out of curiosity when he ended the call. Lucci looked at me and smirked.

"That was Tweety."

I knew my facial expression showed how I was feeling about hearing her call my man, but I didn't care. "What did she want?" My tone was a little harsh.

"I had her looking into some things, and she just called me back with some good news."

"Good news like what?" Lucci asked before I could. "Does it have anything to do with the reason why you wanted us to meet you over here?"

Nav nodded his head. "I couldn't risk having this conversation at the firehouse because I don't trust it ever since Cowboy's ass went missing, and I didn't want to chance it going to your house because of how the Feds have been watching you."

"Okay, so what's going on?" I inquired, wanting to find out why Tweety was still looking into shit for him.

"Well,"—he pulled at his scruffy chin hair—"as you all know, we took a big hit when them niggas got us for our shit. I know you guys were looking forward to getting the fuck outta here with that last job, but now, I don't see how that will be possible. Especially with the fuck shit Stax did to you, Lucci. Bobbi, you good with me and the money I have stashed away, but if I'm honestly speaking, it isn't enough to have us living comfortably for the rest of our lives."

"So, what you trying to propose, my nigga?" Zig wanted to know. Ever since the funeral, Zig and Nav had formed a cool little relationship. They weren't the best of friends, but they trusted each other to the extent that they could talk about certain shit in front of one another.

Nav squeezed my shoulder and looked down at me. "I'm trying to propose one last job if you guys are up to it. It's not going to get us the eighty mil we would've came up on had we not missed the diamond exhibit, but it will get us enough to split and live a good life."

"You want us to try to rob another jewelry store?" I questioned, confusion all over my face. "Are you crazy, Nav? Do you not see how much the news, blogs, and anything else that reports the news is talking about us?

About Diamond? I think it's entirely too soon to try and rob another store. For one, the Feds are already sniffing around. It's only going to be a matter of time before they start looking into our backgrounds. They're already looking into Lucci's and questioning her relationship to Diamond."

"I know, babe. But—"

"But what?" I cut him off, still trying to make my point that his proposition to do another job wasn't a good one. "What about surveillance, Nav? Have you got in contact with Cowboy or found someone else who can get into the system like he could? Or do you want us to go in there blind and end up in the same predicament we did the last time but with the police instead? Make me understand your logic behind wanting to do another job."

"My logic is money," he returned, giving me just as much attitude as I was giving him. "We need to do this one last job to get this money and get the fuck up out of here. I know it's hot right now, but we can't afford to let it cool down and let these stores switch up their security systems and shit. The spot I have in mind, you already know the ins and outs of. Plus, we have an inside man, or should I say woman, who's in on it too."

I thought about what he said for a second. "You're trying to do the BJE job? The diamond exchange is over. All of the millions we could've gotten in jewels is back overseas. At the most, we would only be able to get five million of BJE diamonds, and that split five ways isn't going to be much."

"Now, wait a minute, Bobbi," Lucci interrupted. "I would probably be feeling the same way as you had Stax not run off with basically every single dollar I had stashed away, but I need an easy come-up right now.

Not only did that nigga fuck me over, but he fucked over the connect, too. And since we don't know where that nigga is right now, who do you think those Jamaican muthafuckas are hitting up? Me. Stax ran off with their money and dope too, and they don't give a fuck that the nigga did me dirty. All they care about is their money, which is way more than what you can possibly loan me to pay them back."

I could tell by the look on Lucci's face that she wanted to break down and cry, but the thug in her wouldn't allow it. Zig must've sensed it too, because before a tear could even slip from her eye, he wrapped her up in his arms and started to whisper something in her ear, easily calming her down.

"Look, Lucci, I get what you're saying, and I understand it wholeheartedly, but I still don't think it's a good idea. Maybe Nav can loan you the—"

"Nah, she ain't about to accept money from no other nigga as long as I'm around," Zig interjected. "I already gave her half of what she needed. I didn't have enough to cover the other 250K she owes them. Been busting my ass out here in these streets trying to get it, though."

When his eyes connected to Lucci's, she couldn't hide the blush that rose on her cheeks.

They fucking, I thought as I watched Zig whisper something in her ear again.

"Look, if you wanna sit this one out, Bobbi, I understand, but for the rest of us, the shit is already in motion." He held up his phone. "That was Tweety I just got off the phone with. She said that some sheik nigga is having a shitload of diamonds sent over to your old job to have some necklaces and headpieces designed for his daughter's wedding or some shit like that. According to her, if we pull this off, we could all be splitting five mil apiece. I don't know about you, babe, but five mil in sixty seconds sounds way better than trying to make it working a nine-to-five for the rest of our lives."

All eyes turned to me. When I didn't say anything, Lucci spoke.

"Bobbi, you know I wouldn't ask you to do something like this, but right now I'm begging you. Outside of Tweety's ho ass, you're the only other person in the crew who knows the ins and outs of BJE. I need my sister there, watching my back, just in case something goes down."

"Lucci—"

She grabbed my hands between hers. "Please, Bobbi. Just this one last time. And if this sweetens the deal, I promise to be your full-time babysitter when you and Nav start having my godkids in the next few months."

I couldn't help the laugh that slipped from my mouth. "Girl, Nav and I aren't having kids anytime soon."

"I hope your pussy and his dick knows that."

We shared another round of laughter.

"No, but all bullshit aside, can you do this with me one last time, sis? I need you."

I looked up at Nav, who was intently staring back at me, and then returned my gaze over to Lucci and Zig. All three sets of ears were anxiously waiting to hear my answer.

"If it's just this last time . . . I'm with it," I responded, covering my ears at the same time Lucci let out the loudest scream, scaring her dog and me.

I turned my attention back to Nav. "You sure we can trust Tweety one hundred percent with this plan?"

He nodded his head. "I am, but just in case, I want you to tell me everything you remember about BJE's regular exits, emergency exits, back entrance, front entrance, secret rooms, et cetera."

"I got you."

We discussed this last job with Zig and Lucci for about another hour before they decided to head home. Once they pulled off, Nav and I ate some of my leftover pizza for dinner, and then I was dragged into my bedroom and fucked every which way until I couldn't take anymore. That first round of sex we had before Zig and Lucci came over was like nothing compared to the hurting Nav put on my body for the rest of the night. If I had a slight limp earlier, a bitch for sure was looking crippled now.

Chapter 21

Lucci

"Shit, shit, shit," I hissed, fanning my hand frantically in air. Trying to fry this chicken was starting to become some bullshit. And all because I wanted to impress a man I had no business trying to impress. Well, at least not right now.

Grabbing one of those pitchfork-looking things out of the drawer, I slipped my hand into one of the oven mitts and flipped the chicken over. Grease flowed over the top of the skillet, causing smoke to fill the air, and I started to panic. All I needed was for the house to catch on fire and for Zig to see that I really wasn't about this cooking life. I mean, I knew how to make stuff to get by, but making full-course meals and shit? Nah, I was indeed a shoo-in for that *Worst Cooks in America* show. As if things couldn't get any worse, the smoke detector started screeching loud as hell in the midst of everything else going on. I sniffed the air and smelled something burning.

"My waffles!" I yelled, immediately remembering the sheet pan of Eggos I put in the oven twenty minutes ago. I forgot all about those things. "Fuck!"

As soon as I opened the oven door, more smoke filled the kitchen, causing the other detector in the hallway to go off. Moving as quickly as I could, I opened the window above the sink and turned on both ceiling fans. When that didn't seem like it was helping, I used the dish towel and began waving it back and forth in the air, trying to clear some of the smoke around it.

"Lucci?" I heard Zig's deep voice frantically call through the chaos. "Lucci, what's going on? Are you okay?"

I turned to respond to him but lost my footing and fell down hard to the ground on my ass. I cried out in unbearable pain the second my body connected to the tiled floor.

"Awww, shit." I rolled over and lay down straight on my stomach, trying to control my discomfort. The gunshot wound I had in my lower back was healing, but it wasn't completely there yet. I knew I had fucked something up, though, when I reached back to make sure the incision was still closed and could feel blood seeping out.

"You're bleeding," Zig noticed after seeing the blood on my fingers. "We need to get you to the hospital."

"No." I tried to wave him off and get up by myself, but he grabbed my arms and carefully pulled me up instead. "No hospital. I just ripped the stitches. If you have some gauze and medical tape left, I'll be okay."

Zig turned my body around so my back was to him. Lifting my shirt up, he examined my wound, pressing lightly around it. I felt a bit of pain, but not as much as I did when it first happened.

"Nah." He shook his head and said sternly, "We're going to the hospital."

I tried to object again, but he held his hand up, cutting me off.

"I don't want to hear it, Lucci. You're going, so you might as well go change into some clean clothes and grab your purse. I'll take you to the little urgent care spot down the street. They're pretty fast. Once the nurse or doctor says you're good, I'll bring you back so that you can finish up whatever you were trying to do in here."

The way Zig's eyes darted around his kitchen, taking in the mess I had all over the place, I knew I had to explain. Lifting up the sheet of burnt waffles, I dumped them into the trash, followed by the chicken pieces that were charred just as black as the Eggos.

"I was trying to make you something different for dinner tonight."

He smiled. "Oh, yeah? Ran outta shit to make using hot dogs, eggs, or boxed mac and cheese, huh?"

My cheeks heated, and I laughed. "Look, I never told you that I was a five-star chef. Never said I knew how to fricassee or even flambé some shit. I just know what I know, which is hot dogs, eggs, ramen noodles, Kraft mac and cheese, and takeout."

"You didn't cook for your ex?"

I shook my head. "Nah, not really. We were hardly ever home, and when we were, nine times out of ten, Stax had already eaten or would have me pick something up on my way in."

Zig walked over to his stove and turned off the burners I forgot were still on. "So, why is it so important that you cook for me?"

I opened my mouth to respond, but nothing came out. His question had me speechless for a second. Why was it so important for me to cook for Zig? I could say that it was because he'd been a gracious host in the last couple weeks that I'd been staying with him. I didn't think us cohabitating was a good idea at first, but after seeing the way that Stax was moving and then getting word from the connect that he still wanted his money even though I didn't have it, Zig insisted that I stay with him. I didn't want to be a burden, so I figured since I was chilling at his house all day, I could at least pull my weight by cleaning and making sure he had a home-cooked meal when he came home.

I shrugged my shoulders. "I guess because I wanted to show you my appreciation for how you've been holding me down, from trying to help me figure out a way to pay off the rest of this debt I have with the connect to helping me keep my streets and corners on lock. The one nigga who should've been doing it for me ran off to God knows where, and you're still here. Like you've always been."

I limped over to where Zig was standing and placed my hand on top of his. The spark that ran through my body when our fingers touched had goosebumps decorating my skin. When I tried to pull my hand back, Zig grabbed it tighter and pulled my body into his. We stared into each other's eyes, both caught up in whatever this was between us that we'd been trying to fight for the longest.

When Zig lowered his head and pressed his lips against mine, I released all the pent-up feelings I'd been developing for him and let them manifest in this kiss. A soft moan slipped from my throat, and Zig pulled me into his strong hold tighter. His tongue danced along my lips, begging me for permission to deepen the kiss, but before I could grant him full access, his phone started ringing.

Pressing his forehead to mine, Zig pecked my lips one last time and groaned. "I need to get this. Give me two minutes."

I bashfully nodded my head, missing the warmth of his body when he pulled apart from me and answered his phone.

"What's good, li'l homie?"

When I tried to put some distance between us so that he could have some privacy, Zig hooked his fingers into the elastic part of my yoga pants and pulled me back into his space. With my back toward him, Zig positioned my ass to sit right on his dick as he snaked his arm around my shoulders and placed a tender kiss on my neck.

"Nah. I'm just at the house with Lucci about to run her up to the urgent care spot. Everything good? . . . What did the nigga say? . . . So, was he sure that it was him? . . . Oh, yeah? You got the location, right? Text it to my burner phone. . . . Was he by himself? . . . Then nah, I can handle this on my own. But just in case, have Funk and Ace ride with you in a separate car. Y'all leave now and keep an eye on that nigga. If he steps out onto the balcony to smoke, I want a text telling me that. I'll meet you there in a couple hours. . . . Keep a low profile and don't let the muthafucka out of your sight. . . . Okay, man. I'll tell her. And make sure you give Big Titty Tina the twenty stacks I promised for that information. All right. Gone."

"Who was that?" I asked out of curiosity. I could tell from Zig's part of the conversation that someone he had been looking for was found.

"That was Styles. Nigga just told me some good news. Oh, and he also told me to tell you he said what's up." Zig wrapped his other arm across the lower part of my belly. When I winced, he loosened his hold and looked down at my wound. "Shit, the muthafucka is still leaking blood. We need to get you down to the urgent care and get that tended to now so that I can go handle this other business

ASAP. Go get your stuff so that we can head there and then grab something to eat before I have to leave."

"If you're in that much of a hurry, I can just go by myself. I'll call you once I'm done and on my way back home to let you know what the doctor said. And I can order me something to eat with Postmates, since I don't think I'll be up to trying to cook anything else."

Zig shook his head. "If that's what I wanted you to do, I would've suggested that, but since I didn't,"—he kissed my cheek—"go handle your business and then grab your shit, Lucci. I said I'm going with you, and then I'm going to take you out to eat. All that other nonsense you talking about, cut it out." With one last kiss to my chin, Zig released his hold on me and smacked my ass.

"Oh, and just so you know, we gon' talk about that kiss we just shared while we're eating. You not about to tongue a nigga down and have my dick all hard the way you just did and think we're going to stay on some friend-type bullshit. A nigga been feeling you for a long time, and now that you're fuck-nigga free, I'm about to show you what it's like to be with a real nigga."

I couldn't do anything but smile after hearing Zig say that. Us hooking up had been a long time coming, and I only hoped that if we took it there, I chose the right one this time.

Going into Zig's room, which he designated as mine for the time being, I changed into a fresh yoga outfit and grabbed my purse and phone. When I returned to the kitchen, Zig was on another call. While he finished up his conversation, I tried to clean up some of the mess I'd made so that I wouldn't have much to do when I came back.

"All right. Good looking, man. I'll let Lucci know," he said before releasing the call.

"Who was that?"

Zig turned around from his crouched position in the fridge and eyed me up and down, pulling his bottom lip into his mouth. I could tell that he liked the way my body showed in this outfit.

"If I was one of those insecure-ass niggas, I would tell your ass to go change, but since I like to see other niggas mad that they ain't got it like me, I'm a let you rock that."

"Boy, shut the fuck up. I'm not yours yet." I giggled, and he smacked his lips. "Now, who was that on the phone, and what is that you are supposed to be letting me know?"

"Oh. That was Nav. Said that everything is in place for that new gig and that we make that move in a few days. Also said that he'll send the meetup location the day of and will have everything we need already there, so we shouldn't bring anything with us."

I nodded my head, glad that we were finally about to do this last job. I really needed this money to pay off my debt and finally get my shit back on track.

"What about the call from Styles?" I inquired, remembering Zig never answered my question about that. "You never told me what the good news was that he told you."

Zig grabbed a bottle of water out of the fridge for himself and me. Instead of responding to my question, he began to walk toward the front door after grabbing his keys off the counter.

I followed behind him, wondering why he was being so tight-lipped about that conversation. Zig had never had a problem relaying information to me, so I was confused about what was the issue now. After hopping on the elevator, we rode it down in complete silence, my mind still racing about what this possible good news could be.

Once we made it over to Zig's truck, he opened the door and helped me get inside before hopping in the driver's seat. As always, one of the oldies but goodies he liked to listen to came floating through the speakers as soon as he started the engine. We were five minutes into the ride before I decided to question him again about the call from Styles.

Turning the volume down a bit, I turned my body as far as I could toward him. "So, you're just going to keep ignoring my question?"

Zig bobbed his head to Zapp and Roger's classic hit "Slow and Easy," still not responding to me, eyes focused on the road and lips tightly pulled together.

I didn't know why his attitude had changed so quickly, but it did. I studied his side profile. His chocolate skin was smooth and scar free, lips thick and soft. The only hair on his face was the neatly trimmed mustache above his lip and the groomed coarse patch of hair on his chin. His low Caesar cut was faded on the sides, eyebrows full and naturally arched. I wanted to be pissed that he kept choosing to ignore me, but just looking at his sexy ass and thinking about the kiss we shared a few minutes ago kept me from spazzing out on him.

We pulled up to the urgent care both still in our thoughts while listening to his music. When I went to open the door to get out, Zig grabbed my arm, stopping me.

"What?" I snapped, ready to go get my wound checked out and then head back home. I wasn't in the mood to go eat anymore.

"There's no need for an attitude, Lucci. I have every intention of telling you what that call with Styles was about. I just don't think you're ready for what I'm about to hit you with."

I pulled my leg back into the truck and closed the door. Looking at him, I asked, "What could you possibly say that would have you questioning if I would be ready to hear it or not?"

Zig's phone vibrated with a text, and he responded to it. Handing his phone over to me, I looked down at his open screen and then back to him.

"Eyes on the prize? And an address to some place in Lemon Grove, CA?" I shrugged my shoulders and looked at him with a perplexed expression on my face. "What is any of this supposed to mean to me? And how would this make me mad?"

He scratched at the fine hairs on his chin. "Does that address look familiar to you?"

I looked down at his text thread again. "No. Should it?"

Zig unbuckled his seat belt and took his phone out of my hand when it vibrated again.

"This address is to a house Stax is at right now. Been posted up for a few days, according to Styles. After I take you to get something to eat and drop you off back at the house, I'm heading up that way."

"Wait. So, Stax is back in town?"

Zig nodded his head.

"And you didn't think I would want to go with you to see him?"

He opened his mouth to respond, but I cut him off. "You know what? Don't even answer that, because regardless of what you were about to say, I want in. So, whenever you get ready to leave, I'm rolling with you," I added, not about to take no for an answer.

Zig looked at me and shook his head. "As hard as you're acting right now, I don't think you're going to be ready for what's about to go down. You may hate that nigga's guts in this moment, but deep down you still have some love for his ass. Y'all were together too long for you not to."

I folded my arms across my chest, attitude slowly rising by the second. "Stax and I haven't been good for a while. You think I didn't know about the bitches he been fucking behind my back? How he would have them hoes at the different trap houses, letting them suck his dick while I was handling business in the streets? You don't think I knew how you would run interference sometimes so that I wouldn't catch him in the act? Rotten coochie leaves a hell of a scent in the air, and I done walked into his office a few times and almost threw up." I shook my head and laughed. "Stax's ass started moving real sloppy towards the end. Him not coming to see me in the hospital when I got shot and lost our baby was the last straw for me, though. Then on top of all that, the nigga is snitching and stole my new shipment of work and the money I've been saving? Ain't no coming back from that. As much as I loved that nigga, he has to pay for what he's done."

Zig tapped his fingers against his steering wheel, thinking about something before saying, "I hear what you're saying, Lucci, but I still don't think you're going to be ready for what's about to go down."

"Why do you keep saying that?"

"Because I'm not going up there to look for answers to why this nigga did what he did to you or have any kind of conversation with his bitch ass, Lucci. Stax's ass has violated on so many levels, and he needs to be dealt with before he gets us all thrown under the jail. The nigga is going to die tonight, whether you like it or not. Will you be able to handle that?"

It didn't take me but a second to respond to his question. "Not only will I be able to handle it, but it's going to be a bullet from my gun that ends this nigga's life."

It was way past midnight when we pulled up to the tree-lined street full of manufactured homes where Stax was hiding out. The amber-colored streetlights shone dimly on top of the cars that sat parked close to the curb. The faint sound of windchimes sounding off every couple of minutes whenever the night breeze rolled through had me looking around the area for any signs of movement.

I pulled at the end of the black leather gloves I just slid over my fingers, making sure they were secured. Lifting my ass off the back seat, I tucked a small-caliber pistol in the back of my pants and then placed one in the holster I had around my ankle. After rechecking the extra clips for the 9 mm in my hand, I stuffed those in my pocket and cocked a bullet into the chamber.

"Yo, Ace said it hasn't been any movement for a few hours now. Lights have been out since ten, and no one has come in or gone out since about four," Styles told Zig from his position in the driver's seat. We'd had him pick us up from one of my decoy cars that was parked a few blocks away.

"Do you know how many people are in there?" Zig asked after double-tying his steel-toe boots and checking the clips for his guns.

Styles nodded his head. "Only two since I've been watching. That fuck nigga Stax and some bitch whose face we couldn't see. She had on a cap and hoodie when they went out for food earlier, and then some kind of scarf wrapped around her head when she went out by herself not too long ago. Whoever she is, though, she wasn't trying to be seen."

Zig's eyes scanned over to me. "You sure you're ready to do this? The nigga has a whole 'nother bitch in there with him. If you don't think you can keep your emotions in check, let me know right now. I can go in by myself, get the job done, and then be out in five minutes flat."

"I'm good, Zig," I replied with way more aggression than intended.

"Are you?" His eyebrows came together, and his lips twisted. "Because the way you just responded tells me that you might not be."

I nodded my head. "Look, my tone was wrong, but the meaning behind my words was still the same. Like I told you earlier, Zig, any feelings I had left for Stax don't exist anymore. I can handle this. Trust me."

"We'll see," was all he said before turning his attention back to Styles. "Aye, man, pull up down the street and drop us off at the end of the block where the unfinished homes are. We'll hop the fences in the back until we get to the yard this nigga is in. Once this shit is done, we'll meet Funk on the next street over. I need Ace to stay in his position two houses down, just in case one of these muthafuckas get lucky enough to run out the house before we get a chance to hit 'em."

Styles nodded his head and didn't say anything else as he drove down the street and dropped us off in front of a partially finished home. Once he made his way back down the street, Zig and I hightailed it to the back of the house, dressed in all black, and began hopping over the wooden fences. By the time we got to Stax's backyard, my heart and adrenaline was pumping.

"You ready?" Zig asked one last time. When I nodded my head, he pulled out the tools from the small pouch and picked the lock.

I thought the loud creaking sound the door made would've alerted Stax and whoever he had up in there of our presence, but after not hearing any movement come from the living room or down the hallway, we crept farther into the house. With guns drawn, we checked each of the empty rooms on the first level of the two-story home before making our way upstairs.

Instead of searching the rooms together like we did on the first floor, Zig signaled for us to separate. While he checked the first bedroom on the right, I went to check the second bedroom on the left.

After quietly opening the door, I stuck the nozzle of my gun through the small crack before leading the rest of my body into the room. Slowly walking in, I wasn't expecting to see much, since the rest of the house hardly looked lived in. Imagine my surprise when my eyes roamed over the neatly decorated nursery equipped with two cribs, a changing table, a rocking chair, and shelves full of diapers, wipes, and stuffed animals. I walked farther into the room, which was illuminated by a Noah's Ark nightlight, an exact match to the bedding and pictures on the wall.

My head started to pound, and my heart began to shatter the more I looked around. There was a closet full of baby clothes with cute little accessories to match, a double stroller in one corner, and a double rocker in the other. My breath hitched in my throat the second I laid eyes on the sonogram pictures that sat above each crib, both framed and labeled for each baby.

"Welks baby number one. Welks baby number two," I whispered to myself as a tear slipped from my eye. My hand went directly over my stomach as flashes of the sonograms I had taken of my baby flashed in my mind.

"This is supposed to be my life," I said to no one in particular. "Nigga didn't even care that I lost our baby. Didn't even show up to the hospital to make sure that I was okay after losing our baby, but has the nerve to get somebody else pregnant and give this bitch the life that should've been mine?"

Removing my mask, I raised my gun in the air and aimed it at the first sonogram on the wall, ready to pull the trigger and fuck this whole room up; but when a hard body slipped up behind mine and a pair of strong arms wrapped around my shoulders and belly, I lowered my gun. Turning me around and pulling me into his chest, Zig held me tight as I quietly whimpered over my loss and the hurt he obviously knew was still there.

"Shhhhhh," he whispered into my ear. "I know you're hurting right now, but we still have a job to do. If you're not feeling up to it anymore, I'll text Styles right now and tell him to come ba—"

Before Zig could finish his sentence, I pulled myself from his embrace and shook my head, cutting him off.

"No. I'm good. I can still do this. It's just—" I looked around the room and started to choke up again. "Can we just get this over with so that I can get the fuck out of here?"

Looking into my eyes, Zig gave me a small smile and nodded his head. I was wiping at the tears still falling down my face and trying to get my head back into the game when he grabbed my chin and brought his lips down to mine. The kiss wasn't hurried or rushed, judgmental, or one of concern, but just what I needed to get me back in the right frame of mind for the time being. Once we were done locking lips, Zig placed a kiss to my chin and a final one to my forehead before cocking his gun and walking out of the room.

Following close behind, I trailed Zig until we reached the last door at the end of the hallway. With guns cocked and ready to go, we entered the master bedroom just as discreetly as we came in. The TV, which was muted, had a rerun of *Martin* playing, while the small lamp on one of the nightstands flickered on and off, spotlighting the opened kilo of dope on a fancy silver tray. Residue from the six or so lines already snorted was still visible.

I looked around the dimly lit room in disgust. Although the nursery looked like something out of a Babies R Us magazine, the master bedroom was messy and dirty as fuck. Clothes, suitcases, and big black duffle bags were thrown around every which way. Takeout containers and pizza boxes from different restaurants decorated the top of the dresser and underneath the bed. The rancid smell of day-old vomit filled the air and had my stomach turning.

Two entwined bodies lay haphazardly over the bed, Stax's heavy snoring echoing through the room. I couldn't get a clear view of the woman beneath him, but I could hear light snores coming from her position underneath his arm.

Without warning, Zig walked over to Stax's side of the bed and slapped the fuck out of him. The nigga was so high from the coke that he snorted that he didn't move an inch. However, the chick he was sharing the bed with stirred out of her sleep. Pressing her open palm against Stax's bare chest, she tried to move him over a bit. When that didn't work, she nudged him with her knee until he turned over on his side, giving her room to move around. With her hair spilling over her face, she slowly sat up in the bed. My eyes immediately went to her stomach, which was poking out a little underneath her T-shirt. Scooting to the edge of the bed, she stretched her arms high above her head before standing up and scratching at the spot above her lower back. She stumbled a bit as she began to make her way toward the en suite bathroom, but then froze dead in her tracks when she caught a glimpse of me standing next to the television.

"Lu—Lucci," hoarsely came from her mouth, but I didn't recognize her voice at all. "Wha . . . What are you doing here?"

"What am I doing here?" I asked, stepping forward. "Nah, bitch, the question is what are you doing here, and how the fuck do you know who I am?"

She stood there quiet for a second, and I could tell by the way her shoulders cowered that she was hesitant to answer my question.

I walked closer to her with my gun drawn and decided. "Since you seem to have an issue responding in a timely manner, I'ma give you five seconds to tell me how the fuck you know my name before I put a hot one in your head. One . . ." I counted off.

By the time I got to three, she still hadn't answered my question. Instead, she tucked a few strands of her hair behind her ear before flipping the rest of the long weave out of her face. When she finally looked up at me, I immediately recognized her ho ass and sent a bullet flying through her shoulder.

"Awwww!" She screamed out in pain, her arms immediately circling her belly as if she were trying to protect it. "You said you wouldn't shoot me if I answered you in a timely manner."

"I didn't say shit like that, you trifling-ass bitch." I pointed my gun at her again, ready to shoot, but stopped when Zig called my name. With my eyes still on her, I responded to him.

"What?"

"You're running off of your emotions, beautiful. You told me that you wouldn't do that."

"Nigga, fuck that running off of emotions bullshit. Do you know who this bitch is?" He opened his mouth to say something, but I cut him off. "Do you know how many times I done looked out for this ho since she was a kid? Helped keep her ass out of the system when her mama was out running the streets and Kay Kay was down for those few years? I damn near raised this bitch. Her kids call me auntie. This how you do me, Shauna? Fuck around with my nigga and get pregnant by him?"

In the midst of me going off, a thought occurred to me. "How long have you and Stax been fucking around anyway?"

She began to cry uncontrollably and shake her head. "Please don't do this, Lucci. Please."

I cocked my gun and pressed the barrel to her head. "How. Long. Have. Y'all. Been fucking around?" I repeated my question again, enunciating each word.

Shauna started to cry harder. Leaning against the wall, she lowered herself down to the ground and began to rock back and forth.

The sound of the bed moving grabbed our attention. Stax had finally woken up and was getting ready to sit up, but he stopped all movement when Zig shoved his gun to the side of his face. When what was going on actually registered in his head, Stax's wide eyes began to franti-cally search the room, until he laid eyes on Shauna's ass crying loudly on the floor. When he focused his gaze on me, all the color drained from his face.

"Lucci. What—where . . . Why are you doing this, baby? Put the gun down so we can talk. Please. I promise we can talk about anything you like. Just put the gun down." He tried to look up at Zig but couldn't turn his head to do so. "You too, nigga. And that's an order. Take the muthafuckin' gun out of my face."

Zig chuckled. "Nigga, you ain't runnin' shit in here but your mouth. Now, you shut the fuck up and sit there like a good little bitch until my girl decides to address you."

"Your girl?" he questioned with attitude. "So, you have been fucking with this nigga behind my back?"

I took my eyes off Shauna and looked at him. "Nigga, please. The only person I've been fucking for the last ten plus years of my life is you. But you can't say the same thing, can you? You don't think I know about all them other hoes you thought you were keeping from me?"

Stax's eyes cut toward Zig.

"Don't look at him, 'cause he ain't tell me shit. Your dumb ass started getting sloppy. Must've forgotten about the cameras and shit we had installed in the trap houses when the dope and money started coming up short."

Stax stapled his eyes back on me, and they softened. "Lucci, baby. Let's talk about this. Please. You don't want to kill me. Hell, you don't want to kill her either. You know the Feds are watching me. They're watching you, too. Probably on their way in here right now. Do you want to add a double murder rap to what they're already trying to build against you?"

"Nigga, fuck you and the Feds. Now, where's my money and my dope?"

Stax looked at me like I was crazy. "*Your* money and dope? Bitch, please. You worked for me, so anything you brought in or thought you were stashing away belongs to me. You got me all the way fucked up. *Your money and dope*," he mocked me. "You lucky I left you the little that I did with your rotten-womb-having ass. Oh, shit. I guess we both know some things about one another that we failed to mention?" he taunted when he saw the way my face dropped. I'd never told anybody else about the other miscarriages, not even Bobbi and them. So how did he know?

"I bet you're over there wondering how I knew, huh? Well, let me tell you. It was your pussy that gave it away. Every time you would get pregnant, that pussy would have a vice grip on my dick. Suck the nut right out of my shit on first contact. Your shit would be so wet, warm, and snug for about two, maybe three months. Then it would go back to being that okay shit you thought was hitting for something." He chuckled.

"Yeah, I knew all about those miscarriages you had throughout the years. That's why I didn't care about the one you had a few weeks ago. Then, when I came up to the hospital and saw this nigga at your bedside holding your hand like you was his bitch, it was a wrap for us. When Shauna got pregnant, she told me as soon as she pissed on the stick and it said yes. You, on the other hand—" He shook his head and smirked. "The fact that you were thinking about keeping this baby and didn't say shit to me let me know that maybe this man"—he pointed at Zig—"was the papi. Either way, I was done with your ass. My real baby mama wanted us to be a family, and she deserved it."

His eyes went over to Shauna, and so did mine.

"Please don't kill me, Lucci. I'm so sorry. I promise I didn't mean to start any kind of relationship with Stax. It just happened." Shauna continued to cry and beg.

Stax smacked his teeth. "Man, babe, stop crying and boss up on this bitch. She ain't gon' do shit if she knows the truth. Hell, she can't do shit. The Feds already know—"

Before he got to finish the rest of his sentence, two bullets were sent into his dome. My eyes connected with Zig's as soon as I watched Stax's lifeless body slump over.

"The nigga disrespected you one too many times already, and I couldn't take it anymore. Plus, I could tell that you were starting to let what this fuck boy said affect you, and I couldn't have that. Now, handle ole girl so we can get the fuck up out of here just in case the Feds are on their way. No faces, no cases."

"No faces, no cases," I repeated as I turned back to Shauna and aimed my gun.

She started to scream hysterically now, snot and tears running down her cheeks and chin.

"Please, Lucci, please. Don't kill me. I promise I won't talk." She started stuttering. "The babies. Th–th–the babies aren't even his. They belong to this other nigga I was fucking with. A nigga my sister used to trick off."

"Bitch, don't even mention your sister's name. That girl died trying to clean up your mess, and you still shit on her even in her death."

She held her arms out as if she were trying to shield her face. "Lucci, please. Wha–what if I had some information for you?"

My ears perked up. "Information like what?"

"Lucci, stop stalling and kill the girl, or I will do it for you," Zig said over my shoulder, his gun now pointed at Shauna.

"No, no, no. Please," she cried. "I know who set y'all up."

"What are you talking about? Set who up?"

"You, Diamond, Kay Kay, Bobbi, and the rest of y'all crew. The Diamond Mafia. That last job that you guys did. The one where Diamond was . . ."

"Killed." I finished her sentence. "Just like your sister."

She shook her head. "No. No, Kay Kay wasn't killed. At least that night she wasn't. He promised he wouldn't hurt her."

"Who is he, and how do you know so much about Diamond Mafia?"

Zig and I listened to Shauna tell us about the nigga Doughboy and some mystery person he was working with. She also told us about Kay Kay and her involvement in the whole thing. I didn't believe her at first, but after she repeated specific details of that night, I didn't have a choice but to believe she was telling the truth. When I asked her how she knew so much, she told us it was because her and the nigga Doughboy had been fucking around behind Kay Kay's back for a few months.

After Kay Kay stole that money from him, it was Shauna who told him where to find her sister. The nigga offered her twenty stacks and a new condo in Manhattan Beach to turn that information over. When I asked her about her involvement with Stax, she admitted that they had been messing around for about two years now. The only reason she started fucking with Doughboy was because she found out that Stax was humping one of her hood rat homegirls on the low.

After Doughboy and Kay Kay double crossed us, whoever he was working with made him cut off all communication with Shauna, meaning the condo and her unlimited access to his money was gone. She called Stax and lied about being pregnant by him. He told her that he was getting ready to skip town after talking to the Feds, and her dumb ass asked to come with him just to have someplace other than her momma's house to stay.

Had all of this gone done outside of our circle, I probably would've been willing to help Shauna get back on her feet, but seeing the kind of snake-ass bitch that she was in the flesh changed all of that. Her having a hand in fucking over everybody who had ever loved and tried to help her was something I couldn't let slide.

"Please, Lucci. Please. What about my babies?" she questioned as she started to beg for her life again. "I gotta be here for my babies."

"Bitch, you don't give a fuck about any of your kids, because if you did, my niece and nephew wouldn't be in the system now."

POW!

Chapter 22

Kay Kay

The loud, blaring sound of a train blowing its horn stirred me from what I thought was my death. I could feel the rough fabric of whatever I was lying on pressing against my arms, legs, and stomach. The stench of wet dog radiated through the bundled-up pile of clothes my head was positioned on. I could tell from the scent of freshly wet asphalt in the air that it was or had been raining. The low flame of the fire burning was doing a good job of keeping my hardly clothed body warm.

Slowly opening my eyes a bit, I looked around my surroundings as far as I could while trying not to alert the person I could hear walking around.

"I see you're finally up?" A raspy voice I didn't recognize spoke from above me. "No need to try and act like you're still out. I can see your eyeballs rolling under your eyelids."

Still not trusting who this man was, I remained on the makeshift cot beneath me as stiff as I could. The man's hoarse laugh echoed around me.

"Baby girl, if I wanted to finish off whatever them niggas who threw you out of that car were trying to do, I would have done it two days ago when I brought you to my humble abode."

I could hear the man moving around, his feet slowly dragging across the concrete ground, and the low sound of some radio broadcast playing softly in the background. I wiggled my toes a little before trying to move my feet. Pulling my hands from the position underneath my head, I pressed my open palms against the ground and slowly tried to raise myself up but fell back down when my arms gave out on me.

"Here. Let me help you," the guy offered before slipping his hands underneath my arms and then pulling me into a sitting position. He used his legs to support my back in trying to keep me balanced. Once I was able to sit up on my own, he walked over to the row of grocery carts he had lined up against the wall. "Here. You need to drink something. I've been on one of those near-death binges before, so I know you're thirsty as hell right now."

I looked up at the half-empty bottle of water he was offering me.

"It's all I have for now, unless you want a shot of some of this Jim Beam." He held up the small bottle wrapped in a brown paper bag.

"No." I spoke for the first time. "No, thank you. The water . . . the water is fine."

I accepted the bottle from him and chugged down every last bit of that shit. My throat desperately needed that coating of liquid because it was dry as fuck.

"Thank you," I said softly, and he nodded his head.

While he began to fiddle around with whatever was in the first shopping cart, I took a minute to take in my surroundings. By the patches of tall weeds I could see just outside of the tunnel we were in and the glowing lights from the cars passing on the overpass above us, I could tell that we were underneath some kind of bridge. With the rain now falling as hard as it was and my high still coming down, I couldn't get a clear enough view of which bridge we were under.

"You're in Lynwood," the man answered as if he were reading my mind "We're underneath the overpass just where the 710 and 110 meet. "

"You . . . you said I've been here for two days?" I asked, slowly turning around to face him.

He nodded, his matted salt-and-pepper beard matching the small afro on the top of his head. "Yep. Saw some men dump you on the side of the freeway while I was walking from doing a little dumpster diving." He motioned his hands toward the shopping carts. "I thought you were dead, but when I checked, I could still feel a faint pulse. I could tell from your eyes and them marks on your arms that you must've been doped up. Your night must've been one hell of a good one, huh?"

I shook my head. "Nah. Far from it."

We shared a look before we both returned to our own thoughts. I wanted to ask the man if he had a cell phone or knew where I could walk to get to the nearest pay phone so that I could try to call somebody and ask for help, but thought to wait it out until the rain died down. The cold air flowing beneath this bridge was enough to have my nose and eyes running right now, so I knew if I went out in the rain, it would get a lot worse.

"You hungry?" the guy asked as he placed some debris in the trash can, causing the flame to blaze a little higher.

"Not really," I told him truthfully. "I . . . I could use another drink of water, though. If you have it."

The guy smiled and picked up the empty water bottle next to me. "I actually don't have it. But when God blesses you with all of these natural resources, who are we to not take advantage of them?" I watched as he walked out into the rain and held the empty bottle up to the air. "You see, not only does God answer prayers, but He knows what you're going to need way before you even ask for it."

I scoffed, "I stopped believing in what God was able to do a long time ago. His love for me stopped the second my mama pushed me out of her coochie and I took my first breath. My life has been nothing but constant bullshit ever since."

He handed me the rainwater, and I took a few sips. "Do you think you would be here right now if God didn't love you? Do you think He would've directed me to walk along the 710 that day if He didn't want me to find you?" He squatted next to me. "Baby girl, let me tell you something. I hardly ever go down that way because the people in that area tend to not like when people of my kind rummage through their trash, but for some reason, I kept hearing this voice tell me to go. Not only was I able to find food and things that would last me for a few days, but I happened to stumble across you. Near death. Badly beaten. No clothes on. Had I left you on the side of that freeway, you'd be lying in someone's morgue right now."

"Why didn't you leave me?" I asked, honestly wishing that he did.

He shrugged his shoulders. "I guess because of the oath. Before I became this shell of a man you see before you right now, I was an ER doctor. Lost my license to practice when I came to work so high one day I zoned out and clipped a patient's main artery. Couldn't stop the bleeding, so he bled out and died. I did some time in jail. Once I got out, everything I ever owned and loved was gone. Family, friends, money. Eventually I started using drugs again, but this time, heavier than before. One day, I shot so much heroin into my system, trying to get away from my past, that I almost died. Waking up in that hospital alone, I had enough time to reevaluate my life and talk to God. He told me that it wasn't my time to go, just like he told me it wasn't yours."

"So, God told you to save me?"

He thought about my question for a second. "In my heart, I believe He did. With as much drugs as them guys pumped into your system, you probably should've died, but obviously the man upstairs has other plans for you. Instead of taking you to the hospital, I brought you here. Watched over you and prayed that you didn't have any seizures or anything like that. Just so happened that I had a few supplies in my first aid cart that helped me check your blood pressure and shit, so you were in good hands."

I didn't know what to say. Just hearing him retell this story as if I wasn't one of the main characters had me thinking all kinds of shit. Did God spare my life so that I could help somebody out like He did this man to help me? My immediate thoughts went to Bobbi and Lucci.

"I'm sorry. I don't think I ever got your name."

The guy sat down in his lawn chair and started to eat what looked like some picked-over chicken and bread. He wiped his hands on his pants after eating a few bites and held his hand out for me to shake.

"A long time ago, I used to go by the name Dr. Wendell Thurgood Douglas, but nowadays everyone around here and on skid row calls me Doc."

I shook his hand. "Well, it's nice to meet you, Doc. My name is Khalani, but my friends . . ." I paused for a second, remembering that due to my own selfishness, I probably didn't have those anymore. "Well, people who used to consider me a friend called me Kay Kay."

"It's nice to meet you, Kay Kay. And I'm sure if you apologize and explain to those friends whatever it was that happened between y'all, they might be willing to forgive you for your transgressions."

I turned my gaze toward the fire, my finger absent-mindedly making circles in the gravel. "I doubt that. Not only did I betray them in the worst way, but I got one of my oldest and best friends killed behind my mistake."

"Mistakes can be forgiven. If the mother and wife of the man I killed could forgive me, I'm sure your friends could and would do the same for you."

"I don't know." I shook my head. "I don't think I could forgive myself if I were in their shoes. If anything, I just want to make something right in the chaos that I've caused, even if that means I'll be tapping on death's door for a second time. I have to make sure not one more of my friends die because of me."

Doc ate his chicken and took a sip from his brown paper bag before speaking again. "If you think what you need to tell them will save a life, then I say tell them. That way, you've righted a wrong and can die in peace, if that's what the good Lord has in store for you."

I smiled for the first time since I'd opened my eyes. "You know, Doc, you've managed to teach me more about life in five minutes than my mama ever did. Thank you for saving me. Thank you for looking out for me and thank you for hitting me with some real shit."

We both laughed. "I'm only doing what I can and know how. Plus, I'm finally able to have the discussion about life that I've always wanted to have with my own children."

"You have kids?" I questioned, wondering why they weren't trying to help him off of the streets.

He nodded his head. "Yeah, I got two. But I haven't seen or heard from them in years. Their mother wouldn't even let me speak to them during my time in prison or after."

"Damn. Sorry to hear that."

"Don't be. Because I'm not. I figure me not being in their lives is the reason why they're doing so good now.

I don't have contact with them, but sometimes when the library allows me to use their computer, I look them up. My one son went into the medical field like me. Happily married with two kids and one on the way. My other son, he either doesn't have social media or he uses a different name other than Wendell Thurgood Jr. When he was little, he always said that he wanted to be a hot shot lawyer. Hopefully he made that dream come true."

"Yeah. Hopefully." I looked over my shoulder at the carts against the wall. "Hey, Doc, you wouldn't happen to have a working cell phone over there, would you? Since it looks like this rain isn't about to let up anytime soon, I wanna at least try to call one of my friends and someone who could possibly come get me."

Doc divided a piece of bread in half and handed it to me. "I'll check in a second, but for now, you need to eat something. Your body will need it, especially if you're thinking about getting out of here as soon as the rain lets up."

I took the bread from his hand and took a bite of it.

"Good girl. I got some more chicken if you want a piece of that."

"Thanks again, Doc."

"It's my pleasure, baby girl." He smiled, showing off his yellow-stained teeth full of tartar buildup. "Now, while we wait and eat, do you mind telling what it is that you've done so bad to your friends? Maybe I can give you a bit more insight and let you know whether your act of disloyalty is really that unforgivable."

For the next hour or so, I basically told this stranger who happened to save my life everything about me, from the struggles I went through when I was younger all the way up until the shit I was going through now. Doc didn't interrupt me, question me, or judge me on anything I told him. He just listened and gave his feedback on the whole situation after I was done. Although I didn't agree with some of the things he told me, I knew I had to make things right between Bobbi, Lucci, and me. I also needed to get in contact with Marvin to see what happened with my niece and nephew's court hearing, since I was too drugged-up to make it.

After eating a few more pieces of chicken with Doc and asking him more questions about his kids, the rain finally stopped. Doc didn't have a cell phone in one of the carts, so he walked with me to a nearby liquor store and gave me enough change to make a few calls. When neither Lucci nor Bobbi answered their phones, I tried to call Shauna, whose shit went straight to voicemail. After leaving her a message, I made another call that didn't last long at all. As soon as I explained some of the situation to Marvin, he offered to send someone to pick me up.

Doc stayed and waited with me outside the store until the Uber arrived. Once I thanked him for all of the things he'd done since finding me on the side of the freeway, I made a promise to come back and help him off of the streets if that was something that he wanted to have done.

I watched Doc's full body fade into the background as the driver drove off. He was indeed a godsend, and I hoped like hell I stayed alive long enough to make good on the promise. For now, though, I needed to concentrate on the task at hand and get up with Bobbi and Lucci. They needed to know that I wasn't the only snake-ass muthafucka in the crew. I just hoped it wasn't too late.

Chapter 23

Nav

"I think if we move quick and move fast, then we can be in and out within ten minutes flat." Tweety addressed everyone in the room as she used one of those laser pointers to circle the picture illuminated against the wall.

We were at one of my old lofts that I used for photoshoots when I first started taking pictures. It was the only place I trusted to be low on the radar for now, since it was in my old partner's name.

"I don't like this idea at all. It seems risky. Why can't we go in through the back door and exit through the back door?" Bobbi asked as she walked up to examine the picture closer. "This front entrance right here has the double glass security doors for a reason. Once the alarm sounds, whoever is in there will be stuck."

Tweety huffed and rolled her eyes, annoyance all over her face. "Don't you think I know that?" She pulled a piece of paper out of her pocket. "With me being head of security now, we won't have to worry about anyone getting stuck anywhere. I have every access code BJE uses."

"And how do we know any of those will really work? Josh and his father stay switching those codes up. What's to say there isn't another set needed after you punch those set of numbers in?"

While Bobbi and Tweety continued to go back and forth with their petty shit, I opened up my laptop and started to look over the blueprints I had one of my connects down at zoning send me. Although I hoped Tweety was on the up and up about this job, I needed to know that there were other options for us to escape, just in case her shit didn't go according to plan. I promised Bobbi that I would never let anything happen to her ever again, and I intended to keep my word.

"Aye, man, you better stop those two before they start fighting," Ant said over my shoulder as he came and sat next to me on the couch, eating a turkey sandwich. "In the event that they do, I got a dub on Tweety. Bobbi looks like she can throw some hands, but not like Tweety can."

I chuckled as my eyes scanned the front of the room where the two hotheads were now in each other's faces. With the way both of their eyes kept cutting over in my direction, I could tell that their heated exchange was more than likely about me.

"Y'all need to stop with the bullshit. I already told you two, if this arguing keeps going on, then one of you will need to sit this round out," I stated casually, firing up the blunt Ant gave me and pulling on it a few times. We'd been there for a little over two hours now, and Bobbi and Tweety had been throwing jabs at each other since we walked through the door. "You two need to come to some common ground before we do this job tomorrow night, or risk not getting a cut of what we bring home."

Bobbi was about to say something but stopped when her phone started ringing. She held it up toward me. "This Lucci. I'm going to take this in the other room."

My eyes followed Bobbi as she walked through the loft and headed down the hall that connected to the darkroom. The little yellow sundress she wore was hugging every single curve on her body. I licked my lips and could feel my dick start to wake underneath my laptop. This meeting was for sure over now. Anything else we needed to talk about would just have to be discussed the next night before we made our move.

"Damn," I heard Ant whisper, and my heated glare turned to him. "Bobbi's bad, man. She thick as fuck, too."

"Nigga, unless you want to leave this loft blind, deaf, and with a hole in your chest, I suggest you keep your eyes off of my woman," I said with so much venom dripping from my tone.

Ant nervously shook his head and laughed. "Man, I wasn't trying to be disrespectful or anything like that, Nav. I just got caught up for a second. You know I like that chocolate skin and yellow fabric combo."

I took another pull of the blunt. "Well, nigga, like that shit on some other bitch, because that one right there belongs to me. And I don't like to share, let alone allow another nigga to fantasize about what's mine in front of me."

Ant raised his hands in surrender. "I already know how you get down, man, so my bad. It won't happen again."

I heard the words coming from Ant's mouth, but for some reason, it didn't feel like his apology was coming from a sincere place. Either way it went, though, I would beat Ant's ass if he ever said some disrespectful shit like that again about Bobbi in front of me

"What you two over here talking about?" Tweety asked as she sat on the other side of Ant. They gave each other a one-armed hug and then laughed at something Tweety whispered in his ear. "Nav got that look on his face like he about to beat somebody's ass. What did you fuck up now, Ant?"

"Man, Tweet, I ain't fuck up shit. All I said was that I had a dub on you if a fight were to break out between you and ole girl." Ant pointed his thumb at me. "This nigga got mad because I have complete and utter faith in your fighting abilities."

"Boy, shut the fuck up. You already know what will happen if she and I ever got down."

I opened my mouth to check Tweety's ass, but she held up her hand, cutting me off.

"Uh, you can calm your ass down, Nav, and keep whatever smart-ass remark you were about to say to yourself. I'm not going to fight your little bed buddy or whatever she is to you. I can already tell she got your ass sprung so we can't even joke around anymore like we used to."

"You're right, you can't," I said, getting up from my seat and walking into the kitchen, closing my laptop in the process. "With that being said, you need to stop worrying about my relationship and how my girl has me. Just know that a nigga happy and is okay with being sprung on that one." I pointed down the hall where Bobbi was still on the phone.

Tweety rolled her eyes and turned her attention back to Ant. They were having a conversation amongst themselves when Bobbi finally came back into the room. Her eyes scanned the entire area until they landed on me. Once our gazes connected, it was as if she floated right over to where I was standing. I ran my fingers through her hair before raising her face to meet mine and placing a soft kiss against her lips.

"Does that mean you missed me for the five minutes that I was gone like I missed you?" she joked, and I could feel her lips curl into a smile against mine.

"I miss you whenever you're not in the room."

"Oh, yeah?"

I nodded my head, placing another kiss on those luscious lips of hers. "Well, why don't we head to the bathroom so you can show me how much you missed me? I'm sure Ant"—She cut her eyes over to the couch then looked back at me—"can keep Tweety entertained until we come back."

When her hands dipped into my sweats and her soft fingers began to caress my dick, I almost slapped the empty buckets off the counter and threw her little ass up there. "As much as I need and want to feel your pussy, we need to discuss the rest of this job so these niggas can leave and I can be all up in that wetness for as long as I want," I growled against her lips before hungrily devouring her whole being in another kiss.

My hands slid down the soft fabric of the dress Bobbi hand on until I had a grip on her ass. I pulled her body closer into mine and could feel the heat radiating from her pussy on my thigh. The scent of her arousal was so intoxicating that my mind completely went blank, forgetting about anything or anybody surrounding us. I lifted Bobbi from the ground, and her legs immediately wrapped around my waist. Her grinding her pussy onto my dick in a slow, winding fashion only intensified my need to feel her cum on my shit even more. It wasn't until we heard the sound of buckets falling to the ground that we broke from the trance we were in. When we finally pulled apart from one another, neither one of us could help but laugh.

"You see what you do to me? Just one kiss and a nigga is putty in your hands. I forget all about the outside world and everyone in it."

Bobbi blushed. "I've been known to have that effect on niggas."

I kissed her chin and then her cheek. "Well, I better be the only nigga you affecting in that way from this moment on."

She tapped her finger on her chin and rolled her eyes up into the air as if she were thinking. When she didn't respond fast enough to my liking, I buried my face in her neck and sucked on her cocoa-butter-scented skin until she gave me the response I was looking for.

"Stop, Nav." She giggled, trying to push me off her. "I just said you're the only one. You're going to put another hickey on my neck."

"Only way to let these fuck boys know that this pussy right here is taken."

When the loud sucking of teeth echoed throughout the loft, both Bobbi and I froze and then turned our attention toward the couch. Just that fast, I had forgotten Ant and Tweety were still there. I couldn't tell what the look on Ant's face was, because he turned his head as soon as I looked in his direction, but Tweety had a mug on hers that she wasn't even trying to hide.

"See, this is the shit I was talking about. How can your head be fully in the game when you're so easily distracted by this tramp-ass bitch? It's a whole 'nother nigga in this room, and she up on the counter, ready to bust it open in front of him. I know you said to leave this shit alone, but I can't. Why would you pick her over me? I would never do anything like that to you. Never give the next nigga the chance to catch a whiff of the way my pussy smells if I was yours. But this nasty ho . . . This is who you love and want to be with?"

I removed myself from in between Bobbi's thighs and pulled her dress down before walking around the counter, closer to the couch. "Tweety, I think you need to leave. As a matter of fact, don't forget to grab all of your shit on the way out. This whole BJE thing . . . is dead. You can either find you another crew to work with or do the shit yourself. I don't give a fuck. As of this moment, me and my resources are off limits to you."

"You can't be serious?" she asked in disbelief.

"I'm as serious as a heart attack. I'm not about to allow you to continue disrespecting me or Bobbi. In the beginning, I let shit slide because I understood that your feelings for me wouldn't go away that easily, but now you're projecting your anger on Bobbi, and she ain't got nothing to do with why your feelings are hurt. I should've never crossed that line with you years ago, Tweety, knowing you cared about me in a way that I didn't care for you. And for the one thousandth time, I'm sorry, but you need to get the fuck over whatever this little jealousy thing is you have over my relationship with her."

"Jealousy? Nigga, I would never be jealous of a bitch who could never compare to me."

"You got one more time to call me a bitch before I hop my pretty ass off of this counter and beat the living shit out of you," Bobbi warned.

Tweety cut her eyes in Bobbi's direction. "You ain't gon' do shit, bi—"

Before the words could fully come out of Tweety's mouth, Bobbi spun her body around on the counter and leaped over to Tweety, pummeling her to the ground. Tweety tried to get Bobbi off of her by sending sharp jabs to her side, but the small hits were no match for the adrenaline-fueled Bobbi, who was raining blows down on Tweety's face and upper body.

"Whoa, whoa, whoa. Wait a minute now." Ant stood up from his seat. "We all need to just calm down for a second. Nigga, you not about to stop this?"

I shrugged my shoulders. "I will, but first I think Tweety needs to learn a lesson."

"Learn a lesson? What could she possibly learn from getting her ass beat like that?"

I watched as Bobbi grabbed a handful of Tweety's hair and slapped the shit out of her. "Bitch, I told you you had one more time!" she screamed before slapping her again. "You thought this was a muthafucking game, huh?"

Tweety tried to talk shit back but was silenced with a blow to the lip. When blood started pouring over my hardwood floor and Tweety's shit-talking turned into cries of "Get this bitch off of me!" I decided that she had had enough and pulled Bobbi off of her.

"Next time, I'ma put a fucking bullet through your head, bitch," were Bobbi's last words before I pulled her into the kitchen and sat her back on the counter.

I placed my hands on the side of her head to try to examine her face, but she snatched herself away.

"Nigga, move. I don't need you to baby me."

I chuckled. "I'm not trying to baby you, baby. I just wanna make sure you don't have any scratches or cuts on your face." I didn't know whether the blood marks were hers or Tweety's.

"I'm good." She tried to push me off of her again, but I continued to hold her face in my hands. "Nav, I said that I'm good."

"I know you are." I kissed her lips and then her nose after seeing that she was indeed good. "Now, sit your ass here for a second, Baby Mayweather, and let me handle the rest of this situation."

She sucked her teeth and started fixing her hair. "You better handle the shit before I beat her ass again."

I kissed Bobbi one last time before making my way back over to the living room area, where Ant was helping Tweety get herself together. I stood behind the couch and assessed all the damage the two had just done.

"Don't worry about cleaning any of this up. I'll take care of it later," I said to no one in particular.

Tweety looked up at me with hurt eyes. "So, that's it? Your girl fucks up my face and beats my ass and you still want me to leave?"

I looked over my shoulder at Bobbi, who was looking at herself in a mirror and reapplying some lip gloss.

"Yes," I answered. "Shit hasn't changed. The BJE job is off, and you need to get the fuck out of my shit."

"Come on, man," Ant said. "I know tensions are high, and I get that Tweet probably isn't in the right headspace to voice how she feels correctly. However, while she's dealing with that, we need to revisit this *not doing the BJE job* thing for a second. I mean, I don't know about you, but I need this money. Us losing that last hit put a big dip in my pockets."

"Man, Ant, I know where you're coming from and I hear you, believe me. But I can't work with Tweety knowing she has all this animosity toward me and Bobbi. What if shit goes left like it did the last time? Would she ride for everybody in the crew, or will she let her pettiness put us in harm's way?"

"You think I would let you die, Nav?" Tweety asked, walking up on me, face full of scratches and bruises. Her voice cracked a little.

For a split second, I almost felt bad for her after seeing an up-close look at the damage Bobbi had done to her face. But Tweety grew up in the projects just like I did, so she was well aware of the consequences that came with talking shit, especially to someone you had issues with.

"That's what I'm talking about right there, Tweet. I know you wouldn't let me die, but what about everybody else who's a part of our crew?" Her eyes cut toward Bobbi. "If we moving as a unit, we ride for each other as a unit. All bullshit aside. If you can't separate your hate for what Bobbi and I have going on and you're willing to put her in harm's way because you think that you should have her spot? Then I can't fuck with you like that anymore. You claim that you ride for me, but how can that be when you're okay with taking something that I love away just so that you can be happy? Is that riding for me?"

It was so quiet in the loft that you could hear a rat piss on cotton. Tweety stood in front of me, trying not to break down, while Ant stood off to the side, waiting to voice his concerns about us not doing the job again. Bobbi came and stood by my side, lacing her fingers with mine after hearing me say that I loved her. This wasn't the way I wanted to let her know that she had a nigga sprung bad, but I needed Tweety to understand for the last time that she and I could never be anything more than friends.

"Nav, I'm sorry." Tweety apologized after a few awkward moments. "And I'm sorry for coming at your girl the way that I did as well."

I nodded my head. "I accept your apology, Tweet, but I still don't think that it would be a good idea for us to do the BJE thing with you. Maybe in a year or two, after you've had enough time to accept this." I pointed between Bobbi and me. "Then maybe we can do something."

"A year or two? Now you're talking crazy, nigga. Let's take a timeout for a quick second," Ant stepped between us and said. "Maybe we all need to just leave for now and then reconvene sometime tomorrow. That way, everyone will be in a better frame of mind and we can get through this job. Once we do that, we can then go our separate ways if that's what everyone wants."

"Babe, I kind of agree with Ant." Bobbi finally spoke. "Maybe we all need to cool off and come back together tomorrow. I'm sure by then we will be all in the same head space and can get this job done. Right, Tweety?"

All eyes went to Tweety, waiting on her response.

She stalled for a second before saying, "Yeah. I think that would be a good idea . . . Ant."

I scoffed and wiped my hand over my head, highly annoyed with Tweety and this whole situation. "Yo, y'all get up out of my shit. We'll talk when we talk," I said over my shoulder before shutting down the projector we were looking at and wrapping it up.

"So, does this mean we will meet up tomorrow before the job?"

"Ant, maaaaan . . ." I dragged out, becoming more irritated with him. The nigga was always about his money, I get that, but sometimes you just had to let shit go. "Aye, bruh, I can't really give you a legit answer on that. Let's just leave it how it is until further notice."

"Until further notice? Man, Nav, you and I have been rocking since we were young bulls. We've always had each other's backs and have done a gang of shit together. If you're rocking, then I'm rolling, and I've always agreed with any and every choice you have ever made, but this one right here . . . I think you're wrong with sitting this one out, man. We need to do this job. I have a feeling that if we do, we're going to hit the biggest score we've ever hit."

I plopped down on my couch and laid my head back on the soft cushion. All of this going back and forth had my head throbbing like a muthafucka, and all I wanted to do was get some pussy and go to sleep.

"Look, Nav, we all need this money, and because we do, I am willing to put my personal feelings aside and be for the team." Tweety stood in front of me. "The whole team. And after, if you don't want me in your life anymore, I'm going to have to accept that and finally move on from you."

"I hear what you're saying, Tweet, but it's the same shit you've said before."

She wiped the tear falling from her eye. "It is, but this time it's different. I hate to admit this, but I can tell that you really like this one so . . . I'm going to fall back." Tweety looked at Bobbi. "I'm sorry for what I said earlier, and I won't disrespect you like that again."

Instead of responding, Bobbi just nodded her head, her eyes immediately casting down to her phone screen when the alert for her text messages started going off back to back.

Ant clapped his hands. "All right. So, now that we're finally done with this week's episode of the Thieving Wives Club, can we please get back to the subject at hand?"

We all laughed at Ant's crazy ass.

"Yeah, man, I guess we can get back to it," I said, re-lighting the blunt and still laughing. "Aye, Tweety, hook the projector back up and let's go over your plan again. Bobbi, I wanna hear your ideas on how we should move as well. You two are the only ones who know anything about this jewelry store, and since we don't have Cowboy here to work the cameras and shit, we're all depending on your eyes, ears, and knowledge to make it out of this one scot-free."

For the next hour, Ant, Bobbi, Tweety, and I went over the details of the job, changing some aspects of the original idea with ones we came up with together. I had a real good feeling that this job was going to set us straight for some years. I just hoped that the niggas who got the drop on us the last time stayed clear. If not, bullets were going to be flying and bodies were going to be dropping. I wasn't taking any more chances this second time around, and I would die before them muthafuckas took from me or my girl again.

Chapter 24

Lucci

"Aye, Looch, you sure you don't want to hop in the shower before me?" Zig asked from behind the wall that separated his kitchen and living room.

I finished chewing my food. "Nah, I'm good. Just make sure your long-shower-taking ass leaves some hot water for me." I laughed and looked up at Zig as he handed me a glass of pineapple juice.

His lips tilted into that sexy smirk of his. "Man, I'll try. I can't make you any promises, though." He turned to walk away, but stopped. "Aye, did you take your pills yet?"

I looked at him like he was crazy. "What kind of question is that?"

He looked at me with squinted eyes. "For real, Lucci, did you take them? Because I don't remember seeing you pop any of them muthafuckas in your mouth since we left the urgent care earlier or since we made it home."

I sucked my teeth and rolled my eyes. Ever since we had climbed into Zig's truck to head back to his spot after handling Stax and Shauna, he'd been asking about my pills. I'm not gonna lie, I was in a little bit of pain after we carried those four duffle bags filled with bricks and cash that we recovered from Stax's house to the car, but it

wasn't extreme. As soon as Styles dropped us off at Zig's
ride, I found my purse and took a couple of the pain pills
the doctor gave me without any water. I'd been feeling
better ever since.

I went to stuff a fry into my mouth, but he knocked it
out of my hand.

"What the hell, Zig? That was my last fry."

"I don't give a fuck. I asked you a question. Did you
take your pills?"

I sucked my teeth and rolled my eyes. "Did you not
hear me say yes the first time you asked me? What the
hell, man? Maybe I should've given you my answer in a
different language or something, because obviously you
don't understand English well."

I caught the quick curl in his lip and amused glint
in his eyes that he tried to hide. "Aye, you get on my
nerves, yo. You didn't answer shit. You implied. All you
had to do was give me a simple yes or no and I would've
left your ass alone. Stop trying to be so difficult, because
I'ma get your ass right every time." He chuckled, hitting
me over the head with his bath towel. "But for real, my bad
about the fry. If you still want some after I get out of the
shower, I'll make you some more," he said sincerely after
picking my discarded fry up and throwing it in the trash.

"Nah, you're good." I rubbed my full belly. "I'm
actually stuffed. You're going to have to stop spoiling
me with these late-night greasy burger joint meals. You
might make me fall in love."

I laughed, but Zig didn't, and I couldn't quite read the
expression on his face. When the moment started to get a
little awkward, he continued the conversation.

"I don't mind cooking for you, Lucci, especially since
your ass almost burned down my kitchen earlier trying

to make a nigga some chicken." We shared a laugh. "All right, I'm about to go get in the shower. Oh, and before I forget, I got somebody stopping by in about five minutes. If you don't mind, can you stay in here and let 'em in before you head back to the room?"

"Yeah." I nodded my head, my thoughts still on Zig's facial expression when I said that shit about making me fall in love. "I'll open the door. Oh, wait. Is it Styles coming over or one of the other little soldiers?" I asked, looking down at the tank top I had on with no bra and the short shorts I usually slept in.

"Nah. It's just a friend of mine. No one you're familiar with," he said over his shoulder before disappearing down the hall and into the bathroom.

"A friend of his?" I whispered to myself, hoping it didn't mean what I thought it meant.

Zig and I never got the chance to talk about the kiss we shared earlier, because we skipped going out to eat so that we could pull up on Stax before he got the chance to move again. Lemon Grove was a little over two hours away from L.A. without traffic, so hitting the freeway when we did saved us some time. I didn't know if these feelings I was feeling for Zig were because of how he'd been there for me in the past few weeks, but I'd be damned if he had another woman coming over while I was there.

Zig finally closing the bathroom door and turning on the shower had me breaking from my thoughts. I wanted to question him about whoever he had sliding through, but I started cleaning up the little mess I'd made in his living room instead. Although I hadn't the slightest clue of who was about to stop by, I didn't want them to see Zig's house all out of whack.

(Show me) Show me what I gotta do. And baby, if you love me, I'll do anything for you. (Show . . . Show me)

A small smile formed on my lips as I began to hum along with the Glenn Jones song "Show Me," which I could now hear playing from the mini system Zig had in his bathroom. It was crazy how I wasn't a fan of those classics like that at first, but after being around Zig and constantly hearing them play morning, noon and night, it was only a matter of time before he had me vibing and making my own playlist filled with these oldies.

Ten minutes had passed before I looked at the time and wondered how my ass was still up. We'd only been home for a few hours since killing Stax and Shauna, and the shit seemed to be moving slow as hell. I'd been up for almost twenty-four hours now. I knew that I needed to get some rest in order to be ready for the BJE job later on, but with the way my adrenaline was still pumping and my mind was still racing, I could tell that I wasn't going to be shutting my eyes to the world anytime soon.

After I was done straightening up, I picked up my phone and started scrolling through the millions of pictures I'd captured over the years. I became real emotional when I swiped over the flicks that Diamond and Kay Kay were in. From our girls' night out to our mini impromptu trips to Vegas and Palm Springs, there were so many great memories we'd shared throughout our friendship, and I was going to miss making new ones.

A lone tear fell from my eye when I stopped on this one picture of Kay Kay when we were at the park for her nephew's birthday. She looked so happy and excited as she posed next to the birthday cake with Devon and Dajah. This wasn't the face of a traitor. Nah, not Khalani. Kay Kay was a lot of things, but she was never a snake-ass friend to us.

I shook my head as I continued to scroll through more of her pictures. The shit that Shauna hit me with about Kay Kay being involved with the robbery was something I still couldn't believe. I wanted to call Bobbi and tell her about it right after we left Stax's house, but Zig thought it would be best if I waited until after we got through with this last job. Some news like that would definitely weigh heavy on your mind, and we all needed to be in the right headspace if we were going to pull this off.

I threw my phone down on the couch next to me after swiping through a few more pics and decided to watch some TV instead. I'd just settled on tuning into a repeat episode of *The First 48* when there was a light knock at the door. I knew I was being petty by continuing to sit on the couch for a few more minutes, acting as if I didn't hear the constant knocking, but after I realized that whoever was on the other side of the door wasn't going anywhere, I decided to get up.

A slight vibration on my thigh caused me to look down at my ringing phone. When I didn't recognize the unknown number hitting my line, I sent the call to voicemail and made my way to the door. Looking through the peephole, I wasn't able to see anything, because whoever was out there was blocking the view with their finger. I wasn't about to take any chances and get caught slipping, so before I opened the door, I grabbed the gun Zig kept in the end table drawer, made sure it was off safety, and finally turned the knob.

"Oh." Her bright eyes scanned me from head to toe the second I came into view. "Hi. I um . . . I wasn't expecting you to answer the door." I didn't acknowledge her comment, so she continued when she realized I wasn't about to respond to her. "Okay. Well, my name is Nisha,

and I'm looking for Zig. Are you his sister or something?"
She tried to look over my shoulder and into the living
room, but I closed the door to block her view.

"Do I look like I'm his sister?" I asked in return, looking down at my barely clothed body.

Her eyes scanned me up and down again. "I'm not
sure. Usually when Zig calls me over, it's only me and
him. And we don't really talk about his background
whenever I stop by, if you can catch my drift."

I caught the bitch's drift and was becoming hotter by
the second, but I wasn't about to let her know that.

"Look, I don't know why Zig called you over here, but
whatever you're trying to give him, please believe that I
have it handled."

She started to fumble over her words. "You have it . . .
handled? What does that mean? Are you . . . are you and
Zy'aire a couple now or something? Is he fucking you?"

I walked up closer to her and got all up in her space,
gun still at my side ready to bust if need be. She looked
down at my hand and stepped back, fear all over her
knock-off Alexis Sky face.

"Whether Zig and I are fucking is none of your business. Just know that whatever you were on your way over
here to do is no longer needed. I got it all handled."

I could tell the instant her attitude changed. No longer
was she putting on that shy, innocent girl act when she
realized Zig wasn't around. The bitch dropped the bags
she was carrying in her hand and crossed her arms over
her chest. She cocked her head to the side and rolled her
eyes.

"You got it handled, huh?" She looked down at my
gun. "You think because you're holding that pistol in
your hand that you're about to scare me off? Do you

know how many times a bitch has pulled a gun out on me? I ain't scared of that shit. And you have another thing coming, sweetheart, if you think I'm about to go anywhere. Zig called me over for a reason. Obviously, you're not *handling*"—she used air quotes—"a damn thing, because if you were, he wouldn't have hit my line. Yeah, I can tell you haven't handled anything, because if you had, you'd be in a dick coma right about now with that mammoth-sized dick Zig has swinging between his legs. But instead, here you are answering the door, trying to get rid of me?" She did a little dramatic round of applause and laughed. "Bitch, if you want me to leave, you would need to either whip my ass or take your little play gun and shoot—"

Her words came to an abrupt stop when I pointed my gun at her face and pressed it to her forehead. "It's obvious that you don't know who you're fucking with, so let me introduce myself. My name is Lucci,"—Her eyes became wide at the mention of my name—"and seeing as you recognize the name means you know how I get down. If you value your life and the lives of your family, I suggest you get the fuck from in front of this door and never come back again. Do I make myself clear?"

She quickly nodded her head as she bent over to pick up her things.

"Can . . . can you at least let Zig know that I stopped—"

I cocked the gun. "Bitch, don't make me shoot you."

She finished gathering up all her things and hurried her ass down the stone pathway to her little red Honda Civic. Closing the door, I placed the gun on top of the end table and made my way down the hall toward the bathroom. Without even knocking, I burst through the door and pulled the shower curtain open, getting a full view of Zig's perfectly sculpted body. Even with the scars, bulletholes, and blemished skin, his tall, masculine frame was still a sight to see. Tattoos decorated his arms, chest, and back. The scent of the Old Spice body wash invaded my senses and had my head spinning for a second, but the low rumble in his voice when he called my name pulled me right out of my nasty thoughts.

"Is everything okay?" Zig asked this time, grabbing the gun I didn't notice attached to the wall.

I slowly nodded my head, bringing my eyes to meet his. "I . . . who . . . you called a girl over here?"

His heated gaze stayed on my face as a range of emotions rolled across his. "If you're talking about Nisha, then yes. I called her over here."

"Why would you do that?" I wanted to know, my tone laced with jealousy.

He smirked and dipped his head under the water, the small beads of wetness cascading down his body, removing the soap suds. I watched in admiration as he used his hands to clear away any leftover residue. When I returned my eyes back to his face, Zig was looking right at me.

He stretched his hand out. "You wanna join me?"

The question was so simple, yet I was having a hard time giving him an answer. Well, not until I found out what Nisha's purpose was for being over there.

I shook the nasty thoughts out of my head again and asked in a tone a bit more firm, "Why did you call her over here?"

I saw the slight roll of his eyes but didn't care. "Nisha is who I call whenever I get done handling a situation. My mind and body be so amped up after a kill that I need a way to calm both down, so I hit Nisha's line to come work the magic that she possesses."

"So, you were going to fuck her while I was in your room?" I didn't know why the thought of that had my heart dropping, but it did. Just thinking about Zig making love to someone else had me ready to kill every last female he'd ever fucked.

He frowned. "Nisha and I have never had sex."

"But she said—"

He cut me off. "Whatever she said was bullshit and something to try and make you mad. I mean, she's always hinted around that she would give me the pussy, but I never took her up on her offer."

I was confused. "If she wasn't here so that the two of you could fuck, then why did you call her over?"

Zig stepped out of the shower and stood in front of me. He pressed his wet body against mine, and I could feel the front of my tank top soaking in his moisture.

"Nisha is a masseuse. I pay her to massage the stress of a job out of me and then send her on her way. Although she's a pretty chick, I'm not attracted to her in that way. She doesn't possess the certain type of qualities I like my women to have."

My nipples were rock hard, and if I could feel them pressing against Zig's chest, I knew he could feel them as well. "She knew your first name," I mentioned, remembering her trying to throw that in when we were talking. For as long as I'd known Zig, he never allowed anyone to call him by his birth name, so for her to use it, it had to have meant something.

He shrugged his shoulders. "I paid her a few times using my credit card. That's the only reason why she knows it. Other than that, she addresses me as Zig, just like everyone else."

Although it was silly, a thought occurred to me as Zig placed his hand on the side of my face and began to caress my cheek with his thumb. "Would you mind if I called you Zy'aire?"

Zig studied my face for a few seconds before that sexy smirk showed up on his lips.

"You can call me whatever you want, Lucinda, just as long as you know that you're the only one who could ever get away with it."

Before I could ask him anything else, Zig's lips crashed into mine, and I welcomed everything he was trying to give. I don't remember who took off my clothes, either. What I do know is that within seconds, he and I were both back in the shower, naked as the day we were born while "I'm So Into You" by Peabo Bryson played softly in the background.

Zig pushed my back against the cold tile and covered me with his warm body. His hands traveled from my breasts down to my pussy and up to my breasts again. The way his fingers trailed across my skin caused goose-bumps to cover me inside and out. Our kiss deepened as he wrapped his hand around my loose hair and lightly tugged. The passion igniting from the connection we had was so deep that I lost all train of thought.

For the longest, Zig and I had this unexplainable attraction to each other, and now that we were both free of any other distraction, we were sure about to act on it. Lifting one of my legs with his free hand, Zig didn't waste any time using his other hand to guide his dick between my slick folds.

The second his large, mushroomed head breached my entrance, my world and whole being had unwittingly changed. No longer was I Lucci, the girl who belonged to Stax and ruled the streets by his side, or the girl who thought real love only existed with the one man who betrayed me in the end. Nah, I wasn't that girl anymore. The way Zig made love to me against the shower wall, reaching depths I didn't even know existed had me feeling like a completely different woman. The care and love I could feel in each one of his strokes as he dove deeper and deeper into my love box had me experiencing something I'd never felt before. For the first time in my life, I wanted to be more than just the gun-toting, drug-dealing, money-getting hothead that most people feared in these streets. I wanted to be more than just Lucci, a lost girl who latched on to the first nigga who she thought was showing her what it felt like to have the world at your hands. No, I wanted to feel the way I was feeling right now—cherished, loved, protected, and desired. Zig made me feel all of that, and I wanted more.

"I'm so into you. (I'm so into you) I don't know what I'm gonna do (I don't know, I don't know. I....) I'm so into you. (You, you, you, you)."

The second Zig's voice began to sing along with the bridge of the song in my ear, I was done. My body started to shake, and that feeling in the core of my belly started to spread all over me. By the time Zig and Peabo sang the ad libs for the second part of the bridge, I was cumming all over his dick, wetting his entire front side up while the cold water from the shower head beat across his back.

Once Zig couldn't hold off his nut any longer, he released every single drop of his seed inside of me. When I tried to remove myself from his grip, Zig locked his arms around both of my legs and lifted me into the air, wrapping my jelly-like limbs around his waist, dick still buried deep in my womb.

We stared into each other's eyes as he shut the water off, stepped out of the shower, and walked us to his bedroom still connected to one another. I moved my hips a little to position myself at a better angle and could feel his dick slowly coming back to life.

No other words were explained as he laid me down on the bed and pressed his lips softly against mine. I could tell in this kiss that Zig was opening himself to me and allowing me the chance to take him up on his offer of being with a real nigga. As he began to slowly move inside of me again, my mind was already made up. I was now his and would remain his until he didn't want me anymore. Stax wasn't shit when it came to the love department, but he did show me that I was capable of loving someone. Now that I had Zig, I was sure I would get the type of man I deserved, even if it took me this long to realize it. He was definitely for me, and I would always be for him, or die trying to be.

Chapter 25

Bobbi

"What's wrong?" Nav asked as he positioned himself behind me and placed a soft kiss to my neck.

I held up my phone. "I just got another phone call from another unknown number."

"Did they say anything?" He wrapped his arms around my waist.

I shook my head. "No. It was like dead silence. I said hello a couple times, but nothing."

Since the day before, I'd been getting calls to my phone from all different types of numbers. When I did answer my phone, either the call was immediately disconnected, or the person sat on the other end, just listening to me speak.

"Did you write down a few of those numbers for me?" Nav asked, releasing me from his hold and walking over to the table that held all of the equipment we would need for the job that night. "I can shoot them over to this other nigga I know that's into the computer hacking shit and see if he can find anything out."

"Still no word from Cowboy, huh?" It was as if the nigga had disappeared off the face of this earth.

Nav picked up the Glock 19 with laser sight and aimed it at the wall, the green beam zeroing in on every target he pointed it at. "I haven't heard shit. And for his sake, he better hope I don't hear shit."

Nav was still trying to figure out the whole Doughboy connection. Only someone who was privy to our plans could've told him about the job that night, and since Cowboy had been MIA since it all went down, he was the top person on the list.

The intercom buzzed, and both Nav and I turned our attention to the small TV screen above it.

"That looks like Ant," I said over my shoulder as I walked toward it. "Yeah, that's him. You want me to let 'im up, or are we going to meet him downstairs?"

Nav began to pack some things in the duffle bags. "Let him up. Have you heard anything from Lucci and Zig?"

I looked at my phone screen. "Yeah, Lucci text me about ten minutes ago and said that they were on their way. She'll probably be hitting the buzzer the second Ant gets off the elevator lift." I pressed the button on the intercom. "I'm about to let you up."

Ant looked directly up at the security camera and nodded before burying his head back down into his phone.

We had decided that our meetup point would be at Nav's loft again since the area was pretty much deserted and the firehouse was still off limits. There was nothing but a bunch of old brick buildings on this side of town that at one point in time was considered a part of the garment district in Downtown L.A. The only thing that surrounded his second-floor photo studio now were a bunch of abandoned clothes factories that no one had operated in years.

"Have you heard from Tweety?" I asked as I fastened the gun holster around my upper body. We weren't going to take any chances this time around in case someone tried to rob us again.

"Yeah. She said that she would meet us at the store instead of coming here."

"Why?" I questioned, curious to know why she decided to switch things up at the last minute and didn't inform all of us.

Nav shrugged. "She said that Josh decided to stay after closing for some reason, and she needed to take care of him before we showed up."

I wanted to ask how she was going to do that, but I decided not to. Nav already thought I was having second thoughts on robbing BJE because I still had some kind of feelings for Josh, but that was so far from the truth. I wasn't on board with it at first, but after remembering what that asshole and his father were previously planning to do in order to fire my ass only fueled my desire to fuck them over even more. I was going to try to take them for everything they had of extreme value up in that store tonight and leave their asses out to dry. The money aspect of our take didn't really matter as much to me as it did to everyone else. I just wanted to embarrass those Bernfeld sons of bitches as much as they tried to embarrass me.

The bell alerting us that the elevator lift was opening brought me from my thoughts and now had my attention on Ant as he casually walked into the spot. He dapped Nav up and bumped his shoulder before coming over to me and pulling me into a hug.

I stepped out of his embrace after feeling a little uneasy and created some space between us.

"What's up, Bobbi? You ready to get this money tonight?" he asked, eyeing my body from head to toe.

I rolled my eyes and snorted. "As ready as I'll ever be." I picked up the gun Nav had laid out for me and caressed the cool metal with my fingertips.

"I see you and Nav on y'all Bonnie and Clyde shit again with the matching Glocks," Ant observed, his eyes still roaming my body up and down. "You sure you can handle the big-boy guns, Bobbi? You gotta know how to shoot carrying one of those. Maybe the .22 might be a better fit for you."

Before I could respond to his hating-ass remark with a snappy one of my own, my phone started going off. Thinking it was Lucci calling to let me know she was downstairs, I answered the phone without looking at the screen.

"Hey, Looch, park your car and come up. I think Nav wants to go over a few things before we leave."

"Bob . . . Bobbi."

My body froze the second the voice on the other end flowed through the speaker. I opened my mouth to try and say something, but I was speechless. I didn't know whether to cry, yell, or faint.

"Bobbi, please don't hang up. I really need to talk to you. If . . . if you can go somewhere private for a second. Please. And if you're around Nav and his crew, don't let them know you're talking to me."

My eyes immediately went to Nav, who was now looking at something on his TV with Ant. Both of their backs were to me, so I slipped out of the kitchen and out onto the balcony without either of them noticing.

"Kay Kay," I finally was able to say. "Where . . . why . . . Are you okay?"

She was quiet for a few moments. "I'm good, Bobbi. A lot better than what I should be."

"Where are you? Oh my God. We thought—I need to get Lucci on the three-way. We've been worried sick about you, Khalani. We . . . we thought you were dead."

"I should be," she said under her breath but didn't give me time to ask her what she meant. "Look, Bobbi, I need to talk to you and Lucci. It's really important. Is there any way you guys can meet me at the firehouse in about twenty minutes?"

"The firehouse?" I asked, confused as to why she would pick to meet there. "We haven't been there since someone shot it up. Khalani, what's going on? Are you okay? Do you need me to come get you from wherever you are? You're starting to make me nervous."

"Bobbi, please. Can you guys just meet me there and I promise I'll explain everything then. Like . . . where I've been. What I've done. How sorry I am about Di—Diamond." Her voice began to crack, and I knew she was crying.

"Diamond? Why would you be sorry about Diamond, Kay Kay?"

"Please," she begged, sobbing. "I would rather tell you everything in person. Are you and Lucci together right now?"

I looked over my shoulder at Nav and Ant, who had moved back over to the table with our equipment on it.

"Um, no. Lucci and I aren't together right now, but she should be here in about five minutes or so. Kay Kay, you need to tell me something."

"Bobbi, please just wait until we meet up. I want to tell you and Lucci everything together." She sniffed. "So, can you meet me?"

I thought about her question for a few seconds before answering it. "Kay, can this wait until later on tonight? As happy as I am that you're alive, we uh . . . we're actually about to do—"

She cut me off. "Are y'all about to rob another store? Are you guys about to do the BJE job?"

I took the phone from my ear and looked at the number Kay Kay was calling from. Although I didn't recognize the number as one I knew, I do remember it being a number that had ghost-called my phone in the last few days.

"Kay Kay, where are you calling me from?" I asked, finding her line of questioning about the BJE job odd. Her ass hadn't been around for weeks. Hell, we thought she was dead. But then you call from a number unfamiliar to me and ask random questions about me robbing a store? Something didn't seem right.

"Kay Kay where are you calling me from?" I asked again when she didn't answer the first time.

She hesitated for a second. "I'm calling you from a friend's phone. I've been calling you for a couple days now from different numbers. Some of the times you answered and I didn't say anything because I—I was scared. But now . . ." I could hear her rustling with something in the background. "Listen, Bobbi, I've done some terrible things. And I don't know . . ."

"Some terrible things like what, Kay Kay?" I snapped, becoming more frustrated. Even though I was glad to know that Khalani was alive, she was really starting to piss me off with this cryptic conversation. "I'm going to need you to start talking or tell me something before I up and meet you somewhere. You been gone for what? I don't even know anymore. But then you wanna call out of the blue and ask to meet up so that we can discuss some shit? Khalani, you and I both know what it means when someone you know disappears for a while only to resurface and wanna talk about certain *stuff*."

I didn't say anything about the BJE job or robberies, just in case she was on some funny shit and actually recording this conversation.

"I'm not a rat, if that's what you're trying to imply, Bobbi."

I scoffed. "Shit, how can I be sure about that?"

The silence from inside of the loft caused me to turn around to see what Nav and Ant were up to. When my eyes located them, they were intently staring back at me. I could tell from the look on Nav's face that he was wondering who I was talking to. I lifted my finger to let him know that I would be back inside in a few more moments. I also mentally prepared myself for the interrogation I was sure he would give me as well.

"Bobbi, I would never intentionally hurt you, Lucci, or Diamond. You know that, right? You guys are my sisters. Regardless of all the shit I used to talk or how shitty I acted with you guys after I started doing those drugs, you all have always had my back. Right or wrong." She began to cry again. "And before something does happen to me, I want to make sure that you guys know the truth and will find it in your hearts to forgive me for all of the hurt and pain that I've caused."

When the alert on my phone sounded with a text from Lucci, letting me know that she and Zig were downstairs, I knew that I needed to finally end this call. "Look, Kay Kay, I gotta go. Lucci just pulled up, and we have some business we have to handle. So, like I said, maybe we can meet up later on tonight, or maybe even tomorrow?"

As much as I wanted to see her, I still needed some time to think about this meetup. I could tell that something was definitely off now.

"Wait," she rushed. "Tomorrow's not going to work. What I need to tell you will only take a few minutes. I need for you and Lucci to meet me at the firehouse, though, before I can say anything. I'm already on my way there. Can you come please?"

The way she kept pleading had me going against my better judgment, and I agreed to meet up with her. As much as I was leery about Kay Kay's reasons for wanting to meet us at the firehouse, I still needed to lay my eyes on her to make sure this was real.

"Khalani, we'll be there. I think we have a couple minutes to spare. Just let me tell Nav and—"

"No!" She cut me off, her voice rising a few octaves. "You cannot tell Nav. Think of something, anything, to tell him other than you're coming to see me. For your safety and mine, don't tell anyone where you're going, not even Lucci. Just bring her here, and I'll meet you guys inside."

Now Kay Kay was really scaring me. I turned back around to the sliding glass doors and connected eyes with Nav. Ant was no longer next to him, which meant he probably went to go let Lucci and Zig up. I diverted my gaze and then returned it. The expression on Nav's face this time was unreadable and caused a small shiver to run down my spine. What the fuck did Kay Kay need to tell me about this man who I was falling deeply and madly in love with? The fact that she didn't want him or anybody else to know where I was about to go didn't sit right with me. What was it that I wasn't seeing? Where did Nav fit into all this?

"Bobbi, are you still there?" Kay Kay called, breaking me from thoughts.

"Yeah, I'm here. Lucci and I will be at the firehouse in ten minutes. And Kay Kay, I swear on my life, if this is a setup, I will kill you before anybody can place a handcuff on my wrist."

She was quiet for a second. "I promise it's not a setup. At least not in the way you're thinking. I'll see you guys when you get here. Oh, and Bobbi?"

"Yeah."

"Make sure no one is following you either."

Before I could ask her why, she released the call. I looked down at my blank screen as so many thoughts began to run through my head. Although I used to trust

Kay Kay with my life at one point, I wasn't sure if I should trust her now.

The glass door sliding open grabbed my attention.

"Aye, bitch, you ready to get this money?" Lucci asked as she walked out onto the patio and pulled me into a hug. "What's wrong? Why do you look like you just seen a ghost?" she questioned after noticing the expression on my face.

"Because I just did. We need to take a ride somewhere, but it can only be me and you that goes and knows about it. You think we can get out of here for a few minutes without the fellas asking us too many questions?"

Lucci's bright eyes stared at me for a few seconds. "What's going on, Bobbi? What is it that you're not telling me? Is something going on with the BJE job? Where's Tweety's bitch ass?"

I shook my head and began walking back into the loft, voice low enough for only Lucci to hear. "The job is still on, and Tweety had to take care of a little situation with Josh before everything goes down." I looked at the time on my watch. "It's a little after nine now. We're supposed to hit the store in two hours. That's more than enough time for us to go hear what she has to say and then come back."

Lucci grabbed my arm and turned me toward her. "Hear what who has to say?"

I licked my lips and took a quick glance over my shoulder to make sure Nav, Zig, and Ant were still engaged in a discussion.

"I just got a call from Kay Kay," I said, becoming teary-eyed. "And she said she needs to talk to both of us right now. Said she'll meet us up at the firehouse so that we can have this little powwow, but she doesn't want anyone to know."

Lucci looked over my shoulder toward the fellas.

"The look on your face is the same one I had when I heard her voice. In my heart, I don't feel that it's a setup, but I can't help but feel like it might be. Kay Kay disappearing and then popping up after weeks of being gone is . . ."

"Suspect." Lucci finished my sentence in a heated tone.

"Yeah. Do you think we should go? Tell the guys?"

I could tell by the way Lucci was biting her lip and tapping her foot that she was contemplating my question really hard. It wasn't until the guys laughed at something and then turned their attention to us that she whispered her response.

"I think we should go, because I have a few questions of my own that I need Kay Kay to answer. And as far as the guys go, let's leave them in the dark for right now until we hear what Kay Kay has to say."

"What are you guys over here whispering about?" Nav asked as he made his way to where we were standing and wrapped his arms around my waist, kissing me on the forehead. "Who was that on the phone?"

Lucci and I both shared a look before I turned in Nav's arms and kissed him on his lips.

"That was Shauna's ass begging for some money. I guess with Kay Kay dea—I mean still MIA, she needs someone to fund her lifestyle." The lie fell effortlessly from my lips. It was the only thing I could think of that would be a little believable to Nav. He didn't know the extent of what Kay Kay did for Shauna as a big sister, but he knew enough by way of me.

Zig cleared his throat to get Lucci's attention, and when she looked at him, he was definitely relaying something to her with his eyes.

"She asked for a few hundred so that she could get a ticket out of town. Something about she wants to start all over and get her life back on track so that she can get her kids back." I shrugged my shoulders. "I told her I would loan her the money and would be able to give it to her now, since we had some time before the job."

Nav kissed my temple and then my nose. "Do you want me to come with you?"

I shook my head. "Nah. I think it will better if Lucci goes with me. That way we could say goodbye and send her off with well wishes."

"And where are you meeting her at again?" Nav asked, releasing me from his embrace. He walked over to the large oak table in the dining room area and grabbed his keys. "And take my car since you didn't drive yours."

I grabbed the keys he tossed in midair. "Oh, wow. Thanks, babe. We're only meeting her down the street at the Greyhound station, so it won't take us long."

I looked over at Lucci, who was still silently warring with Zig. "Hey, Looch. Let's get out of here so we can come back. Does anyone need anything while we're out?"

A chorus of *no*'s followed me to the door. I turned to see where Lucci was. Zig had pulled her into his arms and into a hug. I could tell he was saying something to her in her ear, but I couldn't hear anything he was saying.

"Make sure you guys are gone no longer than twenty minutes. Tweety just text me and said that everything is still on like we discussed. I need you back here so we can go over the plan one more time and then be out. Cool?" Nav asked, his head buried in his laptop that he had opened up. His calmness about me leaving was a tad bit alarming to me. What was this nigga hiding?

"It's cool, babe," was the last thing I said before heading out the door with Lucci on my tail.

We took the emergency stairs down to the garage, both silently in our own thoughts. It wasn't until we stepped into the night air and far away from the loft that I spoke again.

"You told Zig where we were going, huh?"

As soon as we slipped into Nav's black-on-black Impala, she said, "I had to. He knew you were lying as soon as you mentioned Shauna's name."

I started the engine and put the car in reverse. "How did he know that?"

Lucci pulled down the visor, flipping the mirror cover up, which illuminated the inside of the tinted car with its small light. She pulled her blond hair over her shoulder and began braiding the end of her ponytail.

"He knew that you were lying because he knows that Shauna's ass is dead."

I swerved a little in my lane. "Wait, what? Shauna's dead? How? When? Kay Kay is going to die when she hears this." I shook my head after hearing that news. Shauna wasn't my favorite person in the world, but she was still a little sister to me.

We were almost to the firehouse when a thought crossed my mind. "Hey, Lucci, I have a question. How did you hear about Shauna dying and I didn't?"

She licked her lips and threw her braided ponytail over her shoulder, flipping the visor back up. "Because I killed the trifling bitch and will more than likely be killing Kay Kay's disloyal ass once we get to this meeting."

Chapter 26

Kay Kay

I nervously paced the broken concrete area at the back of the firehouse. The windows were still boarded up like they were the last time I was there, and the grass seemed to have grown another inch or two, almost reaching the middle of my thighs. Different pieces of trash and debris moved around me as the night air began to pick up a bit. I wrapped my arms around my body a little tighter to shield myself from the cold, as well as to try to stop from scratching at my arm. Weaning myself off this drug was starting to become a little harder than I thought it was going to be, but I had to do it if I wanted to change my life. Had to do it if I wanted to get my niece and nephew back.

Thanks to Marvin, I knew exactly where Dajah and Devon were. The foster family who took them in seemed nice, but I could tell that my babies were ready to come home. Ever since the night he sent a car to pick me up, Marvin had been a godsend. Not only did he foot the bill for the hotel I was currently staying in, but he made sure I had three meals a day, a little money in my pocket, and came to check on me whenever he had a little free time in between court cases.

When I asked him why he was being so helpful to a stranger, Marvin told me how he grew up with drug-addicted parents. At one point, he and his brother were in the system and stayed there for a few years until his mother got her shit together and was able to properly care for them. He told me that I reminded him of his mother and the obstacles she had to go through to try to get them back. Even though Dajah and Devon were not biologically mine, I cared for and provided for them like they were. In Marvin's book, I deserved a helping hand, and he wanted to be the one to give it to me.

My eyes darted down to the ringing phone in my hand. I was half expecting it to be a call from Bobbi, telling me that she and Lucci had changed their minds and decided not to come, but it was Mr. Phillips instead.

"Hey," I said just above a whisper as I placed my back against the brick wall, body shivering again. "Did you make it back to your office?"

Marvin said something to his driver and then spoke to me. "Not yet. I kind of waited around a bit out front after dropping you off. I wish you would've let me wait there with you. I know you believe that your friends won't do anything, but you never know what might happen after you explain everything to them."

I didn't tell Marvin the specifics of what I'd been up to in the past few months, but he knew enough. Of what he did know, he never tried to judge me or anything like that. Surprisingly, he was content with being a listening ear and a shoulder to cry on.

"I don't need a babysitter, Marvin. I'm going to be okay. Bobbi and Lucci . . ." I paused for a few seconds. "They're my sisters. I might get my ass beat for my fuck-up, but that's about it. Just don't look at me all crazy when I hop back into your car and have two black eyes and a couple of broken ribs, okay?" I tried to joke and laugh but was met with silence. "Hello?"

"Yeah. I'm here, Kay Kay," Marvin said after a brief pause. "I'm going to pick up a few files and then come right back to where you are, all right? Even if it's an ass whipping you may have to endure, I don't want you to be out there alone. Plus, if you're not messed up too bad, I want to take you out to the Chinese spot I told you about over there off of Wilshire. I think you will love the combination fried rice." He chuckled.

I smiled at the way Marvin could make me feel like I was worth being cared for. Too bad I wasn't going to be able to experience that shit for much longer. I had a feeling that tonight wasn't going to end on a good note. I just prayed that my friends would at least be able to forgive me for all that I'd done.

"Hey," Marvin said, grabbing my attention. "The other day, you said you wanted to talk to me about the man who saved your life. You said that he and I may know each other or something like that?"

My mind went back to the last conversation I had with Doc, when he told me about his sons that he let down because of his drug habit. I wasn't one hundred percent sure that Doc was Marvin's father, but something in my gut kept insisting that he might be.

"Yeah, about that," I started to say, but stopped when footsteps crunching against the gravel caught my attention. "Hey, I think Bobbi and Lucci are here. Can we talk about this later over that combination fried rice you think I will love? I'll call you as soon as we're done if you're not out front already, okay?"

Marvin tried to say something else to me, but I released the call before he could. Raising myself up off the wall, I took a deep breath and watched as two faces I'd known since I was a young girl came from around

the front of the building, both dressed in all black. I
didn't have to wonder what they were going to be doing
after they left from talking with me. Bobbi, with her new
wavy hair and cute, curvy frame, was the first to stretch
her hands out and envelope me in a hug. As soon as I
wrapped my arms around her in return, our bodies began
to shake uncontrollably as tears fell from our eyes.

"Kay Kay, I—Oh my God. I'm so happy you're alive,"
Bobbi whispered into my ear before pulling back and
placing my face between her open palms, examining my
face like a mother would a hurt child.

"I'm happy too." I looked down at the ground and then
back up again. "I missed you guys."

"We missed you too," Bobbi responded, stepping back
a little and looking me over from head to toe. "You lost
some weight, and your hair needs a relaxer or two, but
you look good, Khalani." She laughed.

I scratched at my scalp, a little embarrassed that they
had to see me like this. My clothes were plain—a simple
white T-shirt I picked up from Wal-Mart, with some
faded, worn jeans I was able to find at the Goodwill. My
hair wasn't in the healthy state that it usually was in. I
had a lot of breakage around my edges, and my ponytail
literally stopped at the nape of my neck. Overall, I still
looked like myself, but you could definitely tell that I'd
been through some shit.

"Thanks. You two look great as well."

Once Bobbi was done making sure I was really standing in front of her and not some mirage, she stepped to
the side, putting more space in between us. It gave Lucci
and me a chance to come face to face. I gave her a small
smile and was rewarded with a frown. The look on her
face was the typical Lucci look, never showing emotions,
always trying to be hard, but still beautiful as ever.

I giggled a little as I stepped up to embrace her next, but before I could put my arms around her neck, Lucci slapped the dog shit out of me. My frail body immediately fell to the ground, giving Lucci the perfect opportunity to pounce.

"Lucci, what are you doing?" I could hear Bobbi yell as Lucci's fists moved like fire over my face, chest, and back. I tried to roll myself into a tighter fetal position and block some of the blows but got kneed in the stomach instead.

"Bitch, you didn't think we would ever find out, did you?" she yelled as she zeroed her hits in on the side of my head. "You didn't think we would find out, huh, Khalani?"

"Lucci, please," I cried and begged. My head and ears were starting to ring. "Please, Lucci, I'm sorry. I didn't know." I wasn't expecting us to hop right into this conversation already, but here we were.

"Didn't know what?" Bobbi finally asked in between her yelling at Lucci to let me go.

Lucci stood up after she was satisfied with the damage she'd done to my face and started to kick me in my sides with her steel-toed boots. "Trifling-ass bitch. Your sister told me you set the whole thing up. I didn't believe her at first, but after taking one look at your crackhead-ho ass, I knew it was true. You're the reason my baby is gone." She began to cry, something I'd never seen Lucci do. "The reason Diamond is dead."

"Lucci, what are you talking about?" Bobbi asked after things started to calm down. "Kay Kay didn't kill Diamond or your baby. It was that nigga Doughboy and whoever he had with him."

Lucci turned her whole body around from us and looked up into the sky, the back of her hands wiping at the tears still streaming down her face. "This bitch was working with Doughboy. She's the reason he knew where we were and had the drop on us. I've been sitting on this little bit of info since I murked Shauna's ho ass. I wanted to tell you the night I found out, Bobbi, but Zig thought it would be better if I waited until after this last job. Finding some bullshit like that out will definitely fuck with your mentals. Believe me, because it's been fucking with mine ever since."

"Shauna's dead?" I asked, not believing what I was hearing. My little sister and I didn't agree on a lot of things, but I would never wish death on her, and although I was trying to get full custody of Dajah and Devon, I was hoping that Shauna would get her shit together one day and be the mother that they needed her to be.

"Yeah, that bitch is dead, and your trifling ass is going to be next if I have any say so in it," Lucci snapped.

"No. No." Bobbi shook her head, still not convinced that I could ever betray them like I did. "You're lying, Lucci. Kay Kay, she's lying, right? You wouldn't sell us out like that. No. Not you, Kay Kay. We're best friends. Sisters."

Lucci scoffed. "This bitch ain't no sister of mine. Nah, she just some bitch off of the street to me. Any type of love I had for her left the day her ho-ass sister told me that she was behind this whole thing."

"Nooooo, Kay Kay. Don't tell me that. Don't tell me you did us like that. Lucci, you're lying, right? That's not the truth."

I tried to sit up but fell back down to my side. My head was spinning, and my eyes were seeing double. I licked my lips to try to catch the drool oozing down my chin but was surprised as hell when I realized it was blood falling instead.

"Believe it, Bobbi. The bitch set us up for some dick."

Bobbi's hurt eyes turned to me. "You. You're the reason why Diamond is dead, Khalani?" When I didn't answer her fast enough, she yelled her question at me again. "Are you the reason? And please, please don't tell me it was behind some nigga and his dick."

"It wasn't for his dick," I said slowly. "I . . . I owed the nigga some money." I tried to sit up again and managed to roll over on my hip. With the support of my arm, I propped myself up a bit and tried to endure the pain radiating all over my body. By the way my sides were hurting and how hard it was for me to breathe, I knew that I had at least three ribs broken and possibly a punctured lung.

"I didn't mean for any of that to happen that night. He was supposed to just take . . . take the money. He . . . he killed Diamond right in front of me." I was able to get out in between sobs. Flashes of when Diamond's brain matter and blood splashed across my face rolled over in my mind. "It . . . it was an accident."

"Accident my ass," Lucci hissed before kicking me in my back, bringing me more pain.

I cried out so loud that I could hear my voice echoing in the distance. My decision to meet them at the firehouse may not have been such a great idea. The fact that we were literally in a rundown area where hardly any activity happened was the perfect spot for Lucci to kill me and get away with it if she wanted to.

"This gots to be some sick joke. I can't believe what I'm hearing. Tell me this is a sick joke, Looch," Bobbi begged after walking around me and standing next to Lucci.

"It's not a joke," Lucci advised, placing her hand gently over her stomach. "This bitch is telling the truth, and so was Shauna. But she did it in her last-ditch effort to keep me from blowing her brains out."

I could feel Lucci's eyes on me, but I didn't have the strength to turn fully around and face her. My breathing was getting worse, and the pain in my side was so bad that I started to fade in and out of consciousness.

"Did you know that your sister was fucking around with Stax, Kay Kay? Did you know that she was pregnant with twins for him, while I sat in the hospital and lost my baby because of you?"

I tried to shake my head but was too weak to do it, so I moaned.

"Bitch, I don't understand that shit. Did you fucking know?" Lucci screamed in my ear while pulling my ponytail so far back that she almost snapped my neck. "Use your words and answer the muthafucking question, Kay Kay. Did you know that your ho-ass sister was fucking Stax?"

I coughed and blood spilled from my lips. "I . . . didn't . . . know," I managed to say between breaths. In all honesty, I probably would've kicked Shauna's ass for my best friend if I had known.

When Lucci let my hair go, I fell to the ground and cried some more. I could feel my phone vibrating in my pocket, but I didn't have the strength to answer it.

"Aye, Bobbi, I think we should get the fuck out of here. It's been a little over twenty minutes, so I know Nav and Zig will both be calling us at any moment now. Plus, we need to get our minds right to go handle that business," Lucci said as she slapped the tears from her face.

"You're right, we do need to go, but not just yet. I still need to hear the other shit Kay Kay had to tell us."

Lucci sucked her teeth. "The bitch can hardly breathe, let alone talk. It took her ho ass damn near ten minutes to say she didn't know her sister was fucking my nigga. I say we go and leave her ass to die out here with the rats and roaches. Fuck this bitch."

"No," Bobbi said, leaning next to me and grabbing my hand. "We can't leave without at least trying to see if she can tell us something." She looked down at me. "Kay Kay, when you called, you said you had some information for us. I know it's kind of hard for you to talk right now, so just squeeze my hand once if your answer is yes, and twice if it's no to the questions I'm about to ask you okay?"

I applied some pressure to her hand.

"Okay. My first question is, does whatever else you have to tell us deal with the night Diamond died?"

Ashamed, I squeezed her hand once, and she nodded.

"All right. Does it have something to do with myself and Lucci?"

Squeeze.

"Okay. Are we in some type of trouble? Have you been talking to the Feds?"

Squeeze. Squeeze.

"Are we in some kind of danger?"

Squeeze.

Bobbi and Lucci shared a look.

"Is someone trying to kill us?"

Squeeze.

She closed her eyes for a second and said something under her breath. "Is . . . is it Nav?"

Squeeze. Squeeze.

A look of relief crossed her face, and she exhaled. "Thank God. Um. Okay. Is it someone we know? Someone from the crew?"

Squeeze.

"Man, Bobbi, this bitch ain't even been around to know if somebody is out to get us. For all we know, this can be another setup."

At that exact moment, the noise of someone stepping on a tree twig and breaking it echoed around us. Both Lucci and Bobbi grabbed the guns tucked in their backs and pointed them toward the side of the firehouse.

"Whoever's there, you need to show your face now or get shot the fuck up. Your choice," Lucci called out. When no one rounded the corner, she made her way over to the brick wall to check things out. After not seeing anyone, she walked back over to where Bobbi was kneeling beside me. "I don't trust being here anymore, Bobbi. We need to go now."

"Okay. Just let me ask her a few more questions." Bobbi looked into my eyes. "Kay Kay, I know you're still in pain, but I need you to try and tell us who from our circle is out to get us. You at least owe us that much after everything you've done."

My eyes searched Bobbi's face, and I couldn't help the tears that began to fall down mine. Even with Lucci peering down at me with the most disgusted look in her eyes, I cried. A whole lifetime of memories I shared with them and Diamond were gone down the drain, and I didn't have anyone to blame but myself. I knew that if things were to ever get back on track somehow, that our friendship would never be the same. So, as much as it was hurting me to try to speak, I mustered up all of the strength I had left so that I could tell my friends who the snake was in their crew.

I opened my mouth as the last tear fell from my eye, ready to let them know who else was in cahoots with Doughboy, but before I could say anything, a loud pop went off, and a burst of heat exploded in my chest. The last thing I heard before my eyes closed for the final time was Lucci and Bobbi yelling and their guns cocking in the direction of whoever had just sent the single shot to end my life.

Chapter 27

Bobbi

Quickly rising to my feet and pointing my gun in the direction that the single shot came from, I waited with bated breath for whoever was about to step out of the pitch-black spot underneath the old oak tree. I could make out a masculine frame as it stood still as night next to the tree's large trunk, but I couldn't quite see who it was.

"Whoever you are, throw your gun down to the ground and step away from the tree slowly with your hands up," Lucci hissed, her eyes trained on the same dark area as mine as she tightly gripped the handle of her gun.

While whoever was contemplating whether they wanted to die as well tonight, I looked down for a quick second at Kay Kay's lifeless body and wanted to shed a tear for my friend. On one hand, her disloyalty deserved some type of punishment, but on the other, was death really the answer? The shit she had just told us about being down with Doughboy and betraying the lifelong friendship that we shared had me a little conflicted. We'd already lost Diamond, and with Kay Kay now gone, our foursome was down to two.

The unknown figure threw the gun they used to kill Kay Kay under the flickering back-door light and finally stepped into view. I couldn't tell you who I was expecting it to be, but it sure wasn't who my eyes were boring into right now.

"Nav?" I heatedly scoffed. "What the fuck are you doing here? How did you even know where to find us?"

He put his raised hands down and slowly walked closer to us. Lucci still had her gun aimed directly at his head, while mine was aimed at his heart.

"Look, I have a tracking device on my car. The second you fixed your mouth to say that you were coming to give Kay Kay's sister some money, I knew that you were lying."

"How the fuck did you know that?"

He tilted his head to the side, eyes squinted low as his eyes rolled over my body from head to toe. "Because you tend to bite that sexy bottom lip of yours when you're unsure about something or not telling the truth."

"I do not," I said, my fingers absentmindedly caressing my bottom lip.

Lucci chuckled. "Unfortunately, friend, you do. Your ass has never been a good liar. That's how me, Diamond, and Kay—" She paused for a second. "That's how we knew when you weren't keeping it a buck, too."

I looked between them and rolled my eyes. "Okay, regardless of if I'm a good liar or not, why the fuck are you here? And why the hell did you kill Kay Kay?"

Nav looked at me like I was crazy. "Your girl just admitted to being the one who set us up that night, and you wanna question me on why she's dead?"

Regardless of what Kay Kay did, I felt that it wasn't Nav's job to kill her. Lucci and I had everything handled. This was the one thing that got on my nerves about him. He always had to have his hand in everything. I'm all for the letting-your-man-lead movement, but sometimes I wanted to be in control, and when I expressed that to Nav, I was surprised that he didn't respond with some kind of slick response. Instead, he walked a little closer to me, pressing his chest into my gun.

"I apologize if I made you feel like I didn't trust you to handle the situation, Bobbi. But you gotta understand, babe." He reached out and caressed my cheek with the back of his hand. "You lied to me. And for no reason. How can we continue to build what we have if you choose to keep things like this from me? How can I fully trust you?"

"You can trust me."

"I know. But why not tell me that Kay Kay was alive or that you were going to go see her? Of course, I probably would've hopped in the car with you even after you told me not to, but that's only because of who I am. I'm a protector, and I always protect what's mine. So, when I saw that you weren't headed to the Greyhound station but here instead, I hopped into the van and followed you. I didn't hear the whole conversation, but I did hear everything Kay Kay said about the Doughboy shit, and although it looked like one of you beat her ass good, she still deserved to die. I told you once and I'll tell you again—I don't do well with snake shit, and I'll kill whoever fucks me over."

I understood everything Nav was saying, but still, I felt like it wasn't his place to handle Kay Kay. I lowered my gun and walked closer to him. Tilting my head back, I puckered my lips and waited for him to place his soft ones on mine. The minute he did, my whole body was on fire. I circled my arms around his neck as he circled his arms around my waist, both of us expressing our sincerest apologies in our lip lock. When the kiss deepened and started to get a little heavier, Lucci cleared her throat, interrupting us.

"So, y'all just gon' act like I'm not standing here, or that Kay Kay's dead ass isn't lying right at your feet?"

Nav and I both looked down at Khalani before looking back at each other.

"I'm sorry about your friend, Bobbi. But she had to go."

Although my emotions were battling inside, I nodded my head. "Yeah, I know. But you should've let me and Lucci handle it. Kay Kay was our friend who betrayed us, so it was our responsibility to right that wrong."

We pulled from each other's embrace.

"I understand, but if it makes you feel any better, it wasn't me who pulled the trigger."

"What?" Lucci and I asked at the same time.

Nav walked to where his gun was and picked it up. "It wasn't me who pulled the trigger. Where I was standing at, I didn't have a good shot."

Lucci finally lowered her gun from Nav, but began pointing it back in the direction that he came from. "If it wasn't you that shot Kay Kay, then who was it?"

The sound of someone walking on gravel caught our attention. I raised my gun back up and aimed it at whoever was coming just like Lucci. With my finger on the trigger, ready to bust if need be, I waited for the next person to reveal themselves.

"Aye, we need to get the fuck up out of here if we're going to get this money. Y'all can cry over this bitch later." He pointed at Kay Kay. "Right now, we need to be on our way to our destination. Tweety just hit me and said everything is in place, Nav, so we need to head out."

Nav removed his phone from his pocket and looked at his screen. "Yeah, she hit me too. All right, ladies." He addressed Lucci and me. "We can discuss all of this later, but for now, I need y'all to get your heads in the game. Put y'all guns away and let's go. We do this one last job, and then we're out."

Lucci didn't lower her gun until she saw me lower mine, and when Ant gave us that conniving little smirk of his, Kay Kay's warning about someone trying to harm us flashed in my mind. I assumed it was going to be Tweety's name mentioned because of the way she'd been coming for us ever since we first started working with Nav, but now that I was starting to see that Ant really didn't give a fuck about us either, I was going to keep my eye on him, too.

"I see you're still mad about me killing your friend," Ant smirked and said later when we were in the car, breaking me from my thoughts. When I looked over at him, he shrugged his shoulders. "She had to go, Bobbi. If she could betray you, Lucci, and Diamond like that, what makes you think she wouldn't shit on the rest of us?"

"Nigga, don't you dare speak on any of my friends, dead or alive. Kay Kay may have been a snake, but she wasn't your snake to kill. You mark my words. You gon' pay for what you did," I hissed, and Nav placed his hand on my thigh.

"And who's going to make me pay?" He chuckled. "My nigga Nav is not about to let you kill me, and he's not about to let me kill you, so we might as well just squash the beef now. Besides, I handled something for you that I know you would've never been able to do. You may be mad at me now, but you'll get over it eventually. Being the reason why your friend took her last breath would haunt you for the rest of your life. Trust me, I did you a favor."

"You two need to squash this petty-ass conversation straight up. We're almost at the jewelry store, and I need both of you on your shit."

I rolled my eyes so hard at Nav that I almost broke them bitches. We were sitting in the back of the getaway van and supposed to be going over the details of the job one last time, but my mind was on something else as Nav gave out orders. From what I could hear, nothing much had really changed from the original layout that we came up with. I just prayed that we got out as quickly as we got in.

We pulled up to the front of Bernfeld Jewelry Exchange and parked the van almost half a block down. A few cars lined both sides of the street, helping us to blend in a little more. I looked at the time on my watch. It was quarter to eleven, which meant the security detail would be swinging by to do their nightly patrol at any minute. While we waited for that to happen, Nav passed out earpieces to everyone seated inside the van.

"All right," he said after making sure his earpiece was positioned snugly in his ear. "Once the security detail rolls by, we're going to wait sixty seconds and give them some time to turn the corner before we hop out and go to our spots. Myself and Lucci will make our way to the back of the store, while Ant and Bobbi go through the front. Tweety already set it up so that the timer unlocks the door 11:05 on the dot, which is usually the time the night guard inside comes to the front to make sure everything is clear outside. Once you two enter into the second security door, you have to wait fifteen seconds before pressing the handle to let you guys into the showroom. If you press the handle before fifteen seconds, the alarm will go off and lock you in. Do you understand?"

I nodded my head when Nav looked at me. "Yep. Got it."

"Now, Ant,"—He turned to his friend—"while Bobbi makes her way to the back to let us in, you will be in the showroom, starting on the smashing and grabbing. The store has the invisible laser beams set in every display. The little black box in the middle of each case is how you tell whether or not the beams are on." Nav held up a replica box. "Red means beams, green means you're good to go. In the event that the green dot turns back red, I need you to grab everything you already have and make your way to the back exit, where the two getaway cars will be positioned."

"Who's driving the getaway cars since we're down two people now?" Ant asked. He cut his eyes at me and then winked.

Nav wiped his hand over his handsome face and let out a frustrated breath. "Zig will be driving the car that's waiting on the north end, and one of his buddies I checked out will be driving the other on the south."

"Zig and one of his buddies? Since when do you recruit niggas and not have me look into them? Can we even trust them?" Ant questioned, disgust in his tone.

"Since when do you think it's okay to question my decisions?" Nav returned. "Nigga, you must've forgotten that this is and has always been my crew. I run it how I want to run it. You work for me just like everybody else in this muthafucking van. If you got a problem with that, you can hop your ass out right now and get dealt with later."

All eyes turned to Ant. When he didn't say anything in return, Nav continued.

"Now, like I was saying, in the case that everything runs smoothly, we will have no more than ten minutes to try and pull this whole thing off. Bobbi, you and Tweety will handle the big vault. I will handle the smaller safes in the offices and keeping track of time. Lucci, you will take care of the room where they store the custom orders ready for pickup. We all have our earpieces in. If you see or hear anything that is out of the norm, speak up and let me know. We need to keep our eyes and ears open and make sure our surroundings are clear. We don't wanna go out like the last time, but just in case, no one is to leave the building until everyone has done their part or I say so. Do you all understand?"

A chorus of "Yes, sir" echoed around us after Nav finished his little speech.

"What about the van?" Lucci asked as she crawled from the front seat and into the back with us. I could see headlights shining in the distance and knew the patrol car was about to roll by.

"The van will be torched and burned by the time we make it back to the meetup spot, so you don't even have to worry about it," Nav informed. "All right, the patrol car is about to pass. Is everybody ready?"

I looked down at myself and made sure my boots were tied and my over-the-shoulder bag was secured. Once I tucked my gun into the holster, I pulled my diamond-studded ski mask over my face. Lucci followed suit and did the same. We shared a quick smile before holding one another's hands and both saying a quick prayer. Once we were done, I released Lucci's hand and looked at Nav. He had a small smile on his face and a look of admiration in his eye.

"I'm glad I came into this store all those months ago and met you. One of the best days of my life." He pulled the strap of my bag and placed his lips against mine. "When this is all over and done, I'm going to give you the world and then some, Bobbi. You deserve it for riding with me through all of my craziness and being the Bonnie to my Clyde."

I kissed his lips one last time before reaching up and pulling his plain black mask down over his face. "I love you, Naveen, and I can't wait to let you spoil me."

He chuckled and placed his forehead to mine. "I love you too," was the last thing he said to me before looking down at his watch and pushing the back doors of the van open.

"All right, it's go time," Nav said over his shoulder. "Everyone knows what they have to do, so let's do it."

One by one, we removed ourselves from the van, checking our surroundings and making sure we blended in with the night. Nav and I shared one last look before he and Lucci took off on the side of the building, while Ant and I made it to the front of the store.

Just like Tweety said, the doors opened at 11:05 on the dot. After waiting fifteen seconds in the second door, Ant pushed it open, and we walked into the showroom.

I looked around the dimly lit room from wall to wall as memories of my time working there started to flood my mind. Nothing much had changed. The place was still exquisitely breathtaking with its modern architecture and luxurious decor.

"Oooh-weee. Damn, it smells like money in here. I can't believe it took you this long to rob these muthafuckas. As soon as they would've offered me a job, I would've been robbing their asses blind," Ant mentioned as he looked around at the different display cases. "I can just imagine the type of muthafuckas that come in and shop here on a daily basis, dropping big bands on some shit they'll forget all about in a month or two."

I ignored his statement as I began to walk toward the back of the store. We had a job to do where the time was limited, and Ant knew that.

"Aye, I know the clock is ticking, but can I ask you something before you go?"

I slowed my pace down a little with my back still facing Ant, my eyes glancing down at the fast-moving numbers on my watch. "What is it?"

He took a few seconds, but then asked, "Hypothetically speaking, had I approached you before Nav had the opportunity, would you have given me the same chance you're giving him?"

I stopped and turned toward Ant with the stankiest look on my face. Don't get me wrong for one second, Ant wasn't ugly in the least. He just wasn't my type—light skin with thin, pink lips, an average-sized body with the boy-next-door kind of looks. I preferred a much darker and smoother blend, a nigga who exuded confidence and a certain kind of cockiness when he walked into the room. Someone who gave the orders instead of taking them. Nav had all of that, which was why he had me at first sight. Ant, unfortunately, didn't.

"No," was my honest answer as we looked each other in the eyes.

"Yeah, okay," Ant scoffed and turned his head away, but not before I caught the devilish curl in his lip. "You better get going before Nav starts to wonder what's taking you so long."

I looked back down at my watch. A whole minute and a half had already passed. Nav for sure was going to question my tardiness. I just hoped he would hold off on wanting answers until we were done with what we had to do.

I damn near sprinted to the back of the store to open the back door, but by the time I got there, Tweety had already let Lucci and Nav in. All eyes turned to me as I froze in place. Tweety had a small smirk on her lips, while Lucci waited to see what my next move was going to be. I opened my mouth to give them an explanation on what the holdup was, but Nav held his hand up, cutting me off.

"Save it for later, Bobbi. Right now, you and Tweety need to get down to the vault, while Lucci and I get to where we need to go."

I wanted to say something but decided to keep it to myself until later. The sooner we got done with this job, the faster I could get the fuck on.

Chapter 28

Bobbi

"So, what took you so long up there?" Tweety asked as we entered the room holding the big vault. "You do know we're on a strict time schedule, right?"

I rolled my eyes as I placed my bag on the floor and walked up to the vault door. "Do you have the access codes?" I asked with my hand stretched out over my back, looking at the keypad. "I know Mr. Bernfeld liked to change them constantly. Are you sure the numbers you have are the right ones?"

Tweety handed me a piece of paper with an array of numbers scribbled on it. "The top row of numbers is the one you put in first, followed by the row of numbers beneath that." She smacked her lips and sassed, "Oh, and to answer your question, yes, I'm sure the numbers are correct. I know Nav probably let this slip a time or two, but I'm good at what I do. Plus, men tend to give you anything you want when your dick-sucking skills have their toes curling and their souls leaving their bodies."

I rolled my eyes again at Tweety's dumb ass and began to type the numbers of the code in. She only said her little comment to try to get some kind of reaction out of me, but I didn't have time for that right now. The bitch was itching to get slapped again, and I couldn't wait to give it to her.

"You can keep rolling your funky-ass eyes all you want. That shit doesn't faze me."

"I wouldn't give a fuck if it did, Tweety. Now, can you please shut the fuck up and stop talking to me? We only got one thing to do down here, and I don't need to hear your hating-ass mouth to do it."

Tweety smacked her lips. "And to think Nav picked you over me."

I laughed. "You still salty even though he's checked your ass over a dozen times about that shit. You know what?" I asked, turning to look at her. "Instead of worrying about what Nav and I have going on outside of this job, did you handle everything you were supposed to handle in here?"

She looked at me like I was dumb. "Girl, this isn't the first time I've robbed a store. Everything has been taken care of. I made sure of that myself. Rigging the security camera feed so that it plays prerecorded footage wasn't rocket science. The guards on duty have been dealt with, and as far as Josh goes, I slipped something into his drink after we fu—I mean, after we discussed some things earlier. That should have him out for at least a few hours. So, the answer to your question is yes, bitch, everything here is handled."

"Yeah, okay," I said sarcastically before turning back to the vault door and rolling my eyes for a third time. I could hear Tweety mumbling something under her breath, but as long as she kept that shit to herself, we were good.

Once I entered the last number into the pad, the locking mechanism clicked behind the large wheel, allowing me to spin it around until the door popped open. After some assistance from Tweety, we were able to pull back the door and enter into the confined space. Diamonds, rubies, and rare jewels from all over the world sat on top of black velvet trays, while the more expensive pieces, like the Heart of the Ocean replica and Red Scarlet necklaces, were draped over black velvet necklace stands.

"Oh my God," Tweety whispered as she picked up the Harry Winston marquise-cut diamond bracelet and wrapped it around her wrist. "I'm going to take this as a parting gift."

I removed the bracelet from her hand before she could fasten the clasp and gently placed it back in its box. "You can't take that. Not unless you want to get us all caught. These pieces right here,"—I pointed to the collection of jewelry sectioned off—"all of these have tracking devices in them. These are the pieces famous people borrow for award shows and shit. Not only do they come with a personal security detail, but you also need a special kind of key to take them off. So please don't try on or touch anything else over here. Our focus should be on the loose jewels and whatever pieces they have in the lock boxes. I distinctly remember telling your ass that at Nav's loft."

Tweety didn't respond. She just walked over to the uncut diamonds scattered on one of the tables and began placing them in her bag. We went around the entire space in less than four minutes, grabbing any and every piece of jewelry I knew would get us our money's worth. By the time we were done, half of the vault was cleared out, and I estimated that we had a little over ten million in our bags.

"Hey, everybody, we have approximately two minutes and thirty seconds before the alarm codes on the doors switch. I need all of you to stop what you're doing and head to the back exit now. Do you copy?" Nav's voice floated through the earpiece.

"Yeah, we copy," I said after looking over at Tweety, who nodded her head in agreement.

We grabbed our things and began to make our way back upstairs. By the time we got to the back exit, Lucci, Ant, and Nav were walking up at the same time.

"Yo, this was one of the smoothest licks we ever hit. I know collectively between the four of us we probably just came up on twenty-five mil easy." Ant rubbed his hands together and laughed. "Aye, Bobbi, how much do you think you and Tweety snatched out of that vault? I know that's probably where all the good shit was."

"Man, shut the fuck up, Ant," Nav snapped. "You talk too fucking much. Right now, your focus should be on getting the fuck up out of here before all of our asses end up in jail."

Ant didn't say anything in return, but the mean mug on his face told me that he didn't like the way Nav had just checked his ass in front of us. When he cut his eyes in Tweety's direction, she quickly turned her head the other way.

"All right. Once we go out these doors, you all know which way to go." Nav looked down at his watch, and I looked down at mine. We had a little over a minute before the code change. "Tweet, are you sure you're gonna be able to pull the rest of the plan off all by yourself?" We all looked over at the three security guards hunched over at the security desk, knocked out from whatever she had injected them with.

"Yeah. Don't worry about me. I got everything on my end covered." She emphasized that last part of her statement before looking over at me. "Y'all just get on outta here. I got it," she advised before removing her bag from her shoulder and handing it over to Nav.

"All right, bet. Lucci and Bobbi, give Ant your bags."
We handed him our things. "You two go straight to the
meetup spot. Once we stash this shit, Ant and I will meet
you guys there. We'll part ways, then catch up in a few
days to divvy up the take. Anybody got any questions?"

When no one responded, Nav nodded his head and
walked out of the door. Lucci, Ant and I followed suit,
while Tweety stayed behind. I looked to the left and the
right as soon as we made it down the small flight of stairs.
Both getaway cars were in position and ready to go.

"Aye, be careful. You owe me a day of spoiling," I told
Nav, and he laughed.

"I always am," he said, turning around to face me.
"Now, stop talking and go get your ass in the—" Nav's
face took on a blank expression after his words were cut
short. His eyes rolled into the back of his head, and his
body fell into mine.

"Nav!" I yelled frantically as I tried to keep him from
falling to the ground. When I looked up to ask for some
help, Ant was pointing a gun in my face.

"Your pistol. Take it from your holster and throw it
over here."

I stalled for a few seconds but eventually did as he
said.

"Now, take both of the bags from around Nav's ass and
hand them to me," he ordered.

"Wait, what?"

"You gotta be kidding me," Lucci hissed.

He aimed the gun at Lucci. "You know, I used to
think you were fine as hell, but your smart-ass mouth
killed all that. Plus, you always wanna be the nigga in
the relationship. I could never deal with a bitch like you."

"A bitch like me?" Lucci smirked. "Why? Because I have more balls than you ever could?"

"You wish you had as much balls as I did."

Lucci laughed. "Says the fraud-ass nigga who had to betray his homeboy to get his hands on some money."

Ant frowned. "Maybe, but I was going to get my hands on this money regardless. This plan has been in motion for years. It just made it a lot easier when Nav decided to have me look into y'all background so that he could add y'all to the team."

"Look into our background?" I asked, and Ant scoffed.

"As articulate as this nigga is, do you really think that he would hire four bitches to help him rob a jewelry store and not know anything about you? You"—He pointed the gun back at me—"were the key to all of this. Nav and I cased this store for a few months before these racist assholes considered even hiring you. We couldn't figure out how we would get the job done without getting caught up, but then you started working here. The first time I saw you, I knew you'd be down. Bitches like you could never resist coming up on some money." He took his vibrating phone out of his pocket and looked down at the screen before answering it. "Yeah, Doughboy. She called you? . . . Uh-huh, it's already done. Bring the vans back here. . . . Okay. Gone."

"Doughboy?" I asked, remembering the name of the muthafucka who killed Diamond and finally putting two and two together. "Wow. So, it was you who set us up that last time too? You're the real reason why Diamond was killed."

Ant rolled his eyes. "Oh, it wasn't just me. Kay Kay had a hand in that shit also. If it wasn't for her, none of this shit probably would've popped off the way it did. When she stole from my nigga Dough and he put that hit out on her head, that was all the ammo I needed to get my plan into motion."

"So, you basically used her?" Lucci asked.

"Hell yeah. Dough wasn't having any luck catching up with her until I pointed him in the right direction. I thought shooting up her mama's house would've made her come sooner, but that didn't work. So, we ended up having to snatch her up. Don't get me wrong, the bitch didn't want to do it, but you know how fiends get once you start taking their candy away."

"You muthafucka!" Lucci lunged at Ant but was stopped when he pointed the gun back in her face.

"There you go again, thinking you can take me on heads-up like a nigga. You better stay in your place, Lucinda, or I'm going to kill you faster than I intend to."

I looked down at Nav when I thought I felt some kind of movement, but I was sadly mistaken. His stiff body lay lifeless across my lap, and I could feel the tears building up in my eyes.

"Why, Ant, after all the shit Nav has done for you?"

"You can be so damn dramatic sometimes, Bobbi. That shit is a major turnoff. You know that?"

I opened my mouth to respond but looked up toward the end of the alleyway when a pair of headlights flashed instead. The black van that slowly crept up stopped next to the first getaway car and let off a few rounds, killing Zig's homeboy instantly. When headlights from the other direction flashed across the wall, I turned around and looked at the car Zig was in and noticed that the driver-side door was already open.

"Yo, boss man," the driver of the van yelled. "Ain't nobody in this car."

Ant shook his head and waved for the driver to come down to where we were. "That means the nigga must've hopped out when he saw what was going down. Take the van and drive around the corner a few times and look for the muthafucka. He couldn't have gotten too far. Make sure when you do find him, though, you kill him. We don't need no loose ends."

"I got you," the Terminator-looking nigga said before reversing the van down the alleyway and disappearing out of sight.

"Your little boyfriend is going to die tonight one way or the other, so you might want to call him and have him come back," Ant told Lucci.

She smacked her lips and crossed her arms over her chest. "I ain't telling him shit. You better hope your little minions know what they're doing by going after him, though. Zig isn't your average nigga."

"Every nigga can get got," Ant said before looking at the other van, which was still at the end of the alleyway. "Aye yo, Dough, bring the van down here and come get these bags."

The van slowly made its way down to where we were and stopped. The fat muthafucka whose face I could never forget stepped out of the driver's seat and opened the side door, where two more niggas hopped out. After grabbing the three bags Ant handed to him, he looked down at the two bags Nav still had over his body.

"What about those bags?" he asked.

Ant took a second from texting on his phone and looked over at me. "Take them off of him, and if she tries to jump bad, shoot her ass in the head."

Doughboy looked at me and smiled as his two home-boys grabbed hold of Nav's legs and pulled him off my lap. Instead of rolling him over to unhook the bags, Doughboy took out a big hunting knife and cut both straps.

"Where the fuck is she?" Ant asked no one in particular before walking back up the small flight of stairs and banging on the metal door. One minute later, Tweety, now dressed in all black like us, came waltzing out of the door looking like a million bucks. I could see the Harry Winston bracelet sparkling on her wrist, as well as a few other of the exclusive pieces I had told her not to touch.

"Hey, baby," she cooed and kissed Ant on the lips. "Is everything taken care of?"

Ant smacked her on her ass and nuzzled his face into her neck, which caused her to giggle. "Yeah, just about. We just need to take care of these two bitches, and then everything is gravy."

Tweety looked at me and Lucci with a smirk on her lips and waved. She walked down the steps with her eyes still trained on us, stumbling a little when she tripped over one of Nav's legs. Her eyes immediately opened in shock when she noticed him laid out on the ground, but she quickly corrected the expression on her face when Ant came and stood next to her.

"Why is he on the ground?" she asked Ant. "And why isn't he moving?"

"Because, baby, we don't need him anymore. I told you when I brought you in on this plan that Nav had to go. You know that nigga would've never let us live a happy life if he was still alive."

"But that wasn't the plan, Anthony. You said we were going to rob the store, frame them, kill them, and then leave the country. You never said anything about Nav not coming."

"Man, Tweety, Nav would've never been on board with any of this shit."

"How do you know that?"

He wiped his hand over his face, frustrated. "Because he loves this bitch." He pointed at me. "This sick fantasy you have about y'all being together, you need to forget about it. Nav would never want you. I'm the one who's always been here for you. It was always my shoulder I let you cry on when that nigga basically said fuck you. Why can't you get that through your damn head?"

Tweety looked down at Nav's body again, and I could see the different emotions crossing over her face. "He wasn't supposed to die, Ant," she said a little above a whisper.

"What did you say?"

"I said he wasn't supposed to die," Tweety repeated before pulling a gun from behind her back.

"Tweety, what the fuck are you doing? Put that shit down before you fuck around and shoot me on accident, pissing me the fuck off even more," Ant said in a cocky tone. "Don't make me second guess bringing your ass on."

"This wasn't the plan," she mumbled to herself. "You would never be Nav. He was always two steps ahead."

"Tweety, what the fu—" was the last thing Ant was able to get out before Tweety raised her gun and shot him directly between his eyes.

As the gunshot rang out, it seemed like time stood still for a few seconds. It wasn't until a barrage of bullets came flying from the north end of the alleyway that reality set back in. The shock of what had just happened turned into pure chaos. Doughboy's friends tried to take cover, but they were hit before they could. When

Doughboy realized that he was by himself and didn't have anywhere else to go, he tried to jump his ass back into the van and take off, but before he could rev up the engine, I grabbed my gun off the ground and sent two hot ones into the side of his head.

Tweety continued to shoot back and forth with the other shooter, who actually turned out to be Zig, until she made it back up to the jewelry store exit. She started to dip back through the door and out of the line of fire but froze when her attention was shifted to something at the bottom of the stairs.

Taking the opportunity I would probably never get again, I raised my gun and aimed it right at Tweety after realizing that Zig had stopped shooting too. The bitch wasn't about to get away from me, especially when she was in on this setup the whole time. Tweety's ass was just as responsible for Diamond's, Nav's, and Kay Kay's deaths as the other muthafuckas lying on the ground now.

I applied pressure to the trigger and was just about to take my shot when something out of the corner of my eye caught my attention. Looking down at my chest, I noticed a small green dot aimed at my heart. When I looked in the direction that it was coming from, I couldn't believe my eyes. I opened my mouth to ask what was going on, but I felt a burst of heat explode through my body instead.

The last thing I remember hearing before falling to the ground and closing my eyes was Lucci screaming my name and the green dot being aimed at my head.

Epilogue

Lucci

"All right, ma'am, so you ordered two two-piece baskets, both breasts and wings, an order of fried clams, extra tartar sauce, a side of rice, potato salad, fritters, and banana pudding. Is that right?" the girl behind the thick glass window asked, repeating my order.

"It is. But can you also add an extra side of potato salad, a two-piece fish basket, and an extra side of fritters? Extra powdered sugar, please."

She nodded her head as she entered my order into the register and then told me my total. After paying for the food, I moved to the side and allowed the customer behind me to step up to the window.

"What's up, Lucci?" One of the corner boys named Thumper greeted me as he walked into the small chicken spot. "I thought you were gone already. Haven't seen you around in the hood in a minute."

I placed my hand over my small belly and smiled. "Now, you know Zig would kick my ass if I stepped foot over there and even tried to chop it up with y'all. That nigga swears I can't hold my own, pregnant and all."

Thumper laughed. "We both know that's a lie. I done seen you beat a bitch's ass for looking at you too long. And do you remember that time you whipped out the pistol on ole boy in broad daylight because he was a nickel short when you came to collect your money? Yo, I ain't never feared no broad before that day, but you, you had my ass a little scared."

"Yeah. Those were the good old days," I recalled, shrugging my shoulders. "But at some point, you have to let it go, especially when things that are far greater than your own life pop up unexpectedly." I gently rubbed my eight-months-pregnant belly when my mini-me started to kick wildly. "Look, she already starting to trip. She ain't heard her daddy's voice all day, and her little bad ass is going to tear my insides up until she does."

Thumper nodded his head. "She already running thangs like her mama. Well, I'm not gon' hold you up any longer. Plus, I need to order this food. I'm hungry as fuck. I'll see you around, Lucci. Congratulations on the baby, and make sure that nigga Styles keep y'all shit running as smoothly as it does when he takes over. My pockets stay fat, and I wanna keep it that way."

"They will," I assured him before hearing the girl behind the window call my number, signaling that my order was ready. After getting all the bags she handed me and making sure that all of my food was in there, I carried the large order over to my car and set it in the back seat. Once I slid into the driver's side, I reached back to grab a few fries and put the car in gear.

Taking a more scenic route, I drove past and around a few streets in L.A. that I surely would miss once Zig and I moved to our new home out of the country in a couple of days. The construction for our six-bedroom, four-bathroom beachfront house was finally done, and I couldn't be more excited to go. Although I loved my city, there were too many bad memories for me there, and I needed a fresh start.

It had been a whole year since Diamond Mafia ended, and I couldn't be happier. The night that we robbed Bernfeld Jewelry Exchange had turned out to be one of our biggest licks. Crazy how we almost lost it again because of Ant's snake ass. But in the end, everything turned out to be more than fine.

With my portion, I was able to pay off the Jamaicans for the product that Stax stole, as well as flood the streets again with that pure-cut shit my crew was known for having. Zig easily transitioned into the head nigga in charge, while I played my part more in the background these days. No longer was I making runs, collecting money, or busting down doors when niggas weren't acting right. Zig made sure I stayed my ass out of the streets. The nigga threatened to shoot me if I didn't.

Pulling up to the house on Sixth Ave., I hopped out of my car and was immediately greeted by all the niggas standing on the porch, shooting dice and drinking beers. A few of the new workers lustfully stared at my pregnant ass as I walked by, while the ones who knew better kept their eyes to themselves.

With food in hand, I ignored the low catcalls as I walked around to the back of the house and punched in the key code. As I entered through the back door, I was expecting to see a kitchen full of people cutting and bagging up dope, but I was surprised when I didn't see anyone. The whole place had been cleared out, and not a single soul was in sight. Product was nowhere around, and the kitchen had been cleaned spotless. I looked around, confused. This was one of my top trap houses. Where the fuck was everyone at?

As I walked farther into the house, I began to notice that a lot of things were different. The old cum-stained furniture in the living room was gone and replaced with some new shit. The dining room had a beautiful eight-chair dining set in it, and the bathroom was clean and decorated nicely.

When I got to the door of the master bedroom I had turned into an office, I knocked lightly before letting myself in. My eyes swept across the large, empty space and immediately started to tear up. There were candles lit all around the room. The smell of lavender surrounded me as soon as I stepped inside.

"Zig," I called out as I made my way over to the massage table and placed the bag of food on top. "Babe, where are you? What is this?"

As soon as the words left my mouth, the sound of wind chimes began to flow through the speakers, followed by the melodious humming of K-Ci Hailey as Jodeci's "Forever My Lady" started to play.

"Babe," I breathlessly said as tears began to build up in my eyes. "Zy'aire."

"What are you in here crying about, woman?" Zig asked from behind me, his deep voice vibrating in my ear. The heat from his body transferred to mine, sending a tingly feeling down my spine.

"I'm not crying," I lied, wiping my tears away. "You know my allergies have been hell during this pregnancy."

He wrapped his hands around my waist and palmed my belly. "Allergies my ass. How's my baby?"

I blushed. I loved when Zig asked me that. "Well, I'll be better once I can dig into that Jim Dandy's. I've been craving those fritters for a few days now."

Zig started rubbing on my stomach when the baby started to kick.

"And as far as she goes, her little butt has been killing my insides since this morning. You know how she gets when she doesn't hear your voice."

Zig smiled and kissed my neck before walking in front of me and kneeling down to the ground. After raising my shirt and lowering my tights a little bit, he pressed his lips to my belly and whispered whatever sweet words he normally did to get our daughter to calm down with the kicking. As soon as he was done, he kissed my belly again, and the little heffa hadn't kicked me since.

"What do you say to her?" I asked as he led me over to the massage table and placed the food on the floor.

"I say what she needs to hear. I tell her how beautiful she's going to be, like her mommy, and how much I can't wait to meet her. I tell her how much I love her already, even though I haven't met her yet. I also tell her to stop hurting my woman or I'm going to whip her little ass."

I playfully pushed Zig's shoulder. "No, you do not."

He started to remove my clothes, and I didn't question it. Hell, I hardly ever questioned Zig's moves. I'd learned a long time ago to follow his lead. Zig had shown me in more ways than one that he would never do anything to hurt me or let anyone else hurt me. This man was so different from Stax, and oftentimes, I got angry with myself for not giving him the chance all them years ago. A lot of things probably would've been different in my life had I chosen Zig instead of Stax when I was younger, but I couldn't keep harping over any of that. He was mine now, and I intended on keeping it that way.

After getting me fully naked, Zig helped me up onto the table and grabbed a bottle of oil. Starting at my feet, Zig massaged every inch of my body until I damn near drifted off to sleep. If it wasn't for my phone ringing, I probably would've been dead to the world already.

"Babe, can you pass me my cell, please?"

Zig stopped massaging my shoulders for a second and took my phone out of my purse. I stretched my hand out so that he could hand it to me, but he ignored the call and turned my phone off instead.

"Why did you do that? That was probably—"

He cut me off. "It was. But you can call back after I finish doing what I'm doing."

"But, babe, that could've been important. Give me the phone. I promise you can have your way with me after this one call."

"Nah. I'm going to finish massaging your body, and then I'ma get me some pussy. You can call back later, like I said."

I blushed again. "A full body massage *and* some pussy. With your horny ass, that means I won't be returning any phone calls until tomorrow."

Zig chuckled. "Aye, blame that on yourself. You know how a nigga zones out when he's knee-deep in your shit. I can't help it."

"Oh, so is that what this is all about, too?" I waved my hands around the room. "Babe, don't get me wrong, I'm enjoying my massage and all, but why did you change the house up? Is everything okay? Where is everybody?"

Zig poured more oil into his hand and started to rub my belly. "Lucci, you know me well enough by now to know that I don't have to butter you up to tell you shit. I'm catering to you right now because you're my woman who's pregnant with my baby, and you deserve it."

"Awww, babe, for real?"

"Real shit. And to answer your question, this house, as well as all of the other ones you used to run work out of, have all been shut down as of last week. The only reason them niggas are outside right now is because they just helped move the last of this furnitue in. I told Styles that he needed to find his own spots to cook, pack, and deal out of. Since we're both getting out of the game, I don't want anything to fall back on us for shit. The Feds couldn't find or come up with enough evidence to charge you with anything, but there's still no telling what that snitch nigga Stax had set up. So, for that reason alone, all of the spots are getting put up for sale. The money made from those properties will go into baby girl's college account, and then that's it. I'll still deal with the connect on Styles' behalf, but other than that, we are officially no longer in the game."

Zig leaned down and kissed my belly, and then came up to my lips. "I asked you to give me a year, and you gave it to me. Did I deliver on my word or what?"

I giggled. "Yeah, you delivered."

Zig looked down at me with a serious expression on his handsome chocolate face. "You know I love you, right?"

I nodded my head. "I do know that, Zig."

He pressed his lips against mine, and my body shivered. "And I would lie, die, steal, and kill for you, Lucci."

"I know. I would do the same for you."

He smiled and nuzzled his nose into my neck, inhaling my scent. "After we move into the new house, I don't care if it's small and intimate or something big and grand, but I want you to marry me. You and my daughter will share the same last name before she enters into this world. You good with that?"

Although the proposal wasn't one most girls would wish for, it was just right for me.

"Yes, Zig, I will marry you," I responded as the tears started to build up again. "Damn these allergies."

We shared a laugh.

"As long as those are tears of happiness, I don't care about you crying at all, Lucci," Zig said before pulling me up, wedging his thick body between my legs, and tonguing me the fuck down. With me already naked, that heated kiss easily led to Zig removing his clothes and ramming his beautiful dick inside of me. He and I fucked in each and every one of the redecorated rooms until my pregnant body couldn't take it anymore. We didn't head to the home we shared until a few hours later, when Zig took me down one last time before he knocked out.

As I sat in our bed and watched him sleep, my mind replayed all the shit that had happened in the last year and a half. Losing my best friends back to back were some of the worst days of my life; however, I could honestly say that I wouldn't trade anything that had happened to me for the world.

Not only were we a group of friends who decided to make a better life for ourselves by robbing jewelry stores, but we were a family. Even with Kay Kay betraying us the way that she had, she was still our sister, and my heart ached every day from missing them. Things probably wouldn't have been the same had we all made it out alive; however, it still would've been Diamond Mafia for life.

Bobbi

"You have reached Lucci. Leave a message after the tone, and I'll call you back whenever I get a minute."

"Damn it, Lucci," I groaned, frustrated. "Answer your damn phone."

I released the call before the beep could sound and threw my phone down on the pillow beside me. This was my fifth time I had tried calling Lucci and the call went straight to voicemail after the first ring. Either she was ignoring my calls, or she let her battery die again. Either way, I needed to speak to her and let her know that the movers were officially done with moving her new stuff in. Because she was still in the States, Lucci and Zig left it all up to me to make sure the building of their new home and the placement of their new furniture was done exactly the way that they wanted. I followed their instructions to a T but did my own thing with the nursery. Zig wanted to surprise Lucci with an explosion of pink for my little niece's bedroom, but I changed that real quick. Lucci hated pink, so I used a soft green and yellow instead.

Standing up from my relaxed position on the bed, I walked over to the sliding glass door that led out to the balcony and looked over the beautiful ocean view before me. I would've never imagined myself being there and living in that moment had it not been for meeting Nav and starting Diamond Mafia with my girls.

My fingers caressed the small wound I had hidden underneath the new tattoo I got a few weeks ago. It was only by God's grace that the bullet meant to pierce me in my heart actually ended up going through my shoulder instead.

It wasn't until I woke up a day or two after I got shot that Lucci recounted everything that happened. Not only did we get away with stealing over twenty-five million dollars' worth of jewelry from BJE, but we also recouped some of the money we lost from the last heist Doughboy and his team got us on.

When Zig rounded up some of his boys and ran up in Ant's house, they found a few duffle bags filled with money, as well as some of the high-end pieces he couldn't get off from the last lick. Ant knew that Nav's jewelry connect wasn't going to fuck with him unless Nav was there, so he had to hock the gems elsewhere. The buyer he found couldn't handle the large transaction and only covered what he could. Not only did Ant fuck over Doughboy and his crew when it came to their cut of the lick, but he ended up fucking over himself. Ultimately, Ant lost a good friend, what could've been a great family, and his life. I hoped the nigga was burning in hell for all the trouble that he caused, and I couldn't wait to see him again. Even in death, I still owed him for the way he did Kay Kay, and that nigga's soul was gonna pay.

The sound of two voices giggling behind me caused me to turn around. When I looked back into my bedroom, both Devon and Dajah were jumping on my bed.

"What did I tell you two about doing that? Get down before I cancel the beach day we're supposed to have today."

Dajah immediately sat down at the foot of my bed, while Devon continued to jump.

"Devon, what did I just say?"

"But Aunt Bobbi, your bed is so bouncy. If you just try it once, you'll see what I'm talking about." He held out his hand for me, and I grabbed it, but instead of joining him to jump on the bed, I pulled him into my lap and started to tickle him.

"Aunt Bobbi, no. Stop. Okay, I'm sorry," he said through his laughter.

When Dajah stood up to help her brother, I pulled her down and began to tickle her too.

I know a lot of people would probably think that I was crazy for taking Devon and Dajah in especially after the way their mother and aunt did us, but the kids didn't deserve to be left behind. Not when I had the means to take care of them the way that Kay Kay always wished that she could. Besides, one of the main reasons why we started Diamond Mafia was to get them and us up out of the hood and into a better life. That would've been some real bitch-ass shit had we left them in the system with their foster parents when we were their real family.

"Okay, okay, okay," I told the kids as I let them go. "Now that we got an understanding about not jumping on the bed anymore, are you guys ready to go out and get in the water?"

They both excitedly screamed, "Yeah!"

"Okay. Well, then go put your swim clothes on and get whatever toys you want to take down there with you. You guys ate lunch already, right?"

Devon was already gone out of the room to get dressed, but Dajah stood in front of me and nodded her head.

"Yes, Auntie Bobbi. We ate already. Uncle Na—"

"Uncle Nav what?" Naveen interrupted as he walked into the bedroom with nothing but his swim trunks on, body looking all the way right as he walked past me and straight into the closet. He grabbed his laptop and a few other things before coming back out and sitting next to me on the bed. "What were you just about to say about Uncle Nav, baby girl?" he asked Dajah again.

The little heffa blushed and walked into his open arms. "I was just about to tell TiTi Bobbi that you made us a sandwich, chips, and yogurt for lunch. She wanted to know if we had something to eat before we go down to play in the water."

Nav kissed Dajah on the cheek and then sat her back down. "Yes, you've been fed. All you need to do now is go put on your bathing suit and grab your floaties, okay?"

Dajah happily nodded her head and then ran out of the room. Once she was out of sight, Nav licked his lips and then turned to look at me.

"So, you still think I'm a sorry-ass nigga, huh? This past year of unlimited ass-kissing and not letting you lift a finger, buying you this big-ass house and keeping good on my promise to take care of you for the rest of my life just don't mean shit anymore, does it?"

I stared into the eyes of the man who had stolen my heart the very first day we met. "It still means something. I'm just enjoying the perks and loving life right now, that's all."

Nav's lips curled into one of the sexiest smiles as he lovingly stared back into my eyes. When the cool island breeze knocked the thin cover up off my shoulder, revealing the tattoo of his name, he traced each letter with his fingers before placing a kiss on my wound.

"Even though it's been over a year, I'm still sorry about how everything went down. I should've listened to you about Tweety, and I damn sure should've had a better eye on Ant. I was so busy trying to stay ten steps ahead of the outsiders that I wasn't keeping a good eye on the ones closest to me." He kissed my wound again and then got up from the bed, pulling me up with him and enveloping me in his arms. "You forgive me, right? I know you've said you have a million times, but I just gotta keep reassuring myself for my own sanity."

I pulled from Nav's embrace and looked up into his face for a second before I responded. I mean, I did forgive him for not listening to my warning about Tweety, and I did applaud him for handling that bitch the last time we were all together alive, but at times, I still felt some type of way. When the green beam from Nav's gun was aimed at my heart, I didn't know what to think, and when the bullet entered my body, I knew at that moment that him shooting me would never be something that I could forgive if I made it through. However, it wasn't Nav's bullet that entered my body. It was Tweety's.

The bitch took the opportunity to try to take my life when she thought that Nav was having second thoughts on doing it himself. The crazy thing was, Nav didn't have any intention of killing me in the first place. When he came to after being shot in the back and tried to get up, he reached for his gun as he heard the bullets flying. He flipped the beam on accidentally. Because he was facing me when he used the bumper of the van to help himself stand to his feet, the gun and beam aimed directly at me. After Tweety noticed that Nav wasn't really aiming his pistol to take a shot, she raised her gun and let off a few rounds, hitting my shoulder and grazing the side of my head. Nav, being the trigger-happy nigga that he was, turned his gun to Tweety as soon as she let the second shot go, and he sent a bullet flying right between her eyes. Lucci said that with all the strength that he had left in him, Nav walked his ass up the stairs and put two more bullets in Tweety's head before collapsing again.

By the time the police did show up after an anonymous call, Zig and Lucci had managed to get me and Nav into the van and away from the scene with our score before anyone even knew we were there. Because of the gruesome scene left behind and the priors on every one of the bodies that they found, the police and news outlets basically assumed that Ant, Tweety, Doughboy, and his friends were responsible for the string of jewelry store robberies that they had no leads on. Josh and his father didn't make it any better once they started doing interviews and blaming everything on Tweety after learning of her involvement.

Now here we were, in the beach house that I'd always wanted, with my family and, pretty soon, my friends living next door. Did I forgive Nav? Yes. Would I make him pay for some of the bullshit I'd experience because of him for the rest of my life? No, and I told him that, too, right before he placed his lips on mine and hypnotized me with a kiss.

"Ewww." Devon said as he ran back into my room, ready to go down to the beach. "Can you guys please stop doing that? Every time I turn around you guys are kissing."

Nav kissed my lips one last time before pulling away from me and turning to Devon. "Li'l man, when you get you a woman like your Aunt Bobbi, you're going to be kissing her just as much as I do."

He stuck out his tongue and acted as if he were throwing up. "Can we go down to the water now? We're ready now, right, Dajah?"

She nodded her head and grabbed hold of Nav's hand. "Let's go, Uncle Nav. I want you to throw me in the water just like you did last time."

Never one to resist her cute, dimpled face, Nav grabbed his laptop and the other stuff he took out of the closet and placed them on the dresser. "I guess I can get some work done once I come back up."

I looked down at the papers that were fanned out. "What is this, babe?" I asked, seeing an unfamiliar name at the top of some of them. "Kazimir?"

"Oh, that's the info one of my guys got on the dude who shot up the firehouse and snatched up Cowboy. I've been tracking him for a few weeks now, but he seems to disappear from time to time. Completely off the grid. I got my best guy looking after him, though. He hardly leaves a paper trail, but he's bound to fuck up one day, and when he does, I'm gon' pay his ass a little visit."

I had all of the faith you could ever have in your man when it came to Nav, but some things I felt needed to be left alone—especially when the person you're trying to hunt down has a Russian last name associated with the mafia. But leaving that discussion for another day and time, I watched as Devon and Dajah both dragged Nav down to the water and tried to dunk him.

As I watched them have fun, I couldn't help but to think about Diamond and Kay Kay. They both would've loved it out here. Especially Khalani. She always talked about visiting an exotic island one day and lying naked on the beach, enjoying the sun's rays. Diamond probably would've made it seem like she hated it since Shine wasn't there to enjoy it, but I had no doubt that they were both in heaven right now, causing all kinds of ruckus. Regardless of the good, the bad, and the ugly, I really did miss my friends and was sad that neither one of them was here to experience this.

A lone tear fell from my eye as memories of the times Kay Kay, Diamond, Lucci, and I shared continued to re-play in my mind. It wasn't until Nav called for me to come down to the water to join them that I broke from my thoughts. After removing the Harry Winston bracelet from my wrist and the fifteen-carat princess-cut diamond ring from my finger, I slipped into my bathing suit and joined Nav and the kids at the water.

I may have done a lot of things in my lifetime that I had come to regret, but one thing that I would never be ashamed of was the love that I had for my girls Khalani, Diamond, and Lucinda. Some of us may not have gone out like we should have, but at the end of the day, we were all sisters, and if I had to do it all over again with each and every one of them, I would.

Diamond Mafia for life, bitches.

Kay Kay

I stood over the plots of two people who I would dearly miss in my life, one of whom died way too early from having a faulty heart, and the other who died all because of me. I wiped the lone tear that fell from my eye and slowly placed my knees on the well-manicured grass of Forest Lawn Mortuary. My head carefully rested on the tombstone of one of my best friends as my mind replayed the events of the night her life was cut short.

If there was one thing in this world that I could ever change, it would most definitely be the night I stole that money from Doughboy. Although I took the twelve *G*s for a good reason, I should've just waited for my cut from the jewelry store jobs to start planning my new future. Yes, my niece and nephew deserved a much better life than what I lived, but so did Diamond. After losing Shine, she deserved some sort of happy ending. Shit, we all did. It's crazy how one choice can fuck up your life in so many ways.

I placed the white calla lilies Diamond loved against her tombstone and a bottle of Hennessy against Shine's. After sending up a little prayer, asking Diamond and God for forgiveness, I stood up from the ground, kissed my fingers, and placed them on the inscribed stone.

I know by now you're probably wondering how in the hell is this girl still alive, right? Well, all I can tell you is that it feels good to finally have a man who cares about and loves me the way that Marvin does. Had it not been for him leaving his office earlier than he intended and showing back up to the firehouse when he did, let's just say that your girl would've really been lying in the plot next to Shauna's, which was a few rows up from Diamond's.

"So, how did it go?" Marvin asked as soon as I slid into the back seat of his truck and intertwined his hand with mine.

"It went as expected."

"So, everything was cool?"

"It was when I went to see Shauna," I said, wiping the fresh set of tears that started to fall. Marvin wrapped his arms around my shoulder and kissed my temple. "But as soon as I stepped in front of Diamond's grave, I kinda broke down. It took me the whole time I was out there to finally get up enough courage to apologize to her for what I'd done."

He kissed my forehead. "I'm pretty sure she heard everything you had to say and has probably forgiven you already. From the things you've told me about all of your friends, Diamond seemed like the one who had the biggest heart."

I nodded my head and grabbed the tissue Marvin's driver, Lee, passed to me. "That's true. Her heart was big. Diamond would curse you out in a second, hate the earth you walked on in the next, but be the first person to open her home, wallet, and arms to you if you were ever in need. She was the provider in our clique. The girl damn near killed herself working two and three jobs to take care of Shine. I remember when that nigga went to the joint for boosting cars when we were younger, and his commissary stayed stacked up. When the nigga paroled a couple years later, he came home with a little over three *G*s in his pocket."

"See. That really shows her character. What roles would you say Bobbi and Lucci played?"

"Bobbi was always the one who had your back. Right or wrong. You rocking, she's rolling. And Lucci, she was the hustler of the group. Always giving us the game and schooling us on how to flip or double our money." I choked up. "I . . . I miss them, babe. I miss them a lot. If only I could turn back time. Just get one more chance to—"

"Shhhhh." Marvin cooed as I sobbed into his shoulder. He held me close in his arms, soothing me as Lee finally pulled off.

I tried to stop the tears from falling down my face, but I couldn't. My mind kept racing with so many thoughts as we passed all the other rows of tombstones and headed out of the graveyard. The guilt of what I'd done weighed heavy on my heart. I longed to be with my friends again.

"Did you hear me, Khalani?" Marvin whispered into my ear, grabbing my attention.

I dabbed at the wet streaks on my face with the tissue. "No, babe. I didn't hear anything. What did you say?"

He raised my chin up so that he was directly looking in my eyes, concern and love written all over his face. "You have to stop blaming yourself for the way that everything went down."

"But—" I started, but he cut me off.

"No. Hear me out." When I reluctantly nodded my head, he continued. "What you did? The way that you betrayed your friends? That was indeed some fucked-up shit. But I bet if you were to talk to Lucci and Bobbi right now and tell them the full story on why you did what you did, they would understand."

"They wouldn't understand, Marvin. Hell, at times, I don't even understand," I responded as I wiped a tear from my eye with the back of my hand. "Diamond isn't here because of me. Because of my actions. Reality will never allow Lucci and Bobbi to understand that."

"But you didn't pull the trigger, Kay. Doughboy did. And if they saw the way you toss and turn at night, crying in your sleep from the nightmares you have about seeing your best friend's head get blown off in front of you, they would understand. If you told them how you only did what you did to make a better life for Devon and Dajah, they would understand. If they saw how many times you cry in a day because of how sorry you are, they would understand, babe. You all wanted to make it out the hood. You just chose a different path to get there before you were flagged over to another one. Baby, Bobbi and Lucci are your family. And sometimes your family can stab you in the back, but running away from the situation will never heal your relationship or friendship. If you want to make this right between the three of you, you have to reach out. Let them know that you're alive and let them know how sorry you are."

I contemplated his words for a few minutes as I nuzzled myself deeper into his embrace. Marvin was right. The only way to try to repair the friendships Lucci, Bobbi, and I shared would be to explain everything to them face to face. I had written both of them a letter while I was recovering in the hospital, but I didn't have an address to send them to.

Ever since the night I was shot by Ant, I didn't know where Lucci or Bobbi were. It was like they vanished off the face of this earth without a trace. Their social media accounts were shut down, homes sold off, accounts closed out, and their cell phones were disconnected. I'd spent the last year trying to find them and hadn't come up with anything.

Marvin's phone began to go off, and I could feel him reaching into the breast pocket of his suit to get it. When he loosened his hold around me to respond back to a text message, I looked up at him.

"What's wrong, babe?" I asked when I noticed the confused look on his face. When he didn't respond, my heart started to beat a little faster. "Marvin, you're scaring me. What's going on?"

His face stayed buried in his phone as he spoke to his driver. "Aye, Lee, change of plans. I need you to head to the airstrip instead of the house."

"The airstrip?" I questioned, now confused. "You have to go out of town?" It was the one-year anniversary of Diamond's death, and I didn't want to be alone that night.

Marvin finally finished responding to whoever he was talking to and looked over at me. "I'm not going anywhere. *We* are going out of town. That P.I. I hired a few weeks ago finally found something."

I sat up straight in my seat. "What did he say?"

Marvin scrolled through a few things on his phone and then handed it to me. "He found them, babe," Marvin excitedly said as a picture of my niece and nephew playing in some pretty blue water came into my line of vision. "He found Devon and Dajah."

I scrolled through the six or seven pictures the P.I. had sent over and couldn't believe my eyes. My babies looked happy, healthy, and well taken care of—everything I'd always wanted for them.

"Where are they at? Are they with their foster family?" I asked.

When I went to look for Devon and Dajah after I felt that I was well enough to take care of them, they were no longer at the address I last remembered them being at. Marvin and I caused all kinds of hell at the social service department and currently had a lawsuit going against them.

Marvin removed his phone from my hand and scrolled through some other emails before handing it back to me. When I looked down at the screen, my eyes teared up.

"They . . . they're with Bobbi?"

"According to the P.I., her and Nav have been caring for them this whole time. Took them from their foster family and have been providing them with the life you always dreamed about them having."

My body started to shake. "But why would she do that after everything that I've done? Devon and Dajah aren't her responsibility. They're mine."

Marvin grabbed my hand and kissed the back of it. "My guess is because she still loves and cares about you in some way. Regardless of all the wrong you've done, she still found it in her heart to take care of Devon and Dajah, something she knows you would have given your life to do."

"But—"

"But nothing, Khalani. Stop questioning this moment and just be happy that we know where your niece and nephew are. Anything else that's bothering you, I'm sure you can find the answer to it once we land in Costa Rica."

I didn't know what to say. Not only was I going to be able to hug my niece and nephew after not seeing them in almost two years, but I was going to finally come face to face with Bobbi and Lucci. From the pictures the P.I. had captured of them, it seemed that they were doing great, too. Bobbi had this certain glow to her, and Lucci looked beautiful as hell with her round belly and puffy face. I don't know how they would react to seeing that I was still alive, but I prayed that they would give me the chance to at least explain my side of the story and sincerely apologize for all of the wrongs that I'd done. God saw fit to save my life one more time, so it was only fitting that I try to mend the friendships that I'd broken and make everything right again.

When we started Diamond Mafia, we were four sisters who had been through so many things together. Now that it was only the three of us left, I had to get us back on the right track, or at least die trying.

The End

Hey, guys . . .

I hope you enjoyed my remix on this '90s classic.
What should've been a short novella easily turned into a
full-blown book that I had a great time writing, especially
since *Set It Off* was and still is one of my favorite movies.
I'm so glad you took the time out of your busy schedule
to give me a chance. Thanks for rocking with your girl,
and I hope to hear from you soon.

With Love,
Gen

Keep in touch:

Instagram & Twitter
@iamgenesiswoods

Facebook
www.facebook.com/iamgenesiswoods

Email
iamgenesiswoods@gmail.com

For book discussions and other shit going on in the literary world, join me and my partner in crime, Shantaé, in our group **Literary Rejects**
www.facebook.com/literaryrejects

If you're interested in more books by Genesis Woods, check out my catalog.

Available in paperback, ebook, and audiobook format wherever books are sold.